CRYSTAL LAKE SERIES VOLUME TWO BOOKS 4-6

CRYSTAL LAKE SERIES

LAURA SCOTT

READSCAPE PUBLISHING, LLC

WORTH THE WAIT

CRYSTAL LAKE SERIES

1
———

"**D**r. Katy?" ER nurse Janelle Larson poked her head through the doorway of the patient's room. "The trauma pager just went off. We have two GSWs on their way in."

Katy Reichert glanced up from the wound she was currently suturing on a young man who'd been sliced by a knife in a bar fight. Now they were getting two gunshot wounds? Barely nine o'clock on a Saturday evening and already patients were pouring in. "Thanks, Janelle. I'll be finished here shortly."

"Sounds good. I'll make sure the trauma bays are well stocked." Janelle flashed a quick smile and darted back out of the room.

Katy concentrated on finishing her task, even as her stomach clenched with anxiety. Hope County Hospital wasn't normally so busy, but with spring giving way to summer, it seemed that locals and tourists alike were determined to celebrate the warm weather by drinking too much and getting into fights. She couldn't remember the last time they'd had so many patients, especially at the same time.

Although, truthfully, she'd had far worse nights when she'd been practicing at Baltimore General.

She shied away from the painful memories of her past and focused on the issue at hand. Her patient, Danny Truitt, snored loudly, no doubt from the combination of the alcohol he'd consumed prior to the knife fight and the pain medication he'd been given here. She finished up Danny's sutures—fourteen in all—stripped off her gloves, washed her hands, then quickly logged in to the computer to complete her orders.

"All finished?" Merry Crain, another ER nurse, asked as she breezed into the room.

"Yes, but we'll need to monitor him closely until he sobers up. We can't discharge him until he's fully awake."

"I'll get him hooked up to the telemetry and pulse ox," Merry agreed. "That way we'll hear the alarms if his condition changes."

"Good idea. We'll need all hands on deck for the traumas." Katy headed over toward the trauma bay, anxious to hear more about their impending arrivals. She looked around but didn't see her colleague, trauma surgeon Wade Matthews. Where was he? He was the trauma surgeon on call; his pager should have gone off by now, alerting him to the GSWs.

Janelle was standing near the computer, making sure everything was ready to go. Katy stripped off her lab coat and tossed it over one of the chairs along the back counter that housed several computers before crossing over to Janelle.

"What do we know so far?" she asked.

"Not much. One patient has a gunshot wound to the upper chest, and the other has a gunshot wound to the arm," Janelle said. "They should be here any minute."

Katy nodded. "We should put University Hospital in Madison on alert for the GSW to the chest."

"I already made the call," Janelle assured her. "It's protocol to let them know about serious traumas. The Lifeline helicopter is on its way. They've agreed to remain on standby up on the landing pad."

Katy nodded, wishing they'd dispatched the chopper to the scene. But it was too late now. She took a deep breath and let it out slowly. Seconds later, the double doors leading in from the ambulance bay burst open, and a bevy of people crowded through.

"GSW to the chest, bleeding badly," the paramedic announced. "We've been pumping O neg blood into him like crazy."

Since there was still no sign of Wade Matthews, Katy had no choice but to step up and take control. "Get the level one rapid infuser," she ordered. "Give four units of O neg, and order some fresh frozen plasma as well. I need a set of vitals as soon as possible."

Janelle deftly connected the tubing and began hanging blood products. Another nurse began connecting the patient to the heart monitor.

"Merry, find Dr. Matthews, *stat!*" Katy drew on gloves and a gown over her scrubs, anticipating blood splatters. She lifted the dressing from the patient's upper-left chest. Blood pooled rapidly, indicating a nicked artery and, likely, a severely injured lobe of the lung. She wasn't a surgeon, but if she didn't take immediate action, this man would bleed to death.

"Get me a chest tray and suction," she ordered. "And start a propofol drip to put him under. I need to explore this wound."

Janelle shoved the chest tray on a bedside table located

to her right, and Katy forced herself to remain calm as she waited for the nurse to begin the propofol infusion so that her patient wouldn't feel any pain. She sent up a silent prayer for strength as she picked up the scalpel. A bead of sweat trickled down the side of her face when she opened the entry wound so that she could assess the damage.

Somehow, she managed to drown out the cacophony of voices surrounding her to focus on the emergency situation at hand. She needed to find a way to stop the bleeding. Through the opening, she could see the bullet was lodged in the upper lobe of the lung, which wasn't good. But when she continued her search and found a lacerated artery, pumping out blood at an alarming rate, her stomach dropped.

She hadn't repaired an artery this large or removed a significant portion of lung tissue since her residency, but what choice did she have? How else could she stop the bleeding and remove the bullet? Performing surgery wasn't her strong suit, but she knew they needed to buy time in order to stabilize the patient so he could be flown to Madison.

"Hand me a scalpel," she forced herself to say, hoping the tremor in her tone didn't betray her lack of confidence. The only positive note was that the injury was located high enough that she didn't need to split the patient's chest.

With the scalpel in hand, she opened the entrance wound and placed small vascular clamps to stop the bleeding. She'd need to work fast, or the surrounding tissue would die from lack of oxygen. She sutured the artery, silently praying for strength and precision. When the artery was repaired to the best of her ability, she opened the clamps and breathed a sigh of relief when the bleeding was contained.

Feeling calmer now that the most tenuous part was

done, she picked up the forceps and began exploring the upper lobe of the lung where the bullet was lodged. She found herself glancing frequently at the overhead monitor, to make sure her patient remained stable. Halfway through the procedure, Wade Matthews finally showed up.

"You're doing fine," he said, as if his absence was no big deal. She glared at him, seriously annoyed, but this wasn't the time or place to vent her frustration. "I'll take it from here," he assured her.

She stepped back, knowing Wade's surgical skills were far better than hers, although he wasn't a cardiothoracic surgeon either. "The chopper is ready to take him to Madison, so the goal is to stabilize him enough for the flight."

Wade nodded but didn't look up from the wound. A glance up at the heart monitor convinced her that their patient was doing all right, not great, but better than she'd expected. Her gaze dropped to the patient's face, and her stomach squeezed painfully when she realized the guy was far younger than she'd originally thought—which might be why he was still alive, despite the serious injuries to his artery and lung.

For a moment, Steffie's all-too-still features flashed in her mind, reminding her of the young patient she'd failed back in Baltimore.

"Dr. Katy? Should we get more blood?" Janelle asked, breaking into her thoughts.

"Yes, keep the O neg flowing," she said. She stripped off her gloves and turned to look for the second GSW patient. Her gaze landed on DNR game warden Reese Webster sitting on a gurney with a field dressing wrapped around his left bicep. She'd taken care of Reese just a few weeks earlier, after he'd been slashed by a wounded bear, so she shouldn't be surprised to see him again. Apparently his job often put him in the path of danger.

As she walked toward him, he didn't glance at her, his gaze focused solely on the patient with the chest wound. He seemed more concerned about the other guy than his own injury.

Katy put a hand on Reese's forearm, the warmth of his skin practically scorching her fingers. She dropped her hand, hoping he didn't notice her hasty retreat. "You should probably lie down so I can take a look at your arm."

Reese's mouth tightened, and he shook his head. "Sorry, Dr. Katy, but I'm fine. Marcus Boyle is the one who needs your medical attention, not me."

She looked over her shoulder to see that Wade had finished with the procedure and was placing fresh dressings over the open chest wound.

"Get those units of blood in, stat, so we can get him up to the helipad," he ordered. "Now!"

Hospital staff and paramedics jumped to do his bidding. Janelle pushed the rapid infuser with the blood transfusions going alongside the gurney, while the other staff members quickly wheeled the patient to the elevators leading up to the roof, where the helipad was located. As soon as they left the trauma bay, an eerie silence filled the room.

"Which hospital are they taking him to?" Reese asked.

"University Hospital in Madison," she replied. "Trust me, he has the best chance of surviving his injury there. They have highly qualified cardiothoracic surgeons on staff. What we did here was a temporary patch job."

Reese stared at the closed elevator door for a long moment. "It's my fault he's injured," he said in a low voice.

"I'm sure there's more to that story," she murmured, feeling bad for him. "Now let me take a look at your arm."

Reese sighed and finally stretched out on the gurney. He was still wearing his forest-green uniform, and he was so tall his booted feet dangled off the end of the cart.

"I shot him," he said bluntly.

Katy unwrapped the bloody gauze from Reese's arm, wincing in sympathy when she saw fresh blood oozing down his arm. His uniform sleeve had been hacked off super short, no doubt by the paramedics to provide easy access to the wound. "I'm thinking he shot you first," she said. "You're lucky the bullet went all the way through. This looks to be mostly a flesh wound."

Reese didn't argue or flinch as she probed the wound, making sure there were no foreign bodies left behind. But when she noted a few threads of fabric embedded inside, she grew concerned.

"I need to irrigate this with antibiotic solution, okay? I can't remember from last time you were here if you have any allergies?"

"No allergies," he said tersely.

All three nurses had gone up with the chest wound patient to the helipad, so she stripped off her gloves to get the normal saline, antibiotic solution, and syringes that she needed.

"Why did he shoot you?" she asked as a way to distract herself from the odd awareness she experienced from being so close to him. She'd come to Crystal Lake, Wisconsin, to get away from the memories of her past failures, not to be distracted by a handsome game warden.

"He was poaching and has been for a long time. I'm sure he injured that bear that clawed me three weeks ago. I've been tracking him ever since, and this time, I caught him in the act of shooting a cougar." Reese's tone was hard and flat. "When I confronted him, he fired at me, so I shot back."

"A cougar?" she echoed in horror. While she loved working in the Hope County Hospital ER, she was a city girl at heart. All this talk of bears and cougars living in the woods that flanked the north side of the lake unnerved her. She enjoyed hiking the walking/running path but wouldn't dare venture any farther. "You're joking, right? There really aren't cougars around here."

A wry grin tugged at his mouth, making him even more handsome. As if his dark hair, hazel-green eyes and broad shoulders weren't devastating enough? "Just a few, and don't worry, they tend to stay far away from people. They're feeding on the overpopulation of deer, which is a good thing."

Feeding on Bambi was a good thing? Katy suppressed a shiver. "If you say so," she muttered doubtfully. "Do you want some pain medication?" she asked, changing the subject. "This is going to hurt."

"No pain meds," Reese said firmly. "I need to drive up to Madison to check on how Boyle is doing."

She wanted to roll her eyes at his macho attitude, but she remembered how Reese had declined pain meds the last time he was here too. With a mental shrug, she went to work, extensively irrigating the wound and then turning toward her suture tray.

"Are you sure you don't want something for pain before I stitch this up?" she asked, stalling for time. Maybe if she waited long enough, Wade would return, and he could do the task. After all, he owed her big-time. Not that Reese's wound needed a trauma surgeon, but for some reason, she loathed the idea of sticking needles into Reese.

"I'm sure."

She stared at him for a long minute before taking a deep breath and picking up the curved needle attached to a suture. Once again, she sent up a silent prayer, knowing she needed extra support from her faith. When she pierced the needle through the edge of his wound, she flinched more than he did. She tried to think of Reese like any other patient, but it wasn't easy. Sweat dampened her scalp and rolled down her back as she placed one suture after another, closing the entry wound and then the exit wound.

And when she finally finished, she stepped back and dropped the suture needle on a wave of relief. For a moment, her vision went hazy, and Reese unexpectedly reached out and clasped her arm in a strong, firm grip.

"Are you all right?" he asked with concern.

She forced a smile. "Of course. You're the patient here, not me."

He lifted an eyebrow, and she inwardly sighed, knowing she wasn't fooling him one bit. She stared down at his hand holding her arm, and he slowly released her.

She forced a smile. "Sorry, I guess I'm a little tired. It's been a busy night."

His expression turned serious. "I know. You were really incredible."

She blushed and dropped her gaze, knowing that if he knew the truth about what had happened in Baltimore, he wouldn't think of her as incredible at all. Her heart squeezed in her chest, and she pulled herself together with an effort.

"Okay, you're all set to go, but I want you to take antibiotics twice daily for the next ten days," she said in a stern tone. "And you'll need to make an appointment with your doctor to get the sutures removed."

"I don't have a doctor," he said with a frown. "Can't I just come back here to see you?"

For a moment, she simply looked at him, wondering if she was imagining the flash of interest in his gaze.

Of course she was. She barely knew the man, had only patched him up twice now. What was wrong with her? She wasn't interested in anything remotely resembling a relationship. She needed to get a grip and fast.

"I'm an ER doctor; I don't have clinic appointments," she managed. "But you can establish care with any of the general medicine physicians here. In fact, I'll be happy to give you a list of names."

He shrugged. "No need, I'll just come back when you're working," he said in a casual tone. He nimbly jumped off the gurney, looming over her from his height of six feet three inches. She craned her neck, tilting her face upward, thinking it was ridiculous that the top of her head barely reached his chin.

"I appreciate everything you've done for me," he said in a low tone. "Thank you."

Their gazes crashed and held. For the life of her, she couldn't manage a single coherent thought. Thankfully, the rest of the medical team returned from the helipad. The moment was gone, and she stepped back gratefully. Wade Matthews disappeared down the hallway while Janelle began cleaning up the equipment and restocking supplies in the first trauma bay.

"Dr. Katy?" Merry called, entering the room with a worried frown etched in her forehead. "I heard the heart monitor beeping and found Danny thrashing around in his room. I think his pain meds have worn off, even though he still reeks of alcohol."

"Okay, don't give him any more pain meds yet. I'll be right over," she promised, grateful for the interruption. She crossed over to the counter, drew her lab coat back on and then rummaged for a prescription pad. Her fingers shook a bit as she filled out the antibiotic order for Reese. When she finished, she carried it over to him. "Here, you can get this filled at any pharmacy, and you need to take these until they're gone. I'd recommend taking your first dose tonight."

"Thanks," he said, taking the script and tucking it in his pocket. "See you soon, Katy."

"Sure," she murmured, distracted by his use of her given name. It took a herculean effort on her part to turn away to head toward Danny's room.

Maybe it was her imagination working overtime, but she could swear she felt Reese's gaze boring into her back as she walked away.

2

Reese walked outside, leaving Dr. Katy and the rest of the ER staff behind. It wasn't until he was standing in front of the ER parking lot searching through the darkness for his car that he realized he didn't have his truck here because he'd been brought in by the ambulance crew.

Idiot. That's what happened when he let his hormones run wild.

He shook his head in disgust. Hadn't he already learned the hard way that relationships weren't worth the trouble? His ex-wife had left him for his best friend after cleaning out every last dime in their joint bank account. Three years later, he was still digging his way out of debt.

The last thing he needed was to start down that path again, especially not with a pretty redheaded doctor who likely made more than twice his salary, and then some.

With a rueful grimace, he focused on the present and pulled out his phone. He could try one of his DNR buddies even though it was almost ten thirty. He grimaced, hating to bother them on a Saturday night. But considering there wasn't any sort of taxi service in Crystal Lake, he didn't have much choice.

Gavin's phone went straight to voice mail. Doug's phone rang a half dozen times before going to voice mail. He tried George's number, too, with no luck.

Where was everyone? Obviously they all had better things to do on a Saturday night than he did. Which was why he'd been working, following Boyle's trail through the woods. If only he'd gotten there sooner, before the idiot had killed the cougar.

He scowled at his phone. So now what? The only option he could think of was to call the Hope County Sheriff's Department to request a ride. The DNR worked closely with local law enforcement agencies—surely someone would be willing to help him out.

As if on cue, a sheriff's department vehicle pulled into the ER parking lot. Reese waited for the deputy to climb out from behind the wheel before walking toward him.

"Hi, Deputy Armbruster, right? I don't know if you remember me, but my name is Reese Webster, and I work for the DNR," he said.

"Yes, I remember and you're just the guy I'm looking for," the deputy said dryly. "I need to take your statement."

Great, he thought with a sigh. "All right, but afterwards, will you give me a lift back to my truck? The ambulance brought me in, and I need a ride."

"I suppose." The deputy didn't sound too thrilled. "Let's go inside. I need to know how the alleged poacher is doing."

Reese wrestled with his temper as he fell into step beside the deputy, whose name tag identified his last name as Armbruster. "The poacher's name is Marcus Boyle, and he's on his way to Madison for treatment. He's a confirmed poacher. I personally watched him shoot that cougar, and when I yelled out to stop him, he shot me. Feel free to add attempted murder to his arrest warrant."

Armbruster glanced at the bandage on his upper arm. "Right now, it's your word against his, isn't it?"

"Since I work for the state, that makes me the more credible witness," he responded sharply. Was this guy for real? "And when I find the body of the cougar he killed, you'll be able to match the ballistics of his gun to the slug in the cat."

"Okay, okay," Deputy Armbruster said, holding up his hand in defense. They entered the ER and crossed over to the waiting area. "I believe you, but that doesn't mean I don't need to tie up all the loose ends."

There weren't any loose ends, but he forced himself to bite back the sarcasm. "Listen, I've been tracking this guy for the last month. I have photos of his boot prints along with the slug we took out of the bear he shot. I've built an ironclad case around this guy, and I'm happy to share everything I have to put him behind bars."

"Once he's out of the hospital, right?" Deputy Armbruster pointed out wryly.

"Yeah, once he's out of the hospital," he echoed. Reese didn't like knowing Boyle could easily die of his gunshot wound, a wound that he was responsible for. He much preferred that the guy recover so he could pay for his crimes.

"What happened after you shot him?" Armbruster asked.

"I called for help and hauled him on a tarp out to the clearing." Reese remembered wishing for help from Duke, his German shepherd, as he struggled to drag Boyle's dead weight. Luckily, the ambulance crew had met him halfway or Boyle might not have made it.

Still might not make it.

"Hmm," Armbruster murmured as he scribbled in his tattered notebook. "I'm sorry, but we have to confiscate your gun, to validate the ballistics report."

Reese ground his teeth together but handed over his weapon. He knew the protocol, and his boss, Gavin Crowley, would have taken it if the deputy hadn't asked for it.

"Thanks. Anything else?"

Reese hesitated, wondering if he should voice all his suspicions. He didn't have any concrete proof that Boyle hadn't been working alone, just a few glimpses of a blond dude in the same area where Boyle tended to illegally hunt. The blond dude was good, though; Reese hadn't even found a boot print or any other evidence that he'd been working with Boyle.

"Nothing else from the incident this evening," he confirmed. He'd glimpsed the blond dude about an hour before Boyle had shot the cougar, so either he'd stayed hidden once Reese had shouted at Boyle, or seeing the guy had been some strange coincidence.

"Okay, thanks." Armbruster flipped his notebook shut.

"So about that ride," he began, but the deputy's radio squawked, and Armbruster turned away to listen.

"Ten-four," he said. "Sorry, Webster, but there's a crash on the highway, and I'm the closest deputy. Gotta run. If you're still here later, try me again." Armbruster rose to his feet and headed back outside.

Reese watched the deputy leave with a sigh. He pulled out his phone again, knowing that if none of his buddies answered their phones, he might be stuck here for hours.

He'd finished leaving another round of voice mail messages and was trying to think of another alternative for a ride when he caught sight of Katy walking toward him, a frown puckering her brow. He abruptly disconnected from the call and rose to his feet.

"What's wrong?" she asked. "Is your arm hurting? Or did you have a reaction to the antibiotics?"

"No, I haven't even picked up the antibiotics yet." He flashed a lopsided smile, hating the thought of asking her for a favor. "I'm waiting for a ride," he added lamely.

Her frown cleared, and she glanced out toward the parking lot. Did he imagine the hesitation in her tone? "My shift is over and I'm leaving now. I'm happy to give you a ride."

"Are you sure?" Her offer was exactly what he needed, but for some reason he felt guilty for taking her up on it. Not that he'd planned to get shot and stranded here. He should have insisted on driving himself.

"Of course I'm sure." Any hesitation she might have had seemed to have evaporated. "We'll stop at the pharmacy first," she added. "I wasn't kidding about those antibiotics."

"I really appreciate your help," he said, quickening his pace so he could hold the door open for her. "Deputy Armbruster was called out to the scene of a crash, so I might have had to wait for hours."

"It's really no problem," she assured him.

Reese followed Katy through the darkness as she headed for her car. His fingers itched to take her keys so he could drive, but he sensed she wouldn't appreciate it. She pressed the key fob, and the lights flashed on. He opened her driver's-side door and closed it behind her, before rounded the vehicle to slide in the passenger seat.

She turned on the engine and pulled out of the parking space. "Any particular pharmacy?" she asked.

"There's one on Main Street, right?" he said, thinking

back to when he'd had to get antibiotics after the bear incident. "I should be on record there."

"Sounds good," she said, turning left toward Main Street, which was all downtown Crystal Lake had to offer.

Reese sat back, trying to think of something to say. He was so out of practice being with a woman it wasn't funny. "I hope I'm not taking you too far out of your way," he said. "My truck is way over on the north side of the lake."

"As long as you protect me from cougars and bears, I'll be fine." Her light teasing tone helped him relax.

"No problem," he agreed. His stomach growled loudly, and he pressed his hand to his abdomen, trying to make it shut up.

"Look, Rose's Café is still open. Why don't we stop for a bite to eat?" she suggested.

He wasn't fooled by her innocent tone, but since the idea of having one of the best burgers in town was too good to pass up, he decided to let it go. "That's a great idea. My treat since you're going out of your way to drive me to my truck."

For a moment, he feared she'd insist on paying, making him a bigger bum than he already felt, but then she nodded, offering a small smile. "All right, it's a deal."

She parked in front of the drug store, which wasn't too far from Rose's Café. She waited for him inside the pharmacy and, thankfully, filling the script didn't take long. He paid for the medication and then tucked the bottle into the front pocket of his uniform slacks.

"All set?" she asked as he returned.

"Yes, Doctor," he teased.

She rolled her eyes. "You'd be surprised how many of our patients are not compliant with their medications."

"I can imagine," he said, wondering if she was reminding him of their patient/doctor relationship on purpose. Not that he really blamed her, since this wasn't anything close to a date.

She fell silent as they walked down the crowded sidewalk toward Rose's. Again, he searched for a safe topic of conversation but realized he didn't know very much about her, other than she was an amazing doctor.

His stomach rumbled again, reminding him that he hadn't eaten since lunch. He opened the door of the café, relieved to notice there were several empty booths.

"Hi, Dr. Katy, and Reese, it's been a long time," Josie greeted them from behind the counter, her eyes bright with curiosity. Josie was one of the biggest gossips in town, and he inwardly groaned at the way she kept glancing between them. "Have a seat. I'll be right over."

Katy slid into the first available booth, and he took the seat across from her. "She'll have us married by morning," he whispered with a wink.

Katy's cheeks turned pink, and she suppressed a laugh. "She's been trying to set me up since I got here," she whispered back. "Maybe now she'll back off."

Reese chuckled. "I'll take the heat for you, no problem."

Josie bustled over, plopping two plastic menus in front of them. "So what can I get you?" she asked. It took her a moment to notice the bandage covering his arm. "Reese, what on earth happened?"

"Just a scratch," he said, waving off her concern. "Nothing to worry about. I'd like a large glass of water, please, and one of your amazing burgers loaded with the works."

Josie preened at his praise. "One burger with the works coming up. What about you, Dr. Katy?"

"Chicken sandwich, and I'll have water, too, please."

"Great. So, I see you're still wearing your scrubs; you

must have come straight from the hospital, huh?" Josie said, clearly prying for more information.

Katy's smile was strained. "Yes, and it was so busy I didn't get dinner. I'm famished."

"Oh, you poor thing." Josie looked appalled at the idea of missing a meal. "I'll get your food going right away. Now you two just sit back and relax for a bit, okay?"

"We will, thanks," Katy said.

Reese shook his head as Josie headed back toward the kitchen. "Talk about being nosy. Nice ploy to get sympathy, though. At least she'll hurry up with our food."

"No kidding," she murmured. She sat back in her seat with a sigh. "But it wasn't exactly a ploy. I really was too busy to eat."

He felt bad, knowing that he'd played a role in her missing dinner. "I'm not sure how you manage to keep so cool under pressure," he said.

The smile faded from her face, and her cheeks went pale moments before she ducked her head, making him realize he'd hit a nerve. "It's nothing."

It was far from nothing, but obviously she didn't want to talk about it. "I hope Boyle is hanging in there. I'd feel terrible if he died after all your hard work."

"I'm sure he'll be fine." She cleared her throat awkwardly. "Tell me how you managed to stumble across him at the exact moment he shot a cougar."

Accepting her change of topic, he explained how he'd been tracking the guy for weeks, gathering the evidence he needed. Josie came out with their food as he finished telling her about his conversation with Deputy Armbruster.

"Here you go," Josie said cheerfully.

"Looks great," he said with a broad smile. "Thanks."

"No problem." Josie walked away and began wiping

down a perfectly clean table well within earshot of their booth.

Katy didn't seem to notice, bowing her head and closing her eyes. Reese was surprised to realize she was praying. Despite the fact that he hadn't been to church since Suzanne had left, he bowed his head, too, respectfully waiting for her to finish.

"Looks fabulous," she said, meeting his gaze without a hint of embarrassment.

"Yeah," he agreed, although he wasn't talking about the food. Katy's deep red hair was pulled back in a fancy braid, but little wisps had fallen down around her face, making her look softer, more feminine. He forced himself to pry his gaze away and to concentrate on his meal.

For the next few minutes, they were both too busy eating to say much, and Josie finally left them alone, returning to her perch behind the counter.

Katy finished before he did, and he gestured to what was left of his burger. "Do you want to try a bite?" he asked.

She laughed and shook her head. "No, thanks, although I'm glad you're enjoying it. Don't forget to take your antibiotic."

"I won't." To prove his point, he drew out the bottle and took one of the pills. His arm still throbbed painfully, but he ignored it, finishing the last few bites of his meal. Josie returned with their check, so he tucked the antibiotics away and pulled out his wallet.

"How was everything?" Josie asked.

"Wonderful," Katy said with a smile.

"Ditto," he quipped, glancing at the bill. He pulled out more than enough cash, leaving a nice tip. "We need to get going, but thanks again, Josie."

"You're welcome," Josie said, tucking the generous tip in her pocket. "You two come back soon, you hear?"

Katy blushed again, and he swallowed a laugh, steering her toward the door.

"With any luck, the gossip will die down in a few days," Katy said with an apologetic smile. "I hope your, uh, family will understand."

Amused, he glanced down at her. "No family, no girlfriend, no one to care about any gossip," he said. "What about you? Is someone close to you going to be upset?"

"No, I'm not really close to my family. No siblings and after my parents split up, they created their own lives with their respective spouses," she said as they approached her car. "I don't hear much from the friends I left behind in Baltimore."

So that's where the slight Eastern accent in her tone came from. The fact that they were both alone here in Crystal Lake ironically made him feel closer to her. Which was stupid, considering they were complete opposites.

"Which way to your truck?" she asked, cranking her key in the ignition.

He gave her directions, hoping she'd be able to make it home okay after she dropped him off.

"Are you sure this is the road?" she asked, frowning as she peered through the windshield.

"I'm sure. My truck should be right around the next curve."

She slowed her small car, taking the curve carefully as if she were afraid she'd miss it. But sure enough, his truck was right where he'd left it.

As they came closer, he frowned, realizing he'd been wrong. His truck wasn't at all the way he'd left it.

Someone had smashed every window, leaving shards of

glass everywhere. The sides were dented in and each of the four tires had been slashed. The vehicle was so badly damaged he couldn't imagine there was any way to repair it.

"What happened?" Katy asked in a horrified whisper.

He let out a heavy breath, raking his gaze around the wooded area. He hoped that whoever had destroyed his truck was long gone, but couldn't afford to take that chance.

"Don't stop," he said sharply. "Speed up and keep going. I'll call the sheriff's department. Unfortunately, it looks as if I'll need a ride home."

"Someone is really mad at you," she said in a shaky voice, punching the accelerator with enough force to pin him to his seat. "That was no accident."

No, it wasn't. And his gut churned with anger as he realized the blond dude he'd seen lurking in the woods near Boyle was likely responsible.

Too bad he had no idea who the guy was or where to find him.

3

———

Katy struggled to relax her white-knuckled grip on the steering wheel. Every nerve in her body was stretched to the breaking point. The violence that had been taken out on Reese's truck had shaken her to the core.

She was used to caring for victims of crimes in the trauma room, but knowing that someone had it out for Reese on a personal level made her feel sick to her stomach.

Listening to his one-sided conversation with the sheriff's deputy wasn't making her feel any better.

"Take a right at the next intersection," he said after disconnecting from the call.

She slowed her car for the turn, wishing the wooded highway had bright streetlights like those she was used to seeing in the city. But out here in the middle of nowhere, she only had her headlights to cut through the absolute blackness of the night.

"My driveway is about halfway down the road. See the little red fire signs? I'm number 872."

"Red fire signs?" She stepped on the brake and peered

through the windshield. "You mean those tiny, narrow red and white markers?"

"Yep, that's exactly what I mean." He was peering through his passenger-side window, and she was very much afraid he was looking for a glimpse of the person who'd demolished his truck.

"Is this your driveway?" she asked, frowning when she saw the barely there dirt road right after the 872 sign.

"Just drop me off here," Reese instructed. "No need to drive up to the cabin."

"I don't think you should stay here," she said, slowing to a stop. "What if whoever trashed your truck figures out where you live?"

"I have my dog, Duke, to help keep me safe," he assured her. "Do you think you can find your way back home?"

"Of course." She brushed away his concern. "But please don't stay here. I'd be happy to take you and your dog to the motel in town."

Reese hesitated but then reluctantly nodded. "Okay, I'll take you up on your offer. Besides, staying in town will make it easier to rent a car in the morning."

She shifted the car into reverse to back up a few feet, and pulled into the rutted driveway, wincing as she bounced around in her seat. No wonder he owned a truck.

The driveway seemed to stretch on forever—a good hundred yards, by her estimation—before she could make out a cozy log cabin nestled in a small clearing. As they approached, she heard the sound of a dog barking. A big dog, judging by the deep tone of it.

She stopped her car at the edge of the clearing, and Reese popped out of the car. "Duke, quiet," he yelled.

Instantly, the dog fell silent, and even though she didn't know squat about pets, she was impressed.

"I'll be right back," Reese promised. "If you see anything out of the ordinary, lean on the horn."

He disappeared inside the log cabin, leaving her to wonder just what he meant by *out of the ordinary*. Since he was at home with cougars and bears, she figured his definition was far different than hers.

No reason to be afraid; she was surrounded by steel. Surely a bear wasn't strong enough to tip over a car. Or was it? The image that flashed in her mind wasn't reassuring.

Stop it! You're only making yourself crazy.

Katy took a deep breath and let go of the steering wheel, trying to relax. She repeated the action several times, pretending she was in her yoga class, willing the tension to leave her muscles.

Her hard-won sense of peace was shattered when the back passenger-side door to her four-door sedan opened and a mammoth dog jumped in, stuffing his wet nose against the vulnerable area along the side of her neck.

"Ack!" she cried, shrinking away from what looked like a moose masquerading as a dog.

"Down, Duke," Reese commanded. Once again, the dog dropped instantly, stretching out along the backseat as if he owned it. Reese set a box, a laptop case and a duffel bag on the floor before shutting the door.

Before she realized what was happening, Reese was tapping on her driver's-side window. Flustered, she pushed the button to lower it. "What are you doing?" Surely he wasn't going to leave her alone with his massive dog?

"Why don't you let me drive?" he suggested. "The driveway isn't easy to back down, and there are a few stumps in the clearing that might damage the undercarriage of your car."

She swallowed hard and nodded. Keeping a wary eye on

Duke lying across the backseat, she awkwardly crawled over the console and plopped in the passenger side. Reese slid her seat back before climbing in.

"Sorry if Duke scared you," he said, expertly backing down the winding driveway. He went slowly, but even so, the car bounced and jiggled as they went over the ruts. "There's no reason to be afraid. He won't hurt you."

"I...um, never had a pet," she confessed. "And he's really big. Are you sure he's not a wolf?" Seemed only natural to add wolves to the bears and cougars roaming around the woods.

"I'm sure." Reese's white teeth flashed in a quick smile. "Duke is a German shepherd, the breed most often used as police dogs. He's well trained, and I promise he won't hurt you."

"Okay. Good. That's good." She gripped the handrest as he turned onto the highway. It wasn't until they approached Main Street that she realized the Crystal Lake Motel might not allow pets, especially one as large as Duke.

The cute two-bedroom house she'd purchased was located just outside of town, on a small parcel of land with lakefront access. Perfect for a single woman living alone, but not nearly big enough for Reese and his huge dog.

Should she offer to stay at the motel so that Reese could use her house? She shouldn't have to leave her home, but truthfully, she'd rather stay in the motel than be confined in a small space with Duke.

Reese pulled in front of the motel. "Thanks for all your help," he said, handing her the keys. "Give me a minute to grab my things."

"Are you sure the motel will allow you to bring Duke?" she asked, dreading his response.

"Yeah, I've stayed here three years ago when I first took the DNR job. It won't be a problem."

She took the keys with a sense of overwhelming relief. "Okay, then. Let me know if you need anything."

"Sure thing." He opened the door, and she was surprised Duke didn't move until Reese gave him the signal. "Come, Duke."

Duke wagged his tail and leaped out of the car, staying close to Reese's side. Again, she had to admit she was impressed, even though the huge animal had scared her spitless.

Reese left with a wave, striding toward the motel with his duffel and computer case slung over his shoulder and some sort of box tucked beneath his arm. Was that the evidence he'd talked about? Or supplies for the dog?

Didn't matter, she told herself. It was well past midnight, and she was exhausted. Right now, she just wanted to go home.

But even in her familiar surroundings, sleep eluded her. She tried to blame her bout of insomnia on the adrenaline rush from dealing with the gunshot victims and then finding the badly damaged truck, but she knew those weren't the real cause.

Her mind kept returning to Reese. Anyone with half a brain would stay far away from him, considering that he'd been shot recently and had his truck smashed to smithereens. He was the kind of guy who lived in a log cabin and protected the wilderness as a DNR game warden. They were complete and total opposites.

So why couldn't she forget about him?

THE NEXT MORNING, sunlight streamed through her

window, waking her from a restless night far too early. She moaned and pulled her pillow over her head, but it was no use.

With a disgusted sigh, she crawled out of bed, grateful she had the next two days off work. She called the chief medical officer to report Wade Matthews, and then called University Hospital in Madison to check on Marcus Boyle.

She was relieved to hear that Boyle was listed in critical yet stable condition. About fifteen minutes later, her boss returned her call about Wade, promising to talk to him. Satisfied, she filled a cup of coffee and took a seat at her small kitchen table, where she could gaze out over the lake. The events from last night seemed surreal in the bright light of the morning.

It took a minute for her to remember that today was Sunday and that she was scheduled to be a greeter for the midmorning church service.

She finished her coffee and got ready for church. She was early, and as she drove past the motel she pressed on the brake, wondering if she should stop by to see how Reese and Duke were doing.

Wait a minute, what was she thinking? They were fine. Reese was more than capable of taking care of himself, and Duke too. She didn't even like dogs, although that might partially be because she'd never spent any time with them. Regardless, pets were not welcome in church.

Giving herself a mental shake, she sped up and approached the tall white-steeple church. As always, the minute she stepped inside God's house, she felt better. Calmer.

At peace.

She greeted the parishioners as they arrived, recognizing many of her former patients, from the occasional bout of the flu to more serious medical concerns such as having a stroke or heart attack.

On days like today, she was glad she'd made the decision to leave Baltimore. And not just because of Steffie, the young patient she'd lost. The ER at Baltimore General was seriously understaffed. The number of patients she'd treated in an average shift was more than double what she cared for in an entire weekend here at Hope County Hospital. And so far, she hadn't made any mistakes or errors in judgment.

Not yet.

She pushed the sliver of doubt away, determined to keep the nightmares from her past buried deep. The last thing the citizens of Crystal Lake and Hope County needed was for their ER doctor to have doubts about her level of competency.

Katy sat alone toward the back of the church when the service began. She enjoyed Pastor John's approach. He had a way of preaching that was interesting and engaging, without the fire-and-brimstone attitude that she'd sometimes heard before. The theme of his sermon today was keeping the Lord in the forefront of their minds and not just when they needed his strength and support. Katy knew she was guilty of doing exactly that and made a silent promise to do better from here on out.

When the service was over, she scooted out the back, avoiding the usual chatter that many of the parishioners enjoyed. She always felt a bit awkward in social situations like this, mostly because she knew most of the people here from the hospital, which some folks didn't appreciate being reminded about.

"Hi, Dr. Katy," Merry greeted her. "You remember my husband, Zack."

"Of course. How are you both doing?" she asked, smiling at the young couple. Merry had gone through a rough patch last fall, but things seemed to have settled down for her and Zack. In fact, she knew they were in the process of building their dream house on the other side of the lake.

"We're good, but you still look tired. We had a long shift last night, huh?" Merry said with a wry smile.

"Yes, but I called Madison this morning, and you'll be glad to know that our patient is stable."

"Good to hear," Merry said, giving her husband's hand a squeeze. "Zack was all worried about the gunshot wounds we had, but I assured him there was absolutely no danger."

"There was plenty of danger," Zack corrected. "You just got lucky."

An image of Reese's smashed truck floated in her mind, making her tend to agree with him. But she forced a smile. "I imagine Zack is always going to worry about you," she said, sidestepping the comment. "After all, you were hurt on the job once."

"That was different." Merry waved away the incident as inconsequential.

"Well, take care, both of you," Katy said, unwilling to be drawn into their good-natured spat. Although watching the way Zack looked at Merry, pure love shining from his blue eyes, made her heart squeeze in her chest, wishing for something she'd never have.

"You too, Dr. Katy." Merry waved as she and Zack headed toward their car.

She shook off the flash of envy. That was not in keeping with the spirit of Pastor John's sermon. She walked to her car, not in the mood to go back to her empty house.

Yet she wasn't going to stop at the motel, either. Besides, she doubted that Reese and his giant dog were still there.

He'd planned on renting a car, and even though it was Sunday, Hank, the guy who ran Billy's Auto Shop, was always willing to open up for a sure sale.

But what if Billy didn't have a car for sale or for rent? Katy found herself turning left at the stoplight so she could drive past Billy's Auto Shop.

When she saw Reese and Duke walking along the side of the road, she slowed down and lowered her window. "What happened? Didn't Hank have a car for you?"

"Hi, Katy," Reese greeted her. He stepped closer, and Duke followed, staying right by Reese's side. The dog was almost totally black in color and, if possible, looked more menacing in daylight than he had last night. "No, he doesn't have one yet but might by tomorrow."

"Do you need a ride?" she asked.

Reese hesitated, then shook his head. "I can walk to the motel, but I had been planning to drive up to Madison."

"I called the hospital," Katy said. "Boyle is in critical but stable condition."

"I called, too, and heard the same thing. But apparently no one has been up there to collect the evidence."

By evidence, she knew he meant the bullet. "Really? That seems odd."

"I know. It might be that the deputies just haven't been up there yet, but I thought it might be good to see for myself."

Katy nodded slowly. "I could drive you up there," she offered before she could talk herself out of it.

Reese smiled, and her heart did a funny little flip-flop in her chest. "Nice of you to offer, but I'm sure you have better things to do with your free time on your day off."

Sad fact was, she really didn't. She forced a smile and shook her head. "My only plan was to maybe take a hike, and it's far too hot for that. I really don't have any other plans."

Hope filled Reese's hazel-green eyes. "Are you sure? I'd be happy to pay for a tank of gas."

"It's really no bother," she assured him. "And this little car gets great gas mileage, especially compared to your truck." There was no way she was going to allow him to pay for her gas. She was fairly certain DNR game wardens didn't make that much money, and she had more than enough to spare.

"Well, then, thanks, I'd love a ride to Madison."

She had to bite her lip when Reese opened the back passenger door for Duke, who nimbly leaped onto the seat. She shrank back, half expecting him to sniff her again, but she needn't have worried. Duke simply stretched out once again, as if he was right at home.

Was she crazy to drive Reese and his dog to Madison? The drive would take an hour, easily. What on earth would they talk about?

When Reese slid into the passenger seat beside her and clicked his seat belt, she knew it was too late to change her mind.

Katy headed for the highway, trying to think of a safe topic to discuss. "How's your arm?" she asked. "Do we need to stop and pick up your antibiotics?"

"No worries, I have them right here," Reese said, patting his pocket. "My arm hurts, but it's nothing I can't handle. I changed the dressing this morning, and I didn't see any sign of infection."

She nodded, thinking it wouldn't hurt to check his incisions herself, just to be sure. Picking up speed on the highway, she kept a keen eye out for signs for the interstate.

Roughly five miles later, she took the on-ramp and relaxed when she reached freeway speed.

"Do you mind if I ask you a question?" he asked.

Surprised, she glanced at him. "Of course not. What is it?"

"Last night, when you were working on Boyle, why did you step back and let that other guy finish up?"

She shrugged, secretly glad the question wasn't too personal. "He's the trauma surgeon. I'm not."

"So basically, he should have been there right from the beginning. You sent that nurse to go and find him."

Reese Webster was far too perceptive for his own good. "Yes. I wasn't sure if he'd received the page."

"But he should have," Reese pressed.

"Yes, but there are a few dead spots in the hospital, so there's no way to know for sure. Why do you ask?"

"I was just curious. You seemed to have everything under control."

She was glad he thought so, even though, at the time, she'd been scared to death of making a mistake. Glancing in the rearview mirror, she noticed a large black truck coming up behind her at a rapid pace. "What in the world?" she muttered, quickly switching over to the right lane to get out of the way.

The big black truck switched lanes too.

Realization dawned, and her hands tightened on the steering wheel. For a moment, panic seized her by the throat. What should she do?

There weren't many options.

"Hang on," she warned, wrenching the steering wheel to the right and stomping on the brake as she headed off the highway.

4

Reese saw the black truck coming up fast and quickly dialed 911 on his cell phone. "This is Game Warden Webster. We're being chased by a black truck, license plate number TXR 990, five miles from Highway Double X."

He pressed his feet to the floor as Katy drove off the highway, bouncing over the shoulder and onto the flat grassy area as the car slowed to a stop. Duke yelped behind them, and Reese winced as he heard the dog slide to the floor. He had a crated area in his truck for the dog but obviously didn't have it in Katy's car. Reese spared a quick glance to make sure Duke was okay, and in a heartbeat, the black truck zoomed past them, having way too much momentum to slow down and stop.

Before he could say anything, Katy stomped on the accelerator. The car jerked forward, and Duke let out another yelp. She pulled back onto the freeway, crossed three lanes of thankfully light traffic to find a turnaround where cops sometimes sat to catch speeders. She executed a completely illegal U-turn and headed in the opposite direction.

"Were you a stunt driver before attending medical school?" he asked dryly as his heart returned to a normal rhythm.

Her smile was strained. "No, but maybe I should have been. How's Duke? Is he okay?"

"He'll be fine." Reese could tell she was badly shaken, and he didn't blame her. "I'm sorry, Katy. I suspect the driver of that black truck was after me."

"You don't know that for sure," she protested.

Oh, yes, he did. He scrubbed his hands over his face, regretting the fact that he'd dragged her into this mess. The blond dude must have been watching his truck last night, waiting for him to show up. Otherwise how could he have known which car was Katy's? The idea that they'd been followed made him feel sick to his stomach.

This had to end. Now. Before something else happened.

"Head to the sheriff's department," he said in a low tone. "We'll file a report, and since we have a license plate, there's a good chance they'll find this guy."

"Are you sure you don't want to head to Madison first?" she asked. "We can always report the near miss later."

"No, it's not worth risking your life." He hated thinking about just how close the near miss had been. The way the truck had barreled down at them, he suspected the driver had been planning to hit them in the rear, hoping they'd lose control while he kept going.

Good thing he'd managed to get the license plate number. At least the sheriff's deputies would have something to go on.

Katy was quiet as she drove back toward Crystal Lake and the Hope County Sheriff's Department. He kept sneaking glances at her, wondering if she might break down now that the danger was over.

But he should have known better. She parked the car in the parking lot and jumped out from the driver's seat before he'd even gotten his door open. He quickly lowered the back window for Duke, commanding him to stay, before following her inside.

"Did you hear me?" Katy said, her voice rising with anger. Reese could certainly hear her, so he had to assume the deputy standing in front of her could, too. "I demand to speak to Sheriff Torretti immediately!"

"Calm down, Dr. Katy," one of the deputies said, holding up his hands as if in surrender. "I understand you're upset, but Sheriff Torretti isn't here. He's out of town with his wife. I'm afraid you'll have to make do with me."

Fury radiated from her in waves, and he hid a smile at her redheaded temper as he stepped forward, putting a reassuring hand on her arm. "We'd like to file a police report against the black truck that tried to run us off the road."

"I'm Deputy Ian Kramer," the deputy said, holding out his hand, looking relieved to have someone calm to talk to.

Reese hadn't met this deputy before and reached out to shake his hand. "DNR Game Warden Reese Webster, and I have the license plate number for you. I'd appreciate your cooperation in finding this guy."

"We'd appreciate it," Katy interjected. "It was my car he almost hit."

"I understand. We'll put out a warrant right away," Deputy Kramer assured them.

It didn't take long for the deputy to take down all the details, and Reese tried not to think about the fact that they didn't have much to hold the guy on, if they even found him.

Reckless driving? That was nothing more than a traffic offense.

"There's a few other things I'd like to discuss," Reese said when Katy had finished her story. "Could we go someplace private?"

Deputy Kramer looked surprised and wary, but nodded. "Sure, this way."

The Hope County Sheriff's Department had two small interrogation rooms, and he pulled out a chair for Katy before dropping into the seat beside her. Deputy Kramer sat across from them, eyeing them expectantly.

"As you probably know, I was tracking a poacher who shot a bear and a cougar," Reese said carefully, unsure of how much Kramer actually knew about his case. "When I shouted at Marcus Boyle to stop, he took a shot at me, and I fired back."

Deputy Kramer nodded. "I read Deputy Armbruster's report."

"I forgot to mention that there was a second man I'd seen a few times while tracking Boyle. A tall blond guy, about six feet tall and weighing roughly two hundred pounds. I'd estimate his age to be in his mid-to late-twenties. The way he moved made me think he might have spent time in the military."

Kramer raised a brow. "You think this is the guy who trashed your truck. Which was towed to Billy's, in case you're wondering."

"I know, I was already over there." His truck was beyond repair, at least according to Hank. But right now that was the least of his problems. "I have some evidence linking the poaching to Boyle. After the incident with the bear, I caught a glimpse of the blond guy, but so far I don't have anything to prove he exists. I even thought that maybe Boyle had done the damage to my truck sometime before I caught him shooting the cougar. But after today, I know that it must have been the blond guy since Boyle is still in the hospital."

Kramer nodded. "All right, let's say the blond guy tried to run you off the road. Why? Just for revenge because you caught Boyle? That doesn't seem logical. You'd think Boyle's partner would take off to poach someplace else. There's plenty of wilderness for the guy to use. It makes no sense to keep coming after you."

"I know it's not logical," he admitted. "Unless he's some sort of relative to Boyle. What have you guys found out about him? Does he have family? Brothers? Friends? There has to be some link to the blond guy somewhere."

Kramer sat back in his chair with a heavy sigh. "Boyle's daddy is dead, and he doesn't have any brothers. Obviously, we'll keep digging, but right now we don't have any leads on who this second guy might be."

If he exists at all. The deputy didn't say the words, but he could read the doubt in his expression.

Great. Just great. Reese ground his teeth in frustration. "All right, but I hope you keep looking. This guy tried to seriously hurt us today. In fact, I want protection for Katy. This guy knows what kind of car she drives. It won't be a stretch for him to find her address, too."

Deputy Kramer grimaced and shook his head. "I'm sorry. As much as I'd like to provide Dr. Katy protection, we don't have that kind of manpower. I'll make sure that the deputies do frequent drive-bys though. She lives close enough to town that it won't be hard for us to keep an eye on her."

Drive-bys weren't at all what he had in mind, but what could he say? He didn't exactly have an alternative.

As much as he'd prefer to bunk down in her living room,

it was clear she was afraid of Duke. No matter how much danger she was in, he didn't think she'd allow him to move in with his dog. And he didn't have a car, so he couldn't very well park outside her house.

"I have a question about the bullet that was lodged in Boyle's lung," Katy spoke up. "Have you sent someone to Madison to pick it up?"

"Deputy Armbruster is planning to do that as soon as he has a chance," Deputy Kramer acknowledged. "Look, Dr. Katy, I understand your concern, especially after the scare you just had on the freeway, but I need you to trust us to do our jobs, okay?"

"All right," she agreed with obvious reluctance.

Reese rose to his feet, wishing there was some way to keep Katy safe.

Because the alternative was too painful to contemplate.

Katy did her best to rein in her frustration as they left the sheriff's department, but it wasn't easy. Her footsteps faltered when she noticed Duke hanging his head out the back window.

"Don't be afraid," Reese murmured, coming up beside her. She liked the feel of his hand in the small of her back a little too much. "If you'd spend more time with him, you'd know there's nothing to worry about."

Despite the soaring temperatures and the sun beating down on their heads, she shivered at the thought of spending time with Duke. "He's the biggest dog I've ever seen in my life."

"And he's probably the best-trained dog you've ever seen in your life, too," Reese argued mildly. "He'll obey me without hesitation. And he'd protect us both with his life."

She sensed Reese was hurt that she was afraid of his dog, but she couldn't bring herself to approach the animal, not even for his sake. "I'm sure you're right, but I think it's best if I take you back to the motel."

"Thanks. We can always walk if that would make you feel better." There was no mistaking the disappointment lining his tone.

"Don't be silly. As long as Duke stays in the back, I'll be fine."

Reese jogged around to open her door for her, and she flashed him a smile before sliding in. No one had ever opened her doors for her, and she suspected Reese's mother had something to do with his gentlemanly manners. On one hand, she was perfectly capable of opening her own doors, but the fact that he cared enough to be polite resonated somewhere deep within.

The last guy she'd dated, Jeff Andrews, had distanced himself in the aftermath of Steffie's death. Even after she'd been exonerated from any wrongdoing, he'd kept his distance. When she'd informed him she was leaving Baltimore General, he'd assured her it was for the best. He'd actually appeared relieved to have her gone.

Looking back, she understood that Jeff had been trying to protect his own reputation in the hospital. But still, he clearly hadn't really cared about her as a woman. Or even as a colleague.

Shaking off the troublesome memories wasn't easy. She glanced over at Reese only to find him watching her intently. She blushed and then mentally bemoaned her fair skin.

"Katy, how would you like to go for a boat ride on the lake?" he asked.

She blinked in surprise. Had she missed something? "You have a boat?"

"Well, actually, Hank has one that he offered to let me use for the day," he explained. "To make up for not having a car ready for me. And the thought of sitting in a motel room doing nothing isn't at all appealing. Please come with me. There's no reason not to enjoy a nice day out on the water."

Katy wanted to say yes, but she couldn't help glancing in the backseat at Duke. "How does Duke like the water?"

Reese flashed a grin. "Actually, he loves it, but I can leave him in the motel room for a few hours."

"Really?" She couldn't keep the relief from her tone. "All right, then I'd be happy to go out in a boat with you."

"Great. Why don't you drop us off and then head home to change into something more comfortable." He gestured lightly to her short-sleeved sweater and flowered skirt that she'd worn to church. "I'll get the boat keys from Hank and meet you back at the motel."

"Sounds good." She pulled into the motel parking lot and kept the car idling while Reese slid out and then opened the door for Duke.

The dog didn't move but waited until Reese said, "Come," before he bounded out of the backseat. Reese flashed her a quick smile. "See you soon."

"All right." After he slammed the door, she put the car in reverse and backed carefully out of the parking space. It wasn't until she was at home, while changing into shorts and a tank top, that she began to doubt the wisdom of spending time with Reese.

Even if she was ready to have a relationship, they would no doubt have completely different schedules to go along with their opposite personalities. She cared for people; he cared about animals. He adored the outdoors while she preferred sitting at home with a good book.

He didn't know anything about the mistakes of her past,

and while he didn't seem the type to judge her unfairly, the fact of the matter was, she still wrestled with guilt.

She'd almost talked herself out of going out on the lake, but the thought of leaving Reese standing at the motel, waiting for her, made her wince. Talk about rude! And going over there just to tell him she'd changed her mind seemed ridiculous. He'd see right through whatever pathetic excuse she came up with, and that would only make him more curious about why she'd backed out of something any number of friends would do.

She stared at her reflection in the mirror. She needed to remember this wasn't a date. They were two adults spending time together, nothing more.

This absolutely wasn't a date.

REESE WAS SWEATING by the time he'd gotten the boat keys from Hank and made his way back to the motel. He risked a quick cold shower before pulling on cargo shorts and a T-shirt. The boat was moored along the public dock, one of the few boats left since most of the others were out on the water.

He was looking forward to relaxing on the lake. Granted, spending the afternoon with Katy was no hardship, either, but he knew he couldn't afford to think of her as anything but a friend.

Any woman who didn't like dogs—or any other animals, for that matter—wasn't for him. Best to remember that fact.

He stopped in at Rose's Cafe, requesting a couple of cold sandwiches to go. Josie's knowing smile made him grimace but even the gossip that would surely follow wasn't enough to stop him. There were already two bottles of water from the vending machine chilling in a bucket of ice in his room.

Katy pulled up mere seconds after he'd returned to the room. "Stay," he said to Duke, who looked forlorn at being left behind. "Guard."

Duke obediently stretched out on the floor, watching him with his dark eyes. Was he crazy to take Katy out on the boat when he could be spending time with his best friend?

As he walked outside, holding their sandwiches and water, the sight of Katy wearing casual shorts and a tank top stole his breath. She was beautiful. No way was he going to regret spending the afternoon with her.

"Hope you don't mind, I brought some food for us," he said as he met up with her. "This way we don't have to hurry back."

Was it his imagination, or was her smile strained? "Sounds great."

"This way," he said, walking down to the community pier. Hank's red speedboat was nothing fancy, but he didn't care. He jumped in and set down the food and water in a small hollowed out area in the bow and then went back to give Katy a hand.

"You know what you're doing, right?" she asked, looking a bit apprehensive.

"Absolutely. I used to own a boat of my own." He didn't add that he'd had to sell it at a loss when Suzanne had cleaned out their joint bank account. He'd managed to get enough for the boat to cover the outstanding loan, leaving nothing extra.

Katy sat down in the seat next to the pilot's chair, watching as he disconnected the moor lines and then started the engine. He put the throttle in reverse and carefully backed away from the pier.

He putt-putted across the no wake zone and then gave it a little gas when they passed the buoys.

"Wow, this is amazing!" Katy exclaimed as the wind whipped at her hair. She once again wore it back in the fancy braid she favored, and he found himself wishing she'd wear it long and unbound for him. Although it was hardly practical while out on the boat.

"Hang on," he said, pushing the throttle forward. The front of the boat leaped up and bounced against the waves. He grinned and steered clear of a boat pulling an inner tube with a swimmer riding inside it.

He pulled back on the throttle, slowing down so he could make a circle around the lake. When he glanced over at Katy, she looked dazed yet happy.

"That was fun," she declared. "I like going fast."

"Me, too. But there are a lot of boats out, so we can't let her rip too much."

"I know; it's crazy busy out here." A shadow darkened her eyes. "I hope the ER doesn't get slammed."

"I'm sure they can handle it, just like you do when you're on." There was a boat coming toward them, so he cranked the wheel to get out of the way.

But the boat didn't move off course. He laid on the horn and pushed up the throttle, trying to get out of the way. At the last possible moment, the boat sped past, missing them by inches.

The boat rocked crazily against the wake, and he pulled back the throttle, glaring over at the careless driver. The boat was heading in the opposite direction now, but he could easily see the broad-shouldered man driving it.

A man with close-cropped blond hair.

5

————

When Reese hit the gas, Katy swallowed a shriek and clutched the edge of the boat, silently praying for safety, relieved when the boat swept past, missing them by inches.

"Did you get a good look at that guy?" Reese asked harshly.

"No, why? Did he look familiar?"

"I don't know. Maybe." Reese grimaced and shook his head. "He had blond hair, but so do dozens of other people on the lake."

She realized he thought the boat driver might be the same guy who'd tried to crash into them earlier. Seemed unlikely, though. How would some stranger figure out that Reese had rented a boat from Hank? A car, maybe, but a boat? "Does Hank lend out this boat often?" she asked.

"Sometimes, but not often," Reese said. "You're right, though, it doesn't make sense that the blond dude just happened to follow us onto the lake."

"It's not impossible," she mused. "Do you think we should report this to Deputy Kramer?"

"Nah, I didn't get the ID number from the boat, and unfortunately, the guy is long gone. For all we know, this was nothing more than some tourist looking for a thrill." The dark shadow in his eyes made her think he'd only tacked on that last statement for her benefit.

"Maybe we should head back," she murmured.

There was a long silence while he steered the boat off into a small cove where there weren't many other boats. When he killed the motor, he turned to look at her with a smile. "I promised you a picnic, so why don't we drop anchor here and eat?"

Since she didn't really want to leave—being out on the boat was so much nicer than being stuck at home—she nodded. "All right."

"Great. Just give me a minute." Reese pulled the anchor out from beneath the bench seat and dropped it over the side. She was surprised at how he seemed to ignore the wound in his left arm. Surely it had to still hurt? He wore a T-shirt today, and it looked like a fresh gauze strip had been wrapped around his arm.

"Seems like you're the type to have a boat of your own," she said, watching him move around with confidence. "You obviously know what you're doing."

He froze for a moment and then shrugged. "Boats cost money, and I work too much to make the investment worthwhile." He avoided her gaze as he pulled up the short canopy to provide some shade. Maybe it was her imagination, but he seemed tense. Or maybe defensive. "You should sit under here so you don't burn."

"Believe me, I lathered up with sunscreen, but thanks." She took the seat directly beneath the canopy, wondering if she'd made him mad. Was he sensitive about money? She had no idea how much DNR game wardens made, but surely he didn't have too many bills living alone.

Not that it was any of her business. She waited as Reese pulled out the sandwiches, chips and two bottles of water.

"I hope you don't mind turkey on whole wheat," he said, handing her a wrapped package. "I wasn't sure what you liked, so I took a guess based on the chicken sandwich you had last night."

"Turkey on whole wheat is exactly what I would have ordered," she assured him. "Why? What do you have?"

"Roast beef." When he grinned, he looked younger, more carefree, and she decided her imagination had been working overtime earlier. Right now, Reese Webster looked as if he didn't have a care in the world, despite being shot in the arm by a poacher. "But if you didn't like turkey, I would have traded."

She laughed and bit into her sandwich, suddenly starving. "Guess today is your lucky day."

"Absolutely," he agreed, and his intense gaze made her wonder if he was talking about being out with her, rather than the sandwich.

She told herself to get a grip. They were friends helping each other out. Nothing more. Averting her gaze, she looked out over the lake, amazed to realize it was actually much larger than she'd originally thought. And so many people. Kids and adults alike were tubing, skiing and playing around on Jet Skis. There were even a few kids swimming, but they were on a floaty thing closer to shore, well out of the way from the motorized toys.

"Is this your first boat ride?" Reese asked.

She grimaced. "Is it that obvious? Yes, this is my first boat ride. I grew up in the city, and even though Baltimore is on the coast, I never had the opportunity to go out on the ocean."

"Crystal Lake is way different than being out on the ocean," Reese said dryly. "The waves get pretty choppy out in the Atlantic."

"Did you live on the ocean?" she asked, curious about Reese's life. He'd mentioned not having any family, no one to worry about him, but she sensed right now he was speaking from experience.

A smile tugged at the corner of his mouth. "I did live on the ocean. On a boat in the ocean." At her puzzled glance, he clarified. "I did a four-year stint in the navy."

"And here I thought your mother drilled those manners into you," she teased. "I should have guessed you spent time in the military."

"Oh, my mother expected manners too," he said dryly. "She's been gone for three years, but I'm sure I'd hear her chiding me if I didn't keep up what she taught."

"I'm sorry for your loss," she said. "Cancer?"

"Brain aneurysm." The words came out clipped. "We were told to be happy she went quickly and didn't suffer." His expression told her what he thought about that idea.

"I'm sorry," she repeated, understanding this topic was treading on shaky ground. She knew from dealing with patients that sometimes the abrupt deaths were the most difficult just because they were so unexpected. Most families grieved about being unable to say good-bye. "I'm sure that was very difficult for you and your family. I hope you can find a little comfort in knowing she's in a much better place now."

He raised an eyebrow and shrugged. "Maybe. Once I might have believed that, although I'm not so sure anymore."

She didn't know what had happened to cause him to lose his faith, but she sensed he had secrets. But what difference did it make? So did she. For a moment, she sat back, wondering if this was the reason that God had thrown Reese into her path.

To help him rediscover his faith.

A mission she couldn't refuse.

REESE FINISHED HIS FOOD, searching for a way to change the subject. How had they gone from sharing a picnic to talking about death? Not exactly a good topic for spending the afternoon on the lake.

"Do you want to swim?" he asked. "I can't because of the stitches, but you could."

She laughed and shook her head. "I don't think so. I didn't bring a swimming suit."

Her laugh made her look innocent, a far cry from the determined doctor he'd watched perform surgery on Boyle. It was difficult to ignore Katy's beauty, the way her hair came loose from her braid, trailing around her face, and her cheeks turning pink from the sun.

"Well, then, I guess we'll do another swing around the lake before heading in." Strange how he didn't want this day to end. Normally he preferred spending time alone, hiking in the woods with no one but Duke for company. His buddies called him a hermit, and maybe that was partially true. He didn't particularly care for crowds, but it was also easier to save money when you didn't go out or do anything for fun.

In fact, the money he'd spent today, gas for the boat and their modest lunch, was the first money he'd spent on something frivolous since Suzanne had left him.

He waited for the flash of guilt, but it never came. Even knowing he'd have to come up with the cash for the deductible on his insurance didn't make him regret the money he'd spent today.

"Here, let me," Katy said, taking the wrapping and napkins from his hands. Their fingers brushed, sending a little zip up his arm.

"I'll get the anchor then," he muttered, edging around her to the bow of the boat. By the time he had the anchor pulled up and the canopy down, she had all the garbage tucked away in a neat little bag.

"Thanks for the picnic," she said. "And for the boat ride."

"You're welcome. Hang on." He pushed the throttle forward, steering the boat back out to the center of the lake.

Katy put her hand up to shade her eyes as she gazed out at the skiers. He'd love to get her up on skis and wondered if she'd be willing. Not now, but maybe in a few weeks or so.

Wait a minute, what was he thinking? This wasn't a date. This was just a way to say thank you for the way she'd helped him out.

"Reese, hurry! Look over there! That boy is having trouble."

Her shout pushed his thoughts aside, and he squinted in the direction she pointed. He caught sight of a kid who looked to be about ten years old, floundering in the water. He cranked the wheel and pushed the speed as far as he dared to reach the boy.

"He's under! Hurry!" Before he realized what she intended to do, she kicked off her shoes and climbed up along the side of the boat.

"Wait, I'll go," he called, but it was too late. Katy dove into the water.

He pulled back the throttle, trying to come up alongside the spot where he'd last seen the child. The lake was murky, mostly from all the mud that had been churned up from the boat motors. He held his breath until Katy's head broke the surface in roughly the spot where they'd seen the boy go down.

She took another deep breath and then went back down in the water. How in the world she'd find the kid was beyond him. He struggled to come up with another plan, but if he dove into the water, who would manage the boat? No, he couldn't risk it.

Suddenly, the boy surfaced, waving his arms frantically.

"Over here!" Reese called, pulling out the round lifesaver. He tossed it toward the boy, but the kid was too panicked and abruptly sank back down beneath the surface again.

"Come on, come on," he urged under his breath. And for the first time in years, he sent up a silent prayer.

Lord, please save him! Save them both!

After what seemed like an eternity, two heads broke the surface of the water, and he felt an overwhelming relief. Katy had the child, but he soon realized the boy was limp, as if he was unconscious.

Not dead. Please, Lord, not dead!

"Grab the life preserver. I'll pull you in." Reese knew they had to move quickly.

Katy grabbed ahold of the life preserver and used it to help keep the boy's head above water. Reese slowly pulled them in, amazed to see that she was trying to do mouth-to-mouth resuscitation right there in the water. It couldn't have been easy, but somehow she was making it work.

"Help me get him up," she gasped when he pulled them

to the edge of the boat. He flipped the ladder down and leaned over the side to grasp the boy beneath his arms. The kid was light, so it didn't take much to yank him out of the water.

He put the boy down on the floor of the boat while Katy climbed in. Water poured off her in tiny streams as she came over to kneel beside the boy. He swallowed hard as she pressed her fingers to the child's neck. "He has a pulse, but we need to get the water out of his lungs."

Reese nodded. "I can help. Tell me what you want me to do."

"Just keep his head turned to the side." She straddled the boy and performed several abdominal thrusts. Then she went back to try and give more mouth-to-mouth breathing, forcing air into his lungs.

Abruptly, the boy started choking, and she quickly rolled him over on his side just in time for him to throw up all the water he'd swallowed. He continued to cough and gag, struggling for air while Katy quietly reassured him.

Once Reese saw that the boy was okay, he stepped over them to take the wheel. Now that he was paying attention to the other people on the lake, he could see there was a boat barreling down on them. Not the blond dude, but several people crowded around, looking anxious.

"Jacob! Are you okay?" one of them called.

"Are those your parents?" he asked.

"My friend's parents," the kid mumbled. "They're gonna be mad at me 'cause I told them I could swim."

Reese met Katy's concerned gaze over the boy's head. She put her arm around the boy's bony shoulders and gave him a reassuring squeeze. "First of all, they're going to be happy that you're okay. But you shouldn't have lied to them,

Jacob. Not about something this important. You almost drowned today."

"I know," Jacob said, his tiny body shaking now that the immediate threat was over. He sniffled loudly. "I'm sorry about the mess on your boat, mister."

Reese flashed the boy a warm smile. "Hey, don't worry about it, I'll get it cleaned up in no time."

"Jacob? What happened?" A woman called out as the boat slid alongside them. "Are you all right?"

"He's fine," Katy assured them. "But he should probably be checked out at the hospital, just to be sure. I'm afraid he inhaled quite a bit of water."

"I'm sorry," Jacob said, hanging his head low. "I should have been wearing a life jacket the way you told me to."

"Yes, you should have, but right now, I'm just thankful you're all right." The woman flashed a grateful smile at Katy. "You look familiar," she said. "My name is Andrea Walters."

"I'm Dr. Katy Reichert. I work in the Hope County ER."

"Lucky for us you were here to help Jacob," Andrea said with a smile. "When we realized he'd fallen in, we swung around but couldn't see him. I'm so glad you were able to find him."

"It's no problem." Katy reached over to hold the boats together so Jacob could get across. The family welcomed him by wrapping him in a towel and then plunking a life jacket over his head and tying it securely.

Katy pushed the boat away and turned back to face Reese. "Do you have a towel, by chance?" she asked, trying to wring out her soaked clothing.

"Right here." He pulled a towel out, and she took it gratefully.

"Well, that was an exciting end to our picnic," she said, pulling the towel across her shoulders and crossing the ends in front of her chest. "Although I wouldn't have minded skipping the water rescue part."

"Once again, you were amazing," he said as he turned the boat toward the community pier. "I nearly had heart failure when you jumped in. Why didn't you let me do it?"

"Did you forget about your stitches? Besides, I don't know how to steer a boat."

Maybe he had forgotten the stupid stitches, but that wouldn't have held him back from trying to rescue the boy. "You must have lifeguard training."

"No, just instincts." She sighed. "But that was too close. I couldn't see anything in the water, and I was so afraid I wouldn't be able to save him. All I could do was pray."

"I prayed too." The words popped out of his mouth before he could stop them.

Katy's quick smile made him feel like a fraud. Just because he'd prayed in a time of crisis didn't mean he was a reformed Christian or anything.

"God is always there for us, Reese," Katy said softly. Even with her matted-down hair and soaking-wet clothes, she still looked beautiful. "No matter what may have happened in the past. I hope you give Him another chance."

"I'll try," was the extent of what he was willing to commit to.

She smiled again, and he forced himself to concentrate on what he was doing. He knew better than to encourage her. Why had he even suggested this picnic in the first place? It wasn't as if he could offer her anything more than friendship. There was no way he could risk getting involved in another relationship. Not when his job required him to be gone for long hours at a time. Maybe it wasn't as long as the stints he'd pulled in the navy, but long enough.

Katy was smart, talented, and a doctor, for heaven's sake.

She saved people's lives every day. Even if he was in the market for a relationship, she was way out of his reach. She deserved far better than a loner who was up to his eyeballs in debt.

The sooner his brain got that message, the better.

6

"Are you sure you don't want me to drop you off at your house?" Reese asked.

Katy shook her head. "As much as I'd like that, there isn't a pier over there. I guess I'd rather not wade through the muck to get on land."

"All right."

She watched as Reese deftly maneuvered the boat along the community pier. Walking back to her house wouldn't take too long, although she knew her appearance would make people curious enough to stare and ask questions. The hardest thing to get used to in Crystal Lake was the way everyone knew everyone else's business.

"I'd offer you my motel room, but I don't have clothes that would fit you," Reese said apologetically.

Had he figured out what she was thinking? She really needed to work on her poker face. "It's not a big deal. Think of the possible rumors. Maybe the citizens of Crystal Lake will assume you tossed me in the water after I broke things off with you."

He chuckled. "Now there's a thought. Or maybe you

were so upset by our breakup that you jumped in the water on purpose."

She wrinkled her nose at him. "Anyone who knows me wouldn't believe that for a minute."

He opened his mouth as if he were about to say something but then must have thought better of it. "Do you want me to walk you home?"

"No need," she responded hastily. "But maybe I should help you clean up the mess first."

"No, just head home to change your clothes," he said firmly. "Duke can keep me company while I clean this up."

She nodded and told herself she was *not* afraid of Reese's dog. But the animal was a reminder that they were friends and nothing more. "All right. Thanks again for the picnic and boat ride."

"You're welcome." He didn't meet her eyes as he helped her off the boat. She was halfway to her house before she realized she still had his towel.

She made a mental note to make sure to get it back to him as soon as she'd washed it. Not that he probably cared one way or the other about a beach towel.

Was she looking for an excuse to see him again? No, absolutely not.

But after she showered and changed, she put a small load of laundry in the washing machine, including the towel and her smelly lake clothes.

Better to return the stupid towel than to keep it as some sort of memento of their afternoon together.

As THE AFTERNOON WORE ON, the weather grew more stifling, to the point that cooking dinner was not a viable option. She was almost out of fresh veggies too, so she couldn't even throw together a salad.

There was an old-fashioned ice cream parlor on Main Street, unfortunately a little too close to the Crystal Lake Motel for comfort. But was she really going to sit here just to avoid Reese? Talk about ridiculous. For all she knew, he was probably back out on the boat, with Duke for company.

She left her house and walked toward town, cringing at the number of people crowding the sidewalks. Not that she should complain—Crystal Lake depended on tourism for a good portion of its financial stability. Summer was the high point, but they saw good business during the fall festival and hunting season. They were even blessed to have tourists come to cross-country ski and snowmobile in the winter.

No doubt the hunting season was the busiest for Reese and the rest of the DNR game wardens. Although she hadn't realized poaching was such a problem until Reese had first shown up in the ER after being clawed by a wounded bear.

She was so lost in her thoughts that she almost went right past the ice cream parlor. Even though she hadn't eaten dinner yet, she decided there was no reason she couldn't start with dessert. When she pushed open the door, a tiny bell jangled, announcing her arrival.

"Hi, Dr. Katy." The young girl across the counter greeted her with familiarity, and she stared for a minute, trying to place the dark hair pulled back in a ponytail. Oh, yes, she was the young girl who'd come in a few months ago with that nasty flu bug. "Hi, Claire, how are you?"

"I heard you pulled Jacob out of the lake," Claire said, her eyes wide with awe. "Timmy's parents said he would have *died* if you hadn't been there."

"Well, I'm just glad he's okay," Katy said, trying to focus

on the various flavors of ice cream. "What's the special today?"

"You just missed Mr. Webster and his dog," Claire went on as if she hadn't heard the question. "Mr. Webster wouldn't buy anything for Duke, though. He said people food would make him sick."

Good grief, had the rumor mill been so busy that even a high school kid thought they were dating? "I'm sure Mr. Webster knows what's best for his dog, but I think I'd like a dish of the mint chocolate chip, please."

This time, Claire heard the order and busied herself with scooping the ice cream into a small plastic dish. The way Claire looked at her expectantly made her think the girl figured she wanted to catch up with Reese and Duke.

Irrationally, that's exactly what she wanted to do.

Stop it!

She pulled her wallet out of her purse and paid Claire before taking her ice cream. When she left the parlor, she decided to head away from the central part of town where the band was playing, assuming that's where Reese and Duke had been headed. She didn't think having Duke would slow him down, not after the way he'd trained the dog to listen.

The cool ice cream tasted wonderful, and she savored the minty flavor as she meandered away from the congestion of tourists. She headed toward the hilly area where the hiking trail began. Not that she intended to hike, but there was a small bench near the base of the hill.

The moment she sat down, she heard voices and tried not to show her disappointment. So much for having a brief moment of peace and quiet.

"Yeah, you're right, I should just forget about it."

The deep male voice sounded familiar, but she was sure that it was nothing more than her imagination.

A moment later, Reese and Duke emerged from the hiking trail. When he saw her sitting there, he looked guilty about something.

"Hi," Reese greeted her awkwardly.

She hid her smile behind a spoon of ice cream. "Were you really talking to your dog?" she asked.

He lifted a shoulder and nodded. "Why not? Duke is a good listener, aren't you, boy?"

Duke perked up his ears and wagged his tail but didn't come over to sniff at her. Instead, he stayed right beside Reese, almost as if guarding his owner from some potential threat. She had the odd thought that it might be nice to have a pet to keep the loneliness at bay.

But even if she did break down to get a pet, it wouldn't be a dog with huge teeth like Duke.

She pushed the idea away, knowing that having a pet with her crazy schedule was out of the question. "So, how come you're not in town, enjoying the band? I figured you'd make the most of your time here." Every weekend a band set up outside, weather permitting, to play for the tourists.

"Nah, too crowded." He stood for a minute, his hand tucked into the pockets of his cargo shorts. He had nice, tanned legs and was wearing a T-shirt that clung to his broad, muscular shoulders. And why was she noticing that, anyway?

"Why aren't you listening to the band?" he asked, turning her question back on her.

Since she could hardly tell him how she'd come this way to avoid running into him, she shrugged. "Country music isn't my thing."

"I thought I heard a rock-and-roll song a few minutes ago," Reese said with a puzzled frown.

"Oh, country rock, whatever." She concentrated on scraping the last bit of ice cream from the dish. "I hope it didn't take you too long to clean off the boat," she said, rising to her feet.

He waved it off. "No worries. I made sure the boat was cleaner than when Hank loaned it to me. And he thinks he'll have a car available by tomorrow afternoon, too."

For some reason, the thought of Reese leaving town to return to his isolated home tucked into the woods made her feel depressed. Which was completely ridiculous. She should be glad that she wouldn't be tripping over him every time she walked down Main Street.

"Good news for both of you," she said, nodding toward Duke. "I'm sure he misses being able to run around in your backyard."

"Trust me, he does. When I call him into the motel room, I swear he gives me a look full of doggy reproach."

She couldn't help but laugh. "I bet." She hated the fact that she was still intimidated by the massive beast. Even though he was an extremely well-behaved massive beast. "Well, I should really head home. Nice chatting with you."

"Sure. Take care," Reese said, matching her offhand tone.

She turned to leave and didn't think it was an accident that Reese stayed right where he was, with Duke by his side. Was the thought of walking with her too abhorrent? She mentally rolled her eyes. No, she was being stupid. Most likely he was trying to give her space. Plus, he seemed to know she was more than a little afraid of Duke.

Okay, so Reese allowing her to walk home alone was his

way of being polite. So why was she feeling so upset and disconcerted?

She took a deep breath and let it out slowly. But even as she walked away, it took every ounce of will she possessed not to turn around to see him one last time.

REESE KEPT his hand by his side, wordlessly telling Duke to stay right beside him since he sensed the dog wanted to follow Katy.

Or maybe Duke was just picking up on his desire to follow Katy.

Reminding himself over and over again that this was for the best didn't make him feel any better. He hadn't gone too far up the hiking trail, mostly because dusk was falling and he didn't want to risk losing his footing on unfamiliar terrain.

Having a gunshot wound in his arm was one thing. Being stupid enough to sprain an ankle would be far worse. His boss was already chomping at the bit for him to get back to work.

So far, Gavin hadn't found the dead cougar, either. They'd had no trouble finding the kill site—there had been plenty of blood marking the spot, so that wasn't the problem. Granted, it was possible a scavenger had dragged it away, but there should be signs of that, too. According to Gavin, he and George had been combing the woods all day but still hadn't found so much as a tuft of fur.

Reese knew with sick certainty that they would never find the cougar because the blond dude had already scooped it up. There was no other explanation for how the carcass had disappeared without a trace.

Taking the bullet evidence with it.

After waiting a good fifteen minutes, he began to walk back toward town. He was extremely grateful that he would only need to stay one more night at the motel. And not just because of the added expense. The noise from people going up and down Main Street at all hours of the night was driving him crazy.

Thinking about the lost evidence from the cougar made him even more anxious to talk to the sheriff's deputies again. They'd get the bullet from Boyle's chest and match it to his gun, but so far, he didn't have as much evidence against Boyle as he would have liked. He had his eyewitness account, sure. And the photos of the boot prints he'd found, along with the bullet from the bear.

Would that be enough? He sincerely hoped so.

Without conscious thought, he ended up outside the sheriff's department headquarters, located a little outside of town. But, of course, the place was shut down to the public this late on a Sunday night.

He considered banging on the door to get the dispatcher's attention but figured the deputies would be busy.

As he turned to leave, a deputy vehicle pulled up and stopped beside him. The deputy rolled down his window, and he recognized Armbruster. "Webster, right?"

"Yeah, that's right."

"Your dog should be on a leash," Armbruster said with a frown.

"He's trained as a police dog. He won't do anything without a command from me." Reese kept his voice even, but he was getting annoyed with this deputy.

"He still needs to be on a leash," Armbruster repeated. "What are you doing here, anyway? Did you need something?"

"Just wanted to check up on where you're at with the

investigation." Reese wished he hadn't come this way since he suspected Armbruster wouldn't tell him anything, even if he had some news.

"No news yet, but we're working on it."

"Okay, thanks." Reese moved as if to leave.

"Heard you and Dr. Katy saved that boy this afternoon," Armbruster said. "Nice work."

He shouldn't have been surprised at how fast news traveled through Crystal Lake, but he was. "Thanks, but Dr. Katy is the one who did the work. I just helped."

"We're lucky to have Dr. Katy working here. She's a very talented lady," Armbruster agreed.

Reese nodded, understanding the unspoken warning. Armbruster didn't want him doing anything to hurt their beloved doctor. And he understood; he would feel the same way. "See you later, Deputy." He lifted his hand in a wave and then turned around to head back toward the motel. Duke, thankfully, behaved himself by walking directly at his side the entire way.

"Don't look at me like that," he said to Duke as he unlocked the door. "I don't like it here anymore than you do."

Duke huffed and crossed the threshold, leaving Reese to do the same. A group of giggling kids walked by, their shrill voices piercing the night air.

Reese sighed and shut the door behind him. This was going to be a long night, in more ways than one.

KATY STARED at the ceiling fan swirling over her bed, trying to figure out why she couldn't fall asleep.

As much as she wanted to blame Reese, she was more tuned in to every little creak and groan of the house. Normal sounds that, for some reason, had never bothered her before.

She closed her eyes and prayed, seeking peace. The church services she'd attended earlier that morning seemed like days ago rather than hours. But instead of remembering Pastor John's sermon, the image of Jacob's still features flashed in her memory.

For a moment, he'd reminded her painfully of Steffie. The young girl had been several years older than Jacob, but her pale, lifeless face had haunted Katy for the past year.

She squeezed her eyes shut and tried to find comfort in the fact that Jacob hadn't died. God had spared his life today.

Why hadn't he spared Steffie's?

To teach her a lesson. To make her realize that she needed to pay more attention to her patients' signs and symptoms. To remind her that patients were people who needed care, not just to be shuffled through the revolving door that the Baltimore General ED had become.

Her chest tightened with guilt, and she blinked back the tears. If she could take back that night she'd discharged Steffie without requesting a surgical consult, she would. But Steffie's pain had gone away after she'd given a fluid bolus, so she hadn't considered appendicitis as a probable cause of the pain, especially since she'd had a waiting room full of patients still to be seen.

And when Steffie's parents had brought her back to the ER four days later, after her appendix had burst, it had been too late. Steffie had died of massive sepsis.

I'm sorry. I'm so sorry! Dear Lord, please forgive me. Please!

Somehow, she must have dozed because a muffled thud woke her up. For a moment, she peered through the darkness, wondering if her mind was playing tricks on her again. Was probably nothing, just someone slamming a car door.

A creak from a floorboard made her sit bolt upright in bed. She recognized that creak from the center of her living room.

Someone was in her house!

7

Katy grabbed her cell phone that she thankfully kept on the bedside table next to her—just in case the hospital needed to get ahold of her—and disconnected it from the charger. Then she slipped out of bed, down onto the floor, hiding behind the bed as she quickly considered her options. The bed was between her and the doorway, and the bathroom was also near the doorway, far too close to the living room.

She had no intention of going anywhere near where the intruder was. Which meant she was trapped.

What should she do? The only thing on this side of the bedroom was a small, barely-able-to-walk-in closet and a window that led to the back of the house.

She could maybe hide in the closet at least long enough to call 911.

The better answer was to go out the window, but she was afraid she'd make too much noise. What if the intruder heard her leave? If he had a gun, he could shoot her from the doorway. The image made her shudder.

No, she should probably call the authorities first and plot her escape later.

Staying low, she crawled on her hands and knees toward the closet. The door was ajar, so she soundlessly opened it farther and eased inside before carefully closing it behind her.

Not the best hiding spot—it wouldn't take long for the intruder to find her—so she needed to act quickly. Slipping a heavy sweater off one of the hangers, she cupped it around her head and the phone in an effort to muffle the noise as she dialed 911.

The phone rang five times on the other end, making her want to scream in frustration before a dispatcher answered. "Please state the nature of your emergency," the woman said in what seemed like an unnecessarily loud voice.

Was the sweater enough to muffle the sound? Or could the intruder hear her? Sweat beaded on her forehead, and she tried not to shake.

"This is Dr. Katy," she whispered. "Someone's in my house."

That got the dispatcher's attention as her voice went quiet. "I have a deputy nearby," the dispatcher said softly. "Stay on the line with me while I send him over."

One good thing about small towns: everyone knew where everyone else lived, so she didn't have to risk telling the dispatcher what her address was. She was already afraid she'd been too loud. Tucking the phone in the folds of the sweater, she leaned forward and placed her ear near the closet door, straining to listen.

There was nothing but silence.

Did that mean the intruder was gone? Was this her chance to escape? Should she make a run for the window?

Or stay put? And if the person was still in her house, why was it suddenly so quiet?

An insidious frisson of doubt crept in as she stayed huddled in the closet. Had she imagined the creaking floorboard? Would the deputy get here and find nothing amiss? She'd feel ridiculous if that was the case, but she was too frightened to open the closet door to look.

Better to be considered a hysterical female than to risk being attacked by a would-be rapist.

Now she was letting her imagination run wild. Rapists didn't run around in small towns like Crystal Lake. Did they?

She reached up to open the closet door when she heard the floorboard creak again. The sound was so loud she knew it hadn't been her imagination. Her heart raced as she thought about what she had in her closet that might be used as a weapon. A coat hanger? Maybe, but the intruder would have to get close for that to be effective, and if he had a gun, she'd be toast.

Too bad she didn't have a baseball bat or some other heavy object.

A book? Hope filled her chest as she remembered storing some of her heavy medical textbooks on the shelf that stretched across the rack of clothes. Throwing a pathophysiology book at him could potentially buy her the few seconds necessary to escape.

Maybe.

Maybe not. Who was she kidding?

Since she couldn't think of another plan, she pushed the sweater-wrapped phone aside, knowing that it would be useless if the intruder found her anyway. Feeling her way in the pitch-black closet wasn't easy, but she forced herself to remember what the items in her closet looked like as she carefully stood. Avoiding the hangers so they wouldn't clang together wasn't easy. Still, she stretched up to feel along the top edge of the shelf.

Inch by inch, she moved her hands until she felt the cardboard box of books. Reaching up, she felt the box's dimensions, making sure it was the right one. She remembered just how heavy the box had been when she'd placed it up there after moving in.

Still, she needed to do something. Imagining the intruder coming into the bedroom was enough to make her lift the box so it wouldn't scrape along the shelf, the muscles in her arms straining with the effort. She pulled it down and swallowed a grunt as she nearly staggered under the weight. She set the box on the floor, grateful for the carpeting, and quickly pulled out one of the heavy textbooks.

Holding it to her chest, she melted back in the corner, wincing as the clothes rustled a bit. She held her breath for another long moment, trying to gauge where the intruder might be. Still in her living room? Or was he making his way through her bedroom?

The wail of sirens split the air, and there was a loud crash as something hit the floor. Katy sucked in a harsh breath, her heart pounding so hard she could barely hear.

She had no idea how long she sat in the closet clutching her textbook, but it seemed like forever before she heard a deep male voice calling her name.

"Katy? Katy! Where are you?"

Maybe her ears were playing more tricks on her because she could have sworn that the voice belonged to Reese. She pushed open the closet door at the same moment that lights flooded her bedroom.

"I'm here," she said, inwardly wincing at her weak voice. It took a minute for her eyes to adjust to the bright lights, but she squinted enough to see Reese and Duke standing just inside her bedroom. She cleared her throat and rose to her feet. "I'm fine."

"Dr. Katy?" She heard Deputy Kramer's voice in the living room and realized he must have been a few steps behind Reese. How Reese and his dog had managed to get here first, she had no clue. "You should have waited for me, Webster," the deputy said in a low furious tone. "Rushing in here like that, you're lucky you weren't killed."

"Duke needed to go out, and I saw the intruder leaving a few seconds after you set off your sirens," Reese said, raking his gaze over her as if to reassure himself she was okay. "I was more worried about what might have happened to Katy than about being shot."

"I should arrest you for obstruction of justice," Deputy Kramer muttered darkly. He glanced at her with obvious concern. "Dr. Katy, are you sure you're all right?" When she nodded, he smiled. "Why don't you come into the living room so you can tell us what might be missing?"

"Okay," she said, taking a deep breath to calm her racing heart. But her feet remained rooted to the floor after Deputy Kramer left the room.

"Pathophysiology?" Reese asked with a raised eyebrow. "A little light reading for when you're trapped in the closet by a prowler?"

"More like it was the heaviest thing I had in the closet to throw at him," she corrected, tossing the book on her bed, refusing to feel embarrassed. She crossed her arms across her chest, belatedly realizing she was wearing only her nightgown. Feeling self-conscious, she turned back toward the closet to search for her robe.

While she pulled on the lightweight garment, she felt Reese come up to stand behind her. "Are you really all right?" he asked in a low tone. "I was worried sick about you."

Tying the belt of the robe, she turned to face him, relieved to see that Duke was sitting calmly where he'd been standing before rather than following Reese. "I was scared, but I'm fine."

For a moment, he just looked down at her, and then abruptly, he pulled her close, wrapping his arms around her in a fierce hug. She could hear the rapid beat of his heart beneath her ear and understood he'd been as scared as she was.

She leaned against him, savoring the strength of his arms surrounding her. The fact that Reese had actually seen the prowler made the whole incident that much more frightening.

Finally, she pushed herself away, at least far enough to look up into his eyes. "Thanks for coming to my rescue," she said softly.

He nodded and then lowered his head toward hers, covering her mouth with his in a kiss that made her legs feel like jelly. She wrapped her arms around his waist, savoring his kiss.

But the brief moment of intimacy was over far too soon. When Reese lifted his head, she gasped for breath and would have pulled his head down again for a repeat performance if not for the fact that Deputy Kramer chose that moment to call her name.

"Dr. Katy? Are you ready to inventory what might be missing?"

With a sigh of regret, she pulled out of Reese's arms, feeling the loss keenly before she turned to head into the living room. She gave Duke a wide berth, although he didn't move from the spot where he was sitting, despite the way his gaze followed her. As she crossed the threshold, she abruptly stopped, unprepared for the mess that greeted her.

Drawers had been pulled open, the contents disturbed as if someone had been searching for something. Books and her personal papers were also strewn about.

"I don't understand," she said, trying to absorb what had transpired. "What on earth was that guy looking for?"

Deputy Kramer sighed and shook his head. "We were hoping you could tell us."

Katy spread her hands helplessly. "I don't know! My television is still here, and so is my laptop computer. I don't keep anything of value, other than some of my grandmother's jewelry, which is in the bedroom."

"I guess it's possible the sirens scared him off before he could search the bedroom," Deputy Kramer said thoughtfully.

But Reese was shaking his head. "I think it's the same blond dude. The one who trashed my truck and tried to run us off the road."

"You mean the second poacher who no one has seen but you?" Deputy Kramer asked dryly.

Reese scowled and nodded. "Yeah, I know it sounds crazy, but I'm willing to bet that once Boyle regains consciousness, he'll be more than happy to turn on the blond guy in exchange for a lighter sentence. And have you forgotten my smashed truck? I was in the hospital. There's no reason for me to trash my own mode of transportation."

"Last I heard, Boyle was still in the ICU connected to a ventilator," Deputy Kramer said in a slow, deliberate tone. "And for all we know, he smashed your truck hours before you shot him."

Reese gaped at him. "You can't be serious."

Deputy Kramer shrugged. "Awfully convenient that there isn't anyone to challenge your story, isn't it?"

Katy glanced between the two men, trying to understand what was going on. It was late, almost two thirty in the morning, and she wasn't in the mood for games. "What are you talking about, Ian?" she asked. "Why wouldn't you believe a respected game warden like Reese?"

Ian Kramer turned to look at her. "How do you know that this isn't all some elaborate scheme to throw suspicion elsewhere? What if Webster is the one actually doing the poaching? I hear some people will pay a pretty penny for bear and cougar hides."

"Don't be ridiculous. Why would Reese do something like that?" she asked in exasperation. She glanced at Reese, a little nervous at the grim expression on his face.

"Maybe because he has massive debts?" Deputy Kramer said in a snide tone. "From what I saw, he has plenty of motive."

She blinked in shock and looked over at Reese, waiting for him to deny the allegation.

But he didn't. Instead, he turned away. "Come, Duke," he said. The dog hurried after him as he left.

And she didn't think it was an accident that the door loudly banged shut behind him.

REESE'S GUT churned with a mixture of anger and hopelessness as he walked back toward the motel. He shouldn't have been surprised that the sheriff's deputies had performed a background check on him. Why wouldn't they? It was pretty much standard procedure.

But somehow, he hadn't expected Kramer to drop the bomb like that, especially in front of Katy.

He told himself it didn't matter, since there wasn't anything more than friendship between them. But that argument would have gone further if they hadn't just shared a bone-rattling kiss.

A kiss he'd desperately wanted to repeat.

His intent had been just to offer comfort, but suddenly he'd kissed her, and even more incredibly, she'd kissed him back. He'd wanted the kiss to go on forever, but he knew that it was probably one-sided. No doubt her response had been in reaction to surviving a horrible experience rather than any true feelings toward him.

Duke nudged his hand with his nose, as if sensing his inner turmoil, and he bent down to scratch the silky spot between the dog's ears, grateful for his silent companion. After the way Deputy Kramer had reacted back there, he wished he'd sent Duke after the blond guy to prove he actually existed. But he'd been too worried about Katy to think clearly.

Not that he had regrets over his split-second decision. Katy's life was more important than his reputation, any day.

He squared his shoulders and told himself he didn't care what Deputy Kramer thought about him. He knew the blond dude existed, and given enough time, he'd find a way to prove it.

As he approached the motel, Duke growled low in his throat. Reese slowed his pace, peering through the darkness.

"What is it, boy?" he whispered. Duke was too well trained to growl for no reason, so he pulled out his weapon, the spare one he'd grabbed from his house when Katy had driven him there, and slid a bullet into the chamber.

The half-moon in the sky offered some light, and a quick glance at his watch verified dawn would be breaking soon. The area around the motel was deserted for once, and he wasn't sure if that was a good thing or not. He edged closer to the brick wall of the motel, trying to stay out of sight while looking for anything out of place.

When he approached the door to the motel room, Duke seemed to tense up, as if ready to spring. Glancing down, Reese could see the broken doorknob.

He considered calling Deputy Kramer but decided it would take too long for the guy to get here, and really, if the blond dude was inside, he wanted to be the one to take him down.

Lifting his foot, he kicked open the door at the same time he commanded the dog, "Attack."

Duke didn't waste a second, leaping over the threshold the way he'd been trained to do.

Reese peered around the edge of the door, his weapon ready, but there was no one inside. He knew for sure the place was empty by the way Duke sniffed along the floor, going into the bathroom and then coming back out again. The dog came right up to where he stood, looking up at him expectantly.

A stab of disappointment slashed deep. He went into the room, looking for anything out of place. Why would the blond guy come here after being at Katy's? What had he been looking for?

Then he remembered the cardboard box that held all his notes and photos of boot prints that he'd taken while investigating the poaching activity.

With a sick feeling in his stomach, he disengaged his weapon and set it aside so he could begin to search the room, trying to remember where he'd left the box. The motel room wasn't very large, and it didn't take long for him to realize it was gone.

The blond dude had stolen it.

Reese sat down hard on the edge of the bed, scrubbing his hands over his face. Granted, the police had evidence, too, but this was his case, and that box had contained his evidence.

He let out a heavy sigh and pulled out his phone to dial the sheriff's department. No matter what they thought, he needed to follow the book and file a police report.

But deep down, Reese knew that Deputy Kramer would only assume this was all part of his master plan. He imagined the deputy would even accuse him of breaking his own motel room door to make it look as if he'd been robbed.

He was the only one who knew the truth. What was that old saying? The truth shall set you free?

Yeah, not so much. Reese had a bad feeling the truth wasn't going to be enough to keep him out of jail.

But what hurt the most would be the stark disappointment in Katy's eyes when she believed what the deputy was saying.

8

———

Katy picked through the mess left in her living room, trying to figure out what, if anything, was salvageable, inwardly reeling from Deputy Kramer's revelation.

Reese was in debt. So much so that the police didn't believe his story about the poacher working with a blond guy.

She didn't want to believe Reese was involved. But he hadn't denied the allegations; in fact, he'd looked guilty. As if the deputy had revealed a secret. And really, why would Ian make something like that up?

Very simply, he wouldn't.

The deputy was still in her kitchen, making notes about the crime scene. She replaced a drawer from one of her end tables, thinking she should probably offer to make a pot of coffee.

Why not? The caffeine wouldn't be the only thing keeping her awake.

She headed into the kitchen in time to hear Ian speaking into his radio.

"He's saying someone broke into his motel room?" Deputy Kramer asked incredulously. "Come on, you've got to be kidding me."

Katy froze in the act of reaching for her canister of coffee. The deputy had to be talking about Reese.

"Yeah, fine. I'll head over there, but I'm sure this is nothing more than a ruse to deflect his guilt."

Katy stared blindly down at the counter. Was it possible she'd been wrong about Reese?

Thinking back, she remembered the grim expression in Reese's eyes when they'd come upon his smashed truck. The stark fear he'd shown when they'd been nearly run off the road by the black vehicle barreling down on them.

The concern in his eyes when he'd told her that Boyle needed her medical expertise more than he did.

"I'm sorry, Dr. Katy, but I need to head over to the motel," Deputy Kramer said with obvious regret. "Make sure you lock up the door behind me."

She looked up and caught his gaze. "I'm coming with you."

His eyes widened in dismay. "I don't think that's a good idea. Better for you to keep your distance from that guy. As far as I'm concerned, he's nothing but trouble."

"I'm coming," she repeated, her mind made up. "You can't stop me from going over to the motel."

"No, but I can stop you from getting anywhere near the crime scene," he said grimly. "Even better, I could have you arrested for interfering with a police investigation."

His threat was nothing but a bluff, and she knew it. He'd never get away with arresting one of the ER doctors for something so ridiculous; he'd never live it down. For one thing, she'd helped a lot of people in this town, earning their respect. Not to mention that her absence would leave the hospital short staffed in the height of tourist season.

The news would spread through the community faster than the gossip that she and Reese had shared a meal at Rose's Café.

Ian turned to leave, which was fine with her. She went into her bedroom to throw on a sweatshirt, jeans and sneakers. After pulling her long hair into a simple ponytail, she grabbed her purse and walked out to her car. Granted, the motel was close enough to walk, but it was the middle of the night, and being awoken from a sound sleep by an intruder made her feel a bit skittish.

Foolish of her to take the car, she soon realized, since the sheriff's deputies had blocked the motel parking lot with their vehicles. She pulled into the parking lot of the Gas N' Go station located right across the street. The night air was chilly despite being June, so she was glad she had on her sweatshirt as she walked over to the motel.

Despite his threat, Deputy Kramer ignored her when she walked up. "So you say the only thing missing is a shoe box full of photos and notes about the poachers," Deputy Kramer said with a hint of sarcasm in his tone.

She tried to catch Reese's gaze, but he seemed to be avoiding her. Duke stood patiently at his side, and she was struck by the knowledge that the dog really would risk his life to protect Reese.

"Yes, that's correct," Reese said in a low tone. The resigned expression on his face indicated that he knew Deputy Kramer didn't believe him.

"But not your notebook computer," the deputy pressed. "Why wouldn't the poacher take that, too? Why just the box? Surely he'd assume you had notes on the computer, as well."

"I don't know," Reese said mildly. "But I'll be sure to ask him if I see him."

Deputy Kramer scowled. "This isn't a joke, Webster. Filing false police reports could land you in the slammer."

"It's not a false report," Reese said. "I know you don't believe me, but I needed to get this on record, in case anything happens to me later."

Katy couldn't help feeling sick to her stomach at the thought of anything happening to Reese. Even worse, it seemed Reese believed it was only a matter of time till the blond guy caught up to him.

"I suppose you believe the guy went to Dr. Katy's house first, to look for the box, and then came here," Deputy Kramer scoffed.

Reese lifted a brow. "Why not? The timing worked out perfectly."

"Is there anyone who can vouch for the fact that this shoe box of evidence even existed?"

Reese glanced at her briefly but then looked away without saying anything.

She thought back to the night she'd taken him to his house deep in the woods after finding his smashed truck. He'd come out of the house carrying a computer case, his duffel bag and, she remembered now, a shoe box.

"I can," she said. "I can vouch for the fact that Reese had a shoe box with him."

Ian stared at her, his expression full of skeptic disbelief.

"You don't have to do this," Reese said in a low tone.

She smiled sadly. "Yes, I do." She turned toward Deputy Kramer with firm resolve. "I gave Mr. Webster a ride out to his truck the night he was shot. We came around the curve, saw that his truck had been smashed to pieces, so I drove him to his house so he could pick up his dog and some things to take with him to the motel. When he came out of the house, he had a duffel bag, a computer case and a small, square box."

Kramer didn't write anything down in his notebook, tucking it away instead.

"Okay, I'll file the report," he said curtly. He turned away to join the other deputy, who was walking around the area, for what purpose, she had no idea.

"I'm sorry I dragged you into this," Reese said, his expression grim. "But hopefully you're safe now that the poacher has what he was looking for."

She nodded, trying to think of something to say. "But he could still come after you," she pointed out.

"Duke and I can handle it if he does, right boy?" Reese bent over to run his hand over Duke's sleek fur. Well, it looked soft, but that was only a guess since she'd never touched the animal. "Hank promised to have the rental car here by noon, so I'll be able to head home. Besides, you'll be safer if you stay far away from me."

The finality of his tone hit hard. She wanted to protest, to tell him that she was willing to take the risk, but she didn't.

Because he was right. She sensed she would be safer with some distance between them. Although, honestly, that wasn't the real problem. The issue was that they were complete opposites for anything more than friendship.

No matter how much she longed to be held in his arms. To share another kiss.

She swallowed hard. "Take care, Reese," she murmured before turning away.

"Wait, I'll walk you home."

"No need," she said, her tone sharper than she intended. "My car is right across the street."

She continued across the street to where she'd left her car. It was only when she slid behind the wheel that she caught one last glimpse of Reese standing there with Duke at his side.

Blinking back ridiculous tears, she drove home.

REESE WANTED nothing more than to chase after Katy, but he forced himself to stay where he was.

He hadn't been lying. Katy would be much safer if she stayed far away from him. And keeping her safe had to be the top priority.

Besides, he knew full well how horrified Katy had been to hear how far he was in debt. Granted, he was making steady progress, but he still wasn't debt free. Katy didn't realize that he'd never take any of her money to free himself from his financial burden. Call it pride, or pig-headed stubbornness, but there was no way he'd accept money from a woman.

Especially not someone he cared about.

Suzanne's mess was his problem alone. Plenty of people had told him to hire a lawyer to go after her, forcing the issue that she should share in the debt since she'd created ninety percent of it, but he'd refused.

The taillights from Katy's car disappeared from view, and he steeled his resolve by turning back toward the motel. Duke trotted off to water a bush, so he waited before heading inside his motel room. The door was still broken, but he wasn't worried. He had Duke and firmly believed that the blond dude was long gone.

Falling asleep wasn't easy; he tossed and turned to the point that Duke padded over, sticking his nose against Reese's chest as if to ask *what's wrong?*

He buried his face against the dog's neck for a moment, wishing things could be different. But wallowing in self-pity was one thing he'd promised himself he wouldn't do, so he lifted his head and gave Duke a nice rub. "Good boy. Lie down, Duke. Down."

Duke dropped down and stretched out on his belly. Reese flopped back on the bed, staring at the ceiling, knowing he should be grateful for what he had. Although at times like this, when everything seemed stacked against him, it wasn't easy.

Somehow, he found himself reaching for faith and God.

Please keep Katy safe and provide me the strength and courage I'll need as I search for the man responsible for all of this. Amen.

He must have slept, because Duke's low growl, combined with bright sunlight, brought him instantly awake.

"What is it, boy?" he asked, blinking the remnants of sleep from his eyes.

Duke stayed right in front of the door, the hair on the scruff of his neck standing upright. Reese dragged on his cargo shorts, T-shirt and running shoes, checking his weapon as he walked over to where Duke waited. He tucked his gun into his holster and grabbed a water bottle.

He found himself hoping the blond dude had returned to finish what he'd started. Getting him in custody would salvage Reese's reputation.

He pulled open the door, and Duke ran through the opening and immediately crossed the parking lot. Reese had little choice but to sprint after him.

"Duke, halt!" he called sharply when several bystanders shied away in fear.

Duke stopped on a dime and turned his head to look

back at Reese. The dog's muscles were quivering, and Reese knew that something was up.

"Search, Duke," he commanded.

The dog sprinted forward again, and this time, Reese ran to keep up with him as he crossed the road and headed in the direction of the hiking trail.

Had the blond dude come this way? If so, Reese was certain that, with Duke's help, he'd find him, proving that he existed once and for all.

WITH HER DAY off stretching long and empty before her, Katy finished cleaning up the mess in her home and then tried to think of something to do.

Something that didn't involve going back to the motel to find Reese. The weather report predicted another steamy day with temperatures reaching ninety degrees or more, and the interior of her house was already too warm and stifling. Opening up the windows helped a little as there was a bit of a breeze coming off the lake.

She couldn't bear the thought of being around other people, her emotions from the night before leaving her raw and vulnerable. She had a few options; stay cooped up in her steamy house on a sunny day, offer to work for one of her colleagues, or take a walk on the hiking trail.

If she called one of her colleagues, offering to work, she'd have to field a bunch of questions about what was going on, so in the end, the hiking trail won. Especially because she needed a distraction from the fact Reese would be leaving town today to head back home.

She changed into a pair of shorts, a loose gauzy shirt, and a tank top. The hiking trail was used by many of the citizens of Crystal Lake, herself included, but that was before she knew about the cougars and bears. Running into wildlife wasn't her idea of fun and was almost enough to keep her home.

But her colleague, Gabe Allen, often ran the trails, and he'd never seen any real wildlife other than the occasional white-tailed deer. And he often told the story about how he'd met his wife, Larissa, on the trail, coming to her rescue when she'd hurt her ankle.

There was nothing to be afraid of, right? Right.

Squaring her shoulders, she lathered up with sunscreen since her fair skin tended to burn and freckle, grabbed a water bottle and headed outside. The hour was early enough that the sun wasn't too brutal yet, and hopefully, she'd be home by lunchtime.

The trail wasn't too far from her house, located in the opposite direction of town, so she decided to walk. No sense in driving to the hiking trail, she thought with a wry grin.

Lifting her face to the sun, she marveled at the warmth seeping into her pores. The scent of burning wood filled the air, reminding her of the campfire they'd had during the one summer she attended Girl Scout camp. A venture that hadn't lasted long. She'd screamed like a banshee when one of her bunkmates had put a grass snake in her bed.

Maybe a grass snake was totally harmless, but she hadn't cared. She'd never gone back to Girl Scout camp after that one disastrous experience. She'd spent her next few summers at the library, reading every book she could get her hands on and enjoying every moment of peace and quiet.

Her camp counselor would laugh herself silly to know that Katy was now living rural Wisconsin, braving a hike along the trail all by herself.

The trail wound around with a steadily rising terrain. The locals called it a hill, but in her opinion it was more like a small mountain, especially surrounded by woods the way it was. She was surprised that the scent of burning wood grew stronger rather than dissipating at the higher elevation.

Where was that campfire anyway? Was someone camping out toward the top of the hill? The idea was enough to make her think about turning around to go back home.

Maybe she should go back to the motel to find Reese? The DNR would be interested in someone camping illegally, wouldn't it? Especially since there was a campground located a few miles down the highway.

She was so lost in her thoughts that she wasn't paying attention to where she was walking. Her left foot stepped in a hole, and she cried out as her ankle twisted in pain.

After hobbling over to a rock, she looked down at her ankle. It wasn't as bad as she'd feared, so she took off the gauze shirt she'd tied around her waist and tried to rip off the sleeves. But the material was strong, and she had to look around for something to use.

She found a sharp-edged rock and used that to rend the fabric. The sleeve came off easily with the rock's help, and she pulled off the other sleeve, too, so that it would match. She wound the fabric around her ankle for support and then took a long gulp from her water bottle.

So much for her hike, she thought grimly. Now, for sure, she'd have to head back down. Which was probably best, since she wasn't too keen on meeting up with the illegal campers. The scent that had started out so nice was almost unbearably strong now. In fact, there was a haze hovering in the air, making her eyes water.

She rose to her feet, swiping at her burning eyes with the remnants of the second sleeve of her gauze shirt. She blinked again, realizing that she could barely see a few feet in front of her face.

What in the world was going on? She couldn't see more than a yard or two of the trail.

She turned in a small circle, trying to get her bearings. She knew she needed to go down rather than head farther up the trail and took a few steps in order to get a sense of which direction she should head.

The downward slope beneath her feet helped provide direction as the smoke was becoming unbearable. Tears pricked at her eyes, and smoke clogged her throat, making her cough.

Half blind, she stumbled down the trail, hoping and praying she was going in the right direction.

But she abruptly froze in horror when she heard a low, menacing growl.

9

Reese desperately searched for a cell signal on his phone, knowing he needed to get help, and fast. Duke had led him farther up the trail toward the scent of a campfire. But the smoke was getting thicker and thicker, making him fear the worst.

What might have begun as a small campfire started by kids or careless adults had somehow gotten out of control into something very dangerous. After almost five weeks of no rain, the level of fire danger in this area was pretty high.

He climbed up on a boulder, holding his phone up, trying to see if there was a signal. Was there one bar there? Hope swelled as he pushed the button to make a call, but after several long moments, there was nothing.

Lost signal.

Sliding off the rock, he continued taking the trail. Duke's growl had him slowing to a stop, every sense on alert. Was the blond guy nearby?

"What is it, boy?" he asked in a low tone.

In answer, Duke let out a sharp bark. But the dog's wagging tail was reassuring. Reese trusted Duke's senses better than his own, especially at times like this. Duke bounded down the trail, disappearing in a haze of smoke.

Reese scrambled to keep up with his dog, wondering what had caught Duke's attention. Right now, all he wanted to do was to call his boss to report the possible fire, but he couldn't do that without a cell signal.

"Help me!" a female voice cried.

"Duke, down," he instinctively shouted, putting on speed. The smoke was so thick he almost trampled over Katy, who was sprawled on the ground staring up at Duke with fear blazing from her eyes. "Good boy," he said when he realized that Duke was actually protecting Katy.

"Good boy?" she wheezed, cringing from the dog. "He scared me to death!"

"I'm sorry about that, but you know he's well trained. He truly was trying to protect you," Reese said mildly. "You can tell by the way he was standing guard. Here, take my hand," he instructed.

She grasped his hand, winced and then coughed as she rose to her feet. He was surprised to see her here, especially after everything that had happened the night before, or rather, just a few hours ago. She tugged on her hand, and he reluctantly released her. She winced again when taking a step back, and he dropped his gaze, searching for the cause of her discomfort. Based on the makeshift bandage around her ankle, he suspected a twist or a sprain.

"What happened?" he asked with a frown.

"It's fine," she said in a hoarse tone. "But we need to get away from here. The smoke is getting worse."

"I know. It's bad up here," he agreed. But he couldn't leave just yet. "Duke will lead you down the trail," he assured her. "I need to investigate that fire, in case there are people stranded up there."

"No, there's nothing you can do," she protested. The frank fear in her gaze and the way she lightly grasped his arm tugged at his heart. The way she looked at him now, it was as if the nightmare from last night hadn't happened. "The faster we get down the trail, the better chance we have of getting help. Surely someone in town has noticed the smoke. Help must be on the way."

True, he'd thought the same thing. Surely the sheriff's deputies had noticed the smoke from the campfire by now. But he couldn't force himself to leave the scene of what just might be another crime.

He'd thought at first that Duke had left the motel because he'd been on the blond guy's trail, but now he knew that it was the smoke that had captured the dog's attention. Maybe the fire was the result of careless kids, but it was also possible the fire had been started on purpose, although he didn't want to tell Katy that. She'd been frightened enough already.

"Duke will show you the way back. I'll join you as soon as I can. I just need to be sure there isn't anyone else trapped up here."

Katy's terrified expression turned grim at the thought of other potential victims, and he was impressed by the way she pulled herself together. "All right, but please hurry," she murmured. "I don't like the idea of you risking your life."

She didn't seem to understand that risking his life was his responsibility. He might be a DNR game warden rather than a cop, but he had much the same kind of training. There could be campers up there in danger, and he wasn't about to leave without checking things out. "I will." He turned to the German shepherd, giving him a signal with his hand. "Home, Duke. Lead Katy home."

Duke seemed to understand, taking a few steps down

the path and then glancing back as if to make sure Katy was following.

Katy looked as if she wanted to argue but reluctantly turned and hobbled toward Duke. He wanted to haul her close and kiss her again but made himself turn and head up the trail instead. The smoke grew thicker the higher he went. The wind shifted, and he sucked in a harsh breath when he saw the orange flames dancing along the tops of the trees.

This was way more than a campfire gone out of control. This was a full-fledged wildfire.

Looking at the blaze, he couldn't help thinking there was no way this was truly the result of careless kids.

Something deep in his gut told him there was a good chance the fire had been started on purpose.

KATY SWIPED at her tearing eyes and stumbled after Duke, trying to follow his bobbing tail. Her initial fear of the dog faded when, on the few occasions she lost sight of him, he doubled back, returning to her side and nudging her gently, as if herding a lost lamb.

She didn't like leaving Reese behind, and she sensed Duke didn't like it much, either. Maybe the smoke was wreaking havoc with her brain cells, but she got the feeling that Duke was trying to rush her down the trail so that he could get back to his owner.

Truthfully, she couldn't blame him.

The toe of her running shoe caught a root, and she stumbled, managing to catch herself before face-planting in the dirt. Duke materialized by her side, nudging her with his head.

"Good boy," she murmured, rubbing the silky fur behind

his ears. She wasn't sure how it had happened, but in the last fifteen minutes, he'd gone from scaring the daylights out of her to being her best friend. She could easily understand now why Reese was so attached to him. And why German shepherds made great police dogs.

The air was slightly clearer down near the ground, and it occurred to her that lack of oxygen was a serious threat. She couldn't deny the fact that smoke filling her lungs might have caused her to stumble in the first place. Carbon monoxide poisoning was no joke, and if she didn't do something, she might not make it off the trail even with Duke leading the way.

Thinking fast, she pulled what was left of her gauze shirt off her waist, dampened it with her water bottle and then tied it over her nose and mouth. Almost instantly, her breathing was easier, without the constant feeling of having shards of glass stuck in her throat, although she sensed the damp fabric wouldn't filter the air for long.

Hopefully long enough to get off this stupid hiking trail.

Duke nudged her again and made a high-pitched whining sound as if urging her to hurry. She rose to her feet and continued following him, trusting in the dog's sense of direction more than her own. In the distance, she could hear sirens and hoped that meant fire trucks were on the way. Maybe once the firefighters arrived, Reese wouldn't feel the need to search for the campers who'd started the fire, handing off the investigation to the professionals instead.

Duke let out several loud barks, startling her badly. Her steps faltered to a stop, as she sensed his barking wasn't a good sign.

The dog appeared at her side, circled around her and then let out three more short barks. The animal was clearly trying to tell her something, but what? He turned and went off the trail, heading south. When she didn't immediately follow, he came back, did that strange whinny sound in his throat and went off the trail again, looking back at her as if to yell, *follow me!*

What should she do? Why would the dog lead her off the trail? She sensed if Reese were here, he'd tell her to trust the dog. Without a second thought, she climbed up and over a boulder, slipping and sliding on the rocky terrain, her ankle throbbing in earnest without the firmness of the trail. It wasn't until she climbed yet another boulder that she could see the flames licking the treetops. And not just the trees behind her but in every direction she could see.

Her heart nearly stopped in her chest as the horror of what she was seeing seeped into her brain.

She and Duke were literally surrounded by fire.

REESE PULLED OFF HIS T-SHIRT, doused it with water and pulled it up over his nose and mouth. Too bad he didn't have eye protection, as he could barely see through the smoke.

He turned around and headed back down the path in the direction of where he'd left Katy and Duke. Rescuing campers was one thing, but seeing the flames of the fire engulfing the tops of the trees put everything in a new perspective. The entire town was at risk if this fire spread farther. And he wasn't sure there even were campers to rescue.

Reese went as fast as he dared, barely able to see through the thick smoke. He was a little surprised he hadn't stumbled across any other hikers aside from Katy. Surely they hadn't been the only ones on the trail, although it was possible the steamy hot temperatures had deterred some of the tourists. Boating, skiing, and fishing on Crystal Lake were the main attractions during the summer months, not the hiking trails.

Reese didn't call out for Duke, hoping that his dog had already gotten Katy off the trail and down to safety. He could hear the wail of sirens indicating that help was coming. But the Hope County Fire Department was far too small to take on a forest fire. Normal protocol was to call the DNR as well as every fire department within a fifty-mile radius. He hoped every single one of them was already on its way.

As he fought his way through the smoke, back down the trail, Reese remembered how calm and peaceful he'd felt after praying. Was God listening to Katy's prayers right now? He wanted to believe that was the case and found himself adding his own prayer.

Please save us, Lord! Save us from the fire!

Three short barks reached his ears, and he paused on the trail, breathing hard through the damp fabric of his shirt. Three short barks from Duke indicated danger, and the realization that Katy and Duke weren't safe at all spurred him into action.

Despite the thick smoke, he slipped and slid down the path in the direction from where he thought the barks had come. Although being surrounded by smoke was disorienting, so he couldn't be sure he was headed the right way.

Sweat, or maybe it was smoke, burned his eyes. "Duke?" he croaked, just in case the dog and Katy were nearby. "Come, Duke!"

There was an answering bark, and he smiled grimly behind the shirt. He couldn't understand why they were still on the hill, unless Katy had fallen again, injuring her ankle to the point she couldn't walk. And if that was the case, he knew Duke wouldn't leave her alone.

Even if it meant succumbing to smoke inhalation poisoning right alongside her.

Despite the overwhelming heat, smoke and sweat, a chill snaked its way down his spine. He couldn't bear the thought of losing either of them, so he shoved the negative thoughts aside and concentrated on following the sounds of Duke's barking.

It seemed like hours but was probably only ten minutes or so before Duke burst out through the smoke to greet him. He dropped to his knees and hugged the animal gratefully.

"Good boy," he murmured. "Good boy!"

The dog wiggled away and barked. He understood the animal was trying to tell him something, so he slowly stood. "Find Katy," he said.

Duke headed off the path, and Reese followed, snaking around rocks and boulders. He trusted Duke, even though he couldn't figure out why the animal wasn't leading them out of the fire.

He slipped and landed hard on a rock but quickly forced himself upright. "Katy?" he called, forcing air through his sore throat. "Are you all right?"

"I'm here." Her reply was so faint he almost thought he'd imagined it. She must be injured, or he was certain she would have come to meet him.

"Hang on, okay? I'll be there soon."

Following Duke off the trail wasn't nearly as easy, as the animal slipped under a fallen tree branch that Reese had to crawl over. He was glad they were still heading downward, if not on the path.

Maybe it was his imagination, but he thought the smoke was thinner as he followed Duke's winding path. At least his eyes weren't burning as much.

"Reese! Over here," Katy called. He caught a glimpse of

her red hair and felt the tightness ease in his chest when he realized she was sitting under a tree about twenty yards up ahead. He was amazed that she'd tied fabric over her face, the same way he had, to protect her airway as much as possible. Most hikers wouldn't think of that, but then again, she was a doctor.

"What happened?" he asked as he made his way closer. "Did you fall and hurt your ankle again?"

"No, Duke led me this way," she said in a stronger voice. "He was pretty insistent about it, too."

"Good boy, Duke," he said, praising the dog again for saving their lives. "We're still heading down, which is good, but I'm not sure I understand why he led you off the trail."

Katy slowly rose to her feet as he came closer. "I'm so glad you're here," she said in a low tone. "I'm not as afraid."

He reached out and pulled her gently into his arms. He was dirty, sweaty and smelly, but he couldn't resist holding her at least for a moment.

She hugged him back, and despite the seriousness of their situation, he found himself smiling.

"How are we going to get out of here?" she asked, her voice muffled against his shirt.

Regretfully, he loosened his grip enough to look down at her. They both looked like bandits from the Old West with their noses and mouths covered, but he figured this wasn't the time to point that out.

"We're going to be fine," he assured her with all the confidence he could muster. "Duke will get us out of trouble, won't you, boy?"

Duke lifted his head, his ears perking up when he heard his name. He wagged his tail and then turned to continue on a convoluted path that only he could see.

"Can you walk?" he asked Katy.

"Yes, but I don't know that it's going to help much," she said as she followed him down the rocky path.

"Why not? Surely you're not still afraid of Duke after all this?"

"No, not at all. He's a wonderful guard dog, and I'm sure I'd already be dead if not for him guiding me." Katy was silent for a few minutes as they carefully picked their way over the boulders and fallen tree branches littering the side of the hill. "Duke pushed me off the trail and I think it's because there's more fire down there."

He snapped his head up and looked over at her. "I didn't see any sign of fire from my vantage point up above."

Katy's gaze was full of despair. "Trust me, I saw it. I just don't see how we're going to get out of this mess."

"We'll find a way," he assured her, even though his mind was reeling at the news. If the fire was truly surrounding them, they were definitely in trouble. But how could the fire have gotten over to the southeast when the wind was coming from that direction? The fire should be heading away from them, which was one of the reasons that he'd sent Duke with Katy to keep her safe.

"It doesn't make sense," he muttered. "There shouldn't be any fire coming from that way, not unless someone set it on purpose."

"Maybe someone did set it on purpose," Katy said. "Because I know that I saw fire. Duke saw it, too, which is why he led me off the trail."

The implication sank deep. Reese knew with sick certainty that this was the work of the blond guy. The same guy who'd tried to kill them on the freeway.

The same guy who'd broken into Katy's house and his motel room.

Was this his final goal? To get rid of him and Katy once and for all?

Okay, he needed to get a grip. Who'd started the fire and why were the least of their concerns. They needed to find a way to get to safety. Duke was still following some sort of trail, and Reese tried to remain positive, although it wasn't easy.

Katy was saying something softly under her breath, and he soon realized that she was reciting the Lord's Prayer. The verse echoed in his mind, drudged up from a distant memory from the last time he'd attended church, before Suzanne had left him for his best friend.

He found himself saying the prayer with Katy as they followed Duke.

And when the prayer was over, a strange sense of peace surrounded him.

"Oomph," Katy said as she slipped and fell on her backside.

"Are you all right?" he asked, reaching out for her at the same time he was trying not to do the same thing.

"I'm fine, but do you hear that?" she asked, her eyes lighting up with hope.

For a moment, he wondered if she'd hit her head, or maybe the smoke had gotten to her. "Hear what?"

"That noise." She hastily scrambled to her feet, looking around in earnest. "It sounds like water."

"Water?" He searched the rocky landscape for Duke and found the dog several yards down near a cluster of boulders. When the dog lifted his head, Reese thought for sure he saw water dripping from the animal's muzzle.

"There is water, see?" Katy said excitedly. "Duke found it! Good boy, Duke! Good boy!"

He followed Katy down to where Duke waited near the

water. As much as he knew water was vital to their survival, he couldn't bear to burst her bubble.

Because even with water to wet their clothes and hydrate their bodies, he knew they were far from safe.

If the fire truly surrounded them on all sides, he didn't know how on earth they'd make it out of here alive.

10

Katy pulled the gauze shirt off her face and cupped her hands in the stream, drinking greedily even though she didn't know if the water was safe for consumption.

At this moment, a parasite of some sort was the least of their concerns. Besides, the way Duke had lapped up the water was good enough for her.

The dog stayed by her side, even when Reese joined them at the stream. When she finished drinking, she leaned over and wrapped her arms around the animal's neck, giving Duke a big hug.

"You're an awesome dog, you know that?" she whispered against his damp fur. "I don't know what we would have done without you."

"I agree," Reese said after he'd finished drinking from the stream. He sat back on his heels and looked at her. A smile kicked up the corner of his mouth. "I'm glad to see you're not afraid of him anymore."

She lifted her head, surprisingly reluctant to let the dog go. "I feel stupid for being afraid of him in the first place," she admitted. "He's amazing. I understand now why people get so attached to their pets."

"Not stupid," Reese corrected swiftly. "He's trained to attack, so being cautious around him was smart. But he'd never hurt you. In fact, he'd protect you with his life."

"Me?" She frowned and shook her head. "No, he'd protect you before me."

"Not if I told him to protect *you*."

The intense expression in Reese's eyes made her shiver, despite the heat and smoke. Was Reese really willing to put his life on the line for her? His dog's life on the line for her? No one had ever done something like that for her before, but then again, she'd never been in this kind of danger before, either.

Thinking back to the way Deputy Kramer had treated Reese, she couldn't suppress a flash of anger. No way in the world would she believe Reese was the poacher, and he didn't deserve the wild accusations the deputy had thrown at him. So what if he was in debt? Half of America was in debt! That didn't mean anything.

Reese had always treated her like a gentleman, and heaven help her, she was beginning to care about him, far more than she should. He was strong, kind and gentle, all at the same time. If things were different...

But they weren't. Besides, this wasn't the time or place for a heart-to-heart, soul-baring discussion. They needed to find a way to get off this stupid hill to safety.

"Do you think Duke can find a way out of here?" she asked, changing the subject. "He's been amazing so far."

"Maybe." Reese bent over the stream, filling his water bottle as much as possible. "Hand me yours, too."

She was surprised she'd managed to hang on to her empty container, especially after following Duke over the rocky terrain. The bottle was badly crumpled, but that didn't matter since Reese could only fill it halfway.

"Now we need to get our clothes wet," he instructed her. "I'll go first and then back off to give you some privacy."

She nodded, understanding his reasoning. Their clothes wouldn't stay wet for long, but since they were surrounded by fire, they needed every possible advantage they could get.

"Maybe we should follow the water," she suggested, averting her gaze, too, as Reese lay down in the stream, face down and then rolling onto his back. He shouldn't be getting his stitches wet, but she decided not to say anything since they were both covered with soot and grime, anyway. If his wound was going to get infected, it didn't much matter what the source was.

She might have laughed at how he looked, like a giant fish flapping around in the shallow water, if their situation weren't so grim.

"Your turn," he said, rivets of water running off him as he climbed back up on the rocks.

Normally she would have felt self-conscious about rolling around in the stream, but the cool water felt so good she couldn't bring herself to care. She had to force herself to get out when all she really wanted to do was to bask in the cool bliss.

Reese had his back turned to her as promised, but she could tell he was searching the landscape around them, no doubt figuring out their next move. A realization that brought her back to their harsh reality.

"Ready?" he asked when she came up to stand beside him.

"Yes." Really, she had no choice but to be ready, but if he was going to maintain a positive attitude, so was she. "Is it my imagination or is there less smoke down here near the water?"

"Definitely less smoke," he said. "But I don't think we can afford to sit here and wait to be rescued. We need to keep moving. I'm hoping we'll run into the firefighters who'll be here fighting the blaze soon."

"That would be nice. Duke could find them, couldn't he?"

"I hope so." Reese shook out his wet T-shirt and pulled it on, drawing the collar up to cover his nose and mouth. She re-tied her freshly dampened gauze shirt over her lower face, too, knowing that they were likely going to see more smoke rather than less as they made their way out of here.

"Home, Duke. Take us home," Reese commanded.

The dog picked his way along the edge of the stream heading south. Their pace was slow since the uneven terrain was difficult even for the dog to navigate.

Her ankle didn't seem to hurt as much, but that could also be the result of an adrenaline rush from being in danger. She knew full well that basic survival instincts would always outweigh the mundane.

"Why haven't you asked me?" Reese said, his voice muffled by his cotton T-shirt.

"Ask you what?" They were walking single file, following Duke, so she couldn't get a good look at his eyes.

"If I'm guilty of poaching. Of planning all this to throw suspicion off me," he said.

"Deputy Kramer doesn't know what he's talking about, that's why. I was in the car with you when you saw your smashed truck, and the shock in your eyes was real. Plus, I was with you when that black truck came barreling down on us, nearly causing us to crash."

He didn't say anything in response, and she risked a

glance over her shoulder. His gaze met hers, and she saw the glint of hope reflected there. He wanted her to believe in him.

And she did.

"Do you remember that first night in the hospital?" she continued. "When I came over to take a look at your injury? You said, 'Marcus Boyle needs your medical expertise more than I do.' This was the guy you shot in self-defense, yet you were more worried about him than you were about yourself."

"I remember," he said. "I'm glad to hear you believe me, but I'm still surprised you haven't asked me any details about why I'm in debt."

She lifted a shoulder in a careless shrug, unwilling to admit she was, in fact, dying of curiosity to know the details. But Reese's personal life was none of her business. "I'm sure you have a good reason."

There was another long stretch of silence as they followed Duke's lead. When the dog crossed the stream, heading to the other side, Reese held out his hand to help her cross, too. Their fingers clung for a long, poignant moment before he released her.

"I was married once," Reese said, breaking the long silence. "While I was still in the navy. I heard the stories about cheating wives, women who were unable to handle the long separations, but I thought Suzanne and I were in love."

The hint of suffering in his tone made her want to hug him. "What happened?" she asked, even though she could guess.

"She proved me wrong. And then some."

"And then some?"

"Not only did she cheat on me, with my best friend, no

less, but she cleaned out our joint bank account and maxed out the credit card. When I came home from being at sea, the divorce papers were the only thing waiting for me. So I signed them and began to dig my way out of debt."

Her chest tightened with sorrow and anger. What he'd told her was so much worse than what she'd imagined. She glanced back at him again but tripped and stumbled. She would have fallen if not for Reese's quick reflexes. She clutched the muscles of his arms and stared up at him.

"I'm so sorry," she said. "What Suzanne did was unnecessarily cruel, and I can't imagine how you managed to get through it. I hope she had to pay at least half of that debt off."

She couldn't see his mouth covered by the T-shirt, but his eyes crinkled at the corners, which made her think he might be smiling. "No, I signed the papers, sold the house to pay off as much as I could and then went to a lawyer to consolidate what was left into monthly payments. I'd be in worse shape if my boss weren't allowing me to live in that log cabin for dirt cheap."

She put a hand on his arm, trying to think of something to say. But in truth, her mind was still reeling from what Reese had gone through. Most men would be angry and bitter and would have dragged their ex-wife through court to force the issue, but he hadn't. He'd taken on the responsibility without complaining.

He'd isolated himself from civilization, choosing to live in the woods with only his dog for company while dedicating his life to keeping the natural resources and wildlife safe.

Now that she knew the truth, it was easier to understand why he'd made the decisions he had.

Duke let out a sharp bark, interrupting the moment. She dropped her hand and turned away, heading after the dog.

They walked in silence for several moments. A coughing fit caught her off guard, forcing her to stop and bend over, bracing herself with her hands on her knees, to catch her breath.

When she stood, the swirling smoke burned her eyes. "It's worse," she croaked. "The smoke is getting worse."

"I know." Reese's grim tone surprised her after his previous determination to remain positive. The serious expression reflected in his eyes couldn't be denied.

She knew what he was trying to tell her. That it was possible that they might not make it out of here after all.

She closed her eyes for a moment and prayed.

Dear Lord, please give us the strength and courage we need to get out of here, and guide us to safety. Amen.

REESE WISHED MORE than anything he could reassure Katy that they would be fine, but he couldn't bear to lie to her. Not now. Not after she'd offered her unconditional trust. Something no one else had done for him, ever.

Maybe that's why he'd spilled his guts about Suzanne, when he hadn't told anyone else the full story, not even his boss.

No, the real reason he'd told Katy the truth was that he didn't want her to think the worst about him, like he was some sort of closet gambler or something. If he were honest, he'd admit that he cared about what Katy thought about him.

Ridiculous to even worry about that now, when they weren't anywhere close to being safe. What did it matter what she thought about him if they died?

No, they weren't going to die. He refused to believe they'd fail. Somehow, someway, they were going to find a way out of here.

Looking down, he noticed Katy's eyes were closed and knew she was praying. He reached out and took her hand.

"Let's pray together."

Her emerald-green eyes opened in shock, but she nodded, holding on to his hands tightly.

"Dear Lord, we have faith in your strength and goodness," Katy said.

"We seek your mercy and guidance to help us find safety," Reese added.

"If it be Thy will, amen."

"Amen," Reese echoed.

"Thank you," Katy said. "I know faith is new to you, but we have to trust in God's plan."

"All right," he agreed. It had never occurred to him before that Suzanne's leaving him for Will Fischer was all part of God's master plan. At the time, he'd been angry and hurt, burying himself in work. But now that he looked back, he knew for certain that if his wife hadn't left him and cleaned out their bank account, he wouldn't be here today.

And he wouldn't have met Katy.

Even in the midst of the desperate situation they were currently battling, he was glad he was here with her.

"We better keep going," she said. Even though they were both dirty, sweaty and smelled like smoke, he wanted nothing more than to kiss her.

Duke barked again, urging them on. "We're coming, boy," he called to the dog. He followed Katy with a renewed sense of peace and determination.

Between Duke's instincts and God's support, he firmly believed they'd find a way out of here.

"The force of the stream is dwindling," Katy said, a frown puckering her forehead. "It can't be good if we run out of water."

He'd noticed the water seemingly drying up too. "It doesn't mean we're headed in the wrong direction," he pointed out. "Could just be that the fire behind us is interfering with the water source."

"Maybe."

He could tell by her tone she wasn't convinced. "We agreed to have faith," he reminded her. "Duke wouldn't lead us into fire."

"True," Katy agreed. "You should have seen the way he kept barking and circling around me when we were still on the trail. It was as if he was trying to talk to me."

"Three barks means danger, which is his way of warning you not to go closer."

"Very effective." She slipped again but quickly regained her balance, with the help of his hand holding hers.

"Is your ankle okay?" he asked.

"As good as your arm, I'm sure," she said dryly.

"Let me know if you need to lean on me." He didn't want to think about how difficult it would be to carry her through the smoky haze, making his way across the rocks and tree branches littering the ground. He would if necessary, but he'd rather she lean on him before her ankle got to the point she couldn't walk on it.

Duke abruptly changed course, heading southwest, a direction that would take them even farther from the hiking trail. As much as he trusted the dog's instincts, he couldn't help a gnawing sense of worry.

"Good boy, Duke," Katy called encouragingly. Apparently her faith in Duke hadn't wavered. "Home. Take us home."

"I think you're going to have to get a dog of your own," he said. "You're going to miss Duke once we're out of this mess."

"I'd love one, but he'd have to be as well trained as Duke," she said. "Although my schedule isn't the greatest when it comes to owning pets."

"My schedule can be challenging, too, but trust me, having a pet is worth the effort."

"I never understood that, until today." Katy's comment ended on another coughing fit, and Reese put his hand on her back, alarmed at the fact that he could barely see more than two feet in front of his face.

He wanted to have faith, but it wasn't easy. Duke wouldn't lead them astray, but it was possible the smoke was interfering with the dog's ability to follow a scent.

"Reese?" Katy's hoarse voice worried him, although his wasn't much better.

"I'm here, Katy. Hang on to me, I'll help you."

"No, that's not what I mean. Don't you hear it?"

He paused, straining to listen. Maybe he was losing it, but he didn't hear anything. "No, what do you hear?"

"A roaring sound, like a fire that's out of control. What if we're heading into more danger?"

He didn't want to think that Duke would lead them farther into fire, but before he could respond, a loud bang pierced the air.

"Get down," he said hoarsely, tugging on Katy's hand.

Katy dropped down to the ground, and Duke rushed toward them, a low, growling noise rumbling in his throat.

"Was that a gunshot?" Katy whispered, her red-rimmed eyes wide with horror.

"I'm not sure," he admitted. "We need to find cover just in case."

"What about over by that fallen log over there?" she said, pointing to a spot near the edge of the dried-up stream.

"That's good. But keep your head down as much as possible," he urged. "You go first, and I'll follow behind you."

"Okay." She stayed bent over as she picked her way back over the rocky streambed. Duke stayed right beside her, while Reese covered her back.

He was thankful that they didn't hear any more gunfire as they moved toward the downed tree. Katy reached it first and sank to the ground. Duke stood beside her, and he had to smile when she said, "Sit, Duke."

Reese sank down beside her. "Down, Duke."

Normally, the dog always followed his commands, but this time, the dog simply stood there for a long minute, nose in the air, his ears twitching as he listened.

Then, abruptly, the dog took off, racing across the terrain like a wolf scenting food. Reese shouted, "Stay, Duke. Stay!" but his voice was little more than a hoarse croak and had no impact on the dog whatsoever.

Duke disappeared from sight, leaving them on their own.

11

Katy gasped and then coughed as she watched Duke disappear into the smoky haze. "Why is he leaving us?"

"I'm not sure. Could be the smoke is making him confused." Reese sounded upset, and she didn't blame him.

She had no idea how they'd get out of here without following Duke's lead. Especially after they'd heard that loud bang. She shivered despite the heat.

"Do you think that was really a gunshot?" she asked, voicing her fears out loud. "Maybe we were wrong and it just sounded like one."

"Maybe. Possibly a branch dropping from a tree or something like that," Reese agreed. "But I don't want to lead you into danger, either."

They were already smack dab in the middle of danger, but she understood what he meant. It was hard enough to battle the smoke from the fire; what could they do if someone was waiting for them in the woods with a gun? She strained to listen, hoping Duke didn't become the gunman's target.

But there was nothing but silence and smoke surrounding them.

Katy wasn't sure how long they huddled behind the downed tree branch—time held little meaning at this point —but there was no denying the smoke was only getting worse.

"I think we'd better keep going," Reese finally said. "We can't stay here forever."

"Which way?" She agreed with his decision to move on. What difference did it make if they died from smoke inhalation or from a bullet? A bullet might be a quicker death.

She shook off the morbid thoughts. They needed to stay positive.

And keep praying.

"The same direction Duke took," Reese said, slowly rising to his feet. He held out his hand to her, and she took it, silently praying they were making the right decision.

Reese didn't let go of her hand, and she found she was grateful for the human contact now that it was just the two of them making their way through the woods.

She found herself reciting the Lord's Prayer again under her breath as they made their way in the general direction the dog had taken. Soon, Reese joined her, their voices gaining strength, despite their hoarse throats.

She stopped praying when she couldn't hear herself anymore because of the roaring sound that seemed to swell in magnitude as they wove their way between trees and over rocks. Katy couldn't help wondering if they were heading straight into the fire rather than away from it.

She wished she knew why Duke had taken off like that. She never would have imagined the dog would totally abandon them.

"Wait a minute." Reese tugged at her hand, halting her progress. "Look at the smoke."

She blinked, her eyes tearing up from the constant assault from the smoky haze. "I know. It's been getting worse all along."

"Not that. It's getting lighter in color. It's not black but more gray."

She shook her head, not understanding. "What difference does that make?"

"When you douse a fire with water, the smoke gets lighter." Reese coughed again. "Come on, maybe this is the way to the firefighters."

She wanted to believe they were close to being rescued, but Reese's color-of-smoke theory seemed lame. Besides, she couldn't really tell much difference.

Woof! Woof!

"Is that Duke?" she asked, half afraid she'd imagined the sound. If three barks meant danger, what did two mean?

"I think so, come on." Reese changed direction, as if trying to aim for the spot where the barking had come from. She followed him blindly, still hanging on to his hand as if it were a lifeline.

A few minutes later, Duke came running out from the trees, heading straight toward them.

Reese crouched low, giving the dog a huge hug. She reached down to pet Duke's fur, overwhelmed with relief.

"He's back," Katy murmured. "Good boy!"

"Look, he's brought the firefighters with him," Reese pointed out.

Sure enough, several firefighters, covered head to toe in black and yellow gear, emerged from the woods directly in front of them. The firefighters picked up their pace, rushing over to meet them.

Her knees buckled as realization dawned.

They were safe! God and Duke had saved them!

Katy didn't remember much of the trip back out of the woods beyond the worst of the fire. Soon she and Reese were placed on side-by-side stretchers, wearing identical oxygen masks. She recognized Sam Torretti, the paramedic who was also the son of Sheriff Luke Torretti, when he bent over her.

"I don't like how red your lips are," he muttered.

"I'm sure we don't have carbon monoxide poisoning," she assured him.

"But you do have a headache, right?" Sam persisted.

She slowly nodded. The headache had only just started after they'd heard the loud noise they'd mistaken for a gunshot.

"Then I hate to tell you, but you might be worse off than you realize, Doc," Sam said in a dry tone. "We're taking you to Hope County Hospital first. From there, you may be transferred to Madison if you need hyperbaric treatments."

She didn't like being on the patient side of the stretcher, and she especially didn't like being told what kind of medical procedures she needed. She knew very well how to treat smoke inhalation.

"Hyperbaric treatments are only for severe cases," she protested. "We're not that bad off."

"I think I'll let another doctor make that decision," Sam said with a stern look. "You're my patient now."

"I'm not going to the hospital," Reese spoke up. "I need to take care of my dog. Can you give me a ride to the veterinary clinic?"

Sam glanced over with a frown. "Your boyfriend needs to go in for treatment, just like you do."

She was about to point out that Reese wasn't her boyfriend, but why bother? The whole town probably knew they'd spent time together. And soon, they'd hear about how they'd been rescued together too. "He's right about the dog needing care. Duke saved our lives." After everything they'd been through with Duke, no way was she leaving the dog behind. "Surely there's some sort of treatment you can do for him."

"Here, we can use a face tent to provide some oxygen," the other paramedic spoke up.

"Try it," Reese urged.

Duke didn't like the mask hanging around his neck, but at least he didn't paw it off his face. Reese kept the dog close at hand.

"Bring him along in the ambulance," Katy said.

Sam looked exasperated. "You know I can't bring a dog to the hospital."

"You can, trust me. Duke is highly trained. He won't be a problem. You can tell everyone he's Reese's therapy dog. Per ADA rules, they'll have to let him in."

"Okay, fine," Sam agreed with a heavy sigh. "But if there's any trouble once you arrive in the ER, keep me out of it."

"I'll make sure you don't get in trouble," Katy promised. Her throat was still sore, but the dull headache that had settled in the base of her skull seemed to be getting better with oxygen. Maybe putting the wet clothing over their faces had helped. She knew there were many potential long-term effects of severe smoke inhalation, especially if their lung tissue was badly scarred from the smoke.

But right now, she was happy to be alive. Safe from the fire and alive.

The ride to the hospital didn't take long at all, or maybe she'd slept for a good part of it. Now that the adrenaline rush had faded, her body felt as if she'd been run over by a truck. Exhaustion weighed on her limbs, and it seemed to take every ounce of strength she possessed just to lift her hand to adjust the oxygen mask on her face.

"What time is it?" she asked when Sam's face reappeared in her line of vision.

"Just past twelve thirty," Sam said. "We're going to have to secure the safety straps to get you out of the ambulance and into the ER, okay?"

"Sure." She kept her arms down along her sides and tried to remain still as Sam buckled the straps across her body. She took several deep breaths of oxygen, thinking how incredible it was that they'd only been in the woods for a few hours when it had seemed like a lifetime.

Sam and his colleague gently set the gurney on the ground and then hit the lever to bring it up to its full height. She craned her neck, trying to get a glimpse of Reese and Duke, but the other ambulance was just pulling in.

They wheeled her into the trauma bay, and she felt dizzy looking up at the bright lights overhead and hearing Sam recite her vital signs. She'd had no idea how vulnerable it felt to be a patient like this. She felt bad that she hadn't done more to reassure her patients in the past.

She wanted to protest that her condition wasn't serious enough to warrant being in the trauma bay, but when she tried to talk, no one was listening.

Since when did patients call the shots? Yeah, since never.

The straps across her chest loosened, and she looked up

to see Janelle leaning over her. "Hi, Dr. Katy, I'm just going to get you connected to the heart monitor, okay?"

She was embarrassed at the thought of being undressed in front of her colleagues, but Janelle did a good job of keeping her well covered as she connected the EKG leads.

"What's my pulse ox?" Katy asked. She wished she could see the display on the heart monitor, but it was located well behind her, out of view.

"A little on the low side, ninety percent right now," Janelle confirmed. "Apparently it was down as low as eighty-seven percent when Sam first checked it."

A normal reading would be closer to one hundred percent, but at least it was improving. She wondered how Reese was doing. She missed having him close by.

Hard to believe she'd only known him for a few days. It seemed much longer.

As the medical staff placed an IV, gave fluids, took blood and discussed x-rays, she battled a wave of helplessness.

She needed to see Reese. To make sure he and Duke were okay.

The thought of not seeing him again was painfully unbearable.

REESE WAS grateful Katy had insisted the ambulance crew provide oxygen to Duke and to bring him along, but he still wanted to find a vet. And soon.

He knew there was a small veterinary clinic located just outside Crystal Lake, but he had no idea if they were even open. Had people been evacuated from the town? Or did the firefighters have the blaze under control?

For the second time in three days, Reese found himself back in the trauma bay of the Hope County Hospital ER.

Only this time, Dr. Katy was in the spot next to him, rather than Marcus Boyle.

"Duke, stay," he ordered. Then he glanced up at the nurse hovering over him. "He won't hurt you," he said.

"I know. The paramedics told us you wouldn't get treatment without your dog," one of the nurses said. He blinked and tried to read her name tag. Merry, that was right. He remembered Merry now from the other night.

"He's well trained," Reese repeated. "And thanks for hooking him up to the oxygen too."

The medical staff gave Duke a wide berth but didn't seem overly concerned with having a dog nearby. He listened as they talked about him in the third person, as if he weren't right there, awake and conscious.

He turned his head to look over at Katy at the exact moment she glanced at him. He smiled at her from behind the oxygen mask and lifted a hand in acknowledgement.

He didn't want to think about the fact that this might be the last time he would see her for a while.

But he couldn't stay, no matter how much the doctors and nurses wanted him to. Even if getting Duke to the vet wasn't an option, he still needed to talk to his boss about the wildfire and his suspicions about the blond dude.

Reese tried to be patient, but it wasn't easy. They cleaned up the wound on his arm and placed fresh dressings over it. When they decided he needed a chest x-ray, he shook his head.

"Listen, Doc, I need to get out of here," he said, glaring at the ER physician on duty. He squinted to make out his name tag. Dr. Allen.

"Your pulse ox readings are getting better, but I highly recommend you stay on oxygen at least overnight, maybe even a few days," Dr. Allen said. "Not to mention, you could use at least three doses of IV antibiotics for your arm, just to make sure it doesn't get infected, but your lungs are the bigger concern right now. You're fortunate that you don't need hyperbaric treatments."

He had no idea what that meant, but it didn't matter. "Can't I get oxygen and antibiotics to go?" he asked. "I really need to take care of my dog and check in with my boss."

Dr. Allen narrowed his gaze. "Your dog is already getting some care. I'll make you a deal. You agree to a chest x-ray and IV antibiotics and I'll treat your dog, too. I can give him IV fluids in the scruff of his neck and keep the oxygen on for a while. How does that sound?"

Reese gave in. His dog was the most important issue right now. But he also needed to call his boss. "All right, Dr. Allen, you have a deal."

The doc waved a hand. "Call me Gabe. Now let's get that x-ray, so we can care for your dog."

The few minutes he was without oxygen didn't seem too bad, as they transferred him from the gurney to a wheelchair. But when they replaced the mask over his face, he couldn't deny that his breathing felt much better. He glanced at Duke, still wearing the face tent thingy around his neck. He was glad the dog didn't look too bad off. Maybe once he got some IV fluids in him, he'd be okay.

He didn't even want to think about what effect this injury might have on his career. Surely his breathing would get better, right? He wouldn't need oxygen forever, would he? Trekking through the woods with an oxygen tank wasn't exactly a viable option.

Pushing aside that pathetic image wasn't easy, but he told himself to concentrate on one issue at a time. Duke came first, and then he could worry about the rest. Besides, he should be glad they'd gotten safely out of the fire.

Praying with Katy had given him the determination to push on. He couldn't deny the power of faith.

The chest x-ray didn't take long, and as he was wheeled back to the trauma bay, he realized he could still lean on the power of prayer for healing, too.

His gut clenched when he saw the two sheriff's deputies waiting for him in the trauma bay. Deputy Armbruster and Deputy Kramer looked ill at ease, maybe because of the way Duke sat as still as a statue, as if waiting for the signal to attack.

He sighed and gave Duke the hand signal to lie down. The dog looked disappointed but stretched out on the floor.

"Deputies," he greeted them in his raspy voice. "What brings you here?"

"We need to ask you about the fire," Deputy Kramer said in a snide tone.

"Then why not talk to both of us?" Katy asked. Reese glanced over in surprise to find her in a wheelchair beside him. She must have come back from radiology, too.

The two deputies exchanged a look, and Reese could tell they weren't too happy with her idea.

Did they think she was going to lie to protect him?

"I'm afraid protocol dictates we'll need to talk to you separately," Deputy Armbruster said in a firm tone. "But we can split up if that makes you feel better."

It didn't, but Reese wanted to get this done and over with. "Fine. Where do you want to talk? I would think you'd want some privacy so we don't try to fix our stories."

"Gabe, are there two empty rooms for us to use?" Katy asked. "I'm sure you'd like to get the trauma bay cleaned up, anyway."

"Sure, take rooms eleven and twelve," Gabe said.

Katy wheeled herself toward a hallway that led farther

into the ER. He waited until Merry disconnected Duke from the oxygen regulator in the wall before he gave Duke the hand signal to come. The dog trotted along beside him.

Merry followed them into room eleven, connecting both his oxygen and Duke's back to the wall. She took a few extra minutes to hang his IV antibiotic before leaving. Reese was a little surprised that Deputy Armbruster took a seat across from him, leaving Katy to talk to Deputy Kramer. He relaxed a bit, trusting Armbruster would be more impartial.

Was it really just twelve hours ago that Kramer had accused him of breaking in to Katy's house? He could barely wrap his mind around it.

"Why don't you start at the beginning?" The way Armbruster sat back in his chair gave Reese the impression he actually intended to listen.

Reese had to think back to what had taken him out to the hiking trail in the first place. He reached over to sink his fingers into Duke's fur.

"Duke wanted to go out, and he headed straight for the hiking trail," Reese began. "I figured something was up, that maybe he'd caught the scent of the blond dude, so I let him take the lead."

"Just so I'm clear, the blond guy is the one you think was poaching with Boyle, correct?"

"Yes." Reese knew Kramer didn't believe him, but it was possible Armbruster was willing to keep an open mind. "I saw him several times when I was tracking Boyle, but I kept losing him."

"Go on," Deputy Armbruster encouraged.

"When I smelled the smoke, I thought Duke was tracking some careless campers, which was concerning since we've had such a dry spring."

"When did you run into Dr. Katy?"

"Duke found her." He stroked the dog's head. "I was going to head back up the trail in case there were people trapped up there, but then I saw the fire engulfed far too many trees, and I decided to get down to safety."

"And then what?"

"The fire surrounded us," Reese said in a grim tone. "We followed Duke to safety. He led us to water, and in the end, he brought the firefighters out to where we were."

There was a moment of silence before Deputy Armbruster cleared his throat. "That dog of yours is quite the hero."

"Yes. He is." Reese lifted his gaze. "I didn't see anyone, but I know that fire was started on purpose. A fire started by a campfire couldn't have surrounded us so quickly."

Armbruster nodded. "Yeah, that's what we think, too."

"Am I a suspect?" Reese asked.

"No." A ghost of a smile flashed over Armbruster's face. "I don't think you'd risk your dog."

Reese chuckled and then started coughing again. "No, I wouldn't. I wouldn't risk Katy, either."

"I know."

Reese felt as if a huge weight had been lifted from his shoulders. He wasn't a suspect anymore, at least not in Deputy Armbruster's eyes.

"Well, if that's all, I'd like to get Duke some treatments while we're here, although it would be better to get him in to see the vet as soon as possible."

"I hate to tell you, but the veterinary clinic isn't open," Deputy Armbruster said slowly.

"Because of the fire?" he asked.

"Yes. It's not just the vet that's closed. The entire town of Crystal Lake has been evacuated as a result of the fire,"

Armbruster said. "The roads have been closed off except for emergency vehicles."

Reese stared at him in shock. "Where did everyone go?"

"The Red Cross has set up tents a few miles outside of town. No one's going back home until we get the fire under control."

12
———

Katy stared at Deputy Kramer, trying to understand where he was coming from. "Reese didn't start the fire," she said firmly. "And I don't understand why you keep accusing him of doing all this stuff instead of trying to find the real culprit."

"You mentioned being surprised to see him on the trail," he persisted. "Why would you think that's a coincidence?"

"Why do you think he'd risk his own life?" she countered, getting angry. "Don't you understand? We almost died back there!"

Kramer's face flushed, and he stared down at his small notebook for several long seconds. "Is there anything else you can remember?" he finally asked.

"No." Katy didn't understand what Ian's problem with Reese was, but she was surprised at how eager he was to believe the worst. Which was strange because she'd worked with Ian before, and he'd always been great.

Now she couldn't wait for him to leave.

"All right, please call me if you remember anything more."

Yeah, right. "Sure," she agreed, which wasn't an outright lie. She'd call some other deputy if necessary, but not Ian Kramer.

After he left, she took several deep breaths in an attempt to calm down. Maybe it was Ian's job to believe the worst in people, but she didn't like the fact that he didn't seem to consider other possibilities.

Like the blond-haired man Reese had seen.

She was in the process of disconnecting her oxygen when Gabe walked into her room. "What are you doing?"

She winced, since there was no denying she'd been caught in the act. "Going over to make sure Reese is okay. Why? Are you here to discharge us?"

"Not exactly. I'm going to admit you both upstairs."

"Do you really think that's necessary?" she asked with a frown. "I'm sure you'll need those beds for real patients."

Gabe pinched the bridge of his nose as if she'd given him a headache. "Katy, you are a real patient, and so is Reese. Besides, you'll both be better off if you stay here since the town has been evacuated."

Her eyes widened at the news, and she wondered why she hadn't considered that earlier. "I'm not sure Reese will stay. He's worried about Duke."

"I've given the dog some fluids. I think he'll be fine."

"I didn't know that you were a practicing vet," she teased, feeling relieved to know Duke had gotten some care.

"I'm not, but thankfully, some of the basics are the same." Gabe took out his stethoscope to listen to her lungs. "Better, but not great."

"I know." She could feel the irritation in her nose and throat, and truthfully, staying on oxygen overnight was probably the right thing to do. "All right, I'll convince Reese we should stay."

"Good plan," Gabe agreed. "I'll get the orders placed, and then we'll get you both transported upstairs."

"Could we get scrubs? We're both in desperate need of a shower and a change of clothes."

"No problem." Gabe left the room, no doubt to find Reese. She finished disconnecting herself from the oxygen in the wall, transferring to the tank on the back of her wheelchair, and then wheeled herself over to join Reese. She could have walked but didn't have the portable oxygen tank on a wheeled carrier to use.

Deep down, she was glad they'd both have to stay the night at the hospital. Pathetic, really, that she was looking forward to spending more time with Reese before they went their separate ways.

"I need to call my boss," Reese was saying when she entered his room. "He needs all the help he can get right now."

"I don't think that's in your best interest, or Duke's, either," Gabe said in a stern tone. "You need oxygen, steroids, antibiotics, rest and fluids, in that order."

Reese scowled and then glanced down at Duke. She noticed the dog had a huge hump on his neck and wondered what had happened. "Is Duke hurt?" she asked.

"No, that's the fluid I injected," Gabe assured her. "It actually works very well. The fluid absorbs subcutaneously into their vascular system. I'll get him some medication, too. Maybe we can give it in some peanut butter or something."

She wasn't sure how Gabe knew how to take care of animals, but she was grateful he did.

"Reese, please stay, for Duke's sake."

He let out a heavy sigh and nodded. "All right, I'll stay. But only if Duke stays with me, and I'll need something to feed him. I doubt you stock pet supplies here."

"I can have Zack head out to get some dog food," Merry volunteered, walking into the room. "He keeps some in his car."

"Dishes, too," Reese added.

"Those I can find in the kitchen." Merry turned to Gabe. "Admission orders have been placed, and there are two inpatient beds available on three west, right next to each other."

Katy could feel her cheeks burn beneath the grime, and she wondered what Reese thought of the arrangements. She hadn't asked to have their rooms next to each other.

But she was secretly glad.

"Good. Call one of the techs to transport them up," Gabe directed. "I'll find clean scrubs for you both."

"Thanks, again, for everything," Reese said in a low voice. "I'm grateful for all the care you provided to Duke."

Gabe smiled. "It wasn't a problem. Easy enough since the dog didn't fight me. Did you train him yourself?"

"Yeah." Reese's smile was strained, and Katy found herself wondering if he'd gotten Duke right after his divorce. She could easily imagine Reese spending all his free time training Duke.

"I wouldn't mind getting a dog if you'd be willing to train him," Gabe continued. "Think about how much you'd charge and let me know."

Reese looked surprised at the offer. "Ah, okay. But you should know that most police-trained dogs go for several grand, so it's not cheap."

"I'd pay that much for a well-trained dog," Gabe mused. "My wife and I have two small children, so I wouldn't even consider a dog unless it was trained by someone who knew what he was doing. Like you."

Reese glanced at her, as if asking if he was for real. She smiled and nodded. Apparently training dogs for other people hadn't occurred to Reese before. And now he'd been handed the chance to make a little extra money.

She hoped he'd take it. Not for her sake but for his own. Because while she could care less about his debt, she knew it weighed heavily on his shoulders.

Reese was too proud to allow anyone else to pay off what he owed. And she figured Reese wouldn't even try to move forward with having a personal life until he'd gotten his financial situation under control.

Truthfully, she didn't mind waiting, if that's what it took. But would he give them a chance? She fully intended to find out.

Because at the moment, she couldn't imagine a future that didn't include Reese and Duke.

REESE TURNED the idea of training a dog for Gabe over and over in his mind as the young tech pushed him in his wheelchair up to his room. He'd never considered there to be a huge market for this type of thing, but obviously he was wrong.

But now that he thought about it, if he trained two dogs a year and kept up with his current frugal spending, he'd be out of debt sooner than he'd anticipated. Maybe even less than a year.

"Here's an admission kit with shampoo, toothbrush and shaving stuff in it," the tech said, pulling out a tub full of personal supplies. "Do you need me to hook up your dog to oxygen again?" The tech glanced at Duke in a way that made him think she might be afraid of the animal.

"I'll take care of it, thanks."

The tech shrugged and walked out of the room. He rose to his feet and took care of Duke before he took the tub of personal items and headed into the bathroom.

The face in the mirror looked far worse than he'd expected. The smoky smell seemed to be imbedded in his airway, and he hoped that taking a shower and changing his clothes would help.

A knock at the door startled him. "Mr. Webster? My name is Amy, and I'll be your nurse. I have clean scrubs here for you to wear."

"Thanks." He opened the door and gratefully took the scrubs.

She frowned. "Did you disconnect your own IV?"

"Yeah. Can't you wait until I finish showering before you hook it back up?"

"I guess, but I also need to put a waterproof dressing over your arm."

"Okay."

Amy quickly wrapped his arm. "Call me when you're finished," she said.

"I will," he promised before closing the bathroom door.

When he emerged a good forty-five minutes later, he felt a lot better. The smoke smell still lingered but not nearly as powerful as it was before. He'd used the cheap razor they'd provided without nicking himself too badly, and he was happy to be wearing clean clothes.

He debated giving Duke a bath, since the dog's fur still smelled like smoke, but decided against trying that feat in the shower. It was difficult enough in a bathtub.

He pressed the call button, and soon Amy returned. "Wow, you look great!"

"Thanks." Actually, he felt like a fraud staying here in

the hospital when all he needed were antibiotics, steroids and oxygen. But when he stretched out on the bed, he realized just how tired he was.

Strange to be so exhausted when he was used to hiking for hours in the woods.

Amy cleaned and reconnected the IV tubing to the catheter in his arm. "I've called for a late lunch tray. It should be here soon."

"Thanks." He glanced over at Duke, who was once again stretched out on the floor beside his bed. "Don't worry. Hopefully your food will be here soon."

Duke's tail thumped against the side of his bed, making him smile.

He hoped Merry made good on her promise. Duke deserved the best. While he waited, he used the phone to call his boss. Unfortunately, Gavin didn't answer. Leaving a message didn't feel right, but what else could he do? No doubt, Gavin was out at the scene of the fire.

Where he should be, too. Making sure the blond dude didn't get away with attempted murder.

Too bad he still had no clue as to the blond dude's identity, which made it difficult to know where to find him.

AFTER CLEANING up and eating the tray of food that arrived courtesy of her nurse, Katy stared out the window, fighting the urge to go over to talk to Reese.

No sense in pushing her company on him. Heaven knew they'd spent over half a day together. No doubt he was appreciating some time alone.

She closed her eyes and tried to rest, but despite her lack of sleep the night before and her bone-deep exhaustion, sleep eluded her.

Another hour dragged by, and finally she gave up and crawled out of bed. She didn't want to use the wheelchair—bad enough to be a patient—so she connected her oxygen to a portable wheeling tank to take with her.

The door to Reese's room was partially closed, and for a moment, she stood uncertainly. Just because she couldn't sleep didn't mean he wasn't.

She'd turned around to head back to her room when she heard him talking. "Gavin, please call me as soon as you get this message. Thanks."

Okay, so he wasn't sleeping. Taking a deep breath to bolster her courage, she lightly tapped on the door. "Reese? It's Katy."

"Come in," he called. His voice was still a little hoarse, just like hers.

"Hi, how's Duke?" She really did care about the dog, even though it was also an easy excuse for her being there.

"He's good. Wow, you look great." The warmth in Reese's gaze made her toes curl.

"Thanks, so do you. Although I can't seem to get rid of the smoke smell," she said, wrinkling her nose.

"Well, you might want to keep your distance from Duke, then, because I haven't given him a bath yet, and his fur still reeks from the fire."

"It's not his fault," she said, sitting in the chair beside his bed. She leaned over and rubbed Duke's fur, wondering again how she could ever have been afraid of him. "Did your boss call you back yet?"

He grimaced and shook his head. "Not yet. Sitting around here is driving me crazy. I feel like I should be out at the scene of the fire."

"I didn't realize that DNR game wardens were also trained as firefighters."

"We have some training, but not to the extent the smoke jumpers do," he admitted. "Still, I'd rather be near the action."

"I get it," Katy said with a sigh. "I'm not used to being at loose ends, either. I keep thinking about the patients who are probably coming in for treatment. I'm sure Gabe could use help, yet here I am, doing nothing."

"You're resting and getting better," he pointed out.

She lifted a brow. "So are you. And so is Duke."

"Touché," he said with a wry smile. But then his gaze turned serious. "I'm sorry you had to get mixed up in all this."

"It's not your fault," she reminded him. "And trust me, I made sure that Deputy Kramer was crystal clear on my opinion."

Reese scowled. "You mean he still thinks I'm involved?"

Maybe she shouldn't have brought the subject up. "I'm sure it's just his usual suspicious nature."

Reese didn't look convinced. "Funny, Armbruster didn't seem to share his opinion. In fact, he told me straight up that I wasn't a suspect."

"Really? That's wonderful!" Katy was thrilled and relieved to hear it. "I'm sure Devon will talk some sense into Ian."

"You're on a first-name basis with him, huh?"

She frowned. "Well, yeah, sort of. I see the deputies all the time, and last year I took care of Devon after he was injured. Ian was there the whole time, so I guess it was natural to call him by his first name."

"Maybe he just doesn't like the way you're always defending me," Reese pointed out. "He might believe the gossip circling around town."

"What, you mean, like, he's jealous? Don't be ridiculous. There's absolutely nothing like that between us."

"Maybe he'd like there to be something more," Reese said in a low voice. "He's not a bad guy, seems to have a solid career."

Her stomach clenched painfully as she realized Reese was trying to subtly tell her that he wasn't interested.

As if the closeness between them, and that heated kiss, hadn't happened.

As if she didn't already care about him, obviously more than she should.

"I'm not interested in Ian that way," she said, forcing herself to meet his gaze head on. "You're the first man I've kissed in well over a year."

A strained silence fell between them, making her wish she'd held her tongue.

"Knock, knock," a female voice called out, breaking the moment. "Reese? Are you decent?"

Katy froze for a second, but then recognized Merry's voice. Merry popped into the room, a half-full bag of dog food in her arms.

"Hi, Merry," Reese greeted her warmly. Katy wondered if he realized that Merry was married to Deputy Zack Crain. "Thanks so much for bringing Duke's dinner."

"You're welcome, and actually, Zack's the one who brought it in." She set the bag down and pulled two silver bowls out. "Do you want me to fill these for you?"

"I can get it," Reese protested, swinging his scrub-clad legs over the side of the bed. "But thanks, anyway."

"Sounds good. Hey, Dr. Katy, how are you feeling?" Merry asked.

"I'm fine. Should be back to work tomorrow."

Merry grinned and shook her head. "I know it's not

easy to be on the wrong side of a hospital bed, but there's no reason to rush back to work. We have it all under control."

Katy smiled, remembering how Merry had suffered a concussion last year after being hit by one of their psych patients. "I'll be back to work tomorrow," she repeated.

"You can fight that out with Gabe," Merry said with a wave of her hand. "I have to run, but let me know if you need anything else, okay?"

The room seemed painfully quiet after Merry left, despite the crunching sounds from Duke enjoying his dinner.

Katy thought that Reese might be trying to avoid a personal conversation, so she rose to her feet and grabbed her oxygen tank. "I'm almost out of air. Have a good night, Reese."

His smile seemed strained. "You, too, Katy. And don't go back to work too soon, okay?"

"I won't." She kept her gaze focused on maneuvering the oxygen tank as she returned to her room.

She crawled beneath the covers, wishing she could forget the awkward conversation with Reese. Her throat felt thick with tears. Ridiculous to cry over a man she barely knew.

So why did she feel so miserable?

Katy closed her eyes and opened her heart and her mind to God. She needed to believe that God had a plan for her, even if she didn't understand what it entailed.

She slept fitfully, getting up several times, not used to hearing the hospital sounds from a patient's perspective. Not that the staff were exceptionally noisy or anything.

She heard a thud when she came out of the bathroom, and she stood for a minute, trying to figure out what was wrong. Had Reese fallen to the floor? Or maybe some other patient had fallen?

The door of her room abruptly swung open, and she stumbled backward in surprise when a tall blond-haired man entered her room. He was wearing scrubs but didn't look at all familiar. He wasn't wearing a name tag, either.

A chill snaked down her spine. Was this the guy who Reese had seen in the woods?

He took another step into the room, and that's when she saw the gun clutched in his right hand. "If you scream, I'll shoot," he said in a flat tone.

She swallowed hard and nodded. Oh, yeah, she believed him. "Who are you?" she asked in a whisper.

"That doesn't matter. You're going to do exactly as I say, understand?"

The chill congealed into ice. She licked her suddenly dry lips. "O-okay."

"You're going to come with me," the blond guy said in that eerily calm voice. "I'm going to keep you directly in front of me so that game warden can't sic that dog of his on me."

Katy didn't want to do as he asked, but what choice did she have? If she'd been closer to her bed, she could use the call light to call the nurse, but she wasn't.

She wanted to believe there was a way to use her brain to get away from the blond guy, but she hesitated a moment too long. Suddenly he was right beside her, grabbing her arm in a grip so painful she felt tears sting her eyes.

"Don't even think about trying anything stupid," he said in a low voice.

Her throat was so tight with fear she couldn't speak. She gave a brief nod, indicating she understood.

"Let's go." He pressed the gun into her side.

She walked slowly toward the doorway, hoping and praying that Reese would figure out a way to get them out of this mess.

Before this maniac killed them both, and poor Duke, too.

13

A low growl from Duke awakened Reese from a restless sleep. How on earth anyone managed to sleep in a hospital bed was beyond him. Of course, the fact that Duke was sleeping on the foot of the mattress didn't help. The hospital bed definitely wasn't big enough for the two of them.

But he'd refused to make Duke stay on the hard floor. Not after the way he'd saved his life. He was glad that the dog had been given the same meds he'd been given, just in a smaller dose.

"What's wrong, boy?" he whispered.

Duke had lifted his head and was staring intently at the doorway. Was someone out there? Duke hadn't growled when the nurse had come in a few hours ago to check his blood pressure and to hang another dose of the IV antibiotic. She'd also checked the oxygen level in his blood. His readings continued to improve, which was good news.

Reese swung his legs over the edge of the bed and slowly rose to his feet. He was hampered a bit by the IV tubing and resisted the urge to pull the stupid catheter out. He hadn't gotten very far when he heard someone call his name.

"Reese?" The whisper sounded like Katy, although that didn't make sense because Duke knew Katy's scent and wouldn't growl at her.

"I'm awake," he said in a low voice. "Come in. Is something wrong?"

The door to his room swung open at the same time Duke rose off the bed, the growl in his throat growing louder. It took a minute for him to realize that Katy wasn't alone. The blond dude was standing almost directly behind her.

"Call off your dog, or I'll kill her."

"Down, Duke." The frightened expression in Katy's eyes ripped at his heart, and based on the awkward angle the guy had on her, he realized the blond dude was holding a gun pressed against her side. His stomach clenched, and he took a deep breath, trying to remain calm. "Duke won't attack unless I give the command. What do you want?"

For several long seconds, the blond guy didn't say anything. Even though it was dark in his room, the muted light from the hall revealed the guy was wearing scrubs.

"We're going to take care of the dog first," the blond stranger said.

"Wait, why are you doing this? I don't even know your name! What's the point of killing us?"

Reese couldn't make out the expression in the blond guy's eyes in the dim light, but his cold, flat tone was not reassuring.

"I have no choice. Boyle would have eventually ratted me out, and you wouldn't stop searching for me."

Reese still didn't understand, but he wanted to keep him talking, hoping someone might come down the hall to find them. "I might not have kept searching for you if you hadn't smashed my truck."

"I needed to keep you from going back into the woods to find the cougar."

Okay, the way this guy answered every question in that same emotionless tone was really eerie. Why was he acting like some sort of robot?

"Look, no one has to die here tonight," Reese said. "I'm sure we can work something out."

"I disagree. Once you're out of my way, I can go back to living in the woods without interference."

Reese had always suspected the guy was ex-military, and seeing him up close only confirmed his original impression. He wished he understood what was going on in his mind. Did he really think that he could kill two people and a dog without being caught? Was he poaching to live off the land to stay off grid? And if so, why kill a cougar?

Unless Boyle had decided to kill the cougar on his own? Suddenly it made sense. "You were tracking Boyle, the same way I was," he said slowly. "You weren't working together at all. You were upset with Boyle because he was drawing unwanted attention from the DNR."

"Too smart for your own good."

Reese would have felt better if there had been satisfaction in his tone, but there wasn't.

How could he get through to the blond guy if he didn't feel anything? There wasn't a hint of emotion for him to exploit. Nothing that Reese could appeal to in order to make him change his mind.

"Dog first," he repeated. He let go of Katy's arm for a brief moment and pulled something out of the pocket of his scrubs. He tossed the syringe on the bedside table and quickly resumed his tight grip on Katy's arm. "Inject him with the contents of that syringe. Don't worry, the sedative will act quickly, and he'll die a painless death."

Reese stared at the syringe and then dragged his gaze up to meet Katy's. Her mouth was pulled together in a terse frown, and she gave her head a slight shake.

She winced as the blond guy pressed the gun painfully into her side. "Don't make me shoot all three of you. Gunshot wounds hurt. But if that's truly the way you want to go, that's fine with me. I can shoot all three of you and still find a way to escape. I won't be taken prisoner again."

Reese stepped forward and picked up the syringe, his thoughts whirling. Again? Had this guy been captured during the war in Afghanistan? Was that what had messed with his mind?

"Let us go, and I'll make sure that you can resume living off the land where no one will bother you," he said, making one last effort. "I promise that you don't have to kill us in order to get away."

"I'll count to three. If you haven't injected the dog by then, I'll start shooting. One..."

Reese wished he knew what was in the syringe. If he only gave a partial dose, would Duke still die? Could he find a way to pretend to inject him? But if Duke didn't go down, then the blond guy would know he'd faked it.

"Two..."

"Okay, stop counting. I'll do it." He stepped closer to Duke and put his left arm around the dog's neck. Tears burned his eyes as he lifted the syringe.

"I love you, Duke," he whispered.

"Jesse, don't! Let her go!"

Reese froze and glanced up in surprise to see Ian Kramer standing in the doorway of his room. The deputy was wearing full SWAT gear and held his gun trained on the blond dude, who still held Katy in a tight grip. It dawned on Reese that the two men had similar facial features, although Ian Kramer's hair was as dark as Jesse's was light. Still, now that he saw them together, he wondered why he hadn't noticed the resemblance before.

They looked similar enough to be brothers.

"Go away, Ian. This isn't your business." Jesse didn't as much as glance at the deputy.

"I didn't want to believe you were involved in this, Jesse." Ian Kramer looked upset, but the tip of his gun didn't waver. "I turned my back on the illegal hunting, knowing how important it was for you to be independent and live off the land. But you went too far when you tried to run them off the road, which I figured out when I ran the license plate tag. Then you set that fire. And now murder? What are you thinking? You know I can't let you get away with this."

Reese palmed the syringe and edged a little closer to Jesse. He wanted to imbed the syringe into Jesse, but he couldn't risk the gun going off and killing Katy.

"You won't kill me," Jesse said in that same eerie voice. "You love me, remember? You told me that at least a dozen times while I was recuperating from being held prisoner."

"I do love you, Jesse. You're my brother. That's why I can't let you do this. Don't you see? There's no point in killing them if we have you surrounded. You can't escape. Please surrender your weapon. I'll make sure you get the help you need."

"The only thing that helps me is to be alone in the woods with nothing surrounding me."

"I know, Jesse. I'll find a way to make that happen. I promise I'll do everything in my power to help you."

Reese wanted to believe the deputy was getting through

to Jesse. Had his hand loosened its grip on the gun pressed against Katy's side? He inched closer.

"Okay, here's another idea," Ian said, sounding desperate. "Use me as your hostage. We can leave the hospital, and I'll take you someplace safe."

Reese held his breath as Jesse seemed to seriously consider the idea. "The other deputies won't let me through, not if I have you."

"Trust me, they will." Ian's voice oozed confidence. "Especially if I tell them to."

"I need to go far away," Jesse said. "The other side of the country if necessary. Maybe Alaska."

"We will. I promise."

Ian glanced at Reese for an intense moment, and he understood the silent message. Ian wanted Reese to use the sedative in the syringe to subdue Jesse.

He gave an almost imperceptible nod. He wished he knew what was in the syringe and tried to squeeze some of the contents out without attracting attention. Duke weighed 95 pounds, and Jesse was obviously closer to two hundred. Surely a half dose wouldn't be as lethal?

"Let her go, Jesse. Katy, I want you to go over to the opposite side of the room, understand?"

"Yes," Katy agreed softly.

Reese tensed and sent up a silent prayer for strength as he prepared to jump. He watched for the moment when Jesse released Katy, then lunged forward and stabbed the syringe into Jesse's thigh.

"No," Katy shouted but he pressed on the plunger at the same time Ian grabbed Jesse's gun. The big blond man let out an animal-like howl as he dropped to his knees.

"Get back. He needs medical attention," Katy shouted. "Call a code blue!"

Reese flipped on the lights. Ian used his radio to call for help. Less than sixty seconds later, the room was flooded with people, mostly deputies.

"Lift him onto the bed," Katy snapped from where she knelt on the floor next to Jesse. "Then I want everyone out of here except medical personnel. I need room to work."

Reese snagged Ian's arm. "Get one of the nurses in here to help her."

Ian left the room and returned with several nurses. A few minutes later, Gabe Allen joined them. Katy pretty much ignored him, barking orders like a drill sergeant.

"I want a full set of labs drawn, including heavy metals. I want an IV going wide open to flush out his system. I want an intubation tray in case we lose his airway. Amy, see if there's any way to get a dialysis unit called in."

Reese was impressed at how quickly the nursing staff jumped to do her bidding.

"He's not breathing," one of the nurses announced.

"Where's that intubation tray?"

"Right here." One of the nurses thrust the tray onto the bedside table.

"He could have used a paralytic combined with a sedative," Gabe said as Katy grabbed equipment from the bin. "That's the most painless way to kill someone."

"Let's hope so," Katy mumbled. "At least I know how to treat that."

With deft skill, she placed the breathing tube with Gabe's assistance.

"We need to get him to the ICU," Gabe said. "We can continue to treat him for the unknown substance better with monitoring equipment."

"Dialysis would be his best option," Katy said with a

sigh. "Especially since we don't know what he had in that syringe."

"There's two more syringes in his pocket," Amy said, holding them up. "We could ask the lab to test the contents."

"Good job," Katy said with a grim smile. "The only problem is that getting them tested will take time."

Reese glanced at Ian, who looked sick to his stomach with the news.

Time was one thing Jesse didn't have.

KATY WANTED to follow Jesse up to the ICU, but Gabe refused to let her. "You're still a patient, and it's not even dawn yet. Go back to bed and get some sleep."

She watched as they left, wheeling Jesse on a stretcher. She lingered in Reese's room, waiting for the nurses to finish putting everything back in order. It didn't take long, and soon they were alone.

"I can't believe it's finally over," Reese said, sitting on the edge of his bed with a sigh. "And now I understand why Kramer was trying to pin this on me. He didn't want to face the fact that his brother was the guilty one."

"I feel bad for Jesse," Katy admitted. She sat down in the empty chair located near the bed. "It's obvious he's been traumatized."

"Yeah, I know. I feel bad for him, too. But at the same time, I know he would have made good on his threat to kill us."

She suppressed a shiver. "You're right. I've never been so scared in my entire life."

Duke made a high-pitched sound in the back of his throat, grabbing Reese's attention. "I think he needs to go outside."

"I understand." Katy reluctantly rose to her feet. "I'll see you in the morning, okay?"

"Sure." Reese surprised her by reaching over and embracing her in a big hug. "I'm glad you're okay," he whispered.

"I'm glad you're okay, too," she whispered back.

She relished his embrace, but of course, it was over too soon. He released her and stepped back. "We'll talk more tomorrow."

Hope filtered into her heart. "Sounds good."

She waited as Reese disconnected himself from the oxygen tubing and the IV so he could take Duke outside to relieve himself.

She headed back into her room and put her oxygen back on before climbing into bed. She hadn't even noticed her breathing while she'd been held captive by Jesse Kramer.

But now that she had her oxygen back on, she could tell her breathing was a little easier. She closed her eyes and somehow managed to fall asleep.

Bright sunlight streamed in through the window, waking her up bright and early. She peered at the clock, thankful to realize she'd slept at least for a few hours.

She slid out of bed, freshened up in the bathroom and then poked her head out of her room. Reese's door was closed, so rather than bothering him, she flagged down a nurse.

"Would you please get me a fresh oxygen tank so I can walk up to the ICU?" she asked. "I want to check on my patient."

The nurse lifted a brow, as if questioning the use of the pronoun. Hmm. Could she have a patient when she was a patient herself? Probably not.

"I'm friends with his brother," she clarified, although it was a bit of a stretch. "Please?"

"I'll get you the oxygen, but you should know that the guy is a prisoner patient, so they might not let you up to see him."

Katy nodded. "Okay, thanks for the warning."

The nurse returned a few minutes later with a fresh oxygen tank in a wheeled carrier. She hooked herself up and then walked down the hall to the elevators. Normally she preferred the stairs, but the oxygen tank took that decision out of her hands.

The ICU was located one floor up. She walked in and immediately saw the deputy sitting outside one of the rooms. No doubt, Jesse's room.

She recognized Deputy Thomas and gave him a nod. "Hi there. How is he doing?"

"About the same," Deputy Thomas said. "Still not conscious."

She gestured to the door. "Do you mind if I go in to see him? I promise I won't stay long."

The deputy grimaced and shook his head. "Prisoner patients aren't allowed visitors. I've already bent the rule for his brother."

Katy smiled. "Yes, but I'm not a visitor, I'm a doctor. I'm the one who put in the breathing tube. I just want to check on his condition."

"Okay, fine, you get five minutes."

"Thanks." She went into the room and noticed that Ian was sitting beside the bed, asleep in the chair, despite the no-visitor rule. She tiptoed farther into the room, trying not to disturb him.

She glanced up at the monitoring equipment, relieved to

notice that his vital signs appeared stable. What had been in that syringe? What if he never woke up?

"I'm sorry, Dr. Katy," Ian said in a low voice.

She glanced at him in surprise. "I think you need to apologize to Reese more than to me."

"I know." Ian scrubbed his hands over his face. "If I had known how bad Jesse was…"

She nodded, understanding his dilemma. "Has he shown any signs of waking up?" she asked.

"Not yet." Ian stared at his brother. "I'm not sure which is worse, having him stay like this or being arrested and sent to jail."

She wasn't sure what to say to that. She sensed that for Jesse, jail would be the worse option.

Ian knew that, too.

"I'll check back later," she assured him. She left the room and walked down the hall, anxious to talk to the nurse caring for Jesse. She wanted to know how his kidneys were doing and if any of the lab work had come back abnormal.

She stood in front of the nurse's desk, waiting for the unit clerk to get off the phone, when a harried woman came rushing toward her.

"You! This is all your fault!" the woman accused harshly. "My son is brain-dead, and it's all your fault!"

Katy froze, staring at the woman in horror. What on earth was she talking about? She'd never seen this woman before in her life.

"I'm sorry to hear about your son, but I think you must have me confused with someone else," Katy said gently.

The woman's face twisted into a mask of pure hatred. "I know exactly who you are," she spat. "You're the doctor who killed my Danny. Danny Truitt was your patient, and you sent him home too soon. Now he's dead! They're taking him off life support!"

The blood drained from her face as she remembered taking care of Danny Truitt, the young man who'd been extremely intoxicated and stabbed with a knife. She'd gotten sidetracked when the gunshot victims had been brought in, but she knew she'd given orders to discharge Danny only when he'd been awake and his vitals had been stable.

Was it possible she was responsible for discharging him too early? Just like she'd discharged Steffie too soon, when she'd been back in Baltimore?

Was she really responsible for the death of another patient?

14

No. This couldn't be happening. Not again. Please, Lord, not again!

Katy reached out for the wall as the room spun around her. In the deepest portion of her mind, she noticed one of the nurses had ushered Danny's mother away.

Is it true? Dear Lord, are her accusations true? Did I fail another one of my patients?

"Katy, sit down." Reese came over and put his arm around her shoulders, but she shrank away from his touch.

The fact that Reese had heard everything only made matters worse. He'd run in the other direction if he knew the truth. And she wouldn't blame him.

"I—can't. Leave me alone. I need to go." Somehow she managed to slide away from him. She grabbed the handle of her oxygen tank and forced her legs to carry her toward the door.

She stumbled down the hallway to the elevator. Leaning heavily against the wall, she waited for the doors to open. She rode back down to the nursing unit where her room was located but headed into the nurse's station and sank down at the closest computer station.

With trembling fingers, she entered her password and opened Danny Truitt's electronic medical record. Tears burned in her eyes, blurring the words on the screen. She swiped them away with the back of her hand and tried to focus on reading the most recent progress notes.

Her heart sank when she realized that at least part of the woman's accusations were true. Danny had been readmitted twelve hours after Katy had discharged him from the ER right at the end of her shift. She reviewed the discharge information. The nurses had documented well. She remembered Danny had been awake and belligerent, demanding to go home. He'd also been demanding pain medication. Not entirely unreasonable, since he had been stabbed. She remembered, now, telling the nurses to go ahead and discharge him.

He'd seemed well enough to leave, and since he was an adult, they couldn't keep him against his will. They'd given enough fluids to help bring down his alcohol level. So what had happened over the next twelve hours? Why had he been brought back to the hospital?

A sick sense of dread enveloped her as she read through Danny's subsequent ER note. He'd been found down and completely unresponsive by his roommates. They'd started CPR and gotten him to the hospital but too late.

He'd suffered severe brain damage.

She slumped forward, burying her face in her hands. Danny's case was different from Steffie's, but the end result was the same.

Only this time, she didn't have a high patient load and understaffing to blame for the mistake.

The blame was hers alone.

. . .

REESE DIDN'T UNDERSTAND what was going on in Katy's mind, but it was obvious the woman's wild accusations had caused Katy to withdraw into herself. He'd followed her back down to the nursing unit and watched her from the hallway as she peered at one of the computer screens.

Surely she didn't believe the kid's medical issues were her fault? From what the nurse in the ICU had said, it sounded more like the kid had overdosed on his pain meds. That couldn't be Katy's fault.

He watched her collapse in front of the computer and decided this had gone on long enough. Ignoring the openly curious expressions on the staff members' faces, he strode behind the desk and went over to Katy.

"Come on, Katy. Let's go. You can't stay here like this."

She didn't acknowledge him verbally or meet his gaze but must have heard him since she rose to her feet. He wanted to put his arm around her but didn't dare, not after the way she'd recoiled from him in the ICU. Careful not to get too close, he stayed behind her as she made her way down the hall toward her room. He wracked his brain for a way to break through the wall she'd built between them.

She walked into her room and sat down on the edge of her bed, staring down at her feet, despair etched on her features.

"Katy, please don't do this to yourself," he urged, sitting in the chair across from her. "That boy's mother is lashing out in her grief. It's not your fault he overdosed on his pain medications."

She swallowed hard and raised her tortured gaze to his. "He came in highly intoxicated. Maybe I shouldn't have given him any pain meds."

"Would you have given any other stab wound patient pain meds?" he pressed. "How many stitches did you put in, anyway?"

"Fourteen," she whispered. "And don't you understand? I have to take each patient's individual history into account before making a medical decision. Knowing that he tended to abuse alcohol means it's not a stretch that he might do the same with pain meds."

He couldn't pretend to understand what the right medical decision would have been, but he still didn't see how she could feel responsible for the kid's overdose.

"Katy, you're a good doctor. You've saved countless patients' lives, including Boyle's. Remember how you saved Jacob from drowning? You were the one who encouraged me to believe in God's plan, remember?"

She nodded but didn't say anything.

"I turned my back on God until you showed me the way back to my faith. While we were stuck on the trail in the woods, I realized that if Suzanne hadn't left me and cleaned out our bank account, I wouldn't have Duke. I wouldn't be a DNR game warden, a job I love. And I wouldn't have met you. I understand that, right now, it's hard to understand why Danny ended up back here, but I have to believe that there's a reason."

Katy's eyes filled with tears. "What if the reason is to tell me I'm not fit to be a doctor? That maybe I should do something else with my life?"

He reached over and took both of her hands in his. "You don't really believe that. Not after all the lives you've saved. You told me that you helped take care of Devon Armbruster last year when he was injured. Don't you think that Danny's situation is more likely a message to other kids his age?"

She drew in a choppy breath. "The reason I left Baltimore General to come here was because of another patient death. Her name was Steffie Moore, and she was only eighteen years old. She came in with belly pain but got better with fluids, so I discharged her. But she actually had a burst appendix. She died because of me. And now Danny is dead, too. All because of me."

He wasn't sure what to say to that, other than he didn't believe either of the patients' outcomes were her fault. "Did the hospital blame you for Steffie's death?"

"No."

"Was there a lawsuit filed against you?"

"Not yet. But there's still time. I dread opening my mail every day, thinking that I'll find the summons and complaint."

"Katy, even good doctors get sued sometimes. I wish I could help you believe this isn't your fault."

"It's not her fault," Gabe said from the doorway. He strode into Katy's room, scowling at her. "Listen to me. Danny's roommates confessed that they saw Danny taking pills and drinking alcohol. They admitted he passed out on the sofa and they thought he'd sleep it off. It wasn't until one of the kids went over to wake him up that they realized he wasn't breathing. Danny's mother is just looking for someone to blame."

"Really?" Katy looked up at Gabe with hope shimmering in her eyes. "You don't think it's my fault for discharging him with pain meds?"

Gabe snorted. "Yeah, like you wouldn't be in worse trouble if you'd refused to give pain meds to a patient with a stab wound. It's not your fault the kid had a huge drinking problem. And I'm sure his mother knows that."

"Maybe, but I still have Steffie's death on my conscience," Katy murmured.

"Don't you think I feel guilty over stabbing Jesse with that syringe?" Reese spoke up. "Especially when he's up there fighting for his life? We're only human. We all make mistakes. God forgives us our sins. Why can't you?"

"Reese is right," Gabe added.

Katy nodded slowly. "I know you're both right. It's just easier said than done."

"Having faith, believing in God's will, handling the ups and downs of life—all of that is easier said than done," Reese reminded her.

A glimmer of a smile toyed with her mouth. "I'll try," she said softly.

"Good. The reason I came up here is to let you know that I've covered your shift, so you have the day off," Gabe announced.

"Thank you. I'll make it up to you sometime soon," Katy said.

"The doctor came by while you were upstairs," Reese added. "He's planning to discharge us both, although he said he needed to examine you first. He should be back any minute."

"That's good, even if we can't go home yet," Katy said.

"You can go home. Sheriff Torretti made the announcement earlier today. After working all night, they managed to put the fire out, and it looks as if there were only a few houses damaged as a result. Everyone else has been permitted to return to their homes."

"I'm so glad to hear that," Katy admitted.

Reese nodded in agreement, although, deep down, he hated knowing that his time with Katy was coming to an end.

He wanted to see her again, but there was still his debt to consider. Even with adding dog training as a way to earn extra income, he still had several months before he'd have the debt paid off.

So maybe this was for the best. As much as he cared about Katy, he didn't have anything to offer her. Not until he was free of debt. No, it was better for her to get on with her life, especially now that the danger was over.

He and Duke would head home. Too bad the log cabin that had once been his sanctuary now only seemed lonely without someone to share it with.

Someone like Katy.

THE DAYS PASSED without Katy seeing any sign of Reese, although he occupied her thoughts constantly. Almost daily, she battled the urge to drive out to the log cabin he shared with Duke to see how they were doing.

She couldn't keep lying to herself. She loved him. Even though they were opposites on many levels, she still loved him.

But she knew he didn't feel the same way. Or maybe it was more accurate to say he wouldn't let himself feel the same way. And while she understood, she also felt sad that he wouldn't at least talk to her about it.

She had to honor his decision, even if she didn't agree.

Spending her free time in church, talking privately to Pastor John, had helped her overcome some of her guilt related to Danny's and Steffie's deaths. Just like back in Baltimore, the quality committee at Hope County Hospital hadn't found her decision making to be at fault.

But she still mourned the fact that two young people had died far too young.

And she often agonized over any discharge that was even a slight bit questionable.

On Wednesday morning, exactly one week after she and Reese had been discharged from the hospital, Katy sat on her porch, staring out over the lake. Only half the woods behind the lake were intact. The rest of the trees had blackened limbs in the aftermath of the fire.

Crystal Lake's income from tourism had taken a hit, although people were still coming to the lake. Despite the annoying crowds and extra workload at the hospital, Katy joined in with the rest of the parishioners, praying for their tourism to return to previous levels.

They prayed for Ian and Jesse Kramer too. Jesse had woken up and was getting psychiatric treatment, but he'd already tried to escape twice, desperate for the freedom of the woods.

"Hi, Katy."

She glanced over to see Reese walking across her lawn toward her with Duke at his side. Her heart filled with a mixture of elation and relief.

He'd finally come to see her!

"Hi, Reese. Hi, Duke."

Reese gave the dog a hand gesture, and Duke came running over to her, his entire body shaking with glee. She bent over to give him a good rub, dodging the licks he aimed at her face.

"Down, Duke," Reese said mildly. "She doesn't want your dog slobber all over her."

"I missed you," she murmured. She glanced up at Reese. "I missed both of you."

"We missed you, too." Reese seemed a little off-balance as he stood there watching her. "I—um, stopped by the hospital, but you weren't working today."

"No, today's my day off." Her previous elation began to waver. "Why? Is something wrong?"

"No, it's just, I think it's been ten days, and I need to get these sutures out. The angle is too awkward to do it myself, and they're itching like crazy."

"Sutures," she repeated, her cheeks flushing with embarrassment. So he hadn't actually come to see her on a personal level. He just needed his stitches removed.

Disappointment stabbed deeply, but she bent her head, hoping he wouldn't notice. "Well, come inside then. Lucky for you, I have a first aid kit here that should do the trick."

"Stay, Duke," Reese said as she opened the back door.

"It's okay, he can come inside," Katy hastened to reassure him. "Has the vet checked him out?"

"Yes, apparently Dr. Allen's treatment was exactly what he needed. What about you?" Reese followed her into the kitchen. "Are you all right?"

"I still have bouts of shortness of breath with exertion, but otherwise I'm fine." Katy pulled out her first aid kit and then gestured toward the table. "Have a seat."

Reese sat down in the kitchen chair and pulled the short sleeve of his T-shirt out of the way so she could see his wounds. The scent of Reese's aftershave teased her senses, and she had to force herself to stay focused on his incisions.

"These suture lines look pretty good, considering everything you went through," she said.

"Thanks to you," he said in a low voice.

She didn't know what to say to that, so she pulled the small scissors and tweezers from the kit and began to snip and pull the sutures free.

"There, all finished," she said, striving for a light tone. "I'm just going to put some antibiotic ointment on it for now, but you should be fine from here. If the wound opens at all, you'll need to come back to the ER for care."

"Thanks, Katy." He rose to his feet, and she took a step back, needing some distance.

"No problem." She hoped he didn't notice the husky note in her tone. She turned toward the table, intending to clean up, but he captured her hand in his, holding her in place. She glanced up in surprise.

"The sutures were just an excuse to come and see you," Reese said. "I've missed you so much. I know that I don't have anything to offer you, but I can't seem to stay away."

"Oh, Reese, you have a lot to offer. You have your heart."

His gaze softened, and he subtly pulled her closer. "You've mended my broken heart, so I guess it's only fair I give it to you. I love you, Katy. More than I thought possible."

Sheer joy flowed through her veins. "I love you, too, Reese. And you've mended both my heart and my soul."

"I don't deserve you," he muttered, but then he captured her mouth in a deep kiss.

She clung to his shoulders, enjoying every moment of his embrace. Finally, he lifted his head, allowing them both to capture their breath.

"Don't you think we deserve each other?" she teased.

"Maybe. But first there's something you need to know."

The seriousness of his tone made warning bells clang in the back of her mind. "Okay," she agreed. "What do I need to know?"

Reese took a deep breath, which only made her more nervous. "I won't ask you to marry me until I'm free of debt."

She was relieved it wasn't something worse, but still, how long would it take him to do that? "Reese, I don't care about money," she began.

"Don't," he interrupted. "The debt is mine, and I refuse to ask you to share it. This isn't negotiable, Katy. I couldn't stay away from you because I love you. I know I don't have a right to ask you to wait for me, but in the end, I decided that was your decision to make, not mine."

Her heart ached for him, but she understood where he was coming from. She didn't like it, thought it was ridiculous, but she couldn't help admiring him.

"I'm determined to start fresh with you," he said when she didn't answer. "So it's up to you where we go from here."

She smiled and stood up on her tiptoes to kiss him again. "I love you, Reese Webster," she whispered. "You are definitely a man worth waiting for."

"Thank God," he murmured.

Woof! Woof!

Katy giggled and glanced down at Duke, who was sitting patiently near Reese's feet, staring up at them as if asking what was taking so long already.

"You, too, Duke," she said, reaching down to stroke his silky fur. "You and Reese are a package deal."

Duke thumped his tail against the floor, obviously in full agreement.

R eese patted the ring reassuringly in his pocket as he strode up to Katy's front door. The last year had been good to him. His boss had given him a raise, and he'd trained two German shepherds for a nice profit. He'd doubled up his payments and had paid off the last of his outstanding bills three months ago.

He'd saved every dime since then for Katy's engagement ring. It was modest, but if she wanted something bigger, he'd oblige. The downside was that he'd be forced to push off any chance of a wedding for another couple months.

Her decision, not his. He'd do whatever she wanted, even if it killed him.

Which it just might.

He knocked at her door and nearly swallowed his tongue when he saw her standing there in an emerald-green figure-hugging dress.

"You look beautiful," he said in a husky tone.

"You look pretty good, yourself," she countered, noticing he'd dressed in the only nice clothes he owned, a pair of black dress slacks and a gray button-down shirt. "I know you said you made reservations, but I decided to cook for us instead."

"Katy, I wanted tonight to be special for you," he protested. As much as he loved her deep red hair, she could be awfully stubborn when she got an idea in her head.

"Trust me, having you over, cooking dinner for you, is special." Her smile faltered a bit. "Are you angry?"

He drew her in for a deep kiss. "Of course I'm not angry," he said when they could breathe. "Thank you for doing this."

She took his hand and led him into the living room, where she had candles lit and fresh flowers on the table. "I hope you don't mind, but I wanted to celebrate."

He thought of the ring he had burning a hole in his pocket. "It is a special day, isn't it? One year ago today, we acknowledged our love for each other."

Her eyes lit up. "You remembered!"

"Of course I remembered." Since the timing seemed right, he dropped to one knee, pulled out the ring and opened the case. "Katy Reichert, will you marry me?"

"Yes! Oh, yes! Of course I'll marry you!" She tugged him up off the floor and threw herself into his arms. It took him a minute to realize she hadn't even looked at the ring. "I love you so much," she murmured.

"I love you, too." He kissed her again and then pulled back so that he could slide the diamond ring on her finger. "If you don't like it, you can pick out something else."

"I love it," she assured him. "But I love you more."

"Good, I hope you don't mind a short engagement. Because I'm pretty much sick of waiting to make you my wife."

She laughed. "I love short engagements. And I'm sure Pastor John will fit us into his schedule as soon as possible."

"I love you, Katy," Reese repeated. "You've made me whole."

"We healed each other," she pointed out. "Now sit down or dinner will be ruined."

He did as she requested but knew that no matter what she served, dinner would be perfect.

Because they were together, at last.

CHRISTMAS REUNION

1

H ope County Sheriff's Deputy Ian Kramer gripped the steering wheel tightly as he maneuvered the treacherous highway through the swirling snow. The citizens of Crystal Lake, Wisconsin were likely thrilled to have a white Christmas, but he was the one stuck working night shift over the holiday and patrolling the county in the middle of a blizzard was not his idea of fun.

Not that he was complaining. After everything that had happened with his brother a few months ago, he was lucky to have his job at all. He was very grateful that after a lengthy month-long investigation, Sheriff Luke Torretti had allowed him to return to duty. The graveyard shift wasn't his favorite, but he was willing to take whatever his boss gave him.

No way was he going to ruin the second chance he'd been given.

The wind kicked up, blowing snow horizontally across the country highway, buffeting his SUV. He was moving at a crawl and, thankfully, didn't see any traffic on the road. He hoped the townsfolk were smart enough to stay home rather than risking their lives driving through this.

No such luck. He carefully navigated a hairpin turn in the road, and caught a glimpse of dim flashers blinking on and off. As he approached he could see that a car was nose down, stuck in the ditch. The vehicle was covered in snow, so much that in another hour, even the flashers would be difficult to see.

If the battery held out for that long.

Ian slowed to a stop and peered through the windshield, trying to read the license plate so he could run the tag through the system. Unfortunately, the information was obliterated with snow. He contacted the dispatcher to let her know that he was responding to a stranded vehicle off Highway ZZ.

Warily, he slid out from the driver's seat, ducking his head and tugging his hat further on his head against the ferocious wind. He approached the driver's side door, but the foggy window made it impossible to see who was inside.

He sharply rapped on the window. "I'm Deputy Kramer," he shouted. "Is everyone all right in there?"

There was a long pause, and he doubted his voice carried above the howling wind. He tapped on the window again and to his surprise, it lowered, revealing the pale face of a woman.

"Kramer? Ian Kramer?" she echoed in surprise.

He bent over to get a better look, and his eyebrows shot up in surprise when he recognized the woman's heart-shaped face framed with long dark hair.

"Sarah Miller," he said in a shocked tone.

Her slight smile faded. "My last name is Franklin now. And that's my five-year-old son, Ben, in the backseat."

Sarah was married. And had a son. The news shouldn't

have surprised him. After all, they'd only spent one summer together and that had been ten years ago. But the three months they'd shared together were forever etched in his memory. He'd fallen for Sarah hard, and ridiculously thought she felt the same way. Yet when summer had ended Sarah hadn't returned his phone calls. After a few weeks, he'd given up since he was attending college in Madison.

He'd never heard from her again.

Disturbing to realize that he'd never forgotten her.

"Hi, Ben," he said to the youngster curled up in a sleeping bag in the backseat. Where on earth was Sarah's husband? She shouldn't have been driving in this storm all by herself.

"I tried to call for a tow truck, but couldn't get through." Sarah shrugged. "I left a message with Billy's Auto Repair."

"Hank owns the garage, but unfortunately he's out of town," Ian said. "He's visiting his daughter in Madison and won't be back until after Christmas."

The spark of hope in her eyes dimmed. "I don't suppose you can somehow pull me out of the ditch?" she hesitantly asked.

He could, but there was no telling what damage had been done to her car, and he doubted that it was drivable. Besides, he'd rather get Sarah and her son somewhere safely out of the storm. "I'll give you a ride, and we'll work on getting your car unstuck later. Do you have a reservation at the hotel?"

"No. I'm heading to my grandparent's cabin. I appreciate you giving us a ride. Would you mind getting our suitcases out of the trunk?"

Suitcases? Ian thought it was odd that she'd come up to her grandparent's place two days before Christmas, but then again, for all he knew, her husband might be meeting her there so they could spend a rustic holiday together.

The idea left a sour taste in his mouth.

"No, I don't mind." He tried not to remember the last time he'd been to her grandparent's cabin, the night he kissed her beneath the stars. Ancient history, he reminded himself as Sarah popped the trunk.

There were three suitcases and several boxes crammed in the trunk without any room to spare. He couldn't help wondering just how long Sarah and her son were planning to stay. There was way more stuff here than what they'd need if they were just visiting over the holiday break from school.

Not that Sarah's plans were any of his business. He fought against the wind and swirling snow, grabbing the suitcases and hauling them over to store them in the back of his SUV.

Sarah joined him, looking cute in her pink parka with matching hat and gloves. "Ian, would you be willing to take the boxes too, if there's enough room?"

"Sure." He saw her son standing beside her, the hood of his coat up over his head and a scarf covering a good portion of his face. "Why don't you and Ben get inside where it's warm? I'll take care of moving everything over."

She nodded, looking relieved. "Thank you."

He trudged through the snow, until he had everything from Sarah's car—including the sleeping bag and booster seat from the backseat. Sarah wrestled with securing the booster seat while Ian kicked the snow from his boots and slid behind the wheel.

"Ready?" he asked as he started the engine and blasted the heat on high.

"Yes," Sarah's voice was strong as she glanced back at Ben, as if to reassure her son. "We're ready, right Ben?"

The boy paused, then nodded. "Right, Mom."

Ian nodded and slowly pulled back out onto the highway. He noticed that Ben hadn't said much, and his instincts warned him that something wasn't quite right with this situation.

He was surprised at how much he wanted to help and protect Sarah from whatever was causing the shadows in her eyes. But unless she was involved in something illegal, which he highly doubted, he needed to remember her problems weren't his concern.

He had his brother to worry about, and that was a huge challenge. Jesse was finally getting the psychiatric help he needed, but Ian was still worried about his brother's emotional stability. The last thing Ian needed was to put his job at risk, especially not for a married woman. He'd get Sarah and her son safely to her grandparent's cabin.

From there, she could call her husband for help if needed.

Sarah momentarily closed her eyes and silently prayed, seeking strength. She'd never in her wildest dreams imagined that Ian Kramer was still living in Crystal Lake. Or that he was a deputy with the sheriff's department.

She'd been seventeen to Ian's eighteen during that summer they'd spent together. They'd been inseparable; swimming and boating in the lake, taking long walks on the hiking trail, and sitting by the campfire roasting marshmallows at night.

Ian had kissed her several times, nothing too heavy until

the night before she had to leave to return home. They'd kissed beneath the stars, passion simmering between them. She was ashamed to admit that Ian had been the one to break things off before their young love spiraled out of control.

"Sarah? Are you all right?" Ian asked, breaking the silence.

She opened her eyes and took a deep breath, forcing a smile. "I'm fine, thanks so much for coming to our rescue."

"I'm surprised you decided to drive up here, despite the storm warnings that have been on the news for the past twenty-four hours," Ian admitted.

She hoped the darkness hid the desperation she knew was reflected in her eyes. The minute she heard David, her ex-husband, was going to be released from jail, she'd loaded up her car and driven north. She hadn't heard the weather reports until she was on the highway, but even then she wouldn't have let the snow stop her.

"I was already on the road when I heard the news," she said, trying to keep her voice steady.

"I didn't realize your grandparents had kept the cabin," Ian said, shooting her a side long glance. "I thought maybe your family had sold it."

Sarah knew what he was really asking, since she hadn't returned his many phone calls ten years ago. And at the very least, she owed him an explanation.

"A week after returning home after our summer together, my mother was diagnosed with stage four uterine cancer. My father," she hesitated, unwilling to speak ill of the dead. "He didn't handle it well. Instead of being supportive he worked longer and longer hours, using every excuse possible to avoid coming home. Six months after my mother passed away, he died of a massive heart attack."

"Oh, Sarah, I'm sorry for your loss," Ian said, reaching

out to take her hand. The simple comforting gesture made tears spring to her eyes and she struggled to blink them back before Ian noticed. "I can't imagine what you went through. Losing both your parents so close together must have been terrible. You should have called me, I would have been there for you."

Looking back, it was easy to see how different her life might have been if she'd garnered the courage to make that call. But then again, she wouldn't have Ben, and she could never regret having her son. Ben meant everything to her.

"I was pretty focused on staying in high school so I could graduate, and being there for my mother," she said softly. "And then so much time had passed, it didn't seem right to call you."

"I would have come, no matter when you called," he said, giving her hand a gentle squeeze before releasing her. She missed his warmth and twisted her fingers together to prevent herself from reaching for him.

Sarah knew she couldn't afford to let her foolish teenage emotions get the better of her. Ian had been the center of her world that summer, but the reality of her mother's cancer and her father's avoidance had caused her to push the memories aside. She'd convinced herself that he'd moved on without her.

And she'd moved on as well. Realizing too late that she'd made the wrong choice in marrying David.

But there was nothing to be gained by rehashing the past.

"Well, anyway, that's enough about my life. What about you?" she asked, eager to change the subject. "I'm so impressed that you're a sheriff's deputy."

He lifted a brow and sent her a sideways glance. "I'm

pretty sure I told you that I wanted to be a cop when I grew up," he reminded her.

And she'd wanted to be a nurse. Regret burned in the back of her throat. She'd only managed to complete a nursing assistant program before her mother passed away.

"Yes, you did," she said softly. "I didn't start my nursing degree. I completed my nurse's aide training, but that's all." Which reminded her she'd need to get a job within the next few weeks, before she depleted her meager savings. But that would have to wait until after the holidays.

"We have a hospital here," he said, as if reading her mind. "Eighteen months ago, I spent more time there than I wanted to."

"What happened?"

He lifted a shoulder. "Gunshot wound, but I survived. The staff there took good care of me."

Sarah swallowed hard, more upset than she had a right to be about his close call. Why was she dredging up her old feelings for Ian? After ten years, they were two completely different people, nothing at all like the carefree teenagers they'd been.

"Are you married?" she asked, striving for a casual tone.

"Nope. Got close once, but things didn't work out."

Her own five year marriage proved that was the understatement of the year. Her divorce had been finalized over two years ago, but that hadn't stopped David from coming after her. And now that he'd been released from jail, her brief respite was over.

"Lucky that you found out ahead of time," she said before she could stop herself. "Less complicated that way."

Ian frowned. "Sarah, what's wrong? Why isn't your husband with you?"

She glanced over her shoulder, relieved to see that Ben

had fallen asleep. "We're divorced," she said simply. "I haven't changed my name because of Ben. It's less complicated to share the same last name."

"I guess I can understand that," Ian said with a nod. "How long have you been divorced?"

"Two years." She had no idea why she was telling him this. It wasn't as if she was interested in picking up where their summer romance left off. The last thing she wanted was to jump into another relationship. Once was more than enough. "Oh, is that the driveway to my grandparent's place?" she asked, changing the subject as the highway marker caught her attention.

"That's it, although it might be tricky getting into the driveway," he cautioned. "Having four-wheel drive isn't fail-safe."

She refused to let the news upset her. She was more than willing to walk up to the cabin if necessary.

Ian gunned the engine and barreled through the snow drifts without stopping until he reached the clearing in front of the cabin. The welcome sight of the familiar rustic dwelling gave her an overwhelming sense of relief.

"Ben, we're here," she said, reaching back to shake her son awake."

He opened his eyes but then groggily closed them again.

"Let him sleep," Ian suggested. "I'll carry him in for you."

"I can do it," she said quickly. "But would you be willing to light a fire for us?"

"Of course. Do you have the key?"

She smiled. "Don't you remember? It's in the flower pot on the porch."

Ian looked surprised, but nodded. "I do remember. Stay here, let me check things out first."

"All right." She sat back in her seat, knowing she shouldn't be leaning on Ian like this. Hadn't she learned the hard way that it was better to stand on her own two feet? She'd vowed never to be dependent on a man again.

With renewed determination, she pushed her door open and tried not to gasp as she was hit by a blistering wave of cold air. Winters in Crystal Lake were far different than summers, that's for sure. Although they had tough winters in Chicago too. She refused to be wimpy.

After trudging around to the back of the police vehicle, she fumbled with the latch. After two tries she finally found the release. She grabbed the smaller of the suitcases and then closed the tailgate so the snow wouldn't get inside before heading up toward the cabin.

The door was open, which was a relief since that meant Ian had found the key. The interior of the cabin smelled musty and was only slightly warmer than being out in the wind and snow. The only light was from Ian's flashlight which was propped beside him.

"I told you I'd carry everything in," Ian chided gently from his kneeling position in front of the wooden stove.

"I know, but I'm not helpless, and I appreciate that you're getting the fire started." She glanced around the cabin, surprised to note that it didn't look all that much different from the last time she'd been here. Of course her grandparents had come up here on occasion over the years, at least until they'd retired in Arizona, but she hadn't been back.

Until now.

She walked into the small kitchenette and opened the drawers until she found a few candles and matches. She placed the candles around the room, the dancing flames helping to chase away the darkness.

When she walked over to the wood burning stove, she

was pleased to see that Ian had gotten a small fire started from the wood that was stacked on the floor beside it. Maybe it was only her imagination, but it seemed like the interior of the cabin was already warming up from the fire.

Ian glanced up at her. "It will take me a while to get this going. Why don't you bring Ben inside? I'll get the rest of your stuff as soon as I'm finished."

She nodded. After all, Ben was her top priority. Before going back outside, she went into the smaller of the two bedrooms, grateful to see that the mattresses were still intact and hadn't been attacked by rodents.

They'd be fine using the sleeping bags for tonight, since she knew she'd have to sleep in the living room to keep the fire going anyway. Feeling certain they were safe here, she eagerly headed back outside to get her son.

After freeing him from the booster seat, she picked him up in her arms. Ben was large for his age, and she staggered a bit as she headed inside the cabin. Ian met her at the doorway and gently pried her son away, easily handling his weight.

"Hang on, I need to gab the sleeping bag." When she returned a few minutes later, her heart melted when she saw that Ian was holding Ben on his lap in front of the fire.

"We're at the cabin?" Ben asked, rubbing his eyes.

"Yes, we're here. You're going to use your sleeping bag tonight. Won't that be fun?"

Her son nodded and yawned. Ian stood and carried Ben into the bedroom, waiting for her to arrange the sleeping bag before lowering her son to the mattress.

She sat beside him, making sure he was tucked in.

"Mom? Dad's not going to find us, is he?" Ben asked.

Her heart clenched in her chest and tears pricked at her eyes as she leaned down to press a reassuring kiss on his forehead. "No, he's not going to find us. Go to sleep, okay?"

"Okay. Good night." Her son closed his eyes and curled up onto his side.

When she straightened, she found Ian's intense gaze boring into hers and knew with a sinking feeling that he wasn't going to leave until he knew the truth.

2
———

Ian tried not to let his anger show on his face even though he knew he should have trusted his instincts right from the start. Of course there was nothing innocent about why Sarah had decided to drive through a blizzard to come back to Crystal Lake after ten years. She and her son were hiding from her ex.

He followed Sarah back to the living room, putting a few more logs into the wood burning stove before closing and latching it shut. When he was calm, he turned to face her. "Okay, Sarah. What's going on?"

Sarah's cheeks were flushed, but she tilted her chin stubbornly. "Nothing is going on, Ian. I came here because I needed a break. The cabin belongs to my grandparents and they don't mind me being here. I didn't lie about being divorced and in case you were wondering, I was granted sole custody of Ben."

The thought had crossed his mind that she'd run off with her son, not that he would have blamed her. The thought of Ben being afraid of his own father made him seethe with fury.

He kept his tone as non-threatening as possible. "I'm glad to hear that, but I am a police officer. You can trust me."

For a moment she looked as if she might tell him, but then shook her head. "There's nothing to tell."

Who was she trying to fool? She'd never been good at lying, a fact that had gotten them in trouble more than once that summer when they'd occasionally stayed out past her curfew. "Fine, I'll figure out what happened on my own. What's your ex-husband's name?"

She hesitated before she responded. "David. But I'm sure he's more interested in getting his life back than worrying about us." The way Sarah avoided his gaze made him believe she was glossing over the details, big time.

He knew very well there was more to this story and it was frustrating that she wouldn't tell him the truth. But before he could ask anything more, his radio went off.

"Unit twelve, we have a report regarding a two vehicle crash on the interstate on-ramp from highway double Z. What's your twenty?"

Ian grimaced, knowing he was the closest deputy. He pushed the button on the side of his radio to respond. "I'm about five miles away. I'll get there as soon as possible."

"Ten-four."

He didn't want to leave Sarah and Ben in the cabin alone, but he wasn't going to shirk his duty either. Especially not when he was still on probation after the fiasco with Jesse. "I have to take this call, but write down my phone number. I want you to call me if you need anything."

"I'm sure we'll be fine," she protested, crossing her arms across her chest.

He suppressed a sigh and dug into his breast pocket for his small notebook. He ripped a page out and quickly scribbled his phone number across the paper before thrusting it into her hand. "Take it, and I'll stop by after my shift is over to check on you."

"There's no need; I don't want to be a bother."

"You're not a bother," he said, even though that wasn't entirely true. He was very bothered by the thought that she was on the run from her ex-husband. And he was bothered by her refusal to let him help. But since he didn't have time to stand there and argue with her, he turned and left the cabin, making sure the door was locked behind him. There were two keys on the ring in the planter so he kept one in his pocket so he could return early the next morning to chop more firewood.

The wind hadn't let up, forcing him to spend a good five minutes brushing the snow off his car before he turned around and headed back toward the road. Several times his tires spun crazily, and he was relieved when he made it back to the highway without getting stuck.

As he headed toward the interstate, it appeared that a snow plow had been through recently, since there was a strip down the middle of the road that wasn't snow covered. He glanced at the time, realizing that it was later than he'd thought, a little past one in the morning.

Six more hours to go until the end of his shift. At least fighting through the storm would help the time go by faster.

Because no matter what Sarah had said, he was determined to go back to check on them.

Maybe she was safe at her grandparent's cabin for now, since he doubted that her ex-husband would be able to find the place in the storm. But the snowy weather wouldn't last forever.

And Ian feared it wouldn't take much for David Franklin to find Sarah and Ben.

. . .

DESPITE THE LATE HOUR, Sarah wasn't the least bit sleepy. She only had a six pack of water and needed to save that for drinking so she searched for several large pots and pans in the kitchen and took them outside to fill them with snow. Then she set them on the table to melt so they'd have wash water in the morning. She blew out the candles, knowing she'd need to save them for the next few days until she could figure out if there was a way to get electrical service hooked up.

The musty smell inside the cabin made her sneeze, and she wished that she could open the windows to air the place out. Since that wasn't an option she snuggled down in her sleeping bag, grateful that she'd washed it a few weeks ago. The day she'd learned about David's parole hearing, in fact.

After all, her mother's illness had taught her to always be prepared for the worst.

She closed her eyes, trying to forget the memories that came rushing back. Memories of the carefree summer she'd spent with Ian. The sobering shock at finding out about her mother's cancer. Her father's subsequent heart attack.

David's slow and insidious betrayal.

After taking several deep breaths, she prayed, seeking peace. She'd sought refuge in church after David's arrest, pleased to discover that faith could fill the holes in her heart and soul in a way she'd never expected.

She only wished she'd found the strength of faith sooner. Before she'd met David. Before her parents had died within six months of each other.

Sarah gave herself a mental shake. Enough with the regrets already. She and Ben were fine. David wasn't supposed to be anywhere near her and he didn't know the location of the cabin. And if by some strange chance he did show up, she'd have him arrested.

Just the thought of David finding them made her shiver with fear, despite the cozy warmth radiating from the wood burning stove. She silently recited the prayers she knew by memory, finally relaxing enough to fall asleep.

A loud bang woke her up and she shot upright on the sofa, looking around in panic. Her gaze stumbled across Ian kneeling next to a pile of fallen logs.

"Sorry," Ian said, as he stacked the logs back up and then slowly rose to his feet. She realized he must have dropped the wood, which explained the loud noise.

She jammed a hand through her tangled hair. "I'm perfectly capable of bringing in the firewood," she muttered.

Ian lifted a brow, looking far more handsome in the early morning light than she remembered. Or maybe she hadn't looked at him closely enough last night. It took her a minute to realize he'd changed out of his uniform, wearing soft denim jeans and a flannel work shirt beneath his jacket.

"Yes, I'm sure you are, but since I'm here, why not let me take care of it? You probably didn't get much rest. And by the way, the storm is over. The snow stopped about an hour ago."

She was exhausted, but refused to let Ian Kramer bulldoze her. When he left the cabin again, she crawled out of the sleeping bag and pulled a heavy navy blue Chicago sweatshirt over her T-shirt. She slipped her feet into her running shoes and then walked over to the table. The pots she'd filled with snow were now more than half full of water, so she carried the largest one over to set it on top of the wood burning stove to get warm. Then she used water bottles to fill the tea kettle.

Digging through one of the boxes she'd packed before leaving home, she found several packets of instant oatmeal and two apples. Maybe not exactly a gourmet breakfast, but enough that they wouldn't go hungry.

Ian returned with another armload of wood. He took the time to stack the logs into neat piles.

"Was anyone hurt?" she asked, breaking the silence.

He glanced up in surprise, and then shook his head when he realized what she was asking. "No, thankfully the drivers of the cars were both driving slow enough that there were no injuries."

"I'm glad," she murmured, going through the kitchen drawers to find spoons. "We're having oatmeal for breakfast if you're hungry."

Her pulse jumped when his teeth flashed in a wide smile. "Sounds great."

She stared at him for a long minute, struck by just how different Ian was from David. How could she have believed herself to be in love with a man who used his tongue like a whip? Constantly cutting her down was one thing, but she couldn't bear it when David began to treat Ben the same way.

And then things had gone from bad to worse.

"Mom? I hav'ta go to the bathroom."

She turned to find Ben standing there, rubbing his eyes and looking adorably sleep-rumpled. Her heart swelled with love and relief when she realized her son seemed more like his normal self after a good night's sleep.

"Me too," she confided. "But we're going to have to use the outhouse, remember? The snow is deep so put on your coat and your boots, okay?"

"Not too deep. I shoveled a path when I first got here," Ian said.

She was grateful she didn't have to do the work, but at

the same time, she didn't like feeling helpless. "Thanks, but I could have done that too. I grew up in Chicago; I know how to deal with snow. And I know what it's like to rough it up here."

"Not in the winter," he pointed out.

She narrowed her gaze, tempted to tell him to get lost and leave her alone, but Ben was hopping from one foot to the other so she quickly helped her son get his coat and boots on before grabbing her own winter things.

"Wow, look at all this snow!" Ben exclaimed when they walked out onto the porch. A good twelve inches had fallen, fresh snow covering the bare tree branches in a way that was breathtakingly beautiful. The sun wasn't quite up yet, but the sky was clear, giving her hope that the blizzard was gone for good.

"Maybe we can build a snowman after breakfast," she suggested with a smile.

"Okay," Ben agreed eagerly.

She took his hand and led him down the path Ian had shoveled to the outhouse. The smell wasn't as bad as she remembered, probably because of the cold and fresh snowfall. She gave Ben the roll of toilet paper, letting him go inside first.

When she emerged a few minutes later, taking a minute to use the hand sanitizer from her coat pocket, she couldn't help but smile when she found Ian showing Ben how to pack a snowball. For a moment she savored the image, wishing for something she couldn't have.

Ian glanced up and captured her gaze and for a long second her throat was so tight she couldn't breathe. What was wrong with her? Her emotions were a chaotic mess. One minute she was grateful to Ian for his kind help and support, but then in the next she resented the way he was trying to take over her life.

She forced herself to take a deep breath. Logically, she knew Ian wasn't really trying to take over anything, but she was afraid to let go of the hard-won control that she'd managed to find after David's arrest.

A snowball hit her in the stomach, and her mouth dropped open in surprise when Ben began to giggle.

"I got you, Mom! I got you."

She laughed and brushed off the snow. "Yes, you did."

Ian scooped up some snow and lobbed it at her, and she let out a yelp as it found its mark. She began to make a snowball of her own, intending to get back at Ian, when Ben beat her to it.

"I got you too, mister!" her son crowed.

"That's Mr. Ian to you," Ian said as he scooped up more snow. But she was step ahead of him, her snowball hitting him high in his chest.

"Hey, it's not fair to gang up on me," Ian protested, although the wide grin on his face wasn't the least bit intimidating.

The snowballs flew back and forth, missing their intended targets about half the time. Sarah tried to dodge a snowball from Ian and ended up falling backward into a huge snow drift.

"Are you all right?" he asked, hurrying over. The concern in his expression made her want to cry.

"I'm fine," she insisted as he helped her up. Ian's hands were on her shoulders as he searched her expression. His green eyes were intense, sending a fission of sizzling awareness down her spine. For several seconds, it was all she could do not to throw herself into his arms.

She couldn't remember the last time she'd had fun with a man. Probably ten years, since the summer she'd spent here in Crystal Lake with Ian. Ironic that he'd given that gift back to her today.

Another snowball hit Ian in the back. He grinned and glanced over to where Ben was giggling as he scraped together more snow.

"That's enough, Ben," she called out.

When another snowball flew by, missing them by a wide berth, Ian shook his head. "Uncle! We're crying uncle."

"Uncle who?" Ben asked in confusion.

Ian chuckled. "That means me and your mom have had enough," he explained. "No more snowballs."

"Ever?" Ben asked, a forlorn expression on his face.

"For now," she clarified, pulling away from Ian's grasp to approach her son. Putting distance between her and Ian didn't help, since she could still feel the warm imprint of his hands through her winter jacket. "How about we get some breakfast?"

"Yes!" Ben exclaimed. "I'm starving."

Ian didn't say anything, so she glanced back to find him staring at her intently. "You're welcome to join us for oatmeal," she offered.

A hint of a smile crossed his features. "Sounds good. I think I have enough firewood chopped for now anyway."

Belatedly she realized there was an entire stack of new wood on the south end of the cabin porch, in addition to the logs he'd already brought inside. And no matter how much she wanted to be independent, she was grateful she hadn't been forced to chop all that wood by herself. "Well then, breakfast is the least we can do."

Inside the cabin she helped Ben take off his winter gear,

making sure to put the scarf, hat and mittens near the wood burning stove to dry. After taking off her own things, she checked the temperature of the water in the tea kettle on the stove.

The water wasn't boiling, but she decided steaming hot would have to do.

Using the hot water that was in the pan, she quickly washed the dishes they would need for breakfast. Ben came into the kitchen to sit at the table, waiting patiently for her to finish.

Ian followed more slowly, as if unsure of his welcome. "Almost ready," she promised. "I just need to cut up the apples."

"Okay," Ian said.

She filled three bowls with dried oatmeal and then poured the hot water from the tea kettle over the oats and then stirred them. Then she topped the bowls with green apple slices. Ian surprised her by coming over to help carry them to the table.

After taking a seat across from Ian, she glanced over at Ben. "We have to pray first, remember?"

Her son nodded and folded his small hands together. She bowed her head. "Dear Lord, thank You for providing this food for us to eat and for the shelter of this cabin. We ask for Your strength and guidance as we follow the path You have chosen for us. We ask this in the name of Christ the Lord, Amen."

"Amen," Ben dutifully echoed.

When she lifted her head, she caught Ian's curious gaze and her heart dropped when she realized he wasn't a believer.

Not that Ian's faith or lack thereof was any of her business. Yes, it made her sad that Ian probably didn't pray or attend church, but then again, she didn't know much about Ian's personal life or how much he may have changed.

Obviously, this was God's way of reminding her that there couldn't be more than friendship between them.

No matter how attractive Ian might be.

I an dug into his oatmeal, surprised to learn Sarah was the type of woman who would pray before eating. During their summer together, attending church hadn't been high on their list of things to do.

Normally he didn't like looking back at the past, wishing things could be different. Yet there was no denying that he'd always had feelings for Sarah. Ridiculous, since they'd been kids back then. Would they still be together if her mother hadn't been diagnosed with cancer shortly after the end of their infamous summer? He had no idea. And there was no reason to think about that now.

For the most part he was proud of the choices he'd made. Fighting crime and standing up for the innocent gave him a sense of purpose. He enjoyed working for the Hope County Sheriff's Department. His record had been spotless until four months ago when his brother, Jesse, had gone rogue, nearly killing two innocent people; a well-respected ER doctor and a DNR game warden. Not to mention, Duke, the game warden's dog.

All because his brother had snapped, believing the game

warden and the doctor were trying to prevent him from living off the land.

After Jesse was hospitalized, Ian had begged the physicians to evaluate his brother's mental health status. One of the female psychologists, Beth Walters, agreed with Ian's concerns and diagnosed Jesse with a severe case of Post Traumatic Stress Disorder from his last tour in Afghanistan. Between the two of them they convinced the authorities to send Jesse to a psychiatric hospital rather than to prison.

Sheriff Torretti declared Ian to be innocent of any wrongdoing and reinstated him as a deputy. Unfortunately, that wasn't entirely true. He hadn't wanted to believe that the brother he'd idolized from the time they were kids had gone off the deep end. If he'd been smart enough to figure out what Jesse was doing before things had gotten so out of hand, his brother wouldn't be sitting in psych hospital right now, a punishment that Jesse believed was worse than death.

Ian tried to remind himself that his brother was getting the help he needed. But was that good enough? Ian wasn't sure. Jesse barely spoke a full sentence during their monthly visits. And Ian figured that his brother blamed him for being locked up again, something Jesse had vowed would never happen.

It took him a minute to realize his bowl was empty and he looked up guiltily, realizing that both Sarah and Ben were staring at him with obvious concern.

"Sorry," he murmured, pushing his bowl away. "I'm used to eating fast between calls."

Sarah's smile hit him low in the gut. "That's okay, but I guess I needn't have worried you wouldn't like instant oatmeal."

He lifted a brow. "What's not to like? And the apple slices were a great touch."

"I'm glad," Sarah said simply. She took another spoonful of oatmeal, as if savoring the taste. It struck him that maybe she'd given him food that she didn't have to spare.

Ian gave himself a mental head slap. Of course her funds would be limited, especially if she was on the run from that jerk of an ex-husband. He'd have to make it up to her by bringing more groceries over later.

Although, first, he'd have to make sure she had the basics, like electricity. He began to make a mental list of things she'd need.

The storm had kept him busy for the rest of his shift, so he hadn't taken the time to run a background check on David Franklin. Of course it would help to have a middle initial or a date of birth to narrow the search.

"I'm all done, Mom," Ben announced.

"Okay, carry your dirty dishes over to the counter," Sarah told him. "I'll wash them, later."

Ian took his dishes over as well, doing a quick inventory on the non-perishable food that Sarah had already unpacked from one of the large boxes he'd brought inside. He was glad to see she'd come prepared with canned beef stew, soup, macaroni and cheese along with the old standby —peanut butter and jelly.

It occurred to him that she may have had some time to plan her escape, since it didn't seem that she'd simply emptied out her fridge. Every food item in the box was something that wouldn't spoil yet appealed to a child.

Feeling grim, he decided he absolutely had to follow up on her ex, and soon. He needed to know just what they were up against. Granted, tomorrow was Christmas Eve, but Ian doubted that any man capable of putting fear in a child's eyes would let a holiday prevent him from getting what he wanted.

Sarah joined him in the kitchen, giving him a concerned look as she took the bowl from his hands. "Ian, you've been up for hours and look dead on your feet. Maybe you should get some rest?"

He was tired since he'd been up for nearly twenty-four hours straight. After a normal night shift, he would go home and fall asleep almost instantly. But this morning after chopping wood he'd gotten his second wind. A burst of energy that was fading fast.

"Soon," he agreed with a crooked smile. "But first I'm going to pick up a generator for you. I don't like the thought of you and Ben being here without power."

A frown puckered in her brow. "I doubt you'll be able to find one until after the holiday, so don't worry about that now. We're fine. I'd rather you get some sleep."

Sarah's concern was touching, he couldn't remember the last time anyone cared whether he was hungry or tired. It was a nice feeling, not that he was looking for a relationship.

"I happen to have a generator at home, and I don't live that far. I'll be back in less than an hour."

Sarah's lips firmed. "You can't keep doing this, Ian. I don't want you to feel like you have to take care of us. I appreciate your concern, but trust me when I say that I'd prefer to do this on my own."

He tried to suppress a flash of anger. "I don't understand what's going through that pretty head of yours, Sarah. Every single thing I've done for you is what I'd do for any other neighbor. This isn't the big city where you don't know the people living next door by name. Here in Crystal Lake, we take care of each other. We're pretty much one big family."

Her eyes widened in surprise and she looked as if she

wanted to say something more, but he didn't give her a chance.

"I have to go." He swept past her and grabbed his coat off the back of the rocking chair. "See you later, Ben," he called, before he walked outside and closed the door behind him.

He didn't remember Sarah having that stubborn, independent streak ten years ago, but then again, they hadn't had any responsibilities either.

Maybe he understood her desire to be independent, but refusing a generator that he wasn't using was downright foolish. Did she have any idea how early darkness fell around here? The sun set by four o'clock in the afternoon, and that was on a sunny day. Refusing light was just ridiculous. He climbed into his car and headed for the highway.

Sarah would take his generator whether she liked it or not. And after he'd hooked it up for her, he'd leave her alone if that's what she really wanted.

Making sure to ignoring the small part of his heart that longed to spend more time with her and her son.

AFTER IAN LEFT, Sarah blew out a heavy sigh and leaned forward, bracing her palms on the kitchen counter.

Okay, she'd handled that badly.

The good news was that not once had she been afraid. She'd known that Ian was getting angry, but she didn't cower away from him the way she once might have. She'd stood up for herself.

So why did she feel so lousy?

She gathered the dirty dishes and put them in one of the large pans filled with water. She quickly washed and rinsed them, trying not to think about how much easier it would be to have the generator Ian had spoken about. Being able to use the electric stove would be amazing.

"Can I go outside to play?" Ben asked.

"Give me a few minutes," she said. "I'm almost finished."

"Why do you hav'ta go with me?"

Her son's innocent question caught her off guard. Not letting him play outside alone in Chicago was a no-brainer considering the crime rate. But they were safe here in Crystal Lake.

Weren't they?

Maybe, maybe not. "Because it's going to take two of us to build that snowman," she said lightly. "There, see? I'm all finished."

Her clothes were still damp, but thankfully Ben's hat and mittens were nice and dry. She bundled him up first and then quickly donned her things. Outside, the wind was cold, but not unbearably so.

"First we have to start with the bottom," she said. "We have to make a nice big snowball."

"Okay." Ben was full of enthusiasm as they made a small ball and then rolled it around in the snow, making it bigger and bigger.

"I think that's good," she said breathlessly, patting the large semi-round base. "Now we have to make another, smaller snowball."

The sound of a car engine caught her attention, and for a moment she froze in fear, thinking the worst. But then she saw the dark brown sheriff's deputy vehicle rolling down the driveway and breathed a sigh of relief.

David hadn't found them.

"Hey, you started without me," Ian complained with a smile as he slid out from behind the wheel.

Her jeans were soaked from the thigh down, making her shiver with cold. "You want to help? Be my guest."

He frowned when he saw how wet she was. "You need a pair of snow pants," he said in a serious tone.

"Pink snow pants," she corrected. "To match my pink jacket." She loved the hot pink color as much as David had once hated it. "Come on, the sooner we get this snowman finished the sooner we can go inside."

With Ian's help it didn't take long to build the rest of the snowman. She sent Ben off to find leaves, sticks and stones to complete the snowman's face and arms.

"Come on, I need some help," Ian said, gesturing for her to follow him behind the cabin. "We need to find a good spot for the generator."

"Okay, but I hope you know what you're doing," she said, walking along beside him. "Because I don't have a clue."

"We need a dry spot roughly fifteen feet from the cabin," he said, looking around the area.

"Wasn't there a concrete slab back here at one point?" she asked, trying to remember. "Like over there, near the electrical box?"

Ian walked over and used his boot to push the snow out of the way. "Good memory. I bet your grandparents had a generator here at one time, which is good news since that will make it easier for me to get this hooked up."

Sarah figured Ian was exaggerating, but working together with Ben helping in small ways too, they soon had the generator set up on the concrete slab with a covered tarp hanging in the trees overhead to protect it from snow.

"Well, let's see if this works," Ian said, rising to his feet.

They trooped inside the house and Sarah held her breath as Ian flipped on the light switch near the door. The light over the kitchen table came on and Ben let out a whoop.

"It works! We did it," her son exclaimed.

"Yes, we helped Mr. Ian, didn't we?" she said, gently correcting Ben. "Now it's time to get out of those wet clothes, young man."

"I'll check to make sure all the lights are working before I head home," Ian said as he shrugged out of his coat. He scrubbed his hands over his face as he walked into the first bedroom.

She listened as Ian tested the switches, noting with satisfaction that every light now worked. Ben pulled off his wet clothes, and she took her time to spread them around the wood stove to dry. There wasn't a washer and dryer in the cabin, so having electricity didn't help there.

"Go find some dry clothes to wear," she told Ben when he was down to his skivvies.

Her son ran off to the bedroom he'd deemed as his own, returning a few minutes later, still in his underwear.

"What's wrong? Couldn't you find your clothes?" she asked with a frown.

"Mr. Ian is sleeping in my bed," Ben said in a loud whisper. "Should I try to wake him up?"

"No, let him sleep. Stay here; I'll get your dry clothes." Sarah tiptoed into the bedroom, nearly tripping over the suitcase Ben had left lying in the middle of the room. She quickly gathered Ben's clothes, but her gaze kept straying back to where Ian was sleeping.

He looked younger, more like the eighteen-year-old she remembered from that summer she'd fallen for him. His mink colored hair was messed up and the dark shadow of his beard covered his cheeks. He was bigger and broader across the chest than she remembered and she was surprised by the urge to reach out and touch him.

She backed out of the room and closed the door behind her.

Enough. She needed to remember that Ian Kramer was off-limits. For one thing, he didn't have faith. But that wasn't the real reason she needed to avoid him.

She'd given her heart to a man once before and David had trampled all over it.

She didn't think she'd survive a second broken heart.

Ian blinked away the remnants of sleep, disoriented by the darkness. The faint musty odor convinced him he wasn't at home.

The ringing of his phone made him realize that's what had pulled him from sleep. Was he late for work? He grabbed the phone from his breast pocket and peered at the screen.

Six o'clock in the evening. He wasn't late, but the number was that of his boss, Lieutenant Greene. And there were at least a dozen missed calls. "This is Kramer," he said, rolling up to a sitting position. "Is something wrong?"

"Where are you?" Jake Greene asked in a clipped voice.

Something about his boss's tone put him on edge. "Why? What's going on?"

"I went to your place to find you," Jake said, sidestepping his question.

Alarm bells went off in the back of his head. For one thing, it wasn't common practice for his boss to seek him out at home. Not to mention, the fact that Greene kept demanding to know exactly where Ian was, told him something was up.

"I'm not at home, I'm with a friend," he snapped, getting angry. "Come on, Lieutenant. Just tell me what happened."

There was a long pause and he imagined Jake Greene was carefully choosing his next question. "How's Jesse doing?"

Ian scowled, wondering if this was nothing more than a weird dream. He pinched himself just to make sure. "He was fine when I saw him two weeks ago at the hospital. Why? Is he sick? Did something happen to him?"

"Where exactly are you right now," Greene demanded.

Ian knew a direct order when he heard it. As much as it went against the grain to tell anyone about Sarah and Ben, he didn't have much of a choice.

"I'm at a small cabin in the woods, not far off highway double Z. Fire marker number two-ninety-eight, to be exact. The cabin belongs to a Sarah Franklin, nee Miller. She's spending the holiday here with her son, Ben."

Another long silence, and he suspected his boss hadn't expected that answer. "Is Jesse with you?"

What? Ian lunged to his feet, sweeping his hand over the wall to find the light switch. "No, Jesse's not with me. I told you I haven't seen him in over two weeks. I only get to visit him on the first Saturday of the month." He drew in a deep breath, trying to remain calm. "Tell me what's going on. Where is my brother?"

"That's what we were hoping you'd tell us," Lieutenant Greene said in a somber tone. "He escaped from the psychiatric hospital sometime early this morning. We've had teams looking for him over the past few hours, but we haven't found him."

Ian sank back down on the edge of the bed, his mind reeling. Jesse had escaped? No wonder his boss had been out to his house. Had Jesse been to his place? Had his brother been hiding in the woods, waiting for Ian to leave with the generator?

"Listen, Kramer, we need to know the minute Jesse contacts you. Understand?"

Ian closed his eyes and shook his head helplessly. "I promise I'll call you if I hear from my brother, but I can assure you that Jesse won't try to get in touch with me. Don't you understand? Jesse blames me for putting him in that psych hospital in the first place, even though I thought it would be better than being in prison. He barely spoke to me when I visited. If he's truly escaped, I'm the last person on earth he'd call for help."

"You better hope that's not true," Greene said in a low, intense voice. "Because I'm taking you off the schedule until we find him."

Off the schedule? Ian knew that Greene wasn't thrilled the sheriff had reinstate him, but this was going too far. Ian disconnected from the call and dropped the phone, staring blindly down at his shaky hands. He could barely comprehend that Jesse had escaped the psychiatric hospital.

And worse that he'd been taken off the schedule because of it.

His career teetered on the brink of disaster.

Because Ian knew better than anyone that no one would ever find his brother. Jesse would disappear, never to be heard from again.

4

———

Sarah was stirring a pot of canned beef stew on the small electric stove when she heard a loud voice coming from Ben's bedroom. Ian must finally be awake.

Although, from the tone of Ian's voice, she sensed something was wrong. His raised, tense baritone seemed to vibrate from the bedroom. She was curious about what was going on but didn't intend to pry. Ben was content at the kitchen table tying scraps of fabric together to make a chain of garland for their Christmas tree. They'd picked out a small pine tree outside that would be perfect to decorate. She didn't intend to cut it down, but Sarah felt strongly that she needed to provide some Christmas spirit for Ben's sake. She had a small gift for him too, tucked away in the bottom of her suitcase.

Not the holiday she'd envisioned, but being safe was more important.

Her son must have heard Ian's conversation as well, as he kept glancing over toward his bedroom. "Mom, do you think Mr. Ian is mad at someone?" he asked in a loud whisper.

"I don't know, but I'll go ask since dinner is almost ready." She set the spoon aside and strode over to Ben's bedroom. As she lifted her hand to knock, the door unexpectedly swung open revealing Ian's tall, muscular frame.

"Hi," she said awkwardly, taking a step back while trying not to notice just how great Ian looked all rumpled from sleep. Her mouth suddenly went dry, as being in close proximity to Ian brought the ten-year-old memory of their last kiss abruptly to the forefront, as if it had happened yesterday. She swallowed hard. "Is everything all right?"

He stared at her for a long moment before he broke the connection and shrugged. "Yeah, I'm fine. Sorry about falling asleep on you like that. Is everything okay here? Did you see anyone around?"

"No, why?" She noticed the way Ian was staring out the windows, not that there was much to see in the darkness. There were no street lights nearby and even the blanket of snow didn't help to provide much illumination. "Are you expecting someone?"

He hesitated, then shook his head. "No, of course not. Just curious."

Sarah wasn't sure why the easy camaraderie they'd had earlier when setting up the generator had vanished, leaving a silted awkwardness behind. She took another step backward, putting even more space between them. "I hope you're hungry, because dinner is almost ready. Nothing fancy, just canned beef stew."

"I am hungry and canned beef stew sounds great," Ian said with a halfhearted smile. She decided that his telephone conversation must not have gone very well. "But, uh, I just need to take a walk outside for a bit."

"Can I go with you?" Ben asked, abandoning his string of garland to rush over to where Ian stood.

"Ben, why don't you give Mr. Ian some privacy?" she suggested, figuring Ian needed to use the outhouse. "You can take a walk tomorrow."

"Your mom is right, it's pretty dark out so there isn't much to see," Ian said to Ben, real regret shimmering in his gaze. "I'll be back soon and then tomorrow we'll take a long walk, see if we can find any wildlife."

"I guess," Ben mumbled, looking disappointed.

Sarah sensed that Ian was determined to go alone, so she walked over to put her hand on Ben's shoulder. "If you're tired of making garland, we can play a game of Go Fish," she suggested. "As soon as Mr. Ian returns we'll have dinner."

Ian sent a thankful glance in her direction. "I won't be gone long," he said, pulling on his jacket and shoving his feet into his boots.

Sarah sensed something was going on with Ian, but was determined not to pry. After all, she had secrets of her own. Granted, Ian knew she was running from David, but she hadn't confided the details of her disastrous marriage.

And frankly, she didn't want to. She'd pulled herself together over the two years since her divorce and, as far as she was concerned, she'd put all of the bad memories behind her.

She'd come to Crystal Lake to start over in the one place she'd always been happy. Ben would flourish here in a small town atmosphere, and she wanted to give her son a chance to have a stable upbringing. He'd blossomed during the year David had spent in jail.

"Okay," Ben agreed, rifling through his backpack to find the pack of Go Fish cards she'd bought at a rummage sale. She turned down the heat beneath the beef stew, then moved the box of fabric off the table to make room for the card game.

As they played, Sarah found it difficult to concentrate, especially when she caught a glimpse of Ian through the kitchen window. She frowned, wondering why he was walking through the backyard. Was he checking on the generator?

When Ian hadn't returned after the first game of Go Fish, she dealt another hand, her stomach knotting with worry. What was taking Ian so long? Obviously he was doing more than using the outhouse. Did he believe someone was out there?

Had he discovered that David was in town?

Her blood pressure spiked at the thought. No, David had been scheduled to be released by noon today. He couldn't know where she'd gone. She wanted to believe her ex-husband would follow the court order and not come after her and Ben at all, but she couldn't afford to assume David had truly changed after his stint in jail. If he did try to find her, he'd likely attempt to call her grandparents first, although she'd already warned them not to give away her location. Her grandparents had never liked David much, and while she hadn't confided any details of what she'd been through, the fact that he'd been sent to jail had only convinced them that she'd made the right decision in divorcing him.

No, she wasn't worried that her grandparents would give her location away.

But she lived in fear that David might remember the brief time early in their relationship when she'd talked about her amazing summer vacation in Crystal Lake. Thankfully, she'd never brought him up here. David had been too busy making her stay home to cater to his every need.

But that didn't mean he couldn't find the location of her grandparents cabin if he really wanted to.

"I won again," Ben crowed.

She smiled wanly and threw her cards down. "Yes, you sure did." Sneaking a subtle glance at her watch, she realized Ian had been gone for almost twenty minutes.

Should she go outside to look for him? Or stay inside and eat dinner with her son?

Eat dinner, she decided firmly. She wasn't interested in living her life around the whim of a man she'd known ten years ago. Ian could eat cold stew for all she cared.

The moment she rose to her feet, she heard the stomping of footsteps on the front porch. Ian came in through the door, his usual smile back on his face.

"Brr, it's cold out there."

An overwhelming wave of relief made a mockery of her determination to remain independent and emotionally distant. "Is there something wrong with the generator?" she asked as he stripped off his coat, hat and gloves.

"It's fine," he assured her. "And there's no sign of anyone else out there either."

For some reason, that statement didn't reassure her the way it should have. Why was he looking around outside in the first place? What had that phone call been about? She wanted to ask, but with Ben sitting there listening to their conversation, she decided to wait until later.

Sarah dished up generous portions of beef stew and set them on the table. This time Ben folded his hands, waiting patiently for her to start the evening meal prayer.

She took a deep breath, closed her eyes for a moment and cleared her mind. She liked the way even a simple prayer could bring a sense of peace. "Dear Lord, we thank

You for providing the food we are about to eat and for providing us with shelter from the elements. We ask that You keep us safe in Your care. Amen."

"Amen," Ben echoed.

"Amen," Ian added.

She opened her eyes and glanced up at Ian, surprised to see that he'd folded his hands and responded verbally to her prayer. He hadn't participated in their breakfast prayer, so what had changed his mind?

Was it possible that he was open to believing in God, after all? She found herself hoping he was.

Since both Ben and Ian seemed to be waiting for her, she smiled and decided to lighten the tone. "Dig in," she said.

Ben grinned and made a big show of taking a healthy bite of his food.

"Hot, hot!" he exclaimed, dropping the spoon back into his bowl and waving his hand in front of his mouth.

"Here drink some water," she urged, pushing in his glass closer to him.

He gulped the water as Ian chuckled. "Ben, I realize you're hungry, but you're supposed to blow on your food to cool it off before you eat it. Like this," he added, demonstrating by gently blowing on his spoonful of stew.

Sarah couldn't help compare Ian's good-natured response to the way David would have responded with a sharp, scathing reprimand.

And while the last thing she wanted was the complication of another man in her life, she realized that not only was Ian smart, funny, sweet and sincere, but he was an amazing role model for her son.

Everything she'd once dreamed of having in a husband.

· · ·

IAN WASN'T sure how he felt about the happiness reflected in Sarah's eyes when he'd joined her evening prayer. He didn't want to pretend he knew anything about faith or God, but as she'd prayed, he found he agreed wholeheartedly with her words.

He was thankful for the food she'd cooked for him, twice now. He was also thankful to be here, spending time with Sarah and her son. And he wanted to believe that God would keep Sarah and Ben safe in His care.

After walking the perimeter of the cabin, he was reassured that no one had been out there. At least he hadn't found any human prints other than his own. Plenty of deer tracks and other small game, but nothing to be afraid of.

Ian knew that if Jesse had been there, his brother wouldn't have left any tracks behind. The Army had taught Jesse well, and Ian knew that in the few hours that he'd been gone, his brother had the ability to cover several miles. His brother was at home in the wilderness, even in winter.

Still, Ian planned to head back to his place tonight, just to make sure his brother wasn't there or that Jesse hadn't left some sort of parting message for him.

Not that either scenario would help him hang onto his job.

For a moment a wave of sheer desperation hit hard. What would he do if he lost his position? If he was let go from the sheriff's department, it wasn't likely that he'd find a job elsewhere. He wasn't even sure any hospital would hire him as a security guard at half his salary.

"Ian, is something wrong?" Sarah's voice interrupted his depressing thoughts.

He realized he'd been scowling and cleared his expression, forcing a smile. "No, I'm fine. The stew was great. Thanks again for making dinner."

"You're welcome. It's the least I can do since you've provided the generator for us to use," she said. "Do you have to work again tonight?"

Regret stabbed deep. "No, I'm off for the next couple of days. But I have to head home for a while to take care of a few things."

"All right. Let me know if you need any help," she offered.

For a moment Ian was tempted to confide in Sarah, but then realized it wouldn't be fair to make her share his burdens. After all, she had personal problems of her own.

One in particular that he needed to dig into for her. He wanted to know more about her ex-husband.

"I'm all done, Mom," Ben announced, dropping his spoon into the empty bowl with a clatter.

"Carry your dishes to the sink," Sarah reminded him. "Why don't you do some more work on the garland?"

"Garland?" Ian echoed in surprise.

"Yes, I found a box of fabric scraps in the main bedroom, left over from my grandmother's quilting days," Sarah explained. "We're going to decorate the small pine tree outside for Christmas."

Ian was humbled to realize that despite everything that Sarah had gone through, she was determined to celebrate the holiday. He thought back to what he might have at his place. He'd never bothered to decorate much for Christmas, but he was sure he had a box of ornaments tucked away in the basement.

"I'll wash the dishes before I leave," he said, when he'd finished his stew.

"It's no bother," Sarah said waving away his offer. "Now that we have electricity, it doesn't take long for the water to get hot."

"I insist," he said firmly. He knew he owed her more than cleaning a handful of dishes for letting him sleep half the day away. He was still embarrassed at how he'd conked out on her son's bed.

She looked as if she wanted to argue, but must have decided not to waste her breath. Instead, she placed a pot of melted snow on the electric stove and turned on the burner beneath it.

When the water was hot, he added dish soap and then quickly washed the dishes. Sarah picked up a towel and dried them, and working alongside her like this made him realize how lonely his life was.

Oh he'd dated on and off, but nothing serious. Joanna, the woman he'd planned to marry, had decided out of the blue that she couldn't stand living in such a small town as Crystal Lake. She'd gone behind his back to find a new job in the Twin Cities and, when he'd refused to move, she'd handed back his ring and left the very next day.

Truthfully, he could look back at that now and admit that Sarah was right. He was glad he'd discovered the truth before getting married.

"Thanks for doing the dishes," Sarah said, taking the last pan from his hand and drying it.

"You cooked," he reminded her. "It's only fair that I clean up."

She glanced at him from beneath her lashes. "So you don't consider cooking and cleaning women's work?" she asked. Her tone was light, but the expression in her eyes was intensely serious.

"Of course not," he said, wondering if that was what her husband had thought. "Living alone, I have to do everything myself. Sharing the cooking and cleanup work is a bonus."

She smiled and his heart flipped in his chest. As crazy as

it might seem, Sarah was more beautiful now than she had been at seventeen.

For a long second awareness sizzled between them. He ached to draw her into his arms, the way he had all those years ago.

"Mom, I hav'ta go to the bathroom."

The urgency in Ben's voice shattered the moment and Sarah instantly turned away to attend to her son. Ian took a deep breath, trying to control the flash of desire.

What was he thinking? The last thing Sarah would need is for him to start acting the way he had back when they were teenagers. She was a mother now, and he wasn't in a position to start a relationship. Not when he didn't know if he still had a career.

He finished cleaning the kitchen and then pulled on his boots and winter coat. He'd head back home to do a little research on David Franklin, to see what Sarah and Ben were up against. And while he believed they were safe for the moment, he didn't like the thought of leaving them here alone all night.

He'd camp out on the sofa, especially since having slept all afternoon, he wasn't tired.

He walked outside, watching from the porch as Ben came running back from the outhouse. "Do you hav'ta go to the outhouse too?" he asked.

"No, I have to head home for a little while," he said with a smile. The kid's enthusiasm was infectious. "But I'll be back later tonight, okay?"

"Okay," Ben agreed readily.

Ian opened the cabin door for him, watching in amusement as the child stripped off his winter coat, hat and boots and left them in a jumble on the floor. He followed Ben inside, taking a moment to hang the boy's coat on the hook near the door. "Take your hat and mittens and put them on the stove to dry out," he instructed.

Ben heaved a sigh but did as he was told.

Satisfied, Ian headed back outside. He was halfway to his truck when he noticed Sarah striding toward him. "You're leaving?" she asked.

"Just for a few hours," he said. "I don't want to impose, but I'd really like to sleep on your sofa tonight, if that's okay with you."

"There's no need, we'll be fine," Sarah said, crossing her arms over her chest.

"I know you and Ben will be fine, but will you please humor me? I won't sleep at all knowing you and Ben are here alone."

There was a long pause before she finally nodded. "Okay, if you insist. But you can't stay with us forever, Ian," she said frankly. "At some point I need to be able to stand on my own two feet."

That was the second time she'd alluded to the fact that she wanted to be independent, and he sensed that her need to do so was tied up in the mess her ex-husband had left behind.

"Sarah, you're doing an amazing job of being on your own," he told her. "There's a big difference between being safe and being independent. My priority is keeping you both safe."

She stared up at him and he wished for light so he was able to read her expression more clearly. "Thank you, Ian," she finally said in a husky voice. "I think that's the nicest thing any man has ever said to me."

Her confession rocked him back on his heels. He

couldn't bear to imagine what Sarah must have suffered with her ex. Before he could think about the ramifications of his actions, he pulled her close and lowered his mouth to hers in searing kiss.

5

Sarah clung to Ian's broad shoulders, quickly losing herself in the heat of his kiss. Passion sparked between them, almost as if the last time they were together like this was just a few months ago rather than ten full years.

He tasted so much better than she remembered, her mouth practically melting beneath his. How was it that she'd forgotten what it was like to be held and kissed by Ian?

As much as she longed to stay in the comfort and safety of his arms, she was all too aware of the fact that her son was inside the cabin. The thought that Ben might be watching through the window gave her the strength she needed to break free of Ian's embrace. She stood for a moment, gasping for breath wishing she didn't feel so light-headed and shaky. Since when did a simple kiss wreak havoc on her equilibrium?

Since Ian.

"Sarah," he began, but she quickly cut him off.

"Don't." She didn't want to hear an apology or, worse, some platitude about how this shouldn't have happened at all. "Please, just don't say anything, Ian. Let's just chalk this up to old times and move on. Besides, I have to go. Ben is waiting for me inside. I'll see you later."

Ian stared at her for a minute as if he still wanted to talk about what happened, but she turned and headed back into the cabin, firmly closing the door behind her. When she found Ben curled up in the corner of the sofa, his eyelids at half-mast, she released a pent up sigh of relief that he hadn't seen them kissing.

Sarah leaned back against the door, listening to the rumble of the engine in Ian's SUV as he drove away. Regret was bitter on her tongue. If things were different...

But they weren't. She needed to remember what was at stake. In fact, knowing that she was here alone with Ben spurred her into action. She pushed away from the door and turned the dead bolt. After taking off her coat and boots, she crossed over to rouse her son. "Why don't you get your pajamas on and brush your teeth?"

Ben rubbed at his eyes and then pushed himself up to a sitting position. "We're camping," he said peevishly. "Don't hav'ta brush my teeth."

It was tempting to let it go, but she also knew that if they were going to stay here for the foreseeable future, she needed to set some ground rules. "We're not camping, we're living in a rustic cabin. And yes, you absolutely need to brush your teeth."

Her son must have been too tired to argue because he slid off the sofa and padded into the bedroom. He emerged a few minutes later wearing his Spiderman footie pajamas and carrying his toothbrush and toothpaste.

"Where should I brush? In the outhouse?" he asked.

"No, of course not. You can brush in the kitchen." She pulled a chair over to the sink so he could reach, and when he finished, she followed him into the bedroom. He crawled into the sleeping bag scooting over so that she could sit on the edge of the bed while he said his prayers.

"Dear Lord, I'm sorry for the naughty things I did today," Ben said, the way he always did. She often wondered what would happen if she asked him to list the naughty things he'd done, because she was sure he had no clue exactly what they were. "Please bless me and my mom and my great grandpa and great grandma. Oh, and please bless Mr. Ian too. Amen."

"Amen," she echoed, surprised that Ian had already been included in her son's prayers. Even though Ben had only met Ian twenty-four hours ago, she knew he'd made a big impression on her son. She leaned over to give him a hug and a kiss. "I love you, Ben," she murmured.

"I love you, Mommy," he said, kissing her cheek.

She hugged him again and then stood up, subtly wiping away the tears burning in her eyes. She was thankful that her son was so resilient. So far, the nightmares he'd suffered right after David's arrest hadn't reappeared.

She hoped and prayed they were gone for good.

As she left Ben's bedroom, partially closing the door behind her, she realized she was glad that Ian had insisted on coming back to sleep on the sofa.

He was right, there was a big difference between being independent and being safe. And she was willing to do whatever was necessary to protect her son.

IAN FELT grim as he took his time walking around the perimeter of his property. His instincts were screaming at him, but there was no obvious sign that Jesse had been anywhere near his small house located on the west shoreline of Crystal Lake. Tucked between the trees, his house wasn't easy to spot from either the road or the lake, which was the way he liked it.

He scowled, stared blindly into the woods, wishing he had the ability to track people the way his brother did. But he hadn't joined the Army the way Jesse had. Besides, tracking his brother wouldn't do any good. He firmly believed Jesse was long gone.

Never to return.

Ian let out a heavy sigh and trudged back inside. He had no idea how to salvage his career. Unless he could set up a one-on-one meeting with Sheriff Luke Torretti? After all, the fact that Jesse escaped from a psychiatric hospital was hardly his fault. He'd been the one to take his brother into custody back in September. Why would he risk his career by helping his brother escape now, three months later?

He wouldn't, although he couldn't blame his lieutenant for thinking the worst. Greene hadn't been happy to have him back in the first place and now with Jesse's escape he had a reason to doubt Ian's ability to be impartial.

Ian wasn't even sure having at least part of an alibi helped his case. He'd been shoveling a path to the outhouse and then chopping wood when Jesse likely escaped. Sarah couldn't say for sure what time he'd arrived. Besides, gossip flew fast through town and once his boss learned that he and Sarah had spent the summer together ten years ago, it wouldn't be a stretch for anyone to believe that she'd agreed to cover for him.

Sarah believed in God and prayer, and he knew with a deep sense of certainty she wasn't the type of woman who would lie for him. But would anyone believe that? Yeah, probably not.

He shook off the depressing thoughts and headed down

to the basement. He still had the boxes he'd taken from his mother's house after she'd passed away. As he headed over to the where they were located, he frowned when he saw the large bin containing his hunting and camping gear.

Was it possible Jesse had stopped by here, after all? Ian crossed over and lifted the lid. Sure enough, several items were missing, including his boots and his hunting knife. But not his shotgun, which was interesting.

Still, he'd have to report this to his boss. Would Lieutenant Greene see this as aiding Jesse's escape? He thought it was highly likely.

Ian replaced the lid with a sigh. He decided to call in the theft directly to the sheriff. The sheriff believed in him once. Ian hoped the sheriff would at least give him the opportunity to explain.

He left a message then disconnected from the call and went down to find the box of Christmas ornaments. He brought it upstairs and carried it out to his truck so he wouldn't forget, then decided to clean out his fridge too. No reason to let good food go bad; he'd rather take it for Sarah and Ben. After all, she'd fed him twice when she didn't even have extra food to spare.

Once he'd filled up a cooler and took that out to his truck, he went back inside and booted up his laptop computer. The generator he'd given her would provide power, but he knew there wasn't any internet service at the cabin and he wanted to gather some information on David Franklin. He logged into the program that allowed deputies to run background checks, grateful to discover his password still worked.

Maybe *off the schedule* wasn't as bad as being suspended.

It took him a while to find the right guy, considering he didn't have a middle initial or date of birth. But then he stumbled upon a David Franklin who'd been arrested a year ago for domestic violence and assault with a deadly weapon. A knife that Franklin had used against Sarah. It was a miracle she hadn't been hurt worse, and yet terrible that her son had been there during the altercation. No wonder the boy had been so afraid of his father.

When Ian dug further, he discovered that Franklin had been released on parole earlier that day.

His heart raced as he stared at Franklin's mug shot. This had to be the right guy, and explained why Sarah had been driving through the storm. And he didn't blame her. No doubt, she'd been desperate to get as far away from this jerk as possible.

Sarah's ex-husband didn't look anything like he'd imagined. Franklin had dirty blond hair and a deceptively innocent boyish face. Only his dark, cold eyes gave any hint of his true nature. The fact that Franklin had cut Sarah with a knife made Ian's temper spike.

He shut the laptop and rose to his feet. Now that he knew exactly what had happened, and who he needed to protect her from, he was anxious to get back to Sarah and Ben. What if Franklin had already found them? Ian wasn't about to wait a second longer. He tucked the computer under his arm, grabbed his jacket and headed out to the truck.

He made the trip back to Sarah's cabin in record time, thankful that none of the deputies from second shift had caught him pushing the speed limit. Sweeping his gaze over the area surrounding the cabin, he remained alert for anything that seemed out of the ordinary. Franklin didn't look like the type of guy who could blend into the forest the way his brother could, but then again, he wasn't going to underestimate the guy either.

Light from a small lamp shone through the living room window, and he found that he liked the idea that Sarah had left it on for him. Especially considering the way she'd abruptly ended their kiss.

He still wasn't sure why she hadn't wanted him to say anything. Did she sense he'd been about to apologize? Not so much for the kiss, but for taking advantage of a moment of vulnerability.

Maybe. But at the same time, he wasn't willing to simply chalk that kiss up to old times and forget about it either. In fact, he very much wanted to kiss her again.

He gave himself a mental shake, knowing he needed to get his priorities straight. This wasn't about him and his feelings. Yes, he was attracted to Sarah. Yes, he could admit now that he'd never completely forgotten her even after all this time. Yes, he liked the woman and mother she'd become.

But as usual, his timing couldn't be worse. She wasn't in a position to be in a relationship, even if she wanted to. And neither was he, considering he had nothing to offer her.

No, his top priority needed to be keeping Sarah and Ben safe.

The hour wasn't too late, barely nine o'clock at night, but he didn't see any sign of Sarah or Ben moving around inside the cabin. Assuming they were asleep, he unpacked his car, bringing everything up onto the porch before quietly unlocking the door, both the main lock and the dead bolt. He smiled with satisfaction when he realized she'd taken his warning seriously.

Moving as silently as possible, he began to unpack the food from his cooler, putting everything into the empty and now working refrigerator. When he finished, he turned around and nearly fell over the cooler in surprise when he saw Sarah standing there, watching him.

"I'm sorry if I woke you," he said, hoping he didn't look as guilty as he felt.

"I needed to make sure it was you out here," she admitted softly.

The image of Franklin's mug shot flashed in his mind and he nodded. "I understand. And I hope you're not upset that I kept a key. I'll give it back to you, if you'd rather keep it yourself."

"No, it's fine. But you didn't have to stock my fridge," she said, a tiny frown puckering her brow. "I was going to ask you to take me to the store tomorrow."

"I'd be happy to take you," he assured her. "But there was no sense in letting my food spoil either."

"Okay. Well, good night then."

"Good night, Sarah."

She turned and then paused when she noticed his laptop computer sitting on the sofa. When she glanced over her shoulder at him, he could see the unspoken question in her eyes.

"I found him," he said, cutting straight to the heart of the issue. "And I'm not going to let him hurt you or Ben, ever again."

She dropped her gaze and bit her lower lip, as if ashamed that he knew the truth. He couldn't stand to see her like that, and he crossed over and tipped her chin up with one finger. "Don't, Sarah. What he did isn't your fault. He was the one who broke his vows. He was the one who used his anger against you. Don't ever think that there was anything you did that justified the way he lashed out to hurt you."

"But you don't know everything," she protested weakly.

His heart ached for her. "I know enough, and I'm glad he

went to jail. He broke his vows and the law. I'm only sorry that he was released so soon."

Sarah's attempt at a smile was pathetic and he carefully drew her into his arms, reminding himself that kissing her was off-limits. She didn't need a kiss right now, she needed comfort. To believe in herself. To know that she'd made the right decision in divorcing that jerk.

He was surprised when Sarah wrapped her arms around his waist, holding him tightly while resting her cheek against his chest. He stroked his hand lightly down her back in a soothing motion. Ian expected her to pull away, but she didn't. And neither did he. He figured he'd stand here, holding Sarah as long as she needed him to.

"Thank you for being here," she murmured, finally breaking the silence. "And you should know that Ben included you in his bedtime prayers."

The idea of a five-year-old boy praying for him was humbling. He searched for the proper words to say. "I'm honored to be included. I only wish I knew enough about God and faith to do the same for you and Ben."

Sarah lifted her head to peer up at him. "I'd be happy to teach you about God and the Bible, Ian," she said. "And praying is easy. You just speak from your heart and God will listen."

She made it sound simple, and yet he knew there was probably much more to faith than that. But maybe as a starting point?

Why not?

He took Sarah's hands in his and bowed his head. Speaking from the heart wasn't as difficult as he'd anticipated. "Dear Lord, please keep us all safe in Your care tonight, Amen."

"Amen," Sarah whispered, her eyes suspiciously bright. Her smile was tremulous. "See? Easy."

"Yeah." His throat was thick with emotion and there were so many other things he wanted to tell her. But he reminded himself this wasn't the time. "Thanks, Sarah. I remember going to church as a young boy, but it's been a long time since I thought about God and prayer."

"The good news is that God is always there, waiting for us," she said. "To be honest, I don't think I would have made it through these past couple of years without my faith and God's support. I'll miss the people in my church."

"I'm glad to hear you had some support, Sarah," he said. "Although I wish I could have been there for you."

She tipped her head to the side. "You're here now, Ian."

Her words made him smile and, despite his honorable intentions, he wanted nothing more than to kiss her again. He even lowered his head to do just that.

But a muffled scream rent the silence.

What in the world? He tensed and jerked his head up, searching for the source of the sound.

Sarah was already one step ahead of him, racing toward the bedroom where he knew Ben must be sleeping. He quickly caught up to her, hoping and praying that David Franklin hadn't somehow gotten in and grabbed Ben.

6

Sarah's heart twisted in her chest when she realized Ben was thrashing around in his sleeping bag, trapped in the horror of his nightmare. She sat on the edge of his bed and drew his small body into her arms. "Shh, Ben, wake up, sweetie. You're having a dream, everything's fine. We're safe here."

She continued to reassure him until he calmed down and burrowed against her, his hands tightly grasping her sweatshirt. For several long moments he struggled to throw off the dream, his sobs quieting to small, intermittent hiccups.

She could feel Ian's gaze on them as he wandered around the room, testing the window to make sure it was secure. Ignoring Ian's presence wasn't easy, but she stayed with Ben long after he'd stopped crying, unwilling to explain the details behind Ben's nightmare to Ian.

Lots of kids had nightmares, but Ian was smart enough to do the math, assuming, rightfully so, that the young boy who feared his father had been dreaming about him.

Ian came to stand beside her, gently resting his hand on her shoulder. "Are you all right?" he whispered.

She nodded. "I'm going to stay here for the rest of the night"

He surprised her by nodding in agreement. "I'll be right outside on the sofa if you need anything."

"I know, but I'm sure we'll be fine." She waited until Ian left the room, closing the door behind him before easing Ben away from her so she could stretch out beside him.

Ben snuggled against her, and she kissed the top of his head, her heart aching for him. He was turning six years old in the middle of January, and she hated knowing that he'd already been exposed to fear and violence.

She closed her eyes, wishing once again that she'd had the courage to relocate sooner. David had stalked her for almost a year after their divorce before making his move. She clearly remembered the crazy intensity in his eyes when he'd attacked her with a knife, slicing her flank while claiming she belonged to him, ignoring how Ben screamed in terror behind her.

She shivered and tucked Ben closer. No, things probably wouldn't have changed much, although there was the possibility that if Ben had been younger, he wouldn't remember that event to the point his subconscious was haunted by nightmares.

Stewing about the past and playing the what-if game wasn't going to change anything so she returned to her faith, praying that Ben would find peace.

Sarah awoke to the dim light of morning with a crick in her neck. Ben was still sleeping beside her so she eased upright and slid from the bed, careful not to wake him.

Stretching and rubbing the muscles in her neck to help ease the ache, she walked into the living room, surprised to find that Ian was already up and puttering in the kitchen.

"Good morning," she murmured, trying not to think about how strange it was to share living space with a man. Although this was nothing like her experience with David. Her ex had never once jumped up to help with kitchen duties the way Ian had. And for sure, David had never attempted to cook breakfast.

After all, that was her job. And if she didn't cook his eggs the way he demanded, he forced her to start over again. The sick feeling in her stomach forced her to quickly slam the door against those memories.

"Good morning," Ian greeted her with a smile. "I don't know if you like coffee, but I brought my coffee maker from home and brewed a pot." He looked so handsome and at ease wearing well-worn jeans and a cable knit sweater in a dark blue that matched his eyes. For a minute she couldn't help reliving the heat of their kiss.

"I'd love some coffee," she confessed, crossing over to the kitchen. "I had to settle for tea yesterday."

He grimaced comically. "Ugh. You should have said something. That's like a coffee emergency. I could have rushed to your rescue, bringing my coffee maker over right away."

She laughed, enjoying Ian's wry sense of humor. "I know. What was I thinking?"

He poured her a steaming mug and then pushed the creamer and sugar containers across the counter so they were within reach. "Better get started before you go into coffee withdrawal."

She added a drop of cream and then took a deep breath, inhaling the aroma before taking a sip. "Crisis averted," she murmured with a sigh. "This is great, thanks."

Ian stared at her over the rim of his own coffee for a long moment, making every nerve in her body tingle in awareness. She had the sense that he was remembering their kiss as well. And she was crazy enough to want to kiss him again.

She couldn't seem to remember any of the reasons that had seemed so important as a reason to keep Ian at a distance. She'd fallen hard for him that summer they'd spent together, but she liked him even more now.

"I've never forgotten you, Sarah," he said in a low tone. "The summer we were together was the best time of my life."

She couldn't find the strength to tear her gaze from his, despite the fact that she knew they were treading on dangerous ground. "For me too," she finally acknowledged. "But I can't regret all the decisions I made back then because I wouldn't have Ben. And my son is everything to me."

"I understand and I'm not saying that I want to go back to change things. We were too young to make any sort of commitment. But now that I've found you again, I don't want to lose you."

She sucked in a quick breath in response to Ian's blunt admission. And even though she'd promised herself she'd never be dependent on a man again, she knew she didn't want to lose Ian either.

"I'm not trying to rush you," Ian said, backpedaling to fill the silence. "Right now, I'm not sure I'll keep my job. But if by some miracle I am still employed, I'd like to spend time with you and Ben."

Wait a minute. What had he said? "What do you mean, if you're still employed?" It was easier for her to focus on the first part of his statement than on the implications of the latter. "What happened between the night you found me in the ditch and today?"

"A few months ago I arrested my brother because he went over the deep end," Ian said. "He was held captive in Afghanistan, and when he returned home he wasn't the same man. He couldn't bear to be indoors. Then he tried to hurt innocent people. Thankfully we stopped him, and I worked hard to get him the psychiatric help he needed. He's been in a psychiatric hospital but apparently escaped some-time early yesterday morning. Probably around the time I was outside chopping wood."

She couldn't believe what he was saying. "Your boss thinks you helped your brother escape? Why would you? And besides, I can vouch for the fact that you were chop-ping wood for us."

"Yet you didn't really see me until I brought the wood in, right?"

She hated the fact that he was right. "Still, I can vouch for you," she insisted.

"I'm not asking you to lie for me, and there's more. Jesse took some of my hunting and camping gear, including a knife, which isn't going to look good for me. But I've already left a message with Sheriff Torretti to request a meeting. Until I clear this up, I've been taken off the schedule."

Sarah scowled truly upset on Ian's behalf. "That's just ridiculous. Maybe I should go with you to meet with the sheriff. I'm sure I can set him straight."

"No, there's no need for you to be involved. I'll be fine," he said firmly. "This is my problem, not yours. I was getting ready to make breakfast," he abruptly offered, and she understood that, as far as Ian was concerned, the personal conversation was over. "Does Ben like French toast?"

"Absolutely," she said, willing to drop the issue of Ian's job for now. Especially since she had more pressing concerns. Like wishing the cabin had indoor plumbing. "I'll be back in a few minutes," she said, heading over to pull her jacket off the peg by the door.

"All right," Ian said, following her outside to stand on the porch. "I'll wait here for you."

She rolled her eyes and ignored him as she followed the path to the outhouse. There was a tiny part of her brain that chafed at how overprotective Ian was acting. Watching her walk to the bathroom? Really?

In the early stages of her marriage to David, she'd thought he cared about her safety and security too. Only to discover that David's true intent had been to control her, isolate her from everyone she knew. And once she was cut off from her friends and family, the verbal abuse started—turning to physical abuse when she'd gotten up enough nerve to file for divorce. And the physical abuse escalated when he'd tried to kill her.

Logically, she knew Ian wasn't anything like David. Ian was a cop, so of course he had strong protective instincts. She needed to stay focused.

But couldn't help wondering if she'd ever be totally free from David's abuse.

When Sarah emerged from the outhouse, she saw that Ben was standing beside Ian on the cabin porch, bundled head to toe in his winter gear. They were talking about something intense, and the way her son gazed up at Ian, with blatant adoration in his eyes, made her heart stumble in her chest.

The feeling forced her to realize that while she might be willing to explore a relationship with Ian, there was more than just her own emotions at stake.

She was potentially sacrificing Ben's too.

IAN ENJOYED COOKING breakfast for Sarah and Ben, and the child's enthusiasm for Christmas was infectious. When Ben learned that Ian had brought ornaments for the tree, he jumped up and down waving his arms excitedly.

"Can we decorate the Christmas tree now? Can we? Please?" Ben begged.

"We have to do the dishes first," Sarah said with a smile. "Remember the rules? Mr. Ian cooked so we have to clean up."

"It's okay," Ian said, but she sent him a stern look.

"No, it's not. We have all day to decorate the tree. We need to do the dishes first," she insisted.

"Oh, Mom," Ben whined.

Ian recognized the stubborn glint in Sarah's eyes and knew better than to interfere with her parenting style, so he nodded and backed off. "That's fine, I need to make a few calls, anyway," he said. He took his phone off the charger and moved into the living room, leaving Sarah and Ben to their cleanup duties.

He called the Hope County dispatcher first, hoping to catch Sheriff Torretti before the holiday, but of course he wasn't there. Ian asked to be transferred to the sheriff's voice mail so he could leave another message.

He stared at his phone for a minute and then called the dispatcher back. "Hey, Kristin, I need you to put an alert out on a guy by the name of David Franklin," he said. "I'll send you the link to his mug shot so you can put the deputies on notice. His ex-wife and son are here in Crystal Lake, and he might be planning to violate the restraining order she has against him."

"Do you have a reason to believe he's in the area?" Kristin asked. "Has he called or threatened her?"

Did his gut instincts count? "No, nothing that concrete but it doesn't hurt to put his picture out there just in case."

"I guess not," Kristin reluctantly agreed. "Okay, shoot the mug shot over and I'll put all the deputies on alert."

"Thanks." He disconnected from the call and then sent the picture through his phone.

Fifteen minutes later, Ben came rushing over. "We're done with the dishes," he announced. "Can we decorate the tree now?"

Ian glanced up and caught Sarah's wry gaze over Ben's head. "I don't know," he said to Ben. "Maybe you need to ask your mom?"

Ben spun in a circle so fast he nearly toppled over. "Can we Mom? Please?"

"Yes, Ben, we can go outside to decorate the tree."

Ian opened the box of ornaments and showed them to Ben. Some were fancy and others were homemade, by both him and Jesse. They had put a clear plastic coating over their school pictures one year and he was surprise his mother had kept them. "Some of these are fragile, so we have to be careful, okay?"

Ben's eyes were wide with awe. "Okay."

Ian carried the ornaments outside to the porch while Sarah helped Ben with his coat and boots. She brought out their handmade garland too, and then walked over to the small pine tree not far off the porch.

"I thought this one would be the perfect size to decorate," she said. "I'd rather not cut it down so we can decorate it next year too."

"All right," Ian said, secretly thrilled to hear that Sarah was planning to stay in Crystal Lake. He only hoped that he could hang onto his job, since he wanted nothing more than to celebrate more holidays with her.

Although Ian knew that even if he was able to stay on with the sheriff's department, he'd have to take things slow. Sarah had every reason to be gun-shy when it came to entering into a relationship. She knew him well enough to feel safe with him. To know that he'd never hurt her or Ben. But that wasn't the real issue holding her back.

Sarah claimed she needed to be able to stand on her own two feet, but she'd already proven that by filing for divorce and surviving David's vicious attack. Ian sensed that the real problem was that Sarah wasn't sure how to care about someone else without losing herself in the relationship.

People who cared about each other, supported and encouraged each other to do better. But she hadn't experienced that phenomenon with her ex.

He hoped he could show her what a true relationship was all about. Obviously the main reason he hadn't found someone else was because he'd subconsciously compared other women to Sarah.

Only to find them lacking.

He smiled to himself as he helped put smaller Christmas ornaments on the top of the small pine tree, leaving Ben and Sarah to decorate the lower branches. He was already envisioning a quiet Christmas Eve in front of the fire. He didn't have gifts to give Sarah and Ben, but somehow he knew Sarah wouldn't mind.

"Oh no, the box is empty," Ben complained.

"Don't forget the garland we made," Sarah said. "And we have time to make more too, if needed."

Ben's grimace made Ian smile. When his phone rang, he pulled it out, his pulse quickening when he recognized the number of Sheriff Torretti on the screen. He connected with the call, moving up toward the cabin porch for some privacy.

"This is Deputy Kramer," Ian said adopting a formal tone. "Thanks for returning my call."

"You left three messages, Ian," the sheriff said dryly. "I figured there had to be some sort of emergency, so I decided to give you a call before leaving for the afternoon. My kids are in the church Christmas pageant."

Ian cleared his throat, a little taken aback by the knowledge that Sheriff Torretti attended church on a regular basis. "Thank you, sir, I appreciate the call. However, I was hoping to discuss my status with you in person. I could be there in fifteen minutes, if that works for you?"

"What about your status?" Sheriff Torretti asked.

Ian was surprised at the question. "Lieutenant Greene took me off the schedule after my brother Jesse escaped from the psychiatric hospital yesterday morning."

There was a long moment of silence, and Ian really wished he was there to see Sheriff Torretti's face. Was it possible he hadn't known about Greene's action? Could it be that his lieutenant hadn't sent the paperwork through yet?

"Did you have anything to do with your brother's escape?" Sheriff Torretti finally asked.

"No, sir, but there's more. I believe my brother got into my house and took some of my hunting gear. And I don't have the best alibi either. I was here, chopping wood at Sarah Franklin's cabin, but she didn't see me until roughly zero eight hundred hours." Ian glanced over to where he'd left Sarah and Ben decorating the tree, frowning when he didn't see them.

"Does Lieutenant Greene know about your alibi?" the sheriff asked.

But Ian wasn't listening. Still holding the phone near his ear, he jumped off the porch, looking all around the clearing for any sign of Sarah or Ben. He even ran down the path to the outhouse, only to find the building empty.

"Kramer," the sheriff said sharply. "Are you there?"

Fear gripped him around the throat, making it difficult to breathe. "Listen, I need you to send two deputies here right away," Ian said urgently. "I also want an APB put out for David Franklin. I believe he's kidnapped his ex-wife and his son."

To his credit, his boss didn't hesitate. "Done. Don't do anything stupid, Kramer. Your backup will be there soon."

"Thank you," Ian choked out before disconnecting from the call. He slid the phone into his pocket and returned to the area where Sarah and Ben had been winding their homemade garland around the tree.

There, behind the tree, closest to the dense woods, he saw extra footprints in the snow. Two sets of footprints, heading into the woods.

No way was he waiting for backup. Ian ran inside the house, grabbed his service weapon and then bolted back outside.

He couldn't bear the thought of losing Sarah or Ben.

7

———

Sarah wanted to claw the smirk off David's face as he held a knife against her son's temple. But she didn't dare let her hatred show on her face, keeping her expression as neutral as humanly possible.

Please, Lord, please keep Ben safe in Your care!

David had emerged from nowhere, grabbing Ben before she knew what was happening. From their position behind the Christmas tree, she could barely see where Ian had been standing and talking on the phone, immersed in his conversation with the sheriff, much less take the risk of calling out to him.

Not when her ex-husband had figured out the best way to get her cooperation was to manipulate her weak spot. Threatening to kill Ben was enough to make her bite her tongue and to follow along with his plan.

"Shut up," David said harshly, when Ben whimpered in fear.

"You're scaring him," she pointed out rationally.

"Too bad. Move it, Sarah. Now."

She did as he asked, following David who was carrying

Ben. Her ex-husband wasn't an outdoorsy kind of guy, but David wove a path through the trees, seeming to know exactly where he was going. As she followed David deeper and deeper into the woods, her mind raced as she tried to think of a way to get Ben away from him. Because, deep down, she knew David didn't want their son.

He wanted her.

But even worse, he wanted to make her suffer the way she'd made him suffer by sending him to jail. Her greatest fear was that David would torture Ben as a way to wound her.

She curled her fingers into fists, determined to do whatever it took to divert David's anger to her, drawing it away from Ben. But how?

"Hurry up," he said in a low tone, when she lagged behind. "The road isn't far."

The road? Was that his escape plan? Did he have his car there? She wished she knew how David had managed to find her location so quickly. Obviously he'd remembered that innocent comment she'd made about vacationing in Crystal Lake. He must have done some research to pinpoint the location of her grandparent's cabin.

It was too late to worry about that now. She risked a quick glance over her shoulder, her heart sinking to the pit of her stomach when she didn't see Ian anywhere behind them. She'd thought for sure he'd notice they were missing by now.

David was moving at a swift pace, which convinced her he had a plan. And she was very much afraid they'd reach David's car before Ian even knew they were gone.

She stifled a scream when her ex-husband tripped badly, letting go of Ben to brace his fall. Her son fell first, partially beneath David. Fearing the worst, she rushed forward and tripped too, landing close to her son. She crawled over the snow to reach her son, pulling him away from David, the sounds of Ben's tortured sobs tearing at her heart.

Gathering Ben close she surged to her feet, preparing to run. But Ian abruptly emerged from the woods, jumping on top of her ex to prevent him from getting up.

"Watch out! He has a knife," she shouted.

Ian dug his knee into David's back, pressing on the back of his head so he couldn't move. "David Franklin, you're under arrest for violating your restraining order," Ian said in a harsh tone. He grabbed David's wrists and snapped on a pair of silver handcuffs.

"He came! Mr. Ian came," Ben whispered.

"Yes, he did." Sarah's eyes filled with tears of happiness. And love.

She loved Ian. How that was possible in such a short timeframe she had no idea, but she loved him more than she'd thought possible. She'd been infatuated with the eighteen-year-old he'd been ten years ago.

And she loved the man he was today.

But Sarah knew that things wouldn't be easy. Especially with his brother's escape hanging over him. But she didn't care. She'd do whatever possible to help him restore his career.

So they could have a future, together.

IAN TIGHTENED his grip on Franklin, determined to prevent him from getting away.

And he silently thanked God for protecting Sarah and Ben.

"I'll get you for this," David said, squirming frantically.

"Was that a threat?" Ian asked, hauling David up to his

feet. "I'll be glad to add that to the list of pending charges. You're not going to get out of jail for a long time. Didn't you know that kidnapping is a federal offense?"

David acted as if he wasn't listening. His gaze seemed to be glued to Sarah. "You're nothing but a whore," he said in disgust. Then he spit at her.

Ian yanked him backward but David's heels became caught on something. Ian scowled and glanced down at the ground. "What in the world?"

Then he saw it, a nearly invisible string of what looked like fishing wire stretched between two large trees.

A trip wire? Where had it come from? Who'd set a trip wire?

Jesse? Ian gave himself a mental shake, unwilling to believe it. Surely his brother was long gone.

Wasn't he?

Of course he was. Why would Jesse stick around? And even if he had, what would have alerted his brother to the danger surrounding Sarah's ex-husband?

Still the trip wire nagged at him.

The sound of someone calling his name made him glance over his shoulder to find two deputies, Devon Armbruster and Jason Thomas, walking toward him.

"Is everything under control?" Dev asked.

"Yeah. I have it under control." Ian stepped on the trip wire so that he could pull Franklin along. "I've read him his rights, but you might want to do it again so that there's a witness." He didn't add that, technically, he wasn't actually *on the schedule* which was a legal loophole they didn't need.

"Violating his restraining order, huh?" Dev asked.

"Along with kidnapping under the force of a deadly weapon," Ian confirmed. "He had a knife, but must have dropped it."

"We'll find it." Dev read Franklin his rights and then searched along the trampled snow for the knife. When Dev found it, he used a plastic bag to pick it up before turning to grin at Ian. "Got it."

"I think he has a vehicle parked on a road too," Sarah said. "At least that's where he seemed to be taking us."

"I'll check it out," Jason volunteered.

Ian let the other deputy go, turning toward Sarah and Ben. His gut clenched when he saw a scratch along Ben's cheek. "Are you sure you're both all right?"

"Thank you for saving us, again," Sarah murmured, her eyes suspiciously bright.

"I never should have turned my back," Ian said harshly. "It's my fault he was able to get close enough to grab you."

"Stop it," Sarah said, putting her hand on his arm. "We can't beat ourselves up about this. It's not your fault any more than it's mine. David did this. He's the one at fault."

Logically, Ian knew she was right, but it wasn't easy to set aside his guilt. If he hadn't been so focused on his career, she and Ben wouldn't have been in danger.

"Mr. Ian?" Ben's voice was thick with tears. "Will my daddy go back to jail now?"

His heart ached for the child who had seen too much violence in his young life. "Yes, he'll go to jail Ben. For a long, long time."

Ben reached out his arms, silently asking for a hug and Ian immediately stepped closer and pulled the child against his chest, holding him close.

Sarah's smile made him realize that this was all that mattered. Not his career, not even the fate of his brother.

But the three of them. The woman he'd never forgotten and her son. A child he'd willingly raise as his own if given the chance.

"Kramer? Armbruster?" The sharp command had him glancing up in surprise.

Sheriff Torretti himself was striding toward them, a deep scowl etched in his face.

Ian handed Ben back to Sarah and straightened to face his boss directly. "Yes sir?"

"I see you have the suspect in custody," Sheriff Torretti said. "Is anyone hurt?"

"Franklin's son, Ben, has a cut on his cheek from the suspect's knife," Ian said.

"We'll be fine, thanks to Deputy Kramer," Sarah interjected in a loud voice. She stepped toward Sheriff Torretti and shifted Ben in her arms so she could extend her hand. Bemused, Torretti took it in his. "It's nice to meet you. My name is Sarah Franklin and my ex-husband, David Franklin grabbed my son and held him at knife point, forcing us to go with him. And I will absolutely press charges to the fullest extent of the law."

Ian choked back a laugh as Sheriff Torretti took a surprised step back at the vehemence of her tone. "I'm glad to hear you weren't hurt and that you intend to press charges."

"And that Deputy Kramer saved us," Sarah added pointedly.

"That too," Torretti agreed.

"Hey, I found his escape car," Jason said as he jogged back through the woods toward them. "Ian, did you find it first?"

He frowned. "No. Why?"

Jason shrugged. "I found the hood unlatched and the distributor cap was missing. Figured maybe you found and disabled the vehicle first, before coming after them."

Another chill snaked down his spine and Ian knew that

the trip wire and the distributor cap must have been the work of his brother, Jesse. Nothing else made sense. "It wasn't me," he said sharply. "I followed Sarah's and David's tracks through the woods, making a wide circle so I could come at them from the side."

"That's true, because I was surprised to see Ian coming at us from the west rather than from the south," Sarah agreed.

Sheriff Torretti lifted a brow. "Then who pulled off the distributor cap?"

Ian shook his head. "I don't know sir, but I found a trip wire which is what stopped Franklin from getting away." When he realized he was still covering for his brother, he forced himself to voice his suspicions. "We need to consider the possibility that Jesse might have done this."

The minute the words left his mouth, he wished he could take them back. Up until now he'd looked like a hero.

Now he could tell his boss and his colleagues were looking at him as if he were guilty by association.

"Did you see your brother?" Sheriff Torretti asked, breaking the strained silence.

"No sir."

"I didn't see anyone either," Sarah said. "And trust me, I was looking for help the entire time David was holding a knife on my son."

Ian wished Sarah wouldn't keep jumping in to help support him. Dev and Jason had already exchanged a knowing glance, obviously wondering about their relationship.

He hated the thought of her good name being dragged down by his.

But since he'd gone this far, he figured he may as well tell them everything. "Sir, remember I mentioned that some of my hunting things were missing? It's possible that I had fishing line in there. The same type used as the trip wire. Jesse easily could have followed me here to Sarah's. Maybe he stumbled across David and watched him grab Sarah and Ben. In fact, he might still be nearby."

There was a long pause as Sheriff Torretti pondered their next move. "Okay, fine. I'll call for reinforcements to help search the woods. Kramer, get the woman and her son back to the cabin. We'll take their formal statements later. Armbruster, you and Thomas take the perp into custody."

"Yes sir." Armbruster and Thomas gladly hauled David Franklin away.

Ian took Sarah's arm, thinking it was odd that Sheriff Torretti didn't order them to begin searching the woods immediately, although it was also important to get Franklin safely secured in jail too.

Still, didn't he realize that even a slight delay would help Jesse escape?

"I wanna walk," Ben said, squirming in Sarah's arms.

"Will you let me carry you?" Ian asked. "We'll get back to the cabin sooner that way."

"Okay." Ben's eagerness brought a wry smile to Sarah's lips.

"You'll always be his mother," Ian said in a low voice.

"I know." He was surprised when she tucked her hand beneath his elbow as they covered the distance back to Sarah's grandparent's cabin.

When they reached the clearing, he stopped and stared at the Christmas tree. There weren't lights, but seeing his mother's ornaments amidst Sarah's homemade garland made him catch his breath in awe.

"Beautiful, isn't it?" Sarah whispered. "I'm glad we didn't cut it down."

"Me too. Especially since we can see it from the living room window." He walked closer, and then stared when he saw Jesse's homemade ornament, the one sporting his photograph, sitting prominently at the top of the tree when Ian had originally placed it somewhere in the middle.

Jesse had been there.

What did the placement of the ornament mean? That Jesse had forgiven him? Had Jesse saved Sarah and Ben as a way of telling Ian that he was doing better mentally?

No, it wasn't possible. No one could get over PTSD that quickly.

But maybe, just maybe, Jesse had learned how to control the flashbacks. At least enough not to be a danger to anyone else.

"Ian? Is something wrong?" Sarah asked.

He tore his gaze from the Christmas tree and shook his head. "Nothing is wrong. I just realized how lucky I am to have found you again, Sarah. The entire time that jerk had you were the longest moments of my life. I was so worried that I wouldn't get to you in time."

"I knew you'd come after us," she said with confidence. "Come inside. We'll drink some hot cider and read the story of Christmas from the Bible."

"That's an offer I'd never refuse," he said, carrying Ben up to the cabin porch.

But even as he set Ben on his feet, he swept his gaze over the clearing in front of the cabin one more time.

But there was no sign of Jesse.

And Ian found himself praying that his brother would be safe so that one day he could have what Ian had found with Sarah and Ben.

Peace. Love. Family.

.   .   .

Sarah sat in the rocking chair as she read the story of Christmas while Ben snuggled next to Ian on the sofa. When she finished, she pulled the gift she'd gotten for Ben out from the hiding spot behind the pile of wood. "Merry Christmas, Ben."

"A present?" Ben's eyes widened with excitement and he jumped off the sofa to cross over to her. "For me?"

"Yes."

He quickly tore off the wrapping paper, letting out a squeal of glee. "A remote control truck!" he crowed. "Can I play with it Mom? Please?"

"Sure," she said, glad she'd purchased a pack of batteries too. She sipped her cider while Ian helped Ben get the truck out of the package so he could insert the batteries.

"Here you go," Ian said, handing Ben the remote. "Be careful that you don't break anything."

"I won't," Ben promised, moving the lever to make the truck race across the room. He followed, making the truck spin in circles and then sending it tearing off into the bedroom.

"Why don't you sit over here?" Ian suggested, patting the sofa.

She set her cider aside and went over to sit beside him. When he wrapped his arm around her shoulders, she leaned against him. "This is the best Christmas ever," she murmured.

"Really? Even though David found you?" Ian asked.

"Yes. We're finally safe now that he's back in jail." She inhaled Ian's musky scent. "And I'm thrilled to be here with you."

"I didn't get you a gift," Ian said.

She tipped her face up to his. "Spending time together is the only gift I need."

"Sarah," he murmured before lowering his mouth to hers in a soft kiss.

She reached up to pull him closer, trying to show him how much she cared. She was lost in his kiss for a long moment before Ian lifted his head.

"Sarah, I love you so much." Ian said, tucking a strand of her hair behind her ear. "I know it's probably too soon for you, after everything you've been through with David, but I need you to know how I feel."

Her heart swelled with joy. "I'm glad, Ian, because I love you too. More than words can say."

Ian's smile slowly faded. "That makes me happy, Sarah, but I can't ask for anything from you until I know what my future holds."

"Don't be ridiculous. I don't care about your job. Besides, if that sheriff of yours has a brain, he won't let you go. You were honest and upfront with him about your brother. And you did your job, even while you were suspended."

Ian shook his head. "There's that stubborn streak again. Funny, I don't remember that from ten years ago."

She wrinkled her nose at him. "I've always been stubborn; you were just too nice so there was nothing to argue about."

Ian chuckled and then shifted in his seat to cup her face in his hands. "I love you, Sarah Miller. And I hope that one day you'll do me the honor of becoming Sarah Kramer."

Tears pricked at her eyes. "That depends. Me and Ben are a package deal."

"I'm counting on it," Ian said, leaning forward once again, to seal his promise with a kiss.

EPILOGUE

E *ight weeks later...*

I̤AN̤ H̤EL̤D̤ one of Ben's hands, with Sarah holding the other, as Ben skipped between them. They'd just come from church and were stopping by the post office to pick up his mail before heading home.

Sarah had become his wife ten days ago, on Valentine's day, and they were now living in Ian's cabin. They were having one of the worst winters on record, but even that hadn't put a damper on his spirits.

Ian knew he was the luckiest man alive. Sheriff Torretti had taken his suspension off his record and had given him his former shift back, so he wasn't working graveyard any more. Sarah was working as a nursing assistant at the hospital, and Ben was flourishing in his new school.

And he'd started the process of formally adopting Ben as his son.

The only shadow hanging over him was that there had been no sign of Jesse since the incident with the Christmas tree ornament.

"Can we get ice cream?" Ben asked.

"Ben, it's only ten degrees out here," Sarah protested. "How about hot chocolate instead?"

"How about a hot fudge sundae?" Ben countered.

Ian bit his lip to keep from laughing. He knew that kids needed structure and discipline. He tried hard not to interfere with the way Sarah raised her son. But the way Ben tried to use logic to get his way always cracked him up.

"No ice cream," Sarah said firmly.

They walked into the post office, stomping their feet to get the snow off. Ian took off his gloves to get the key to his post office box and then went over to get his mail.

When he opened the box, he found the usual bills and junk mail, along with a postcard.

He frowned and turned the postcard over, but the side where messages where normally written was blank. Only his name and address were neatly printed on that side.

Along with a postmark out of Alberta, Canada.

What in the world? He flipped the card back over to peer again at the glossy photo. There was a lake surrounded by forest and the words Lake Louise, Canada.

Jesse. This was his brother's way of letting him know he was still alive and had made it to Canada.

Was he trying to get to Alaska, the way he'd wanted to? Maybe. Or maybe he'd stay in Canada.

Ian couldn't help feeling relieved as he tucked the postcard into his coat pocket. At least he knew that Jesse was safe.

And maybe being free to live off the land would heal

him better than being in jail or in a psych hospital ever could.

He walked over to join Sarah and Ben.

"Ask your father," Sarah said with a sigh.

"Dad, can we please have ice cream?" Ben begged. "Mom says it's too cold."

Ian knew he'd never get tired of hearing Ben call him dad. He glanced at Sarah who shrugged, as if to say it was his call.

"It is too cold. No ice cream, but we'll stop at Rose's Cafe for hot chocolate, okay?"

Ben groaned but didn't complain as they made their way back outside.

Sarah surprised him by pulling him down for a quick kiss. "Thank you," she murmured.

"For what?" Thinking was impossible when she kissed him like that.

"For being the best husband and father."

"Always," he promised before he kissed her again.

Yeah, he was the luckiest guy in the world. And he vowed to never take his family for granted.

IF YOU ENJOYED THIS STORY, please check out the first chapter for the last book in my Crystal Lake Series, Second Chance.

SECOND CHANCE

1

———

Sheriff's deputy, Devon Armbruster, half-carried half-dragged the highly intoxicated Jimmy Campbell into the ER of Hope County Hospital. This was the third time in the past eighteen months that he'd pulled Jimmy over for driving without a valid license and driving under the influence.

"Gotta get home," Jimmy mumbled as he tripped, and would have fallen flat on his face, if Dev hadn't been hanging onto him. "Sally's gonna be mad."

Yeah, that was a massive understatement. Especially since Jimmy wasn't going home anytime soon. He was going to spend time in jail, and considering this was Jimmy's third offense, he was looking at a good six to twelve months behind bars.

Devon held onto his temper with an effort. After losing his fiancée to a drunk driving accident five years ago, he didn't have a lot of patience for Jimmy's plight. Although Dev was glad he'd pulled Jimmy over before he'd hurt anyone unlike the person that had taken his fiancée's life.

Dev shook off the flash of anger and helped Jimmy over to the desk.

"We're here for a legal blood draw," Dev said to Eve, one of the ER nurses who glanced over when they walked in.

"Take room three," she said with a wave of her hand. "I'll be right over."

"Can I call Sally? Please?" Jimmy asked, slurring his words. "Gotta tell her I'm sorry."

"Not yet, but soon," Dev promised.

Thankfully Jimmy wasn't an angry or belligerent drunk, so Devon didn't need back-up to get the legal blood work that would prove what he already knew, that Jimmy was well beyond the legal limit.

It was frustrating to arrest the same people over and over again. As much as he'd enjoyed living in the small town of Crystal Lake, Wisconsin, lately he didn't feel as if he was making enough of an impact here.

Not compared to his older brother, Steve Armbruster, who had assisted in breaking up some serious crime rings in Milwaukee, before he'd lost his battle with pancreatic cancer.

What would be Dev's legacy? Nothing close to his big brother's, that was for sure. His brother's death six months ago had spurred him into action. He'd applied for jobs within several big city police departments.

So far, no one had called to follow up on the applications he'd submitted in both Madison and Milwaukee. Maybe he'd have to go out a little farther, for example the Twin Cities. He'd rather avoid Chicago, but maybe he was being too picky.

Shaking off his maudlin thoughts, Dev tried to focus on the issue at hand. Eve came and drew Jimmy's blood, putting the vial in the chain of custody kit so it could be submitted as legal evidence.

"No problem."

Dev looked down at Jimmy who was slumped over in his seat, snoring loudly. Obviously, getting him outside and into the back seat of his squad wouldn't be easy.

"Help! Please, help!"

Dev glanced over in surprise to find Janelle Larson, one of the ER nurses, dressed in street clothes, and rushing into the arena holding a young blond haired boy in her arms. "Sebastian is running a fever of a hundred point four despite acetaminophen."

Dev frowned, wondering what was going on. He'd always had a soft spot for Janelle, especially after the way she'd taken care of him two years ago when he'd been shot in the line of duty. There wasn't anything but friendship between them though, since she'd been seeing some guy, whose name escaped him at the moment. Larry? Lance? Something like that.

Dev quickly cuffed Jimmy to the chair, just to be sure he didn't try to leave on his own, and then followed Janelle. Not to intrude, but to offer support if needed.

"Let's get him into a room," Merry Crain, one of the ER nurses said in a calm, soothing voice. "Dr. Gabe is here, and will be in soon."

"I'm Sebastian's legal guardian. He has kidney failure and receives peritoneal dialysis three times a day," Janelle said, a worried frown furrowing her brow. "I'm afraid his catheter site might be infected."

"Let me get a quick set of vital signs, okay?"

Janelle nodded and moved to the side so that Merry could examine the boy. Dev stepped up beside her.

"Hey, are you alright?" he asked in a low voice. "Is there something I can do to help?"

Janelle swung around to look at him, her eyes bright with tears. "Hi Devon, thanks for the offer. Sebastian has already gone through so much, more than any four-year old should have to endure. I can't bear the thought of anything happening to him."

"Try not to worry, you know better than anyone the staff here will take good care of him. Isn't Sebastian your sister's son? When did you become his legal guardian?"

Janelle swiped away her tears and shrugged. "Since Lisa died three weeks ago. Sebastian's father lost his parental rights about a year after he was born, and I have to say I'm glad he's been locked up in jail."

His heart squeezed in sympathy. "So of course you stepped up to take the little guy."

She sniffled and nodded. "The state social workers were so glad, because I'm a nurse and wasn't put off by his medical issues. It's been a steep learning curve, but so far we're hanging in there."

Dev couldn't imagine what it must be like to become a mother overnight, not to mention for a child with medical needs. For a moment the night he'd lost Debra flashed in his mind. She'd been pregnant when she was killed in the head-on collision. In fact, if the baby had survived, the child would be close to the same age as Sebastian.

He swallowed hard and pushed the painful memories away. This wasn't about him, but about Janelle. And he owed her for saving his life. "Are you sure there's nothing I can do for you?" he asked. "Do you have someone helping you?"

Janelle flashed him a lopsided smile. "Thanks, I appreciate the offer. But we'll be fine."

The way she avoided his direct gaze gave him the impression there was something she wasn't saying. "Why are you here alone? Where's your boyfriend?"

She lifted a shoulder in a careless shrug. "Lane wasn't interested in sticking around once he knew that I was taking custody of Sebastian. Which is fine with me, things weren't all that great between us anyway. Sebastian and I are better off without him."

Dev reined in a flash of anger. No doubt she was better off without the idiot, but still, talk about being cold and callous. Turning your back on a sick four-year old? What was up with that?

Before he could say anything more, Dr. Gabe Allen came into the room. Dev backed off so that Janelle could participate in the conversation about the boy's medical care.

"We'll send a culture from the peritoneal catheter site, give him another dose of acetaminophen, and then start some IV antibiotics," Gabe said. "I'd like to keep him here in the hospital overnight so that we can watch him closely for the next twenty-four hours."

Janelle nodded. "Okay, but I plan to stay here with him."

"Of course, that's no problem," Gabe assured her.

Dev watched as Janelle moved closer to Sebastian, bending over the side rail of the gurney to talk to him in a low reassuring tone. With Sebastian's blond hair the exact same shade as Janelle's, they looked enough alike to make the average person think they were mother and son, instead of aunt and nephew.

Glancing at his watch, Dev was glad to see the time was almost eleven-thirty at night, which meant his shift was just about over. He'd drive Jimmy to jail, then maybe come back, see if there was anything more he could do for Janelle and Sebastian.

Just as friends. Despite the fact that Janelle wasn't seeing that jerk of a boyfriend any more, Dev was in no position to get emotionally involved. There was more at stake than his plans to move to a big city police department.

Unfortunately, Janelle and Sebastian were a painful reminder of everything he'd loved and lost.

JANELLE CAUGHT a glimpse of Devon leaving the ER with an obviously intoxicated Jimmy Campbell. It had been nice of Dev to come over to offer support.

She closed her eyes for a moment, praying for strength. Leaning on God and faith would help her get through this. She loved Sebastian very much, but that fact alone hadn't made the transition of becoming a mother overnight any easier.

For the first few days, Sebastian kept asking about his mommy, and no matter how many times she explained that his mommy was up in heaven, he didn't seem to grasp the concept. Finally she bought a stuffed angel and convinced him that his Mommy was an angel in heaven. Sebastian had calmed down after that, and slept with the angel every night. Janelle wasn't sure if the fact that he'd stopped asking about his mother was a good thing or not.

She bent down to press a kiss on his soft hair, breathing in the sweet scent of baby shampoo. He was such a good little boy, tolerating his peritoneal dialysis treatments better than she'd ever expected. Surely he'd pull through this latest threat without a problem.

When Merry returned to start Sebastian's IV, Janelle's stomach clenched at the realization she'd have to help hold him down. Funny how different it was to be on this side of the bed. Usually, she was the one urging parents to help hold their kids during medical treatments.

"Shh, Sebastian, it's okay. I'm here. It won't hurt for long," she whispered as Merry inserted the catheter.

Sebastian's crying ripped at her heart, making her eyes well in sympathy. She hated knowing that he had to suffer more pain on top of everything else.

"All done," Merry said cheerfully, once the catheter was in place and the IV fluids running.

"No more ouchies," Janelle murmured to Sebastian.

"Nana," he whispered, cuddling close.

She held him for a few minutes, until the trauma of being stuck with a needle passed. Sebastian used to call her Nanelle, but since she'd taken custody of him, he'd shortened it to Nana. She didn't mind in the least.

In fact, she hoped one day he might call her mama.

"Anything else?" Merry asked as she adjusted the rate of his IV fluids.

"No, but go easy on the fluids, remember he has kidney disease," Janelle warned.

"I haven't forgotten, but fluids are key to battling infection. We may opt to do an extra exchange if necessary."

Janelle bit her lip and nodded. Of course Gabe and Merry knew what they were doing. When had she become such a worry wart?

Since taking custody of Sebastian, she tried to tell herself to back off a bit, but then something like this happened, and she was right back to where she'd started. She was so afraid of doing something wrong, of failing as Sebastian's surrogate mother, the biggest, most important role of her life.

She couldn't stand the thought of anything bad happening to Sebastian. She loved him so much. In just three weeks she'd found she couldn't imagine her life without him.

After about fifteen minutes Sebastian finally drifted off to sleep. His forehead still felt too warm, but she hoped his fever would come down once the fluids and antibiotics kicked in.

She stroked a hand over his hair, then made sure the side-rails were locked on the gurney, before sinking into a chair and wearily rubbing her eyes. Sebastian had been fitful all day; she probably should have realized there was a problem sooner, but the catheter site had looked fine until the last exchange, right before bed. She'd never expected that the small amount of redness could become a raging infection so quickly. She was a nurse, but had needed to read up on kidney failure, to make sure she was well versed in Sebastian's treatment plan.

For some reason, she felt woefully inadequate to be Sebastian's guardian. She tried to tell herself that her nursing background was a bonus, and other foster parents couldn't provide the same care she could. At times like this, though, it was easy to have self-doubts. Especially since she still had a lot to learn about the nuances of Sebastian's kidney failure.

"Everything okay in here?" Merry asked in a whisper.

Janelle raised her head and forced a smile. "Sure, we're fine."

"Phoebe will be your nurse on the night shift," Merry whispered. "She'll be in shortly."

Janelle nodded, knowing they were in good hands. All the nurses in the hospital were great at their jobs. One of the things she enjoyed most about working here was the easy camaraderie amongst the staff, even the physicians. That hadn't been her experience at the large Madison hospital where she'd worked prior to moving to Crystal Lake.

Sebastian was on the kidney transplant list, which meant either moving back to Madison or enduring long commutes back and forth for treatment after his transplant. A problem she didn't want to think about at the moment.

Her stomach rumbled with hunger and she remembered she hadn't eaten much more than the low sodium soup she'd tried to get Sebastian to eat for dinner.

The cafeteria was closed for the night, though, so her only option was vending machine food; not the least bit appealing.

Sebastian moaned in his sleep, and she shot to her feet, crossing over to make sure he was all right. Was it her imagination or did his forehead feel a bit cooler?

She straightened out the IV tubing then bent over to brush a kiss across his temple, her heart aching for him. He had endured so much adversity in his short lifetime. She prayed again, this time for Sebastian to heal quickly and for the possibility of a kidney transplant, one he so desperately needed.

There was a soft tapping on the doorframe, causing her to glance over her shoulder. She'd expected Phoebe, but it was Devon who stood there dressed in casual clothes: well-worn blue jeans and a soft long sleeved T-shirt, instead of the brown uniform he'd worn earlier. He was handsome no matter what he wore, with his thick dark brown hair, broad shoulders, and deep brown eyes. Something she hadn't really noticed until just this minute.

A realization that caught her off guard.

What was wrong with her? Sebastian was fighting off a life-threatening infection and she was thinking about how handsome Devon looked. She should be ashamed of herself.

"Hungry?" he whispered, holding up the bag. "I brought enough for both of us."

Touched by his thoughtful generosity, she nodded. "Yes, but how did you know?"

He shrugged and gestured for her to come out of Sebastian's room. "I feel bad eating in front of him, maybe it's better if we head down to the cafeteria." His voice went up on the end, as if he were asking a question.

She hesitated, then shook her head. "How about the ER staff break room? That way I won't be too far away if Sebastian needs something."

"Sounds good." Devon smiled and gestured for her to lead the way toward the break-room.

As they passed by the central nurse's station, she caught a glimpse of Sebastian's night nurse, a pretty girl with dark hair and wide light gray eyes. "Hey, Phoebe, Sebastian is sleeping. I'll be in the back room if you need anything."

"Sounds good. We're working on getting him an inpatient bed. I'll let you know once we have one assigned."

"Thanks." Janelle darted around the nurse's station to the small break-room located in the back corner of the ER.

"Do you want the cheeseburger or the chicken sandwich?" Dev asked, when they were seated next to each other at the table.

She lifted a brow. "I'm fairly certain you want the cheeseburger, right?"

"I like them both," Devon said firmly. "Seriously, you pick."

"I'll take the chicken sandwich," she said.

"Are you sure?"

"Yes, I was just giving you a hard time." She picked up

the sandwich and silently thanked God for providing them with food, before taking a healthy bite. "Hmm, this is great. How did you know I was hungry?"

"I assumed that taking care of a sick kid would be time consuming and that you might not have remembered to eat dinner. Besides, I was hungry, too."

Janelle stared down at her sandwich for a minute, before raising her gaze to meet his. "It was nice of you to think about me, Devon," she said in a soft tone. She couldn't remember the last time anyone had done something nice for her. Certainly not Lane, since he'd always been primarily concerned with himself. Something that should have clued her in much sooner than it had.

"You're welcome," he responded lightly, although his intense gaze held hers for a long second.

Flustered, she pulled her gaze away and focused her attention on eating, knowing that she couldn't afford to read attraction into Devon's kind gesture. He was being a good friend, nothing more.

She didn't have time for anything else, even if she wanted to get involved in another relationship. Which she didn't.

Nothing was more important than Sebastian's health and well-being. Certainly not her personal life.

The little boy deserved every ounce of her attention, and then some. Maybe she hadn't helped as much as she should have while Lisa was still alive, but she was bound and determined to make up for her lapse in judgment now.

No matter what the cost, personally or professionally.

2

Devon tore his gaze from Janelle's, staring blankly down at his cheeseburger for a long moment. What was wrong with him? Why was he suddenly so acutely aware of Janelle?

And where on earth had that flash of sizzling attraction come from?

He gave himself a mental shake, trying to get things back on an even keel. He needed to stop thinking about how beautiful Janelle looked and concentrate on keeping her in the friend category."So how long do you think your nephew will have to stay in the hospital? Did Dr. Gabe give you any sort of timeline?"

Janelle let out a heavy sigh. "I'm not sure, I'm hoping he'll be able to kick this infection pretty quickly. But that might be simply wishful thinking since Gabe mentioned there is a possibility of Sebastian needing surgery."

"Surgery?" he echoed with a frown. "For what?"

"He has a catheter in his abdomen which is what I use to infuse his peritoneal dialysis solution. If the infection in the catheter site doesn't clear up, they may need to put in a new one."

"Poor little guy," Dev murmured. He wasn't an expert on medical issues, but obviously, the boy's condition was more serious than he'd realized.

"Yeah, I know." Janelle set her chicken sandwich down, as if she'd lost her appetite. "And if that happens, he might need to go on hemodiaylsis, which is something I can't provide for him at home. He's not having any significant problems as a result of his peritoneal dialysis, and I've heard the side effects are worse with hemodialysis. I guess at this point, all I can do is hope and pray he gets the opportunity for a kidney transplant, soon."

Devon glanced up in surprise, somehow he hadn't known that was an option. "I take it you're not a match?"

Janelle shook her head slowly. "No, although you have no idea how much I wish I were. Apparently he's blood type B negative, which is relatively rare, something heinherited from his father."

Devon scowled. "And his father won't donate?"

Janelle grimaced. "His father used to be an IV drug addict, so he's not eligible to donate. Which is fine, since I don't really want Sebastian to have anything to do with his father. I don't trust Grant one bit. He's in jail because he physically abused Lisa and Sebastian, then took all her money and valuables. I'm afraid if he gets out of jail, he'd only try to use the situation to his advantage."

Devon shook his head. Hard to believe how much little Sebastian had the deck stacked against him. "I'm sorry, Janelle. All of this must be tough to deal with."

She abruptly straightened in her seat and picked up her sandwich with determination. "I'm fine and so is Sebastian.

I firmly believe God is watching over us. Sorry if I was wallowing in self-pity there for a minute."

"You weren't," Dev protested, impressed with her inner strength and fortitude. He wasn't so sure he believed God was watching over her, though. Debra had believed in God, but that hadn't prevented her from dying too soon, taking their unborn child with them.

They ate in silence for a few minutes, before one of the nurses poked her head into the break room.

"Janelle? Sebastian's been assigned a room on the third floor. I've already called a report up to Shannon, the nurse who will be admitting him. We're pretty much ready to leave as soon as you are."

"I'm finished," Janelle said, jumping to her feet and quickly wrapping up what was left of her sandwich. "I'll eat the rest, later."

Devon rose to his feet, wishing there was more he could do for her. "Please call me if there's anything else you need," he murmured.

"Thanks Dev." She gave him a brief hug before turning to follow Phoebe towards Sebastian's room.

He watched her from the doorway, the faint citrus scent of her still clinging to his skin. He told himself that he should go home and get some rest. But for some reason, he couldn't seem to force his feet to move.

He stayed right where he was, watching as both Janelle and the gurney carrying Sebastian moved out of sight.

JANELLE DIDN'T GET much sleep that night, waking up every couple of hours when the nurse came into the room to check on Sebastian. His fever broke about six in the morning, which was a huge relief.

But she knew the little boy wasn't out of danger, yet. The fact of the matter was that he was four and a half years old and no matter how many times she told him to leave the catheter alone, she still found him picking at it, sometimes unconsciously.

Was Sebastian destined to have more infections then? If so, then maybe hemodialysis was a better option. She'd be willing to do whatever it took, even driving an hour one way to Madison three times per week.

"Nana, I'm hungry."

"Okay, let's order breakfast, shall we?" She was glad Sebastian was hungry. "What would you like? French toast sticks?"

"Yeah!" Sebastian nodded eagerly.

She placed a double order, so that she could share with him, and then decided she may as well give up on getting any more sleep. Besides, nothing else mattered as long as Sebastian was feeling better.

She was washing up in the bathroom when Sebastian's physician arrived. When she heard talking out in the room, she tossed down her hairbrush and quickly joined them.

"Hi, I'm Janelle, Sebastian's guardian," she introduced herself.

"Dr. Rawlings, nephrology specialist," he said giving her hand a shake. "I see you recently transferred Sebastian's care here."

She bit her lower lip and nodded. "I live here and work here, so I thought it was best to transfer his care. Why, is that a problem?"

"Not a problem, exactly, but you do realize if a kidney becomes available, you'll need to take him to Madison."

"Yes, I'm aware of that," Janelle said, meeting Dr. Rawlings serious gaze with one of her own. "However, I was led to believe it could take years before a kidney might become available."

"True, blood type B negative is a difficult match," Dr. Rawlings agreed. "And Sebastian isn't very high on the list at this point, since he's been tolerating peritoneal dialysis so well."

"I don't necessarily agree," Janelle said, trying not to display her frustration. "He's only four and keeping his catheter site clean is a challenge."

She thought Dr. Rawlings would argue, but he nodded his agreement. "I know, and I'm sure you're doing the best you can. But the fact is, his kidney failure just isn't bad enough right now to move him up the list."

She was glad Sebastian's kidney failure wasn't that bad, but the thought of waiting years for a transplant was just as daunting. She let out a heavy sigh. "I understand. What about hemodialysis? Is that an option?"

Dr. Rawlings hesitated, then shook his head. "I'm afraid not. Again, his creatinine, BUN, and electrolytes just aren't bad enough for that either. Truly his best option is to continue with peritoneal dialysis."

"All right," she murmured, determined to do whatever was best for Sebastian.

"Has the fluid been dwelling in his abdomen all night?" Dr. Rawlings asked.

"Yes. I was waiting for you to arrive before draining the fluid in case you wanted to see it."

"Great, then let's take a look, shall we?"

Janelle washed her hands and then manipulated the peritoneal dialysis catheter so that the fluid that was in Sebastian's abdominal cavity could drain out. This was the least invasive of the treatments available for kidney disease, and while it wasn't at all difficult, she still hadn't found anyone willing to do the task while she was at work.

"Looks good to me," Dr. Rawlings said, as the clear yellow fluid drained into the bag.

"Do you think we need to send it for culture?" Janelle asked.

"No need, probably won't grow anything with the antibiotics on board but I'd like him to get one more dose of IV antibiotics before you head home."

"Home?" Sebastian echoed, his attention momentarily deviating from the Disney channel when he heard the doctor's news. "We get to go home?"

Janelle's heart swelled at the excitement in Sebastian's eyes. She was so glad he was settling into his new life here in Crystal Lake. She sat down on the edge of his bed and gathered him into her arms. "Yes we do. Isn't that great news?"

He nodded and nestled against her. "After breakfast?" he asked.

"Maybe after lunch," Dr. Rawlings corrected as he logged into the computer to write his note.

"But that means I can't go to school," Sebastian protested, his lower lip trembling.

"Today is Saturday, there's no school on Saturdays remember?" Janelle reminded him. She was glad that Sebastian liked the four-year old kindergarten program she'd enrolled him in. The hours worked perfectly with his dialysis schedule, and so far the kids seemed to have accepted him, catheter and all.

"Can I play wif my friends?" he asked.

"We'll see," she promised, hoping that one of the little boys who lived close by might be able to come over for a few hours at least.

"Any other questions?" Dr. Rawlings asked as he logged off.

"No, I don't think so," Janelle said slowly. "He was so sick last night, I'm amazed at how well he's doing this morning. And I was afraid he'd need a new catheter."

"Kids are pretty resilient," Dr. Rawlings said. "They get sick fast, but then get better fast, too. Still, I'd keep a close eye on his temperature for the next few days, just in case. And make sure you give him all the oral antibiotics until they're gone."

"I will, thanks." When she was alone in the room with Sebastian, she tried to think of how she'd manage when she had to return to work next week. She'd used up every vacation day she had, and had dipped into her meager savings account too. Even if her boss did extend her leave of absence, how much longer could she go without a paycheck?

Not very long, that was for sure.

She closed her eyes and took several deep breaths, reaching out in prayer. God would show her the way. She just had to trust in Him and continue following His path.

When breakfast arrived a few minutes later, a sense of peace settled over her. Watching the way Sebastian dug into his meal with enthusiasm was enough to make her smile. Obviously Dr. Rawlings was right. Amazing how quickly Sebastian had returned to his old self.

The day shift nurse came in to check on Sebastian's abdominal dressing and to do a brief assessment. "Are you feeling better, Sebastian?"

He nodded, his eyes glued to the Disney movie on the television hanging on the wall.

"He's much better, thanks," Janelle said. "Dr. Rawlings mentioned being discharged after lunch."

"He gets his last dose of antibiotic around one o'clock, so as soon as that's infused you'll be able to take him home on oral medication."

"Sounds good," she agreed, even though she knew it wouldn't be easy to get Sebastian to take the oral medication in liquid form.

Shortly after the nurse left, there was another knock at the door.

"Come in," she called.

Her jaw dropped when she saw Devon enter the room, smiling sheepishly as he carried a huge box. "Hi," he greeted her awkwardly.

"Hi, what's in the box?" She rose to her feet and crossed over to greet him, surprised he'd come back to visit.

"This is a Play-Station that I had lying around, thought Sebastian here might be able to use it."

"Play-Station?" Once again, Sebastian's attention was pulled away from the television. "Can I see it?"

"Absolutely." Devon pulled the console out of the box and handed over the remote controls. Janelle didn't know much about how they worked, but clearly Sebastian knew all about them as he helped Devon put the pieces together.

"There, now you're all set," Devon declared with a grin.

"Aren't you gonna play with me?" Sebastian asked.

Devon glanced at her, with a questioning look in his eye.

"It's okay if you have things to do," she said, letting him off the hook. "I'm sure Sebastian can teach me how to play."

"I don't have to work until later this afternoon," Devon said in a low voice. "And I'm happy to play with Sebastian for a while if you have errands or something that you need to get done."

His generosity was touching. And even though he was giving her some free time, at the moment she couldn't even think of one thing that needed to be done. "Thanks Devon, I'm sure Sebastian would love to play with you for a while."

"Okay, Sebastian pick your game and I'll take you on."

"Goody!" Sebastian jumped up and down on the bed with enthusiasm. "Mario! I wanna play Mario!"

"You got it," Devon said picking up the game and inserting it into the console. He pulled up a chair next to Sebastian's bed and within minutes the two of them were in the throes of the video game.

Janelle ran her fingers through her hair, feeling self-conscious. Maybe she should take advantage of Devon being here with Sebastian. She could run home, take a shower and change out of her wrinkled clothes.

It took her a minute to realize that she secretly wanted to look nice for Devon. Which was ridiculous. He was here out of friendship, after all, she knew only too well that men weren't interested in a woman who happened to be the legal guardian to a young boy with special medical needs.

So instead of running home, she stayed where she was, curled up on the sleeper sofa that doubled as a twin bed for parents staying overnight. She dozed off for a while, startling awake when the nurse came into the room, interrupting the marathon game.

"Time for Sebastian's peritoneal dialysis exchange," Andrea announced.

Janelle rubbed the sleep from her eyes. "I can do it," she said stretching out her cramped legs.

"No!" Sebastian shouted, his gaze glued to the game. "Don't wanna do my exchange. Me and Dev are playing a game."

"We can pause the game, Sebastian," Devon explained in a low patient voice. "We'll start right back up where we left off."

"Don't wanna," Sebastian repeated stubbornly.

Janelle stepped forward, putting a reassuring hand on Sebastian's back. "Come on, Sebastian, you know doing the exchange only takes a few minutes."

Devon hit the pause button, despite Sebastian's protest. "You need to listen to your Aunt Janelle, Sebastian."

Ironically, the authoritative tone in Devon's voice worked. "Okay," Sebastian repeated reluctantly.

"Game time is just about over anyway," Janelle said as she set out the supplies she'd need. "We need to eat lunch and then once you get your last dose of antibiotic we can go home."

"Hey, that's great news," Devon said. "That means no surgery, right?"

"Right." She concentrated on making sure she didn't contaminate the catheter tip as she connected the new peritoneal dialysis solution so that it could slowly infuse into Sebastian's abdomen. A process that didn't hurt him at all, so normally he never seemed to mind.

Janelle was keenly aware of Devon's gaze watching her. She'd done this exchange three times a day for the past three weeks, but her fingers suddenly felt awkward and clumsy.

"So the fluid stays in his abdomen for the next few hours?" Devon asked, the expression on his face showing genuine interest.

"That's right," she said with a smile. "Then we drain out the old fluid and infuse a new bag that dwells overnight. Since Sebastian's kidneys don't work as well as they should, this helps draw toxins out of his blood stream."

"Amazing," Devon murmured.

She finished her task and then cleaned up the supplies

and washed her hands. "What would you like for lunch, Sebastian?"

"Chicken fingers," the boy said automatically picking his favorite.

"Why did I bother asking?" Janelle asked with a sigh. She glanced at Devon. "We're allowed to order parent trays, I'm happy to share one with you."

"No thanks, I ate a huge breakfast before I came and I like to eat just prior to the start of my shift. But please, eat something. You didn't get much last night."

The memory of the simple meal they'd shared in the break room of the ER flashed in her mind. The sudden intimacy that sprang between them had lingered in her mind, long after he was gone.

She ordered a salad, and when their food arrived, Devon still didn't show any sign that he intended to leave. Not that she wanted him to, but still, she felt bad taking up all his free time.

When the nurse came in to hang Sebastian's antibiotic, she glanced at her watch. "Good news, Sebastian. We'll be able to head home in less than an hour."

"Great, we'll have time to play one more game," Devon said, settling back in his seat.

"You don't need to stay, I'm sure you have other things to do."

Devon shrugged. "I'll follow you home that way I can connect the game console to your television for you."

"Oh, no, I couldn't possibly accept such an expensive gift," she protested.

Devon raised a brow. "It's not a gift, I'm letting you and Sebastian borrow it for a while. My nephews are older now and it's not doing any good sitting at the bottom of my closet."

How could she refuse to allow Sebastian to *borrow* the game? Very simply, she couldn't. "Thank you," she murmured.

The hour flew by and soon they were packing up to leave. Janelle tucked the bottle of oral antibiotic solution in her purse, as Devon packed the game back into its box.

She felt bad taking Devon out of his way, but since she had no clue how to set up the game, there wasn't much she could do about it. "I live in the Crain's townhouse just off Main Street," she told him, as they walked out into the bright April sunshine. The air was a little cool, but she was thrilled that spring was on the way. "I rent one side, but the other side is empty at the moment. The doctor who was living in the other side just bought a house."

"I know exactly where the townhouse is," Devon said. "I'll meet you there."

She was blessed to have such good friends in Julie and Derek for letting her rent the townhouse, and in Devon who had gone out of his way to support her with Sebastian. For the first time since Sebastian's fever had risen out of control, she felt optimistic about the future.

This was what she loved most about living in Crystal Lake. The sense of community; everyone helping each other as needed.

It took a few minutes for Janelle to get Sebastian secured in his car seat, so when she headed home, she wasn't too surprised to see that Devon had beat her to the townhouse.

When she pulled up the driveway, Devon approached her vehicle, a frown deeply furrowed in his brow. "Janelle, I need you to stay inside the car, okay?"

"What? Why?" She craned her neck in an attempt to see around him.

"Someone broke into your house," Devon said in a grim tone.

"What? Are you sure?"

"Yes, I am. Sorry, Janelle, but it looks like you've been the victim of a robbery."

3

———

"A robbery? Someone broke in? Why?" Janelle's horrified facial expression tore at his heart. After everything she and the boy had been through, this was the last thing she needed.

Devon flashed a reassuring smile. "I don't know, but please stay here, okay?" He glanced at Sebastian who was looking a little sleepy. "I don't think anyone is still hanging around, but it would be best to make sure."

"Alright," Janelle agreed, her expression troubled.

He stepped back from the car, shaking his head and wondering why bad things always seemed to happen to good people. He turned and walked back up to the front porch.

Devon carefully examined the smashed door frame, taking care not to touch anything. It looked as if the door knob had been smashed with a blunt object, like a baseball bat or a hammer.

Or the heel of someone's boot. To be honest, the door-jamb wasn't the sturdiest he'd ever seen. There wasn't a lot of crime in Crystal Lake so nobody really paid for high level security systems.

Although it would have been nice if Janelle had used the dead bolt.

Still, he knew that if someone really wanted to get inside, they'd find a way. Either through the patio doors overlooking Crystal Lake or through a window. Kids? Maybe. He'd know more when he was able to investigate what was taken.

Either way, being robbed was hardly Janelle's fault.

He scowled and raked a hand through his hair. There hadn't been any reports of robberies discussed in their roll call yesterday, but he imagined there would soon be others. These types of home invasions tended to happen in clusters, especially if teenagers were involved.

Thankfully, Janelle and Sebastian hadn't been home. Just the thought of what might have happened if they had been brought a flash of anger.

The wail of sirens echoed through the air, indicating reinforcements were on the way. Good thing, because he was having a hard time playing the civilian role.

He wished he had his weapon, but he'd left it at home. He knew the hospital wouldn't allow him to carry it inside since he wasn't officially on duty. Besides, carrying a gun around a four-year old wasn't smart.

When Deputy Zack Crain pulled in behind Janelle, Dev walked down to meet him. Zack was Julie Crain's brother and the two of them owned the side-by-side townhouses, even though neither one of them lived there any longer. Zack and Merry had gotten married about eighteen months ago and now lived on the other side of the lake.

"What happened?" Zack asked with obvious concern.

"I don't honestly know. Janelle spent the night at the hospital with Sebastian, so she wasn't here. I was planning to meet her here, and arrived first. That's when I found the front door smashed in."

"Sebastian? Is he okay?" Zack asked, crossing over to peer into Janelle's back seat. He waved at the little boy who glanced up at him with a tired smile.

Dev couldn't help wondering if the child was tired from the peritoneal dialysis treatments or if this was just a normal part of having kidney failure? "He's fine, although you should probably get all the details from Janelle."

As if on cue, Janelle slid out from the driver's seat. "Hi Zack. Can I go inside to see what, if anything, was taken?"

"Not yet, but soon," Zack promised. "Just give us some time to make sure it's safe, okay?"

"Why would anyone pick my place to rob?" she asked, rubbing her hands over her arms as if chilled. "I don't have anything worth stealing."

"I'm sure it's nothing personal," Zack assured her.

"Have there been other reported robberies?" Dev asked.

Zack hesitated and shook his head. "Not that I'm aware of. But maybe others haven't been noticed yet either."

Dev nodded, and couldn't help thinking the timing of the robbery was significant. Janelle and Sebastian had been gone for roughly sixteen hours, and it was likely that the break-in had happened sometime during the night or the early morning.

Or was it possible the crook had watched her leave the house with Sebastian and then took advantage of the fact they were gone to rob the place?

He scowled, not liking that scenario.

"Let's go," Zack said, clapping Dev on the shoulder.

Dev followed his colleague into the house, sucking in a harsh breath when he immediately noticed the empty spot where the television had probably been.

Zack whistled under his breath. "I hope Janelle has good insurance."

Yeah, somehow Dev wasn't so sure she did, but he didn't say anything as they continued sweeping through the townhouse. It didn't take long to verify the place was empty.

"I'll get Janelle," Dev offered, heading back outside. The moment he stepped out on the porch, Janelle stepped forward, holding Sebastian in her arms.

"I'm sorry, but your television has been stolen," Dev said, wanting to warn her. "The good news is that the robbers didn't trash the place."

Janelle nodded, although she went pale when she saw the missing television. "It wasn't even an expensive one," she said in a low voice.

"Anything else missing?" Dev asked.

She nodded slowly, tears welling in her eyes. "My notebook computer. And my router."

Devon hated seeing her so upset. "You might want to check your room, in case any jewelry is missing."

She sucked in a quick breath and rushed into her bedroom. Dev watched from the doorway, battling a wave of helplessness.

"Lisa's ring is gone," Janelle whispered, lifting tortured eyes to his. "The only thing I had that belonged to my sister. I was saving it for Sebastian."

Dev didn't know what to say to make things better. He crossed over and put a reassuring arm around her shoulders, grateful when she leaned against him.

He silently vowed that he'd do whatever was necessary in order to find the jerk who did this.

. . .

JANELLE LEANED AGAINST DEVON, mentally as well as physically exhausted. She couldn't believe Lisa's ring was gone. It wasn't super expensive, but it was gold and had a ruby stone, the birthstone shared by both Lisa and Sebastian.

"Nana? Can me and Dev play Mario again?" Sebastian asked in a plaintive tone.

She swallowed hard and straightened up, knowing she couldn't afford to lean on anyone, no matter how nice Devon had been over the past twenty-four hours. "I'm sorry, but we don't have a television. It's broken," she added hastily, unwilling to give Sebastian a reason to be afraid.

His tiny brow puckered in a frown. "Who breaked it?"

"Hey, how about I bring my television over for a while?" Devon offered. "I can't use it while I'm at work anyway."

Janelle began to shake her head, but Sebastian's face lit up with excitement. "Goody," he cowed, bobbling up and down in her arms to the point she had to bend over and set him on the ground. "Go get it, Dev. Go get it!"

She wanted to protest but sensed that would be a fruitless endeavor. "Thank you, Devon," she said in a soft tone. "I'm not sure why you're being so nice to us, but I want you to know how much I appreciate it."

Dev shrugged, the tips of his ears turning red with embarrassment. "It's really not a problem, but I don't like leaving you here alone with a broken front door."

"I've already called Frank from the hardware store," Zack said entering the room. "He's on his way to fix it, until I can get a new door in." He glanced at her and took out a small notebook. "I'll need a list of everything that's missing."

"I'll be back in a few minutes," Devon promised, leaving

the room. Janelle had to fight back the urge to beg him to stay.

Ridiculous, really, for one thing Zack was also a cop and a great guy. For another, he happened to be her landlord. She gave herself a mental shake, chalking up her wacky emotions to a night without much sleep.

The list of missing items was pathetically short, and when Zack asked the name of her insurance company, she was forced to admit she didn't have renter's insurance.

Zack groaned. "I don't think my insurance is going to cover your things," he informed her.

"I understand," she hastened to assure him. "It's my fault, Zack, I certainly know better. It's just that I've been more focused on my sister and Sebastian..." her voice trailed off on the pathetic excuse.

The truth of the matter was that even though renter's insurance wasn't expensive, she hadn't been able to afford it. Not when she wasn't working nearly as many hours as she used to.

Zack sighed and turned away. "Okay, I have someone coming to dust for finger prints on the area around the door, where the television was, your computer and the jewelry box."

"Sounds good." Janelle forced a smile. "Thanks again for coming so quickly."

"It's no problem, after all, I don't like the thought of anyone breaking into my townhouse any more than you do," Zack admitted. "Crystal Lake is normally a safe place to live."

Janelle nodded in agreement, because the small town family atmosphere was one of the main reasons she loved living here. "Well, I'm sure you'll find out who did this."

"How is Sebastian?" Zack asked as they walked back into the main living area.

"He's fine, had a little infection but is already doing much better." She eyed the clock, making a mental note to give her nephew his antibiotic at dinnertime.

Zack's phone rang and he stepped away to answer it. Janelle could tell he was talking to his wife, Merry, and she couldn't help the ping of envy at the love that shone brightly between the two of them.

An old rusty blue pick-up truck pulled to a stop in front of her house and she smiled when she saw Frank Gebheart get out from behind the wheel, his tool belt cinched tightly beneath his round belly.

Zack finished his call and strode out to meet with Frank, making it clear what he needed done. Soon her small town-house was full of people, techs dusting for fingerprints, Frank hammering on the door, and Devon setting up his wide screen television along with the video console in the space where her smaller TV once sat.

The entire process didn't take long. The crime scene techs and Frank left first, followed by Zack. Devon had returned already dressed in his uniform so he could head directly to work.

"Thanks again," Janelle murmured as he handed Sebastian the hand-held controller.

"Not a problem," he assured her with a smile. Their eyes locked and just like the night before, she found herself mesmerized by the intensity of his gaze.

She forced herself to look away, afraid he'd notice the longing in her eyes. "Well, at least I know the robbers won't be back since they've already taken everything of value."

Devon scowled as he headed for the door. "Trust me, I'll

be driving by frequently throughout my shift to make sure they don't."

"Thanks." She stood by the door, watching as Devon strode confidently toward his cruiser. The way he tipped his hat to her before sliding in behind the wheel made her blush with awareness.

Watching him drive away, she felt more alone than ever.

DEV HATED LEAVING Janelle and Sebastian in the townhouse, even though logically he knew they'd be perfectly fine after the repairs Frank had done to the front door.

Roll call didn't take long and he was disturbed to hear that Janelle's place was the only reported break-in. They were lucky to get some fingerprints, but it would take a while to get them processed through the database.

The only other item of interest was a small bag of crystal meth that was found in the bathroom of the school. Dev couldn't deny the fact that the two incidents could very well be related. Drug addicts were known to steal anything in sight in order to support their habit.

He hated the thought of drugs being brought into their small town. Of course, drugs were just about everywhere, so he couldn't say he was completely surprised.

Once roll call was over, he headed outside to his vehicle and made his usual sweep of the lake. They didn't have a huge influx of tourists yet, that would come in the summer months. Although they used to get hikers, but they'd dwindled off since the big fire along the hiking trail last fall.

Dev was glad to see that there were signs of spring. Some slender seedlings were sprouting amidst the blackened soil. It would take several years for the trees to grow back, but at least the process had started. And the woods overshadowing the north side of the lake were miraculously untouched.

As he drove around the area, he couldn't help thinking about what Janelle and Sebastian were up to. He liked the idea that the two of them were sitting and playing his game on the television he'd loaned them.

If anyone deserved a break, they did.

The hours seemed to drag by more slowly than usual, and when it was time for dinner, he had to force himself not to drive straight to Janelle's townhouse.

Instead, he pulled over to park on Main Street and headed into Rosie's diner. Josie, the owner and waitress hailed him from the doorway.

"Hey, Dev, should I get you a plate of the usual?"

Since his usual was the special pot roast, potatoes, and carrots, he nodded. "Absolutely, thanks."

Josie placed his order then came over with a pitcher of water, filling his glass for him. "I heard about the break-in at the Crain place. Do you have any suspects yet?"

He shouldn't have been caught off guard at her blunt question. Josie was the town gossip, and he often wished the police network was as good as the town grapevine.

"Not yet, but we'll figure out who's responsible, don't worry." He purposefully infused confidence into his tone. The last thing they needed was for the town folk to go into panic mode.

"Such a shame," Josie went on. She set down the pitcher and propped her hand on her hip. "To think that someone would take a television away from a young child and a sickly one at that! What is this world coming to?"

He didn't have a good answer and honestly, Josie didn't need one.

"Well, I sure hope you find that no-good son-of-a-gun as soon as possible."

"That's the plan."

Josie glared at him for a moment, then grabbed the pitcher of water and swept away. But before he could relax, she came back, this time carrying a large plastic container.

"Dev, I need you to take this over to Janelle and Sebastian for me."

He eyed it warily. "What's inside?"

She rolled her eyes. "Fried toad-skins." When he blinked in shock, she roared with laughter. "Tonight's special, on the house. Will you take the time to run it over to her?"

How could he say no? "Of course, Josie. It's nice of you to think about them."

"They're one of us, and we take care of our own." With that, Josie disappeared back behind the counter.

Devon couldn't deny that he'd miss this place if he ever did get a response from one of his applications,but carrying food to a young mother in need and trying to find kids who were breaking into empty homes to steal or doing drugs wasn't exactly what he had envisioned for the rest of his life, either.

He wanted to fight real crime, to make a difference. The same way his older brother Steve had.

By the time he finished his meal, dusk was falling over the horizon. He carried the heavy container of Josie's special outside, and decided it would be easier to walk the couple of blocks to Janelle's townhouse than to drive over.

As he approached her townhouse, he noticed a dark silver sedan parked on the other side of the road. He frowned, trying to see if the car was empty, when abruptly the headlights flashed on, momentarily blinding him.

He shielded his face, and tried to catch the license plate

number, but was a second too late. The car backed up, turned around and quickly disappeared around a curve.

A chill snaked down his back. Was he imagining things? The actions of the driver seemed suspicious. Had he parked there in order to watch Janelle's house?

And if so, why?

4

Janelle was thrilled to see that Sebastian seemed to be doing so well, he'd been so enthralled in his game that he hadn't even asked for a friend to come over.

She'd finished cleaning up the mess the crime scene techs had left behind and now stood in the kitchen, trying to think of something to make for dinner. Her fridge was pretty empty, she'd need to grocery shop in the morning. A loud knock at her front door startled her from her thoughts, and she took a moment to put a hand over her racing heart, before crossing over to peer through the window to see who was out there.

"Devon?" she asked as she opened the door. She tried to squash a wave of pleasure at seeing him again. "What are you doing here?"

He lifted a container. "Josie sent you a healthy serving of her Saturday night special."

"Pot roast?" she asked with a smile, opening the door and gesturing for him to come in.

"Yep."

"Dev!" Sebastian abandoned his game to come rushing over to greet his new hero. "Did you come to play wif me?"

"I'm sorry, Sebastian, but I'm working tonight," Devon said. "Are you hungry? I brought dinner."

"Will you stay to eat with us?" Sebastian asked.

"Sweetie, Devon already told you he's working," Janelle quickly interjected. "But if you eat all your dinner and take your medicine, I'll play another game with you before bedtime."

"Okay," Sebastian agreed, although she could tell the little boy was still disappointed that Devon wasn't going to stick around.

"Janelle, do you know anyone who drives a silver sedan?" Dev asked as she carried Josie's container of food into the kitchen.

She glanced at him in surprise. "No, why?"

He shrugged and shook his head. "No reason, I don't want to alarm you."

She stared at him. "I'm already scared, Devon so just spit it out already. Why are you asking about a silver car?"

He winced. "I'm probably making a big deal out of nothing," he warned. "But I noticed a silver car parked across the street from the townhouse. Could be someone staying at the Crystal Lake Motel, though."

She shivered and tried not to let her imagination run wild. "The motel has a parking lot, why would they choose to park along the road?"

"Listen, just ignore me," Devon said, rubbing the back of his neck, looking embarrassed. "I'm sure it's nothing. I promised you I'd drive by frequently and I will continue to do that. No need to worry."

Janelle wished it was easy to shut down the worry gene, but unfortunately it seemed that she'd only gotten worse in the weeks since she'd taken custody of Sebastian, rather than better. "I'll try," she said, trying to hide the doubt in her tone.

"I'm sorry, Janelle," Devon said with a grimace. "I shouldn't have mentioned it."

She lifted her troubled gaze to his. "There's no reason for the robbers to come back here, right? This wasn't a personal attack against us."

"Absolutely not," Dev assured her. He crossed over and put his arms around her in a quick hug. It disturbed her how much she longed to lean against him, absorbing his strength. "Don't think about it, okay? I promise to watch over your place."

It was on the tip of her tongue to point out that he wouldn't be on duty twenty-four seven, but she forced a smile and stepped back. "I appreciate your support, Dev."

"I only wish I could do more," he said in a serious tone. "Call me if you need anything."

"I will," she agreed although she knew that Devon had certainly done enough for her and for Sebastian. She walked him to the door, sneaking a glance up and down the street to make sure there weren't any strange cars lingering.

Which of course there weren't.

"Where's your car?" she asked with a frown.

"I walked over from the café," he said. "I'll see you later," he said as he walked back out toward the road.

She lifted her hand in a nonchalant wave as Devon glanced back at her, then closed the door, locked it and shot the dead-bolt home.

The rest of her evening flew by, and soon she finished infusing his last bag of peritoneal dialysis. She quickly cleaned up the supplies and then crossed over to tuck Sebastian into bed.

"Are you ready to say your bedtime prayers?" she asked, sitting on the edge of his bed.

He nodded, pressing his tiny palms together and squeezing his eyes shut. "God bless Nana, Devon, and my angel Mommy," Sebastian said sleepily. "Amen."

"Amen," she echoed, blinking the moisture from her eyes. She leaned down to press a kiss on Sebastian's forehead and when his arms wrapped tightly around her neck, she pressed him close, savoring the embrace.

"I love you, Sebastian," she whispered in his ear.

"I wuv you, too, Nana."

In that moment all her fears about her finances, her job, even being the victim of a robbery, flew right out the window. Nothing was more important than this little boy. Sebastian was a precious gift she'd cherish forever.

"Goodnight," she said when he finally drew away.

"G'night," he answered, turning over and throwing his arm around his stuffed angel.

Janelle made sure the nightlight was glowing in the corner of his room before she left, leaving the door ajar the way he preferred.

A wave of exhaustion hit hard, reminding her that it had been a long day and that she hadn't had much sleep the night before. Even though it was early, she moved through the townhouse, shutting off the lights and double checking the locks on her doors, before getting ready for bed.

As she walked past the living room window, a pair of headlights coming down the street made her stop abruptly, her heart leaping in fear. But then they passed by without stopping.

Idiot, she admonished herself. There was no reason to be afraid.

Devon would protect her.

.   .   .

Considering it was Saturday night, Devon was glad things weren't too busy. He'd been called to a fight at Pete's Pub, but by the time he'd arrived, the two men had been separated by the townsfolk, leaving him with nothing more to do than to take care of the paperwork. He didn't hesitate to issue assault and battery charges and disorderly conduct charges to both men, one sporting a black eye, the other a fat lip.

Apparently they'd been fighting over a woman, who'd wasted no time in high-tailing it out of the place once the fight broke out. Not that he blamed her.

Devon dutifully filled out the paperwork, and then made sure both men were sober enough to drive themselves home. He also jotted down their license plate numbers along with the make and model of their vehicles, just in case.

Not that he suspected either one of them of being the perp who'd performed the robbery. Still, it didn't hurt to be cautious.

He felt terrible for scaring Janelle, earlier. He'd driven by her townhouse several times and hadn't seen anything the least bit suspicious. He shouldn't have mentioned the stupid car, especially when he hadn't gotten a good look at it anyway.

As the end of his shift approached, Devon took one more leisurely drive down Main Street, making sure things were quiet and peaceful before heading to the Sheriff's department headquarters.

He headed home and changed his clothes, but wasn't the least bit tired. Moving restlessly around his house, he found he couldn't settle down.

Logically he knew Janelle and Sebastian weren't in danger. He'd imagined the driver of the silver car was staking out her townhouse. And there really wasn't any reason for the robber to return.

So why couldn't he relax?

Dev forced himself to climb into bed, where he tossed and turned for the next hour. Finally he gave up. He threw on a comfy sweatshirt and jeans before heading back outside to his personal vehicle.

He drove back to Janelle's townhouse, reassured that all was quiet. The windows were mostly dark, although there was a dim light coming from Sebastian's room.

He pulled in front of her house and shut off the engine. The spring air was a bit cool, but not enough to bother him. He ratcheted back his seat and stretched out, making sure he could see her front door.

Dev let out a pent up sigh, feeling calmer now that he was close at hand, on the off-chance that Janelle would need him. He told himself he wouldn't stay too long, just long enough to unwind after his shift.

The stars twinkled overhead and he couldn't help remembering the way Debra had believed God was watching over them from the heavens.

It had taken him a long time to realize the pain of losing her and their unborn child wouldn't ever go away completely. Granted he didn't think about them every day, not any more.

But there were times like this, when he felt alone in the world that the bitter-sweet memories would return.

He tore his gaze from the velvet-black sky and looked over at Janelle's townhouse.

Letting go of the past wasn't easy, but he knew he needed

to keep focused on the present and on dedicating his life to making a difference in the world.

Janelle woke up early, feeling refreshed after having a decent night's sleep.

She couldn't hear any sound from Sebastian's room and quickly freshened up in the bathroom, enjoying a few moments of privacy. Not that she resented caring for her nephew, but becoming a full time mother had been a bit of an adjustment.

Okay, make that a massive adjustment.

She ran a brush through her hair and then headed into the kitchen to start a pot of coffee. Sebastian would be up soon, the kid had an amazing internal alarm clock, and she began to make a mental list of things she needed to get done.

Making breakfast and attending church were her priorities, followed by grocery shopping if they wanted anything to eat for the rest of the week. But then she really needed to figure out a daycare situation of some sort in order to return to work on Monday morning.

She headed into the living room to tidy up the controllers from Devon's play-station, in case he wanted to come and pick it up in the near future. Glancing out the front window had become a nervous habit and when she noticed a black truck sitting directly in front of her house, she stifled a scream.

The robbers were back!

She rushed to the front closet and pulled out a baseball bat. She yanked open the front door and rushed outside, prepared to scream loud enough for the entire Crystal Lake population to hear her.

"Leave us alone!" she shouted brandishing the baseball bat like a sword. "The police are on the way!"

To her horror the driver's side door popped open and a dark haired man climbed out. "Janelle, calm down. It's me, Devon!"

"Dev?" She stood there for a moment, as the fear drained away leaving her feeling weak and foolish. Then she got mad. "What are you doing here? You scared me to death!"

"I'm sorry," he said holding his hands up as if to reassure her he wasn't armed. "Did you really call the sheriff's department? If so, we'd better let them know it's a false alarm."

She slowly lowered the bat, letting out her breath in a sigh. "No, I didn't call them. I reacted without thinking."

He opened his mouth as if to chastise her, but then closed it again. He scrubbed his hands over his face and for the first time she realized he must have been there all night.

"Why in the world did you sleep in your car?" she asked, truly bewildered. Hadn't he told her she wasn't in danger? Or had something happened late last night?

"I didn't mean to fall asleep," he admitted with a self-depreciating smile. "I only intended to be here for a couple of hours."

"So you didn't see anything suspicious?" she pressed, needing to know the truth. Heaven knew, she'd already planned to be on the alert for any sign of a silver car following her.

"Nothing," he said with confidence. "And really, I'm sorry I scared you."

"Well, since I scared you, too, I think we're even." She gestured toward the townhouse. "I have coffee if you'd like a cup before heading out."

His face broke into a relieved grin. "I would love some coffee. Cars are not meant for sleeping, that's for sure."

She laughed and shook her head. "I still can't believe you did that."

"Me either." He came up beside her and gently pried the bat from her clenched fingers. "You really should have called the police first," he murmured.

She sighed. "Yeah, I know."

Their arms brushed as they headed inside and she tried to tell herself that the tingling sensation was nothing more than her overactive imagination. She headed into the kitchen and pulled two coffee mugs out of the cupboard.

"Cream or sugar?" she asked, glancing at him over her shoulder. Her breath caught in her throat at how handsome he looked standing there with his shadowed jaw and sleep tousled hair.

Whoa, what was wrong with her? She needed to stop thinking of Devon as a man she was interested in. He was simply a good friend, nothing more.

"Black is fine," he said, his gaze lingering on hers. Was it her imagination or was there a flicker of awareness in his eyes?

"Dev!" Sebastian said in excitement as he padded into the room, clutching his stuffed angel like a lifeline. "You came back!"

She tried to hide a wince, certain that it hadn't been Devon's intention to be sucked back into another game with Sebastian.

"Sure did," Dev said with a broad smile. "But I think you have a few things to take care of first, don't you?"

"No I don't," Sebastian said defiantly.

"I'm pretty sure you need to drain your peritoneal dialysis first and then eat breakfast, right Janelle?"

She was amazed he remembered. "That's right. I need you to lie down on the sofa for a little while to drain while I make breakfast."

Sebastian's lower lip trembled. "I don't wanna."

Her heart ached for the little boy, but at the same time, she knew she needed to be firm, for his own good.

"Come on, champ, I'll sit next to you for a while," Dev offered.

"Really?" Sebastian's blue eyes instantly brightened. "Why can't we play a game while I'm draining?"

Dev glanced at her curiously and she lifted her hands up in a helpless gesture. "No reason, I guess. Does this mean you want to stay for breakfast?" she asked.

"I don't want to put you out," he hedged. But she had to smile when the rumbling in his stomach gave him away.

"Can we have French toast?" Sebastian asked as he climbed onto the sofa and obligingly stretched out giving plenty of room for her to access his catheter.

"Sure," she agreed. She pulled out the necessary supplies and then returned to the kitchen to wash her hands. She was keenly aware of Devon watching her every move. He gave the impression that he was truly interested, not simply gawking as she opened the clamp to allow the fluid in his abdomen to drain.

"I'm amazed that something so simple can be lifesaving to a child," Dev said in a low voice.

"It really is incredible," she agreed. "And it's not that difficult to do the exchanges. Unfortunately, the concept still scares people off."

He frowned. "So who watches him while you're at work?"

She bit her lower lip and shrugged. "No one yet," she said, avoiding the full story of how she was out of paid time off allowed under the family/medical leave act. She didn't want to dump her problems on Devon, so she quickly turned and headed into the kitchen to start breakfast.

She enjoyed listening as Dev and Seb played video game as she cooked. This was what how she imagined her life would be like with Lane. Only he hadn't wanted anything to do with her young nephew.

His loss, but she couldn't deny his rude departure still rankled. Being angry at him was useless, but she was upset with herself for wasting the last year of her life dating him. Lane hadn't been worth five minutes of her time, but obviously she'd been blind to his faults.

When she finished with the French toast, she washed her hands once again and went back over to disconnect Sebastian's drainage bag. She expected Dev to be disgusted by the yellow fluid filling the bag, but as before he intently watched everything she was doing.

"Just give me a few minutes, and we can eat breakfast," she said, carrying the bag toward the bathroom.

When she emerged a few minutes later, she was surprised to see that both Devon and Sebastian were in the kitchen waiting for her. She'd already washed up, so she pulled out her chair and sat down.

"I'm hungry," Sebastian said, eyeing up the stack of French toast.

"We need to pray first," she reminded him. Devon looked surprised, but he took his cue from Sebastian, clasping his hands together and bowing his head. "Dear Lord, we thank You for this wonderful food we are about to eat. We ask that You watch over us and guide us on Your chosen path as we begin our day, Amen."

"Amen," Sebastian and Dev said simultaneously.

She smiled, pleased at their response.

"When are you scheduled to go back to work?" Dev asked, as he held the plate of French toast out for her.

"Tomorrow morning. But I'm sure I can get one of the nurses I work with to cover my shift if I can't find someone to watch Sebastian."

"I'll do it," Devon offered.

Her mouth dropped open in shock and she wondered if she'd really heard him correctly. "Do what?"

"I'll watch Sebastian tomorrow. I have Monday and Tuesday off work, so it's no problem."

She was stunned speechless by his generous offer. As much as she didn't want to take advantage of Devon's friendship, she also knew that she needed to get back to work in order to pay her next month's rent.

"I don't know what to say," she finally managed. "Are you serious?"

"Absolutely. I've been watching you and it doesn't look that difficult to do his exchanges. Of course, I'll need to practice, but I'm sure I can manage."

Janelle stared at him for several seconds. Was Dev's offer an answer to her prayers? Or a complication she couldn't afford?

She was afraid she'd end up depending on him, far more than she should.

5

Devon watched the play of emotions across Janelle's face, wondering if he'd overstepped his bounds.

Why had he offered to babysit anyway? Just looking at Sebastian made his heart ache for what he'd lost. Before he could try to backpedal, she slowly nodded.

"All right, then. Thank you, Devon."

"You're welcome." He stared down at his plate of French toast for a moment before picking up his fork. Two days wasn't the end of the world. He just needed to help her out until she found someone to watch Sebastian on a regular basis.

"Yay! I get to play with Dev!" Sebastian shouted.

"That's right, but now it's time to eat breakfast, okay?" Janelle said. "And then we have to get ready to go to church."

Dev shouldn't have been surprised by the announcement, after all, most of the town went to church on Sunday. He swallowed hard, wondering if she expected him to come along.

He hadn't been inside the church since Debra's funeral.

"Dev?"

He jerked his head up, realizing Janelle had been talking to him. "I'm sorry, what did you say?"

She tipped her head to the side, regarding him thoughtfully. "I asked if you were working again today."

"Yeah, I'm on duty tonight, starting at three in the afternoon. That's the main reason I have the next two days off."

"I work the early shift on Monday and Tuesday, seven to three-thirty, so you'll still have some time to relax." She paused, then continued, "I owe you, big, Devon. I'm out of paid leave and really need to work to avoid going into debt."

The puckered frown in her brow made him glad he'd impulsively offered to help. "It's no problem, Janelle. You don't owe me anything, you saved my life two years ago, remember?"

"The doctors saved your life," she corrected with a smile. "I just helped."

He clearly remembered the way she'd held onto his hand in the ER, talking to him and reassuring him that everything would be okay. Yeah, the doctor's skills had helped, but emotionally, he'd clung to Janelle's voice like a lifeline.

"Are you going to come to church wif us?" Sebastian asked around a mouthful of food.

"Chew and swallow first, then talk," Janelle told him.

Dev felt trapped by Sebastian's wide blue eyes. He hadn't intended to attend church services, but then again, he needed to learn how to do the peritoneal dialysis exchanges too. It would look pretty obvious if he left before church and then came back afterwards.

"I'm sure Devon has things he needs to get done before work," Janelle said, giving him an out. The intensity of her gaze, as if she knew exactly why he didn't want to attend, made him feel vulnerable.

Janelle had been here in Crystal Lake long enough to know he'd lost his fiancée. But she'd never asked him about his loss.

And no one knew that Debra had been pregnant. He'd never told anyone about that fact.

"I, uh, don't know," he hedged. What was wrong with him? Why hadn't he taken the excuse Janelle had offered?

"Finish your breakfast, Sebastian. We have to infuse another bag through your catheter before we go."

"Okay," Sebastian agreed, popping another large bite of French toast in his mouth, smearing maple syrup across his chin.

Dev was impressed at how well the boy accepted the treatments he needed to have—what had Janelle said—three times a day.

"More coffee?" Janelle offered, rising to her feet and walking toward the pot.

"Yes, please." Sitting at the kitchen table, sharing a meal with Janelle and Sebastian gave him a pang in the region of his heart. This was what he should have had with Debra and his own son or daughter.

No point in looking backward besides, this cozy family scene wasn't what he wanted anymore. He needed to make a difference in the world. He wanted to fight crime and to help keep cities safe for other kids.

The same way his brother had.

When breakfast was finished, he stood and then carried his dirty dishes over to the sink. He hid a smile when Sebastian copied his actions, even though the little boy couldn't even reach the counter.

"Thanks Sebastian," Janelle said, taking the plate from

him. She took a clean dishcloth and efficiently wiped down the child's sticky hands and face. "Time for your medicine."

Sebastian scrunched his face into an expression of distaste. "Do I hav'ta?"

"Yes," Devon spoke up firmly. "No games until you take your medicine."

Sebastian gamely swallowed the thick liquid, wrinkling his nose at the taste before dashing into the living room.

"I'd like to watch the exchange," Dev said.

"Watch?" She echoed, lifting a sardonic brow. "You need to actually practice doing the exchange."

He knew she was right. "Okay, but you're going to walk me through it, right?"

"Of course." She rinsed the dishes and set them in the dishwasher. "Wash your hands and I'll show you how to set up the supplies."

She talked him through the entire process and his fingers felt large and clumsy as he disconnected the catheter and hung a new bag.

"The biggest threat is infection," she said quietly. "That's why you have to be careful not to contaminate anything."

Remembering how sick Sebastian had been made him realize just how high risk this process really was. Oh, it didn't look complicated, but one wrong move could cause a life threatening infection. He held his breath as he worked, feeling a bead of sweat trickling down the side of his face. He didn't breathe normally until he was finished.

"Good job," Janelle said. "Now open the clamp on the tubing, just part way because if the fluid runs in too fast it will cause stomach cramps."

He carefully adjusted the flow and then stepped back, curling his fingers into fists to stop his fingers from shaking.

He felt as if he'd run five miles. He wiped the sweat from his brow with the edge of his sweatshirt.

"How long will it take to run the fluid in?" he asked.

"Sebastian tolerates about an hour." She gathered up the empty wrappers and carried everything over into the kitchen.

"Can we play a game while I'm waiting?" Sebastian asked in a plaintive tone.

"Sure, why not?" He shot a quick glance over at Janelle. "That is, if your Aunt Janelle doesn't mind."

"One game," she cautioned, giving Sebastian a stern look. "Just remember, we have to leave for church once the fluid has infused."

"I know," Sebastian said. "Let's play the racecar game!"

Dev didn't mind playing video games, but as they raced around in their respective cars, he couldn't help wondering if it was okay for Sebastian to play outside. Granted he knew that the child probably shouldn't run around too much, considering the fluid that would be dwelling in his abdomen, but surely he could play on a swing-set and maybe play catch.

He made a mental note to ask Janelle since the weather was predicted to be decent over the next few days.

After forty minutes, Janelle returned to the kitchen wearing a knee-length tangerine skirt and matching sweater. He was so distracted by how pretty she looked that he crashed his racecar into the wall.

"I win, I win!" Sebastian shouted.

He blinked, and hoped the back of his neck wasn't too red with embarrassment. "You sure did."

Janelle crossed over to check Sebastian's infusion, seemingly unaware of how she'd managed to cause him to lose the game. "Just a few minutes to go. Then you'll need to get dressed for church."

Sebastian gazed up at him with his wide blue eyes so much like Janelle's. "I want Devon to come to church with us. Please?"

He hesitated and then nodded, unable to refuse the child's simple request. "Okay, I'll come with you. But then I need to get home, okay?"

"Goody!" Sebastian beamed, as if he'd been given a precious gift. Dev shoved his misgivings aside. If going to church with them brightened this kid's day, then it was worth braving the shadows of his past.

Janelle walked him through the rest of the procedure and then sent Sebastian to his room to change.

"You really don't have to go," Janelle murmured once they were alone.

He searched her eyes, trying to read her thoughts. "Would you rather I didn't?"

"Of course not, I'd love for you to attend services with us. I just don't want you to think you have to do every little thing Sebastian asks of you." She hesitated, then added, "I want him to have as normal a life as possible and that means not always getting what he wants."

"I get what you're saying," he agreed. "But it seems like such a little thing to do to make him happy."

She regarded him steadily. "And what about doing what makes you happy?"

He found it difficult to tear his gaze away. Somehow, Janelle seemed to look all the way through him, down to the center of his soul. "I think it's time I put the past to rest, don't you?"

She smiled, her entire face lighting up. "I'm so glad to hear you say that, Devon. God has been waiting for you."

He wasn't so sure, but Sebastian returned just then preventing him from needing to answer. He glanced down at his own attire, knowing he couldn't show up in worn jeans and sweatshirt.

"I'll meet you there, okay?" he said as they walked outside. "I need to change my clothes."

"No problem," she agreed, opening the car door so Sebastian could climb into his booster seat.

Devon slid in behind the wheel and headed home. Without giving himself time to change his mind, he quickly donned a button-down shirt and dress slacks. He couldn't remember the last time he'd dressed nice for a woman.

Not that he was dressing up for Janelle. No, he was only going with them to service because of Sebastian.

Yeah, right. Who was he kidding?

He was going to church with Janelle and Sebastian because he wanted to. For the first time in almost five years, he wasn't allowing sorrowful memories of Debra to hold him back.

In fact, he felt certain that spending time with Janelle and Sebastian would create new memories.

And oddly enough, he found himself looking forward to them.

JANELLE WASN'T sure if Devon would really meet them at church or not. She knew he hadn't been to church in several years, and had been surprised that he'd agreed to come at all.

Obviously he hadn't wanted to disappoint Sebastian. She was troubled by the way her nephew had glommed onto Dev, idolizing him. She told herself it was good for

Sebastian to have a male role model, especially since his father wasn't allowed anywhere near him.

But she couldn't help thinking that Sebastian would be hurt once Dev moved on. She'd heard through the town grape-vine that he was applying for jobs outside of Hope County.

Not that Devon's career choices were any of her business. Still, he'd become so close to Sebastian in such a short time. The child would be devastated once he left.

She really needed to find someone else to babysit Sebastian while she was at work. Dev could help her out for the next couple of days and she had Wednesday off. But then she needed to figure something else out.

The sooner, the better.

"Hi Janelle, hi Sebastian," Merry Crain greeted her cheerfully as they approached. "Looks like you feel much better, young man," she said addressing Sebastian.

"Yep," the little boy nodded. "All better."

"Will you be at work tomorrow?" Merry asked.

"Yes, I have day care set up for Monday and Tuesday," she agreed. "But I still don't have anyone regular lined up."

"Something will work out, you'll see." Merry only worked very part-time because of her own baby. She swapped child care with her sister-in-law, Julie Ryerson.

"I'll keep praying," Janelle said. "Come on, Sebastian, let's go inside."

"We hav'ta wait for Dev," the little boy protested, hanging back.

"Devon Armbruster?" Merry echoed, her eyebrows lifting in surprise. "He hasn't been here in a long time."

"I know, and I'm honestly not sure if he'll make it after all." Janelle glanced down at Sebastian. "How about we go inside and save him a seat?"

Sebastian reluctantly went along with her plan, dragging his feet. Several pews were already full, so she slipped into an empty space near the back.

The organist was playing a soothing hymn and she closed her eyes, letting the music wash over her. Instantly she felt a sense of peace, as if God had lifted each heavy burden off her shoulders.

She silently prayed that God would send her someone to watch over Sebastian so she could return to work. And she prayed that Sebastian would stay healthy, getting the kidney transplant he needed. Lastly, she prayed Devon would find his way back to church and faith.

Sebastian fidgeted in the seat beside her. Her sister hadn't taken him to church, and learning to sit still and listen was a trial for him.

She reached over to put a hand on his shoulder, trying to tell him without words that he needed to sit still.

It took a moment for her to realize that Sebastian had caught a glimpse of Devon striding toward them. Dev looked so handsome in his charcoal gray button down shirt and black pants, her heart squeezed in her chest.

He flashed her a hesitant smile, and then settled in on the other side of Sebastian. She wanted to reach over and clasp his hand reassuringly, but that wasn't possible with her nephew between them.

She was humbled by his presence, especially after he'd been away from church for so long.

As Easter had just passed, the theme of Pastor John's sermon was life after death. She hoped Devon would find the peace he deserved.

It wasn't easy to concentrate on the service, she must have glanced over at Dev at least a dozen times. The parishioners glanced at them curiously, no doubt wondering if they were a new couple.

She hoped Devon wouldn't mind the rumors that would no doubt ripple through their small town. If he noticed their interest in the fact that they were sitting together, he didn't let on.

The service was over far too soon. She knew Devon had to work, so she steeled herself to say goodbye.

"That was nice," he said as they walked back to their respective cars.

She knew she was grinning like an idiot, but couldn't seem to care. "I'm so glad to hear you say that. I thought maybe you'd change your mind about coming."

His brows pulled together in a small frown. "I told you I would," he murmured. "I keep my promises."

"Are you coming to our house?" Sebastian asked, tugging on Devon's belt loop.

"Devon has to work today, remember?" She didn't want Dev to feel as if he had to keep entertaining her nephew. When Sebastian's face fell, she hastened to reassure him. "But he'll be back tomorrow morning to play with you while I'm at work, okay?"

The little boy kicked a rock and shrugged. "Okay," he agreed, his tone mirroring his disappointment.

Dev accompanied them to her car. "How about I give you a call, later?" he suggested. "We'll finalize things for tomorrow."

"Uh, sure, of course," she said, feeling flustered at the thought of Devon calling her. He pulled out his phone and looked at her expectantly. She rattled off her number and he quickly punched it in.

She licked her lips, and told herself to get a grip. Devon was a friend, nothing more. He was sweet enough to help her out of a jam. She had to stop reading something more into his motives.

"Talk to you later," she said, helping Sebastian get into his car seat.

"Will do." Dev waited until she slid behind the wheel to walk over to his truck.

She wrapped her fingers around the steering wheel, biting back the crazy urge to ask him to come over to spend the rest of the day with them.

Ridiculous since she had to make phone calls to possible babysitters anyway.

It didn't take long to drive back to her townhouse, but as she approached she noticed there was a silver sedan parked on the opposite side of the street, directly across from the townhouse.

The same one Devon had noticed last night?

She lifted a hand to shield the sun, trying to see the plate number. But the vehicle abruptly pulled away from the curb, tires screeching as the driver took off.

Her heart leaped into her throat as she pressed hard on the accelerator.

This time, he wasn't going to get away!

6

———

Janelle was all too aware of the fact that she had Sebastian in the car with her as she tried to close the gap between them.

If only she could get the license plate number!

The silver sedan flew past a stop sign, and Edna Cole, one of the elderly women from their church, lifted a fist and shook it at the vehicle.

Janelle stopped and tapped the steering wheel impatiently as the elderly woman strolled across the street heading toward Rose's café. When the cross walk was clear, she pushed the accelerator, narrowing her gaze as she scanned the area for the silver car.

Her shoulders slumped in defeat when she realized it was gone. No doubt, the driver had taken advantage of her delay at the stop sign to disappear.

With a heavy sigh, she turned around in the parking lot of Pete's Pub and made her way back to the townhouse. When she pulled into the driveway, she was shocked to discover Devon was waiting for them.

"Where did you go?" he asked, as she slid out from behind the wheel.

She hesitated, debating whether or not to tell him. She suspected he wouldn't be happy with her, then again, it wasn't as if they'd been in any danger.

"I saw a silver sedan parked across the street, so I tried to follow." She opened the back passenger door, allowing Sebastian to scramble out.

"You, *what*?" he practically shouted.

"I just wanted to get the license plate number," she said defensively. "But he blew past the stop sign, and I had to wait for Ms. Edna to cross the street, so I lost him."

Dev stared at her for several long moments and she shifted restlessly beneath his glare. "Janelle, please don't do something like that again," he finally said in a soft tone. "You have no idea who that guy is or what he wants. I promise I'll keep an eye on things for you, okay?"

She nodded, but tilted her chin stubbornly. "I know you will, but it is broad daylight on a Sunday afternoon so I highly doubt we were in any real danger."

"Maybe not, but I'd rather you didn't take any unnecessary chances."

Okay, he did have a point. After all, Sebastian had already lost his mother; the poor kid didn't have anyone else in the world but her. "What are you doing here?" she asked, changing the subject.

He rubbed the back of his neck, giving her the impression he was a bit embarrassed. "I just stopped by to practice Sebastian's exchange one more time. You mentioned that he gets one in the early afternoon."

"That's true." She was touched by the fact that Devon was taking his role in performing Sebastian's exchanges seriously. "But we have plenty of time before it's due, so there's no need to hang out here the entire time if you have something else to do."

He hesitated and shrugged. "Nothing more important than this. But I do have a question for you, is Sebastian allowed to play outside?"

She glanced down at her surrogate son. "Yes, he can play outside, as long as he's careful. Running is difficult for him and I wouldn't want him to fall down and injure himself."

"I totally understand, but I was thinking we could maybe walk to the park and swing on the play set." His earnest gaze met hers. "I promise to be careful with him."

Janelle gave herself a mental shake, knowing that she was being over-protective to always think of the worst case scenario. "I trust you, Devon. If you want to walk down to the park with Sebastian I'm fine with that. And I forgot to mention that Sebastian goes to pre-school in the morning, so you'll have to drop him off there after his exchange, around eight-thirty, and then pick him up by eleven-thirty. But that would give you time to head over to the park in the afternoon."

"Great," he said with a relieved smile. "If the weather is nice, we'll give it a try."

Dev's smile transformed his features, making him even more attractive. She tore her gaze away from him with an effort. "Well, looks as if you have everything planned out for tomorrow, then."

"Come on, Dev," Sebastian said, tugging on Devon's slacks. "You said we could play a game."

"We have to check with your Aunt Janelle, first," Devon reminded him.

"Puleeze, Nana," Sebastian begged, his wide blue eyes imploring her to agree.

"All right," she relented. "I have a few phone calls to

make anyway." She was determined to think positively about her chances of securing reliable daycare for Sebastian.

Sebastian let out a whoop of joy, waiting as Janelle unlocked the door before dragging Devon inside the townhouse.

She pulled out a crumpled slip of paper from her purse with a list of names and phone numbers of potential babysitters. One teenage girl in particular had just finished a nursing assistant program and was looking for a part time job. Janelle knew Tina Jamison would be in school during the morning hours, but maybe she could take care of watching Sebastian on the weekends.

Every little bit would help.

But after several calls, she began to lose hope. Tina's mother had promised to pass on the message, but everyone else she spoke to had declined, too afraid of doing the peritoneal dialysis exchanges. One of the older women, Alice, who was a retired nurse hadn't been home, so Janelle had left a message.

She set aside her phone with a sigh and dropped her head into her hands, fighting a wave of despair.

She'd prayed during church, and did so again now.

Dear Lord, please, please help me find a way to provide for Sebastian!

DEV TRIED to concentrate on the game, but he couldn't help overhearing Janelle's failed attempts to line up a babysitter for Sebastian.

Her dejected tone shot straight to his heart and it was all he could do to prevent himself from tossing the controller aside to go over and gather her into his arms.

He forced himself to stay where he was, since he knew that it wouldn't be fair to act on his attraction to her. Especially since staying in Crystal Lake wasn't part of his plan.

But he couldn't deny the need to give her a shoulder to lean on. For her sake? Or his?

Giving himself a mental shake, he tried to think of anyone he knew who might be willing to help out. Getting someone with medical background would be nice, but it wasn't a necessity. Parents without medical background had to learn how to do this kind of thing.

To be fair, he understood the hesitation to take on something as important as performing the child's peritoneal dialysis treatments. He wasn't exactly oozing confidence at the thought of doing them, either.

"Finish up your game," Janelle said, interrupting his thoughts. "We have to get ready to do your exchange."

"No! Don't wanna!" Sebastian argued, his gaze never wavering from the television screen.

Devon hit the pause button, stopping the game. "That's not a nice way to talk to your Aunt," he said mildly.

Sebastian glanced over at Devon, his lower lip trembling. "None of the other kid's hav'ta get exchanges."

His heart squeezed painfully in his chest. What on earth could he say to that? "I know, champ, but you were the one who told me that they didn't hurt, right?"

Sebastian stared down at the controller in his hand. "Right," he mumbled.

Janelle crossed over and dropped onto the sofa beside the child. "Honey, you and I talked about this, remember? We're going to keep praying that God will give you a kidney transplant so that you won't need these exchanges anymore. But until then, this is the best way to keep you healthy so you can play with your friends."

"I know." Sebastian turned and burrowed into Janelle, seeking comfort. She pulled him closer and pressed a kiss to the stop of his head.

Devon couldn't tear his gaze away from the pair, despite how much they reminded him of everything he'd lost. During church services he'd tried to take comfort in the fact that Debra was up in heaven with their unborn child, but it hadn't been easy to let go of the anger at the senselessness of her death.

Why hadn't God spared her life? Why had He taken her away? Dev knew that Janelle would say this was all part of God's master plan, but he wasn't entirely convinced.

Although it had occurred to him that it was possible God wanted him to follow in Steven's footsteps, doing something important to make a difference in the world.

"Ready to do your exchange now?" Janelle asked softly.

Sebastian's head bobbed up and down.

"Great. Stretch out on the sofa and let's see if Dev can remember all the steps."

He groaned. "A test? You're making this a test?"

Sebastian glanced up with a reluctant smile, getting into the spirit of things. "Are you ready?"

"Sure," he said, infusing confidence in his tone. It didn't take him long to set the catheter to drain, that was the easy part. He studied the supplies, trying to remember everything he'd need. He glanced over toward Janelle. "He drains for a half-hour, right?"

"Right."

He played another game with Sebastian while they waited, keeping an eye on the clock. Then he washed his hands again, and began the process of disconnecting the drainage bag. He clamped the open end, then set it aside so he could begin the new infusion. This time wasn't nearly as stressful, and when he finished, he felt a surge of satisfaction. "All set."

"Nice job," Janelle praised him. "You were awesome."

He grinned like a fool, then carried the old bag into the bathroom to dispose of the contents in the toilet. After disposing of the used equipment, he washed his hands again.

"I don't think these hands have ever been so clean," he joked upon returning to the living room.

"Tell me about it, you have no idea how many times I wash my hands at work."

He could well imagine. When he glanced at the clock, he winced. "Listen, I have to run or I'll be late for work."

"I completely understand," Janelle said, rising to her feet. "I'll finish up the exchange, no problem."

He felt guilty for leaving before it was finished, but didn't have much choice. "All right, then. I'll call you later."

"Sounds good." Janelle walked with him to the front door and he noticed she gave a quick glance outside to make sure there were no cars lingering in the street.

"Try not to worry, okay? I'll drive by every hour to check on you."

"Okay, thanks again, for everything."

He didn't want to leave, but forced himself to turn and walk away, her citrusy scent staying with him even after he changed into his uniform.

During roll call, he expected to hear about more robberies, but there was no mention of anything suspicious. In fact, it appeared that other than breaking up a drunk and disorderly and handing out a couple of speeding tickets, nothing much had happened on the previous shift.

Dev knew he should be glad there wasn't a lot of crime in Hope County, especially in the downtown area of Crystal

Lake, but all this proved to him was that he was right to have put in his application at all the big city police departments. He absolutely needed to do something more important with his life than driving around small town, Wisconsin.

Although for some reason the thought of leaving Janelle and Sebastian behind bothered him.

Far more than it should.

JANELLE DIDN'T SLEEP well that night. Not because she was afraid of the silver car, but because she was anxious about leaving Sebastian alone with Devon to return to work.

She loved her job in the ER, and knew Dev was more than capable of doing Sebastian's exchanges. However, she still tossed and turned, waking up to every little noise and glaring at the clock as she ticked off one hour at a time.

At five o'clock in the morning, she gave up trying to sleep. She jumped in the shower and quickly dressed in her forest green scrubs. She pulled her hair back into a pony tail, mostly to keep it out of the way. A patient had once grabbed her by the hair, yanking hard enough to bring tears to her eyes. Not an experience she cared to repeat.

She brewed a pot of coffee and then decided to make breakfast, figuring it was the least she could do for Devon. She owed him far more than she could ever repay, considering he was giving up his two days off to babysit her son.

Her son.

She loved Sebastian more than she thought possible. She smiled as she mixed pancake batter. Hard to believe how much her life had changed in the last month.

For the better.

Granted she still had obstacles to overcome, the largest one being finding a babysitter, but despite the trials she and

Sebastian had been through, she wouldn't give him up for anything.

She poured round circles on the electric griddle and then sipped her coffee as she kept an eye on the pancakes. Glancing at her watch, she wondered if Sebastian would wake up before she had to leave.

The pancakes didn't take long to cook and she stacked them on a plate and covered them with a clean dishtowel to help keep them warm. At six fifteen, there was a soft knock at the door and her heart leapt with anticipation.

Ridiculous, she admonished herself, smoothing her hands over her scrubs before heading over to answer the door. Devon was only here out of kindness, nothing more.

"Good morning," he said, his low husky voice sending a fission of awareness tingling down her spine. He looked amazing, and smelled even better. His dark hair damp from a recent shower and the woodsy scent of his aftershave made her long for something she dared not name.

"Good morning," she responded, striving for a light-hearted tone. "I just finished making breakfast."

"You didn't have to do that," he protested as he crossed the threshold. He sniffed the air and grinned. "Pancakes. Let me guess, another of Sebastian's favorites."

She chuckled. "Of course. I should mention that I have been keeping him on a low salt diet because of his kidneys so that's the only reason I haven't made ham, bacon or sausages for you."

"Am I complaining?" he asked with an arched brow.

"No, you haven't." But Lane had, bitterly. Just another reason she should have gotten rid of him sooner. "Coffee?" she offered, as they walked into the kitchen.

"Sure." He glanced around in surprise. "Sebastian isn't up yet?"

"No, but if he's not awake by six forty-five, you'll need to go in and start draining his catheter. The entire process takes a good ninety minutes."

"Okay, no problem."

She finished her coffee and then set her mug in the sink, feeling self-conscious under his intense gaze. "I'm going to head into work early, if that's okay. You have my cell number, right?" He nodded. "Call me if you have any questions."

"I will," he assured her. "Don't worry, I can handle this."

"I know. Thank you for doing this, I'm not sure how I'll ever repay you."

"No need to repay me," he quickly interjected. "This is what friends are for."

Friends. The word shouldn't have made her depressed. She slipped her purse over her shoulder and headed outside, shoving aside a wave of guilt.

Sebastian and Devon would be fine. She had patients to take care of.

DEVON MANAGED to do Sebastian's exchange, feed him breakfast, get him dressed, and dropped off at pre-school with one minute to spare.

He nearly collapsed in his truck, wondering how on earth Janelle had coped with this all by herself.

Three hours of free time didn't seem like much, but he knew he couldn't afford to waste a minute. He dashed home, threw in a load of laundry and then paid a few bills and balanced his checkbook. Small tasks, but necessary if he was going to spend the afternoon playing babysitter. Two loads of laundry later, he estimated he'd have just enough time to stop at the grocery store for a few basic essentials before he was scheduled to pick Sebastian up again.

He was feeling pretty confident when he arrived at the pre-school with five minutes to spare. So far, so good.

Sebastian came outside with several other boys, and he was glad the kids seemed to accept him as one of their own. Sebastian's face puckered in a frown, but then he noticed Dev and broke into a relieved smile.

"Hey, champ, how was school today?" he asked as he helped Sebastian climb up into his booster seat.

"Good," the boy answered. "Joey's mom is going to take him to the park after lunch, can we go too?"

"Yes, as long as you take your medicine and do your exchange without argument."

Sebastian wrinkled his nose at the medicine, but once they were back at Janelle's townhouse, he swallowed the antibiotic without complaint.

He made Sebastian a grilled cheese sandwich for lunch and then focused on doing the exchange. Dev thought it would be easier without Janelle watching over his shoulder, but he was so afraid of missing a step, or contaminating something, that he kept double checking his work.

"There, all finished," he said in relief. "Once the fluid is in, we'll head over to the park."

"Goody," Sebastian said on a wide yawn.

"Rest for a bit before we go," he suggested. "I have to clean up the kitchen."

The fact that Sebastian didn't put up a fight proved the boy was truly tuckered out. Janelle hadn't said anything about the boy needing a nap, but maybe she assumed he'd know that?

Sebastian dozed in front of the television, but when Dev crossed over to disconnect the bag, his eyes popped open. "Is it time to go to the park?"

He had to suppress a laugh. "Yes, we can go now."

The park wasn't far away, and Dev was glad to see there were other kids playing there, too. Sebastian ran over to meet with his friend Joey.

Dev swept a glance over the area, searching for the silver sedan but didn't see anything. Last night, he hadn't seen the vehicle, either.

The boys played on the swing set and then ran over to the small merry-go-round. "Give us a push, Dev," Sebastian shouted.

He did as they asked, putting a little muscle into it. The merry-go-round spun in a circle and the boys squealed in glee.

"Again! Do it again!"

He spun them around again, but suddenly Sebastian went flying backward, landing on the grass with a thud, and letting out a high-pitched scream.

Dev rushed over, his heart thundering with fear. What if he'd hurt Sebastian?

Janelle would never forgive him.

He'd never forgive himself.

Janelle's shift flew past, one minute she was worried about how Devon was doing with Sebastian, the next she was focused on a steady stream of patients coming in through the ER.

A glance at her watch confirmed that it was well past lunch time, and since there seemed to be a break in the action, she decided to take advantage of the moment to get a bite to eat.

And to call Devon.

She grabbed a sandwich from the cafeteria and took it back upstairs to the ER break room. She took a bite while scrolling through her contact list. Then she switched over to her recent calls.

Dev had called her the night before to finalize things and to check in on her. She found his number and added him to her contact list before she pushed the button.

The phone rang several times before his voice mail message came on. She frowned and asked that he call her back.

Weird, she thought, as she took another bite. Maybe he

was at the park, playing with Sebastian and hadn't heard his phone. Although surely he would have expected her to call?

Then again, maybe not. She'd told him she trusted him. Which she did. And she might have caught them in the middle of a game.

She finished her lunch, and then sighed when she was notified of a new arrival. Ten minutes to eat was better than nothing, so she tossed the wrapper in the garbage and headed back out to the arena.

"Janelle, your patient is in room three," Eve informed her.

She nodded and crossed over. When she pushed back the privacy curtain, her heart leapt into her throat when she saw Dev standing beside Sebastian who was lying on a gurney.

"What happened?" she asked, crossing over to put a hand on Sebastian's forehead. "Is he sick?"

Devon's face was full of anguish. "I spun him on the merry-go-round and he fell off. I'm so sorry, it's totally my fault."

For a moment the urge to lash out at him was strong, and she swallowed the harsh words with an effort. "It's okay," she said with a strained smile. "Sebastian? Can you tell me what hurts?"

"My tummy," he whimpered.

She tried to control her shaking fingers as she lifted his shirt and examined his abdomen. The catheter site looked fine, clean, dry and intact. He didn't have any obvious bruises or contusions that she could see, although it was possible they would show up later. She glanced up at Devon. "Did he land on his stomach?"

"No, he landed on his backside."

She was relieved by the news. "Okay, I'm sure he'll be fine, but I'll ask Dr. Katy to take a look."

As she moved around to the foot of the gurney, Dev's hand shot out and lightly grasped her arm. "Janelle, I'm truly sorry about this."

He looked so distraught that her initial annoyance faded and she covered his hand with hers. "I don't blame you, Devon. Sebastian is a child, he's going to fall down or get hurt sometimes."

"I pushed them too fast," he insisted. "You warned me to be careful and look what happened."

"Nothing has happened that we know of," she reminded him. "We'll see what Dr. Katy says, but I'm sure he's going to be just fine."

Dev's dark gaze clung to hers, as if seeking reassurance. Finally he released her and nodded. "Okay, send the doc in."

She strode into the arena and swept her gaze over the nurse's station, searching for Dr. Katy's auburn hair. The ER doctor was seated in front of a computer, scowling at the screen. Janelle approached her, wondering what was wrong. "Dr. Katy? Do you have a minute to examine my patient in room three?"

"What?" Dr. Katy glanced up and her expression cleared. "Sure, I'll be right in."

"Anything I can help you with?" Janelle asked, glancing at the computer screen over Katy's shoulder.

"No, just don't like the look of this CT scan on the patient in room eight but I have consulted the neurologist; just waiting for him to get here." Dr. Katy pushed away from the computer desk. "Let's take a look at your patient. What's going on?"

Janelle filled her in on Sebastian's medical history and was glad when Dr. Katy didn't seem too concerned.

When they walked into the room, Devon was sitting next to Sebastian's gurney, smoothing a hand over her son's head.

"Hi Devon," Dr. Katy greeted him. "Is Sebastian your son?"

Dev looked stunned by the question and Janelle quickly spoke up. "No, he's actually my son. I'm his legal guardian, Dev was just helping me out by watching Sebastian today while I was here at work."

"Oh, of course, I should have known. Now that you mention it, I did hear something about you adopting your sister's son." Katy bent over Sebastian. "Hi, my name is Dr. Katy, can I take a peek at your tummy?"

Sebastian nodded and pulled up his t-shirt. Dr. Katy gently palpated his abdomen and glanced over at Janelle. "He's dwelling, right?"

She nodded. "Yes, that's right. He's not scheduled for another exchange until later tonight."

"I think we need to make sure the fluid in his abdomen is clear," Dr. Katy said, stepping back and stripping off her gloves. "So let's get him drained, then we'll get a CT scan. If it looks good, I'll discharge him home."

"Do we need to infuse another bag?" Janelle asked with a frown. She didn't like the idea of skipping an exchange.

"I don't think so, he should really be fine for a couple of hours. Just start his nighttime exchange an hour early."

Janelle nodded and quickly connected the tubing to Sebastian's catheter. She held her breath and released the clamp, hoping, praying there was no blood in the fluid as a sign of trauma.

She could feel Devon's intense gaze, both of them waiting to see what would happen. When the fluid appeared clear, she smiled. "Looks good."

"Yeah." Dev glanced up at her. "I've been praying the whole time that he'd be okay."

She was touched by the fact that he'd prayed for Sebastian, especially considering how he'd kept his distance from church and faith. Maybe yesterday had helped mend that fence. "Me, too. But as you can see, he's fine."

"Can I go home, now?" Sebastian asked. "I wanna play the race car game."

"Not yet, but soon." Janelle glanced up at Devon. "I have a couple of other patients to check on, but I'll be back in a few minutes."

He nodded. "I'm not going anywhere."

She kept busy with her other patients, while Dev accompanied Sebastian to the CT scanner. She wanted to be there for him, but she couldn't just walk away from her patient care responsibilities, either.

When Dr. Katy gave them the all clear, she glanced at her watch, realizing she only had thirty minutes left in her shift. "I can't leave just yet," she told Dev. "But I'll meet you soon, okay?"

"Sure, no problem." Dev looked exhausted, as if the events at the park had taken a toll on him. "We'll play video games while we wait, right Sebastian?"

"Right. And I'll beat you, too."

She smiled at Sebastian's determination, glad to see he was back to his old self. She kept the discharge paperwork for herself, watching as Sebastian skipped beside Dev as they left the ER.

As fast as the beginning part of her shift passed, the last thirty minutes dragged painfully slow. When she finished giving the oncoming nurse a brief report about the patients who were still waiting for their disposition, she hurried to grab her purse out of her locker.

Thankfully, the ride home didn't take long, and for once there was no sign of any silver sedan hanging around. She found Dev and Sebastian playing a game, but was equally shocked to see that there was a large crockpot of beef stew on the counter.

"You made dinner?" She glanced at Dev in surprise.

"I used a low salt recipe so it should be fine for Sebastian," he responded from his spot on the sofa.

She didn't know what to say, certainly she hadn't expected him to cook for her.

For them.

This was how she'd once envisioned her life.

Before Lane had walked out on her.

She told herself not to read anything into Devon's kind gesture. After all, he was probably just returning the favor since she'd cooked breakfast.

Yet she had no idea what to do with the extra time on her hands. Time she'd slotted to prepare dinner.

She ducked into her bedroom to change out of her scrubs into a comfy pair of soft denim jeans and a pull-over T-shirt.

When she returned to the kitchen, Devon was standing at the counter, stirring the stew. He turned when she approached.

"What do you want to do about tomorrow?" he asked in a low voice.

Her stomach sank to the soles of her feet. The way he avoided her gaze made her realize he'd changed his mind about watching Sebastian. She could barely force the words past her constricted throat. "What do you mean?"

"Can you still trust me, after everything that's happened?"

She licked her dry lips. "I'll be honest, Devon, I was

angry at first. But then I realized that this could have happened to anyone."

"But not to you." He finally lifted his gaze to hers.

"I've probably been a little over-protective of him," she admitted. "But what I said to you in the ER was the truth. He's going to run and play with other kids. He's going to fall down and get hurt. You were right to take him to the park to play. He shouldn't spend his days playing video games."

"Do you really mean that?" he asked, his dark brown eyes searching hers.

She couldn't stop herself from stepping closer and putting her hand on his forearm. "Yes, I do. Please don't let what happened today bother you."

"How can I not?" Dev's tone was husky with pent up emotion. "Sebastian could have been seriously injured."

"Yes, but he wasn't."

He pulled her close, wrapping his arms around her. She linked her arms around his waist and rested her head on his shoulder. They stood there for several long moments, drawing strength from each other.

When Dev finally loosened his grip, she stepped away, feeling a bit self-conscious. They were friends, but in the past few days, she was beginning to think of him as something more.

"Thanks for making dinner," she said, desperate to change the subject. "I hope you're planning on staying to eat with us."

He hesitated for a moment before nodding. "Sure, I'd like that."

It was on the tip of her tongue to ask what they were doing, but just then Sebastian called out for Dev, asking if he was going to return to the game.

"Go ahead," she urged, distracted by the ringing of her cell phone. "I have to get this anyway."

Dev headed back into the living room and challenged Sebastian to another game. She picked up her phone, frowning when she didn't recognize the number.

"Hello?"

"Hi this is Alice Beckstrom, returning your call."

Janelle was thrilled to hear from the retired nurse. She explained her situation with Sebastian and asked if there was any possibility she'd be willing to babysit for him, which included performing his peritoneal dialysis exchanges three times a day.

There was a long pause and Janelle's hope deflated like a balloon.

"I know it sounds like a lot," she hastened to fill the silence. "But he goes to preschool in the morning, so it's really not as bad as it sounds."

"How many days a week would you need me?" Alice asked.

She caught her breath, trying to rein in her excitement. "I'm working just part-time hours for now, usually two to three days per week, and every third weekend."

Another long silence. "I don't do weekends."

At this point, she would be willing to take what she could get. "That's okay, I'm hoping a young high-school student who's already a certified nursing assistant will be willing to do them." She took a deep breath and pressed on. "I would really appreciate your considering the position. I have to be able to pay my rent and I'm running out of options."

"All right, then I'll watch your boy two or three days per week. But it's been a long time so I'll need a refresher on how to do his exchanges."

Janelle closed her eyes on a wave of relief, resisting the urge to dance a little jig. "I'm off work on Wednesday, but work again on Thursday. I can show you how to take care of his exchanges on Wednesday if you're willing. I only need you Thursday of this week, and then not again until Monday the following week."

"Wednesday is fine. I'll need directions to your house."

Janelle rattled them off and then disconnected from the call, letting out a heavy sigh of relief. She sank into a kitchen chair, trying to absorb what had just happened.

God had answered her prayers! She had a babysitter for Sebastian. For during the week at least.

She'd have plenty of time to worry about the weekends later.

Suddenly full of energy, she jumped up from the table and began pulling glasses, bowls and silverware out of her cupboards, setting the table. Devon's beef stew smelled delicious and she was acutely aware of how hungry she was.

"Dinner's ready," she called.

"Not yet," Sebastian protested, leaning into a curve as if he were actually riding the race car.

Devon hit the pause button. "Yes, now," he said, firmly. "We can finish the game after dinner."

As much as she was glad to have his support, she couldn't help wondering just how long Dev planned on staying. He had a right to eat the meal he'd cooked, but surely he had other things to do.

Other ways to spend his evening off work.

Her stomach knotted at the thought of Devon dating someone else, even though she knew he didn't belong to her. And after tomorrow, she wouldn't even need his help any more with watching Sebastian.

So why was she feeling depressed by that fact?

She filled their bowls with the steamy stew, and once everyone was seated she clasped her hands together and bowed her head.

"Dear Lord, we thank You so much for this wonderful food and for keeping Sebastian safe today when he fell. Also thank You for answering my prayers for a babysitter. We ask that You continue to show us Your path, Amen."

"Amen," Sebastian said.

She glanced at Devon, surprised at the somber expression on his face.

"You found someone?"

She forced a smile. "Yes, Alice Beckstrom, the retired nurse that Pastor John referred to me. She doesn't want to do weekends, but at least I have part of my problem solved."

"That's great news," he said with an odd lack of enthusiasm.

She nodded and picked up her spoon, wondering what was going on in his mind.

Was it possible Devon would miss spending time with Sebastian?

With her?

8

———

Devon knew he should be happy for Janelle's having a solution for her babysitting problem. However, he couldn't deny a twinge of regret that she wouldn't need him anymore.

Ridiculous to think that way, this wasn't about him. Both Janelle and Sebastian deserved a break.

"Delicious," Janelle murmured after tasting his stew. "Thank you so much for making dinner. I wasn't expecting you to do that."

"It was really not that big a deal," he said, wishing she wouldn't be so nice to him. The image of Sebastian lying on the ground beside the merry-go-round and the shrillness of his scream were firmly implanted in his memory.

He hadn't prayed that hard since Debra's death.

Cooking dinner had been his feeble attempt to repay her. It was the least he could do.

"Actually, it is a big deal," Janelle countered. She reached across the table and lightly put her hand on his forearm. "You've been so supportive over these past few days, Devon. I'm not sure how I'll ever repay you."

He stared at her slender hand for a moment, aching for something he didn't dare name, then dragged his gaze to her face. "You supported me the night I was shot, Janelle," he managed. "So how about we just consider ourselves even?"

The smile that bloomed across her features made his breath catch in his throat. "Okay, then. It's a deal."

He nodded and began to eat. The stew wasn't half bad, and he was glad to see Sebastian and Janelle both seemed to like it too.

"Have you heard any news from Zack about the break in?" he asked.

Janelle scowled and shook her head. "No, but I'm sure these things take time."

They did, but he thought Zack would have tried to put a rush on the fingerprints at least. Although the robbery had been discovered on Saturday, the evidence was probably only first being processed today.

"Everything can be replaced," Janelle said with a shrug. Then her expression clouded over. "Except for Lisa's ring."

"I can check out some of the pawn shops and jewelry shops in the area," he volunteered.

She looked up at him in surprise. "Won't Zack do that?"

"Maybe," he acknowledged. "But it won't hurt to have both of us making phone calls."

"I'd appreciate that," she said softly.

Dev couldn't help thinking he'd do anything to make her happy, but then pulled himself up short. Wait a minute, what was he thinking? They were friends.

Good friends. Helping each other out in a jam.

So why did he have the insane urge to kiss her?

Devon tried to push the troublesome thoughts out of his mind, but it wasn't easy. When they finished dinner, Janelle insisted on cleaning up. He decided he should head home, after all, he'd be back in the morning.

"I'll see you tomorrow, Janelle. Same time, right?"

"Right."

"Noooo," Sebastian wailed. "Don't go, Dev. Don't go!"

He was surprised when the little boy wrapped his arms around his legs, in a meager attempt to keep him from leaving.

"Hey, champ, I need to get going, but I'll be back in the morning, okay?"

"Can't you stay and play wif me? Puleeze?"

"Sebastian," Janelle said in a stern, warning tone. "That's enough. You need to get your jammies on, Dr. Katy said we need to do your exchange an hour earlier tonight."

"Don't wanna!" Sebastian abruptly let go of his legs and ran down the hall toward his bedroom. The door slammed shut behind him.

"I can stay for a little while," Devon began, but Janelle quickly interrupted.

"No, the sooner Sebastian realizes that he can't get everything he wants, the better."

She was probably right, what did he know about raising a child? Not much. But he was still hesitant to leave. "Are you sure?"

"Yes, I'm sure," she said firmly. "He's tired, but he'll get over being upset soon enough." She made her way over to the front door, leaving him little choice but to follow. "See you in the morning."

"I'll be here." He couldn't resist the urge to touch her, so he gave her a quick hug, and then left the townhouse. He could feel her gaze on his back as he walked to his truck.

The minute he returned home, he booted up his

computer and did a search on the closest jewelry stores that advertised buying gold.

He picked up his mobile phone and began dialing, determined to find Janelle's missing ring. He'd try the jewelry stores first, as they were closer, then move on to the pawn shops, most of which were located in either Madison or Milwaukee.

As he worked, he was all too aware that his need to make Janelle happy came from a personal need, rather than a professional one.

THE NEXT MORNING, Janelle wasn't up quite as early, so she wasn't able to make breakfast. Devon didn't seem to mind, but she still felt a bit guilty for rushing out and leaving him to face Sebastian's exchange alone.

This time, there were no crises to worry about. Her shift dragged by slowly, but when she checked in with Devon he assured her everything was fine.

A heart attack victim came in through the ER right before shift change, so she ended up staying a little later than usual to help get the patient settled. When she was free to leave, she sent Dev a quick text telling him she was on her way home.

The ride home didn't take long, but when she walked into the townhouse, there was no sign of Sebastian or Devon. She frowned, her heart racing. Had they gone to the park again?

Then she heard Sebastian giggle, and realized the patio door was open, allowing a cool breeze to wash in through the screen. Dev and Sebastian were outside in the back yard, standing a few feet apart on the grassy area over-looking the lake. She stood in front of the patio doors for a moment, watching as Devon gently tossed a baseball to Sebastian, who tried to catch it in a too big leather baseball glove.

"That's it, good job," Dev was saying.

Sebastian glowed under his praise and threw the ball back in Devon's direction. Dev did a good job of leaping to the side to catch the ball.

For a moment she simply watched them, loving the way Devon was so patient with Sebastian, the way a father should be with his son.

Would Devon find someone else to marry one day? Would he have a family of his own? The thought was bittersweet.

"Nana!" Sebastian caught sight of her in the doorway. "We're playing catch!"

"I see that," she said with a smile.

The next ball Devon lobbed at Sebastian he dropped, but the one after that managed to land awkwardly in his glove. Sebastian threw it back at Devon with more force causing Dev to scramble in order to prevent it from hitting the side of the house.

Janelle tried not to wince. "Good catch," she said to Dev.

He grinned, looking younger and somehow more carefree. "Sebastian is keeping me on my toes."

"Clearly," she said in a dry tone. "Thanks for staying, sorry I had to work late."

"No problem. Are you hungry? I was planning to cook burgers and brats on the grill for dinner."

Janelle knew that Sebastian was already becoming too attached to Devon, but at the same time, she enjoyed spending time with him. Probably a little too much. "Sure, if you don't mind."

"Of course not, or I wouldn't have offered."

"Throw me the ball, Dev," Sebastian said, hitting the center of his glove like some pro baseball player.

Janelle stepped back from the doorway, and turned to head into her room. She changed out of her scrubs then returned to the kitchen, checking to see if she had enough veggies in the fridge to make a salad to go with the burgers and brats.

The fact that this was their last night together wasn't lost on her as she shredded lettuce and chopped up tomatoes. Of course she could always invite Devon over for a meal, but that would be difficult since he worked second shift, while she primarily worked dayshift.

Crazy to worry about when she'd see Devon again, considering that up until four days ago, she'd hardly spent any time with him. How was it that he'd become such a fixture in their lives in just a few days?

Dating Lane for a year hadn't given her the same feeling of closeness that she experienced now with Devon.

As if on cue, Dev opened the screen door of the patio and came inside. "Looks great," he said, eyeing the salad bowl.

"I'm trying to get Sebastian to like vegetables as much as he likes macaroni and cheese," she said dryly. "I don't think my sister was big on healthy cooking."

Dev snatched a cucumber, drawing his hand away quickly when she playfully swatted it. "You don't talk about her much."

She shrugged. "Don't get me wrong, I loved Lisa, but she didn't always make the best choices. Like living with Grant and getting pregnant. But she was getting on the right track after Sebastian was born."

"I didn't mean to dredge up painful memories," he said.

She sent him a sideways glance. "We both have painful memories, don't we?"

He nodded and turned away, to gaze out through the patio doors. She sensed he wasn't quite ready to talk about the loss of his fiancée, and she didn't blame him.

Was that the reason he wanted to move out of Crystal Lake? Her heart squeezed in her chest and she realized just how sad she would be to see him go.

"How's the job hunt going?" she asked, striving for a casual tone.

He swung toward her in surprise. "How did you know about that?"

She arched a brow. "Seriously?"

He rolled his eyes toward the ceiling. "Let me guess, Josie said something to you."

Her lips twitched in a smile. "Bingo."

"How does she find this stuff out?" he asked, truly baffled. "It's not like I told very many people about my plan."

"She eavesdrops on her customer's conversations," she responded with a smile. "She mentioned overhearing Sheriff Torretti making a comment about getting a reference call about you."

"Really?" Devon's eyes widened. "He got a reference call?"

"According to Josie. She thinks you can't bear to live here anymore because of all the reminders about your fiancée."

"That's not the reason," he protested. "It's just—I feel the need to do something more with my life. Something important. Truly making a difference."

She wanted to point out that he was making a difference to her and Sebastian, but knew that wasn't what he was talking about. "I understand," she said, putting the last of the cucumbers into the salad bowl.

"You do?"

She nodded and opened the fridge and placed the salad bowl inside. "I used to work at the big level one trauma center in Madison for the same reason. But eventually I realized that seeing nameless faces day in and day out wasn't really what I wanted. Even at church I didn't necessarily feel as if I truly belonged. I wanted a sense of community. The minute I arrived in Crystal Lake, I knew this was home."

Devon didn't say anything in response to that, so she finished cleaning up the cutting board and then crossed over to stand next to him in front of the patio doors. "What's Sebastian up to?" she asked, changing the subject.

"Practicing," Dev said with a smile. He was so close she could breathe in the woodsy scent of his aftershave. "I taught him to toss the ball up in the air and practice catching it."

"Hmm, maybe I should get him a smaller glove," she said, watching as Sebastian dropped more balls than he managed to catch. "That one seems way too big."

"I think I have one of my nephew's gloves somewhere so don't buy anything until I have a chance to search the basement."

She was touched by his willingness to loan his nephews things to Sebastian. Of course, the fact that she'd told him all about her money problems was likely a factor, too. "Okay, thanks. But there's no rush, I've taken up more than enough of your free time."

He turned to look down at her with his deep brown eyes. She caught her breath, unable to tear her gaze away. He lifted his hand and lightly brushed a stray strand of hair off her cheek. "I like spending my free time with you," he said in a low voice.

She parted her lips, trying to come up with some sort

of response, not easy when all she could think of was kissing him. And then he slowly bent his head toward her, giving her plenty of time to back away if she were so inclined.

She wasn't.

Instead she found herself leaning forward, meeting him halfway. The moment his mouth covered hers, every logical thought slid right out of her brain. He tasted amazing, like chocolate and peppermint rolled into one.

When Devon deepened the kiss, she found herself clinging to his broad shoulders, drowning in sensation. Somewhere nearby, an odd buzzing sound nagged at her, but she ignored it.

Devon lifted his mouth from hers, breathing heavily. "I think that's your phone," he said.

She didn't want to let go, but of course, the buzzing continued. Remembering she'd set the device on vibrate, she forced herself to release him.

Her legs were shaky as she crossed over to the kitchen table. The name on the screen was Zack Crain, so she picked it up and pushed the talk button. "Hello, Zack."

"Did I catch you at a bad time?" he asked.

Yes, she wanted to shout, but of course she didn't. She glanced over at Devon, who stood with his shoulder propped against the doorway, watching her. "Just getting ready for dinner," she said, sidestepping his question. "Why? Did you find something out about the robbery?"

"Actually, we do have a clue, but is Devon there? Apparently he's the one who did most of the work."

Color rushed into her cheeks. "Um, yeah, he's here. Do you want to talk to him?"

"No, that's not necessary, but tell him thanks for the tip."

"Here, I'll put you on speaker," she said, taking the

phone from her ear to push the button. "Go ahead, Devon's here, too."

Devon crossed over to stand next to the phone. "Hey Zack, what did you find out?"

"Did you call and leave a message at Gretchen's Goldsmith shop about a ruby ring?" Zack asked.

"Yes, I called Gretchen's among others," Devon admitted.

Janelle's heart leaped in her chest. "Lisa's ring? Did you find it?"

"The owner of the goldsmith shop let us know she did buy a gold ring with a red stone," Zack said. "But don't get too excited, we don't know for sure it's the same ring."

"Do you have a picture of it?" Janelle asked excitedly.

"Yeah, I can e-mail it to you."

"Wait, I don't have a computer, remember?" Janelle said. "The thief took that, too. Can you text the photo to me?"

"Send it to both of us," Devon spoke up.

"Okay, here it comes."

Devon's phone chirped and he quickly pressed on the text button to see what Zack had sent. He maneuvered the photo so it was larger in size and then turned the phone to show her. "Is this the ring?" he asked.

She stared in shock at the photograph. "Yes, that's Lisa's ring," she said in a choked voice.

"Did you hear that?" Dev asked Zack. "Janelle has positively identified the ring. Did the owner give you a description of the guy who sold it?"

"She did, said he was tall and skinny, with dirty blond hair and a scruffy beard. He wore a green T-Shirt and worn blue jeans that appeared to be a size too large on him. Any idea who he might be?" Zack asked.

Janelle tried to picture the man, but honestly that

description could have been anyone. "I'm sorry, but I can't think of anyone who matches that description."

There was a long silence. "Okay, don't worry about it, I'm sure we'll find him eventually," Zack assured her.

She nodded, wishing she could be so sure. When Zack disconnected from the call, she saw that Devon was pulling his car keys out of his pocket. "Where are you going?"

"We're going to get Lisa's ring back." Dev turned and called through the patio doors to Sebastian. "Come on, Sebastian, we're going for a ride."

She wanted to protest, first because she didn't have any spare money to buy Lisa's ring back, and second she had no idea how long it would take. She needed to get back in time to do Sebastian's exchange.

But when Devon held out his hand, she found herself taking it, liking the way his warm fingers gently cradled hers.

She found herself agreeing with his impromptu plan. "Let's go."

9

____

Devon did his best to concentrate on driving, but his mind kept going back to reliving their kiss. He had no idea why he'd kissed Janelle, but there was no denying she'd kissed him back, sending sparks of electricity zipping along his nerve endings.

He hadn't felt this level of attraction for any woman in a long time. Not since Debra.

And unfortunately the memories of his former fiancée were growing distant, which made him feel bad.

But not enough to make him regret kissing Janelle. And not enough to think about how much he'd like to kiss her again.

"Just give me a minute to pack some supplies," Janelle said, before rushing toward Sebastian's bedroom.

Supplies? He belatedly remembered Sebastian's need for dialysis. He hesitated, wondering if he should offer to go and pick up her sister's ring alone. No reason to drag Janelle and Sebastian along.

When she returned with a small backpack full of

supplies, he put a hand on her arm. "Why don't you and Sebastian stay here? I'll get the ring and bring it to you."

Indecision flashed across her features, but then she shook her head. "No, I'd like to come. And I'm only dragging all this stuff along just in case. We'll probably be back in plenty of time."

He relented. "Okay, is there anything else you need?"

"Nope, all set. Well, except for Sebastian."

He glanced through the patio doors. "Store that stuff in the car, I'll get him."

Janelle nodded, and he crossed over to the sliding doors. "Sebastian? Come inside, we're getting ready to go for a ride."

The little boy didn't waste any time tossing aside his baseball and glove.

"Oh, no. You need to bring your things inside," Devon instructed.

Sebastian let out a heavy sigh, but did as he was told. Within five minutes, the boy was tucked into the booster seat and they were on the road, heading for the interstate.

Dev glanced at Janelle. "Are you sure that description didn't sound familiar?"

She pursed her lips and then lifted her shoulders in a helpless shrug. "Not one bit. I've been trying to go through the teenagers I happen to know around town, but that description doesn't fit."

He wasn't so sure the burglar was a kid from town, but there was no point in pushing the issue. Hopefully, the goldsmith shop would have security cameras that would give them a decent angle. If the guy had been smart enough to avoid them, maybe the owner would agree to work with a police artist to create a sketch.

And why were the fingerprints taking so long? They

should have had something back by now. Unless of course the perp wasn't in the system.

His truck ate up the miles as Janelle and Sebastian sang nursery rhymes. Twenty minutes later, he pulled up in front of Gretchen's Goldsmith.

"Are you ready?" he asked Janelle, as she unbuckled her seatbelt.

"Absolutely." She hopped down from the truck and reached up to get Sebastian.

Inside the shop there were rows and rows of glass cases containing all kinds of jewelry. It was a nice place, looked as if they sold high end jewelry. Odd that the robber would choose a nice place to sell the gold ring.

Unless he sold it to someone else, first? The possibility of this being a dead end made him frown.

A woman with an athletic build and weathered skin came out of the back room to greet them. "Janelle Larson?"

"That's me," Janelle said, stepping forward.

The woman smiled. "My name is Gretchen, I understand this is your ring?"

Janelle glanced at the ring, then down at Sebastian. "Actually, it belonged to my sister, Sebastian's mother. It's the only thing of value she possessed and I was saving it for her son."

Gretchen's expression softened. "That's very nice." She held out the ring. "Here, take it."

Janelle didn't move, so Dev stepped forward, reaching for his wallet. "How much did you payfor it?"

Gretchen waved him away. "Really not that much, and I wouldn't have given that guy any money at all if I had known it was stolen."

Janelle reached for the ring. "At least let me pay what you spent, it's not fair for you to lose money on the deal."

"Don't worry about me, I have insurance. Besides, business has been good. I have no complaints."

Devon was touched by Gretchen's kindness. "Are you sure?"

"Positive, just remember me if you're ever in the market for jewelry." Gretchen's eyes softened as she watched Janelle cradle the ring. "Glad to help out."

"You've been wonderful, thank you," Janelle said, slipping the ruby ring on her right hand.

"Can we take a look at your security cameras?" Dev asked.

"Sure." Gretchen led the way over to her office. She brought up the camera feed and went in reverse to find the guy who'd brought the ring in.

He wore a baseball hat pulled over his hair, and a scruffy beard covered the lower portion of his face. Dev sighed. "Not very useful, but will you save it on a disk?"

"Of course." Gretchen shrugged. "Sorry I couldn't be much help."

"You were a huge help," Janelle said, fingering the ring. "Thanks again, for everything."

Devon placed his hand in the small of her back as they headed out to the truck. "So what do you think? Do we have time to stop for dinner? That way, you can do the exchange right when you get home."

"Sounds good," Janelle agreed. "Right Sebastian?"

"Right," the child echoed.

Devon drove toward a family style restaurant, rather than a fast food place, knowing it would be easier to find something lower in salt for Sebastian.

When their food arrived, Janelle folded her hands together and bowed her head. "Thank You, Lord, for providing this food for us and for bringing my sister's ring home. We ask that You continue to keep Sebastian healthy as we follow Your chosen path, Amen."

"Amen," he murmured. When Dev lifted his head, he caught Janelle's gaze and smiled. Praying with her didn't feel awkward or forced. Instead, it felt right.

For the first time, he realized that leaving Janelle and Sebastian behind just to work on some big city police force wouldn't be as easy as he'd once thought.

He didn't want to leave her at all.

JANELLE WAS RELIEVED they'd made it back home in time to do Sebastian's exchange. Devon hung around for a while, but once Sebastian was tucked into bed, he made his way to the front door. She reluctantly followed him.

"Thanks again, Dev."

He stared down at her for a long minute, and she held her breath, hoping he might kiss her again.

But he didn't. "I'm glad you were able to get your sister's ring back," he said in a low, husky tone.

"Me, too. It was nice of Gretchen to just give it to me."

He nodded and rubbed the back of his neck. "Take care, Janelle. Let me know if you need anything."

She curled her fingers into fists to prevent herself from reaching out to him. Obviously, Devon considered their brief kiss a colossal mistake. She forced a smile, trying not to think about how lonely it would be to not have him around. "I will."

He turned away and strode to his car. She watched, waiting for him to turn back. But he slid behind the wheel and backed out of the driveway.

She stepped back inside and closed the door, feeling bereft, even though she knew she had no reason to. Despite how she'd responded to his kiss, it wasn't as if they were dating.

Devon was likely still mourning his fiancée.

And she had a young boy to care for.

Janelle didn't sleep well that night, tossing and turning, imagining that the silver car was parked once again outside her house. Crazy, since she hadn't seen the vehicle in well over twenty-four hours.

The next morning, she performed Sebastian's exchange, then cleaned up the house in preparation for Alice's visit. Janelle didn't know Alice, but when the woman arrived, just after noon, the woman wasn't anything like what she'd imagined.

Alice had a rotund frame and wasn't smiling, in fact she seemed to have a permanent frown etched on her forehead. Her gray hair was pulled back into a harsh bun, and she moved slowly when Janelle opened the door to let her in.

"Sebastian," Janelle called, trying her best to ignore her misgivings. "Ms. Alice is here."

Sebastian glanced over and then scowled when he saw the retired nurse standing there. "Don't wanna do my exchange," he said, turning his attention back to his game.

Janelle forced a bright smile. "Come on, Sebastian, we need to show Mrs. Alice how to do this."

She feared he'd throw a tantrum, but he tossed aside the controller. "Okay, let's get this over with," he said in a resigned tone.

Janelle was glad to see that Alice at least appeared to be paying attention as she walked through the steps. The woman didn't say much, but after they finished, she reached for her purse.

"What time tomorrow?" she asked in an abrupt tone.

"I have to be at work by seven, so if you could get here by six-thirty that would be great."

"Okay, fine. I'll see you then." Alice clomped her way back toward the door.

Janelle told herself not to panic at her abrupt departure, after all, the woman was a nurse. Surely she'd do fine.

"Where's Dev?" Sebastian asked a few minutes later. "I don't like her, I want Dev."

Oh boy, this was exactly what she was afraid of. Sebastian had already grown too attached to Devon Armbruster.

And if she were honest, she'd admit she'd grown attached to him, too.

"He's working as a police officer," she reminded Sebastian. "Mrs. Alice is going to be your babysitter from now on."

Sebastian's face crumpled. "No! Don't want Mrs. Alice! She smells funny!"

Since the scent of mothballs had clung to Alice's badly wrinkled clothes, she couldn't exactly argue with him. "I'm sorry, Sebastian, but Devon has to work."

He thrust out his lower lip. "Then you stay home with me."

A wave of guilt hit her hard. "I can't, I have to work, too."

"NOOOO!" Sebastian screeched in a voice loud enough to shatter ear drums.

"Stop it," she shouted in a sharp tone. "That's enough. Go to your room."

He scrambled off the sofa, tears rolling down his chubby cheeks and ran into his bedroom, slamming the door loudly behind him.

Janelle collapsed on the edge of a kitchen chair, burying her face in her hands. She probably could have handled that better. Thankfully, no one was renting the townhouse next door. She could only hope that no one else had heard the shouting match, the last thing she needed was an unexpected visit from child protective services.

The worst part of it all, was that she couldn't even blame Sebastian for not liking Alice. Truthfully, she hadn't been overly thrilled with the woman's demeanor, either. She'd seemed so nice over the phone, but in person, ugh. But what could she do? The rent was due in just three weeks, and she'd be lucky if her paycheck covered the amount.

The urge to call and cry on Devon's shoulder was strong, but somehow she managed to hold back. He didn't need to listen to her sob story when he was busy getting ready for his shift. Besides, there really wasn't anything he could do.

No, this was one mess she had to deal with alone.

Sebastian's wails grew louder to the point she covered her ears. Then she abruptly pushed away from the kitchen table and let herself out through the patio doors.

The lake was calm just a few boats dotted the water. The sun was out, but it wasn't quite warm enough to swim or ski.

She walked until she couldn't hear Sebastian's crying anymore, stopping at the edge of the lake, in front of the white pier. She drew in a deep breath and let it out slowly, seeking peace.

Lots of kids had temper tantrums, this wasn't Sebastian's first, nor would it likely be his last. She closed her eyes and prayed that the Lord would continue to provide strength and wisdom.

Maybe she needed to keep searching for another babysitter for Sebastian. Obviously she had to work tomorrow, so she'd need to use Alice for that, but then she had another three days off to work on a replacement.

Someone other than Devon.

Although she'd already gone through her entire list, and she still hadn't heard back from Tina, the teenager who'd finished her nursing assistant training, either. She'd had high hopes for Tina, since she could only assume Sebastian would like having a younger woman watching over him.

She sat down on the grass and wrapped her arms around her knees. She'd give Sebastian some time to calm down, and then she'd offer to take him to the park. This was nothing more than a minor setback.

They'd get through this. They had to.

She and Sebastian only had each other.

Janelle forced herself to sit there, gazing at the lake for a full fifteen minutes. When the timeframe was up, she pushed herself to her feet and walked back inside the townhouse.

She stood in the kitchen, straining to listen. But she couldn't hear any evidence that the child was still crying. Satisfied that he must have fallen asleep, she poked in the fridge to figure out what they'd have for dinner.

The salad from the night before was still inside, so all she needed was a main dish. Something that Sebastian would like.

A peace offering.

He'd been excited to have the hamburgers Devon was going to make the night before, so she decided to go with something simple. She pulled out the ground beef, and then headed outside to start the grill.

It wasn't easy, but she managed. She watched the flames for a long moment, steeling herself to go in to confront Sebastian.

Back inside, she made her way down the hall to his room, which happened to be adjacent to hers. She opened the door, expected to find him cuddled up on his bed with his stuffed angel.

But he wasn't in the bed.

With a frown, she registered the fact that the stuffed angel wasn't there, either, which meant he must have taken it with him. To her room? She quickly went over to check.

When she didn't find him in her room, she went back into his bedroom. This time she searched everywhere, beneath the bed, in the closet, anywhere a small child could hide.

But she didn't find Sebastian, anywhere.

Panic swelled in her chest, but she tried to remain calm. He was only four and a half, he couldn't have gotten very far.

She spun on her heel and went back to the front door, mentally kicking herself for not locking it after Mrs. Alice had left.

A chill snaked down her spine when she noticed the heavy inside door had been left open. She jerked it out of her way, and burst through the second screen door, and out onto the porch.

"Sebastian? Sebastian!" Janelle didn't hesitate but ran out to the street, half expecting to see the little boy walking along the side of the road with his stuffed angel tucked beneath his arm.

Surely he couldn't have gone far?

But when she didn't see any sign of him, the panic she'd tried so hard to hold at bay erupted into a full-fledged attack.

"Sebastian!" she screamed at the top of her lungs. Rose's diner wasn't far, so she sprinted in that direction, telling herself she'd find Sebastian inside, enjoying a cup of hot chocolate. Right now, Josie was probably trying to call her to let her know Sebastian was there.

But when she barged into the diner, there was no sign of Sebastian's blond head.

"Janelle, honey, what's wrong?" Josie demanded, planting her hands on her ample hips.

"Have you seen Sebastian?" Her heart was pounding so loud she could barely hear herself speak. "Did he come up here to see you?"

"No, I haven't seen him. Why, is he missing?"

Tears welled in her eyes, blurring her vision. "Yes," she choked. "I can't find him. I—I think he ran away."

"Listen, go back home," Josie told her in a no-nonsense tone. "I'll call the sheriff's department."

Janelle nodded, and swiftly turned to head back outside. She broke into a run, trying to get back home in case Sebastian was actually there, waiting for her.

Maybe he'd been hiding somewhere else in the townhouse. But where? The place wasn't all that big.

Then she remembered the empty side of the townhouse. Had he found a way to get inside? Was it possible that Zack Crain hadn't locked up the night after the robbery?

She checked the front door, but it was locked. She ran around to the lake side and pulled on the patio doors.

They were locked too.

Without wasting a second, she hurried inside her own townhouse, this time checking each room systematically, looking anywhere a small child may try to hide.

But a few minutes later, she knew there was no escaping the truth.

Sebastian was gone.

She'd lost her sister's son.

10

———

Devon tapped his fingers on the desk, waiting for Zack Crain to answer his cell phone. He wanted the fingerprint results and couldn't understand why Zack hadn't kept him in the loop. Surely, they were back by now?

"Crain," Zack's clipped voice carried across the line.

"It's Dev. I hear you have the fingerprint results from the break-in at Janelle's place."

There was a small pause before Zack responded. "Yeah, I just got them about an hour ago. I needed to check a few things out before breaking the news to Janelle."

A wave of apprehension made Dev grip the phone tightly. "What news?"

He could hear Zack's sigh. "Does the name Grant Gardner mean anything to you?"

"Janelle mentioned that Sebastian's father's name was Grant, but I have no clue what his last name is. And he's supposed to be in jail."

"Yeah, well the finger prints in her house belong to

Grant Gardner and he just happens to have been released from jail, three days before the break-in."

He swallowed hard. "That's no coincidence."

"I don't think so either," Zack admitted. "And it's pretty interesting that he found her so quick. Not only that, but I showed his mug shot to Gretchen and she positively identified him, too. We have him on the burglary, if we can find him."

Dev stood and headed out to his squad. "I'm going over to talk to Janelle. Any chance you can find out if this Grant dude is driving a silver sedan?"

"I can try, but why? What makes you think he's driving a silver car?"

He resisted the urge to smack himself upside the head. He should have gone with his instincts. He knew that silver car parked near Janelle's was a sign of trouble. "I've seen a silver car hanging around outside the townhouse."

"That jerk," Zack muttered harshly.

Yeah, his feelings exactly. "Anything else? Do we know where Grant might be staying?"

"The Crystal Lake motel isn't far from Janelle's, I'll try there first." Zack hesitated, then added, "The guy has a history of domestic violence. Do you think he's going to try and hurt her?"

"I don't know," Dev forced himself to answer honestly. "But I'm not going to wait to find out. Call me if you find him at the motel, okay?"

"Sure thing."

Dev disconnected from the call and almost immediately another call came in, this time it was Janelle. He didn't want to believe that Josie could have gotten the scoop already, but crazier things had happened. "Hi Janelle," he greeted her cheerfully.

"Dev? Sebastian's gone. I need your help to find him!" The hysteria in her voice caused his gut to clench with fear.

"What do you mean, gone?" He jammed the key into the ignition and quickly started the engine. He figured he could be at Janelle's place in ten minutes flat if he used lights and sirens.

"He's gone, I left him alone in his room after his temper tantrum and now he's gone! I—I think he ran away from home. I need you and the other deputies to help me find him."

The timing of the boy's disappearance bothered him. "I'm on my way," he promised. "But Janelle, listen to me. Have you seen the silver car lately?"

"No, why?" she asked with a sniff.

The image of her crying was like a kick to the chest, but there was no time to. "We know the identity of the burglar, Grant Gardner, Sebastian's father. We matched his fingerprints. And Gretchen identified him, too."

"Grant?" There was a flash of anger in her tone. "You think Grant is here in Crystal Lake?"

"Yeah, we do. Just hang tight, I'm on my way."

"Hurry," she begged, before disconnecting from the line.

He punched the gas and took the turns that lead to Janelle's townhouse as fast and safely as possible. He couldn't believe that Sebastian was missing. Janelle had every right to be frantic.

The thought of the little boy in the hands of his father made Dev's blood run cold. Did Grant understand Sebastian's medical needs? Did the guy realize the child needed peritoneal dialysis exchanges to stay healthy? And what on earth possessed the guy to try and play father to Sebastian now?

Dozens of possibilities flashed through his mind, but at

the end of the day, Dev didn't think Grant really wanted custody of Sebastian. With his history of being an IV drug user, he was very much afraid the guy had something else on his mind.

Like kidnapping for ransom.

JANELLE PACED the sidewalk in front of the townhouse, trying to formulate some sort of plan as to where Sebastian might have gone. Was it possible Grant had something to do with his disappearance? She'd initially feared the little boy had decided to run away, especially after their fight over Mrs. Alice, but that was before Devon had told her that Sebastian's father's fingerprints had been found inside her house.

Grant had broken into her house. Had stolen her television and her computer. Pawned Lisa's ruby ring.

For money? Highly likely. It wouldn't be the first time Grant had robbed the people closest to him.

Hard to believe the authorities actually let Grant out of jail, but obviously everything she'd read about the problems with overcrowding within the prison system was true.

She heard police sirens long before she caught sight of Devon's squad car blazing up the road, red and blue lights flashing. He was barely out of the vehicle when she launched herself at him.

"We have to find Sebastian!"

"I know, we will." His strong arms held her close and she tried to calm her racing heart by filling her head with his familiar scent.

But even having Devon there wasn't enough to soothe her ragged nerves. She pulled out of his embrace, staring up at him intently. "How will we find him? Are you sending out search parties? What can I do to help?"

"First I need you to tell me exactly what happened," Dev said. "When was the last time you saw Sebastian?"

She swallowed a wave of frustration. Talking was not high on her agenda right now; she wanted, needed to *do* something. But she forced herself to think through the last few hours and tell Devon what she remembered.

"Mrs. Alice came to watch Sebastian's exchange around 12:30 in the afternoon. She left shortly afterwards, maybe close to 2:00 or so. Sebastian had a bit of a temper tantrum, so I sent him to his room." Her throat closed and her eyes welled with tears. She knew that Sebastian's disappearance was all her fault. She'd handled things badly and now the little boy was gone.

As if he could read her mind, Dev put a hand on her shoulder. "You did what hundreds of parents do when their kids throw a tantrum. Being sent to his room isn't anything to feel bad about."

She swiped at her eyes and shook her head. "It's worse," she said hoarsely. "I could still hear him screaming so I went outside to sit down by the lake."

"Don't, Janelle," Dev said softly. "Don't beat yourself up over this. You didn't do anything wrong."

"Then why is Sebastian missing?" she asked sharply. "Of course I was wrong! If I hadn't left the house he'd still be here."

"Stop it," Dev's tone was firm. "Blaming yourself isn't going to help. I need you to focus, okay? How long were you outside?"

He was right, she knew logically he was right. But that fact didn't make her feel any better. She took a deep breath and thought back. "Fifteen minutes, maybe twenty. I went back inside the house and went to listen by his door. I didn't open it, because I thought he might have cried himself to sleep. I started dinner, and then went to wake him up. But he was gone." The image of his rumpled, yet achingly empty bed was firmly etched in her mind.

"Okay, so Sebastian was in his room for less than an hour all told, right?"

An hour didn't seem long, but in reality it was an eternity. "Yes," she whispered. "Forty-five minutes, an hour at the most."

"So then what?" Devon prompted.

"I thought he'd run away, so I ran outside calling his name. He wasn't anywhere along the road, and I thought he might have made his way down to Rose's café, so I went there. But Josie hadn't seen him." The hysteria building inside threatened to explode.

Sebastian!

Devon lightly clasped her shoulders, forcing her to meet his gaze. "Don't panic, there's still plenty of light. We'll find him, okay?"

She wanted to believe that, and forced herself to nod.

"Let's go inside for a minute, I want to be sure there wasn't a note left behind."

A note? "Sebastian can't write," she protested, as they walked up to the front door.

"A note from Grant," Dev clarified.

"I searched the house for Sebastian, under his bed, in the closet, anywhere he might think of to hide," she protested. But she followed him inside, hoping she'd missed something.

Rushing down the hall, she flung open his bedroom door and stood on the threshold, peering around the room as if a note might have materialized in her absence.

But there was no note. Nothing of any sort left behind that she could see.

Janelle put a hand to her chest, fighting to breathe normally. Devon was right, self-recriminations and panic weren't going to help find Sebastian.

"What's this?" Devon asked, walking toward one of the bedroom windows.

She blinked, surprised that there was in fact the edge of a piece of white lined paper taped to the outside of the window, near the window frame. When the spring breeze blew past, the edge of the paper lifted up and away from the window, making it difficult to see.

Before she could move, Devon had brushed past her to head back outside. She followed in his wake, hope blooming in her chest. The note was a positive sign, right? This could be a clue that Devon and the other officers could use to help them find Sebastian.

Dev stood outside her son's bedroom window, reading the note. When she reached up to take it, he lightly caught her wrist, preventing her from touching it. "We need to check for fingerprints, Janelle."

She couldn't suppress a groan of frustration. "But that will take days, Devon." They didn't have days. They didn't even have hours.

There was no telling what might happen if Sebastian didn't get his next peritoneal dialysis treatment.

"Janelle?" Dev's voice broke through her torturous thoughts. "Does this look like Grant's handwriting to you?"

She stared at the note that appeared to be written in haste. *I have Sebastian. It will cost you ten grand to get him back.* There was a phone number with a Milwaukee area code scribbled along the bottom.

"It could be," she said. "But to be honest I only glanced at the letters he sent my sister from prison, begging her to give him a second chance."

"Do you still have those letters?"

Tears threatened again as she shook her head. "No, I didn't keep them. He physically abused Lisa, especially when he was under the influence, and to be honest, I didn't want him to have contact with Sebastian. I was afraid he'd do something drastic. And now-he has."

"It's okay, we can still compare his writing to court documents he would have needed to sign. But at this point, I think we can rule out the possibility of Sebastian running away on his own. It could be that Grant was hanging around and happened to hear the argument. Maybe he even used bits of the fight to get Sebastian to come along with him."

She could easily see how that could have worked, despite the fact that Grant was virtually a stranger to the boy. Grant was still Sebastian's biological father regardless of the fact the courts had severed his custody rights secondary to the abuse. She tried to think back. "Sebastian was wearing blue jeans and a red t-shirt with a dinosaur on the front. He also took his stuffed angel with him."

"Stuffed angel?" Dev looked confused.

She sniffled and swiped at her face. "When I first brought Sebastian home with me, he kept asking about when his mommy was coming home. I told him she was in heaven, but he couldn't grasp the concept. So I bought him a stuffed angel and told him that his mommy was up in heaven with God but that she sent the angel for him to hug and to hold at night when he was afraid."

This time when Dev reached out for her, she collapsed against him, pressing her face into the hollow of his shoulder.

"I can't lose him, Dev, I just can't," she whispered.

"You won't. I promise I'll do everything in my power to find him."

She nodded, knowing that Devon was a good cop, all of the Hope County Sheriff's deputies were good cops. But the relentless fear continued to gnaw at her. "Will you pray with me?"

"Of course I will." Devon pulled her hands up to the center of his chest and held them there. He bowed his head. "Dear Lord, we ask You to please keep Sebastian safe and healthy in Your care. Please grant us the wisdom and guidance to find him, so we can bring him home, Amen."

"Amen," she responded. Lifting her head she gazed up at him. "Thanks, Dev."

"You're welcome." Another cop car pulled up in front of her house and Janelle was relieved to see two more deputies making their way toward them.

She recognized Ian Kramer and Zack Crain. "Have you found something?" Zack called.

"A note taped to the outside of the kid's window." Devon gestured toward it. "I think we have to assume this is a kidnapping."

"Ten grand?" Ian echoed with a frown. "This dude isn't asking for a million dollars, so that means he knows Janelle wouldn't have that much."

She didn't bother to point out that she didn't have the ten grand, either. "We think Sebastian's father, Grant Gardner, took Sebastian. Grant is a known IV drug user, and he was hooked on Heroin before he was arrested for beating and robbing my sister three years ago."

The deputies exchanged serious looks. "Okay, and we think the suspect might be driving a silver sedan?"

"Yes, that's our theory," Devon replied. "There's a phone number on the note. I'm guessing he didn't have Janelle's cell number. I'll give him a call."

Janelle reached out to stop him. "Wait, I think I should

be the one to make the call. He doesn't need to know I've involved the police, does he? He might open up more to me."

Devon scowled, but reluctantly nodded. "Okay, you call, but let's go inside, I want you to put him on speaker, and we can't have any background noise."

Thankful for something to do, she waited while Devon took down the phone number from the note, leaving it right where they'd found it, and then headed back inside.

"Okay, here's how this works," Devon said as she pulled out a pen and paper. "You're going to ask for proof that he has Sebastian, insist on talking to him, okay? Then we'll take notes on what he says."

"What if he wants me to meet him with the money?" she asked.

"Go ahead and agree to make the arrangements. If he's using again, there's a good chance he'll make a mistake." Devon stared at her intently "Any questions?"

Too many to voice so she simply shook her head. The deputies crowded all around her in the kitchen, watching as she punched in the numbers and then set the phone in the center of the table. She waited with her pen poised above the paper.

The phone rang several times before going straight to voice mail. She took a deep breath and then spoke into the phone. "This is Janelle, I found your note and I have the money you requested. Please call me back at this number..." she said each number slowly, as if speaking to a child. "Please, I need to know Sebastian is all right."

She disconnected from the call and slumped in her chair. "I can't believe he didn't answer." She resisted the urge to throw the cell phone across the room.

"He'll call back," Devon assured her. "In the meantime, we'll try to figure out where he might be holding Sebastian."

She dropped her head into her hands, and did her best to put her faith and trust in God.

And Devon.

She had to believe that they'd find Sebastian, before it was too late.

11

———

Devon crossed over to where Zack and Ian, the other deputies, were standing off to the side in Janelle's kitchen. "Did either of you check the Crystal Lake Motel?"

"I did," Zack confirmed. "I flashed Grant's mug shot, no one remembers seeing him and there was no one registered under his name."

Dev had figured as much, but they needed to cover all bases. "What about the campground located down the highway?"

"I drove through it on my way here," Ian spoke up. "No sign of a silver car, but I didn't check every single camper."

"We need a game plan, and we can't wait forever for this guy to return Janelle's call. We need to spread out, try to figure out where he's hiding with Sebastian."

The other deputies nodded in agreement. "I'll head back to the campground," Ian volunteered.

"I'll flash Grant's photo up and down Main Street, see if anyone else recognizes him," Zack added.

"I'll drive around the lake," Dev decided. He turned back

toward Janelle, hating the thought of leaving her here alone. "We're going to start searching the area," he told her. "You have my cell number, right?" When she nodded, he continued, "I need you to call me the minute you hear from this guy. Don't try to do this alone, okay?"

"I won't," she promised, glancing toward the door as the other deputies left. "But isn't there something I can do, too? Sitting here doing nothing will drive me crazy."

He hesitated then nodded, realizing there was no reason she had to be here to get Grant's call since she'd left her cell number. In fact, it would save time if they were together. "Okay, you can ride along with me, an extra pair of eyes couldn't hurt."

"Thank you," she murmured.

He led the way outside, but then she stopped him with a hand on his arm. "Wait, let me get Sebastian's dialysis supplies so that I have them when we find him, just in case this takes longer than we expect."

"Sounds good." He was glad Janelle was maintaining a positive attitude about the outcome of the search. Logically he knew Grant had no reason to hurt the boy, but that didn't mean the guy would take good care of him, either. In fact, there was no telling what Grant might do, especially if he's under the influence.

Or worse, going through withdrawal. Was that why he hadn't answered Janelle's call? Maybe he wasn't capable of having a conversation? And if so, what was Sebastian doing? The poor kid would be scared out of his mind.

He slammed the door on that train of thought, knowing that it wouldn't help to think of the worst case scenario. Grant would call Janelle back. He'd give instructions on where they could meet in order to exchange the cash for the boy.

They'd get Sebastian back safe and sound.

When Janelle returned carrying the familiar backpack bulging with supplies, he opened the passenger door for her. "First thing we need to do is to stop at the bank."

"The bank?" she echoed, staring up at him in confusion. Then realization seemed to sink in. "Dev, I don't have ten thousand dollars. I barely have two thousand left in my savings account, I've been living off that money for the past few weeks."

"I know, but we need some cash to make it look good and we have to get it now, since the bank closes in less than an hour. I'll front the money, no problem." He closed the car door and jogged around to slide in behind the wheel.

"I can't let you do that," she said as he backed out of her driveway. "I'll use my money. Maybe if we get small bills it will look like I have the entire amount."

He wanted to argue, but held his tongue. In the end it didn't matter how much cash she took with her, Grant wouldn't be in a position to argue for more, he'd likely take what he could get.

Although Dev was equally determined they wouldn't lose one dollar of Janelle's money. Grant had already taken enough from her, the television, the computer, the ring. Seemed impossible that he could have blown through all that cash in just a few days, although Dev knew that he probably hadn't gotten very much for any of the items in the first place. Drug addicts generally only looked as far ahead as their next fix.

The trip down Main Street to the Hope County Bank didn't take long. It took some fast talking on his part to convince the bank to hand over the cash, and it wasn't until the bank owner, Edward Finch got involved that they were able to obtain the cash they needed.

Devon hauled the bags of cash out to the car and carefully stored them in the trunk.

Minutes later they were back on the road. "Okay, we need to keep an eye out for any sign of the silver car, and any possible remote hiding spots where Grant could be holding Sebastian. Also, let me know if you see any places for sale, those could be potential hiding places."

"Understood," Janelle said, gripping the cell phone tightly. She plastered her face against the window, taking her job of searching for the silver car very seriously.

He drove slow, giving them both plenty of time to scan the area. On occasion a call would come through the radio, making Janelle jump.

"The bartender at Pete's Pub recognized Gardner, but can't validate that he was driving a silver vehicle," Zack reported. "Last seen two nights ago."

"Ten-four," Dev responded, glancing over at Janelle who was obviously listening intently. "I'm approaching the north side of the lake."

"Campground all clear," Ian said a few minutes later. "No one claims to have recognized our guy, but I have my suspicions related to a couple of guys who I believe may have seen him. I found a small amount of dope in their camper, so I'm hauling them in to headquarters to book them for possession."

"Try to pressure them for the truth," Dev said. "Offer a lighter sentence and fine, if necessary."

"Ten-four," Ian responded.

"Do you think those guys sold Grant drugs?" Janelle asked, a small frown puckering her brow.

He gave her a grim nod. "Yeah, that's what Ian was insinuating. Hopefully Ian will convince them it's in their best interest to cooperate."

"Maybe we should check out the area closer to the campground?" she suggested, a flash of hope brightening her blue eyes.

"After we circle the lake," he agreed. "One step at a time."

She let out a heavy sigh and turned back to peer out the window. She understood that it wasn't easy to have patience, especially when a young child with medical needs was missing. But if Grant really had a car, then he could literally be anywhere.

Even someplace outside of Hope County.

Dev didn't want to think along those lines, at least not yet. He was determined to be thorough in their investigation, which meant checking the surrounding areas first. Besides, Grant would want to be close enough to Crystal Lake in order to make the exchange to get his money.

As Devon continued to drive, he found himself silently praying. Please, Lord, guide us to Sebastian! Keep this little boy safe in Your care, Amen.

JANELLE TRIED to focus her energy on finding the silver car, or any properties that were listed for sale, even though she kept remembering the argument that she'd had with Sebastian.

Ruminating over what she could have done differently wouldn't help. She needed to work with the Hope County Sheriff's Deputies to find her son.

It seemed that there were hardly any cars out on the road, and certainly no silver ones. Which was odd, since silver was a popular color.

She caught a glimpse of a small hand-made sign that

read *For Sale By Owner*, stuck in the ground near a tree-lined driveway on the north side of the road, across from the lake.

"Look, there's a for sale sign," she said excitedly, reaching over to grasp Devon's arm. "We should check it out."

"Good eye," Dev said, making an abrupt right hand turn onto the property. The squad car bumped over the uneven gravel driveway, as they approached the small cabin.

Janelle searched for any sign of life within the building, but the place appeared to be deserted. When she reached for the door handle, Dev stopped her.

"No, you need to wait here. Let me take a look around, first."

"Alright," she reluctantly agreed. She understood Devon's rationale, but that didn't make sitting there while he examined the place any easier.

But it was better than being stuck at home. She kept her eyes peeled on the building, hoping, praying she'd see Sebastian's face in a window.

Devon took his time, walking around the small cabin first, before making his way up to the front door. He knocked, but no one answered.

She held her breath, thinking he might break the door down, but instead he appeared to be speaking through his radio. She wished she could hear the conversation.

Minutes passed with agonizing slowness, and when he walked back toward the car, she wanted to scream in protest.

"Aren't we going to look inside?" she demanded, when he slid in behind the wheel. "Sebastian could be in there right now!"

"Calm down, Janelle. There's no evidence that anyone has been here in the past week, because it hasn't rained and there's a film of dirt on the front porch. There aren't any footprints other than my own."

His explanation caused her shoulders to slump. "Really?"

"Zack is running down the owner now, to see if we can get inside. But I wouldn't hold out any false hopes. I think if Grant and Sebastian had been here, we'd see some indication of that. I can't imagine Grant is that good at covering his tracks."

"So now what?" she asked, trying to hide the depths of her despair.

"We keep looking," Dev said calmly. "Are you still game? Or do you want me to take you back home?"

"I'm sticking with you."

"Good. Let's go." Dev executed a three point-turn so he could head back down the driveway toward the road.

They made a slow circle around the lake, ending up back on Main Street. Janelle couldn't help being discouraged by their lack of progress, especially when Dev returned to her townhouse.

A tiny flicker of hope in her heart convinced her Sebastian may have returned in her absence, but when she rushed back inside, she found the townhouse as empty as they had left it.

"What's next?" she asked, turning to face Devon.

"Zack is getting ready to send me a list of properties that are for sale in the area," he said, glancing down at his smart phone.

More properties? They hadn't found anything encouraging at the last few they'd looked at. She tried not to sound as tense and irritable as she felt. "Isn't there something else we can do?"

Dev didn't take umbrage with her tone. "Listen, we know

that Grant likely purchased drugs at the campsite. What if he took a tent and pitched it on some property that happens to be for sale? If it's a big enough lot, with trees for cover, no one would see them."

"That sounds like a possibility," she admitted, feeling better at his logic.

Devon's cell phone rang, and he quickly answered it. "Armbruster," he said in a formal tone.

She fell silent, able to hear a bit of the other person's conversation. "Confirmed drug buy."

"Good to know, what else did they have to say?" Devon asked.

She realized the campers must have admitted to selling drugs to Grant. The thought of him using again made her feel sick to her stomach. Especially since he had Sebastian with him.

Lost in her thoughts, she missed what the other deputy said. "Okay, thanks, Ian. It's good to know that we're on the right track. I'm waiting for a list of properties from Zack, once I get them we can split them up."

"What kind of drugs did Grant buy?" she asked when Dev disconnected from the call.

He grimaced. "Heroin," he admitted. "But again, the last time they saw Gardner was two days ago, the same night as the bartender. And one of the campers happened to be the one who sold Lisa's ring to Gretchen. We have a good connection and theory here, but we still haven't found anyone who has seen him in the last forty-eight hours."

Forty-eight hours to create a plan to kidnap Sebastian.

A lifetime.

She drew in a choppy breath. "It's past dinnertime," she said in a low tone. "I'm sure Sebastian is hungry."

"Don't, Janelle," Devon murmured. He stepped closer

and put his arm around her shoulders. "Don't think the worst. For all we know, Grant has food tucked away, especially if he's been camping up here."

She nodded and rested against him, trying to absorb some of his strength. "Why hasn't Grant called me back?" she asked, her voice rising in helpless frustration. "What's taking him so long?"

"I don't know," Devon admitted. "Maybe he's waiting for darkness to fall. Or maybe he thinks that the longer he waits, the more frantic you'll be to pay the money. There's just no telling what's going through his mind."

"He's on drugs, which means he might not be thinking clearly at all." She shivered and burrowed closer to Devon's warmth. "For all we know he could be passed out, leaving Sebastian unattended. That poor little boy is probably scared to death, wondering what will happen to him."

"Janelle, please," he begged, reaching down to lift her chin, forcing her to meet his gaze. "Please stop thinking like that. Fear will only paralyze us. We need to remember that Sebastian is smart. He'll manage just fine."

She really, really wanted to believe that. She forced a lop-sided smile. "Okay, you're right. Thank you, Devon. I couldn't handle this without you."

He stared down at her with fathomless deep brown eyes, and she almost thought he was going to kiss her, but the moment was broken when his phone chimed with an incoming message.

"This might be Zack's list," he said, releasing his hold on her.

She stepped back and rubbed her hands over her arms. What was wrong with her? She shouldn't have been thinking of kissing Devon. Not when Sebastian was out there, alone and afraid.

"Ian? It's Dev, I have the list of properties and am sending it to you, now." There was a moment of silence as Dev hit the message on his phone. Then he said, "I'll start at the top, you start at the bottom and we'll meet in the middle, okay?"

Janelle grabbed a jacket then decided to gather more things for Sebastian, in case they found him. She tossed his coat over her arm, and then went into the kitchen to pull out a box of cheesy fish crackers.

"I'm ready to go," she announced.

"Great." Devon glanced down at his list, then led the way outside to the car. "The first property isn't that far from the cabin that was listed for sale, we'll start there."

She nodded, grateful for something constructive to do. Although she couldn't help thinking that time was not on their side. Her phone hadn't rung even once, and her nerves were stretched thin with fear and worry. Yet as Dev drove, she continued to search for any sign of a silver car.

"What else did Ian have to say?" she asked. "You mentioned something about how it was good we're on the right track."

"The campers claimed Grant was driving a silver car, and that he had a tent, along with other camping gear."

She sucked in a quick breath. "So he was watching me for the past few days."

"Yeah." Devon's expression turned dark. "I wish I gotten his plate numbers long before this."

"No sense in looking back," she reminded him. "I've been doing that enough for the both of us."

He glanced at her with a wry grin. "Yeah, easier said than done, isn't it?"

"You got that right. I keep wishing I would have handled Sebastian's anger differently."

He tilted his head to the side. "You never mentioned what caused Sebastian's temper tantrum in the first place."

She swallowed hard then decided it was better to be honest. "You."

Dev did a double take. "What do you mean? What about me?"

"Remember how I found that retired nurse to babysit Sebastian?" When he nodded, she continued, "Well he didn't like her. He kept telling me that he only wanted you to babysit him. And when I told him that wasn't possible, he lost it." The argument seemed so petty now that Sebastian was gone.

Devon was silent for a long moment. "I'm sorry. I had no idea."

"It's not your fault. Sebastian has never had a father figure. Grant went to jail when he was barely a year old." She sighed, and then added, "To be honest, I didn't much like Mrs. Alice, either. She was old and crabby and as Sebastian put it, she smelled funny."

Devon's lips twitched with repressed humor. "So I should forgo showering the next time I visit you both?"

She managed a small smile. "I don't think that will help, Sebastian will still love you anyway. Ms. Alice smelled like moth balls."

The shrill ringing of her cell phone interrupted them. Her heart pounded in her chest as she glanced down at the screen, recognizing Grant's number.

"Hello?"

"I have—the boy," Grant's voice was slurred. "Got money?"

"Yes, I have the money," she said, speaking slowly and clearly so that he could understand her, despite whatever drugs he'd taken. "I'll pay you to get Sebastian back. Where can I meet you?"

"The woods..." his voice trailed off the rest of his speech garbled to the point she couldn't figure out what he was saying.

"Where in the woods? Tell me where to meet you?"

Seconds passed and then the line abruptly disconnected. She stared at the device and quickly pushed the redial button.

But Grant didn't answer, neither did Sebastian.

And she still had no idea where they were hiding.

12

Devon hated hearing the panic in Janelle's tone. "I can't believe it! Grant didn't tell me where to meet him!"

Devon understood her angst, but couldn't think of anything to say that would make her feel any better. He struggled to remain calm. "Take a breath and tell me exactly what he said."

"He said he had Sebastian and asked if I had the money, but he was clearly under the influence. When I asked where to meet him, he simply said, the woods, and then his voice trailed off. Now he's not answering the phone!" She thumped her fist on the phone as if that would help.

Devon tightened his grip on the steering wheel, battling a wave of frustration. Janelle had every right to be upset, but she needed him to be strong, so he did his best to maintain his professionalism.

"I grew up here, Janelle. I know these woods and so do the other deputies. We'll find him," he said, knowing that the mantra was likely getting old.

But he needed to believe it just as badly as she did. Despite the fact that Sebastian originally reminded him of what he'd loved and lost, he cared very much about the little guy.

The sun was dipping down on the horizon and he knew that it would be dark soon, making the task of finding Sebastian difficult, especially if they were hiding in the woods.

The wooded area along the north side of the lake covered a good twenty-thirty acres and since it wasn't damaged by the fire, the evergreen trees were thick and dense. The only good news was that the rest of the trees only had early spring buds on them, which might make it easier to find a tent.

Who was he kidding? Finding a tent in thirty acres would be nearly impossible. Especially since Sebastian's exchange was due soon.

In less than an hour.

So they had to try. Using his radio, he updated the rest of the deputies, asking them to meet him at the corner of Lake Drive and Elmhurst. From there, they'd have to formulate some sort of search plan.

But hiking through the woods at night wouldn't be easy. He radioed into the dispatch office. "Ask Sheriff Torretti if he'll call in a K9 search and rescue unit."

"Ten-four," the dispatcher responded.

Maybe he should have requested this earlier. He'd thought for sure that Grant would return Janelle's call to set up a meeting. But once they discovered how Grant had bought drugs from the other campers, he should have altered their game plan.

He'd made the wrong call, and both Janelle and Sebastian would pay the ultimate price for his mistake.

Dev did his best to shove his useless guilt aside. Focus. He needed to focus on saving Sebastian.

The meeting point was up ahead and he was glad to see that Ian was already there, waiting for them.

Devon rolled down his window. "Do you have extra flashlights?"

"Yep. I'm ready when you are."

"Where's Zack?" Devon asked, as he pushed open his car door and climbed out of the vehicle.

"I think that's him now," Ian said, gesturing to the twin pair of headlights approaching from the east.

Dev blew out a heavy breath. "Okay, we need to figure out where this jerk is hiding with Sebastian. The only clue we have is that there's a possibility they're in the woods. Although it doesn't make a lot of sense that he'd arrange for a meeting there."

"Guy's a druggie, who knows what's going on in his head?" Ian muttered darkly.

Dev silently agreed. Addiction was a terrible thing. It took good people and twisted them into someone who would do anything to get what they needed. Obviously Gardner wasn't thinking logically or rationally.

So if he was a drug user and had kidnapped a child, what would he do? Where would he go?

His radio buzzed. "Sheriff approved the K9 unit, should be there within twenty minutes or so," the dispatcher informed him.

Twenty minutes was too long. Although he wasn't going to turn down the offer of help, either. Glancing at Janelle's pinched features, the phone she held so tightly in her hand, he knew he'd search all night if necessary.

"Ten-four." He turned his attention to the other two deputies. "Are there more deputies coming?"

Zack nodded. "I reached the two night shift deputies, they're coming in early to assist."

Five deputies to cover thirty acres. It could be worse, but he felt as if twenty deputies wouldn't be enough. "All right, let's split up the area evenly between the five of us and spread out. The K9 unit will be coming soon, too. Once the dog is able to pick up the child's scent, our search field will narrow considerably."

"I want to help search, too," Janelle said, coming up to stand beside him.

He shook his head regretfully. "I'm sorry, but you'll need to wait here for the K9 unit. You have Sebastian's coat, they'll need that for the dogs. And being in the woods at night is dangerous, I don't want you to get lost, or worse, run into a hungry bear."

She shivered and crossed her arms protectively across her chest. "You're making that up, aren't the bears still in hibernation?"

"I wouldn't count on it," Ian spoke up. "We've had decent weather for the past week; I suspect they're up and about by now."

She blanched. "What if Grant and Sebastian run into a bear?"

Dev wished he'd have kept his mouth shut about the wildlife. Bears weren't the only threat: game warden Reese Weber had found bobcat tracks recently, too. Thankfully the deer and other small game wouldn't pose much of a problem.

"I'm sure they'll be fine," Devon said reassuringly.

Zack spread out a map of the area on the hood of Ian's squad car and glanced at Devon. "Okay, how do you want to split this up?"

Devon stared at the map for a moment, then tapped the

area to the west. "I'll start here."

"Okay, I'll take this one," Ian put his finger on another part of the map.

Zack nodded in agreement. "I'll take this area." He scribbled their names on the map, so that when the other deputies arrived they wouldn't end up in the same place. "Janelle, you're going to be our point person, okay?" He handed her a radio. "When the K9 unit arrives, you let us know. And when the other deputies arrive you show them this map. We're counting on you."

Janelle clipped the radio to the edge of her sweatshirt. "Okay. I can do this."

Dev was proud of the way she set her fear and panic aside to assist in any way possible. He wanted to pull her close and kiss her, but managed to hold back sensitive to the fact they weren't alone.

He lifted the heavy flashlight and headed into the woods on foot. As he made his way through the trees, listening intently for any human sounds, he abruptly remembered the shallow cave where he and Steven had played as kids.

The cave was little more than a crevasse in the side of a large hill, too shallow for a bear to consider using it as a place to hibernate. Not only was it a perfect hiding spot for a human, but it also happened to be in his search area.

He decided to check there first, especially since the hill wasn't too far away. Using his compass he made his way in a north-east direction.

Slowly sweeping the flashlight from side to side, the beam cut through the darkness. In the daylight, he might be able to find Grant's tracks, but searching in the dark wouldn't be easy and he didn't want to waste precious time.

The radio remained silent as he made his way through the woods. Devon tried to walk fast without making too much noise, but the sound of a twig snapping beneath his heel echoed like a gunshot through the darkness.

It took longer than he anticipated to reach the crevasse in the hill. When he saw the area reflected in the beam of his flashlight, he aimed his light down on the ground, covered the lens with his hand to dim the light and slowed his pace, moving as quietly as possible.

He debated calling for Sebastian by name, unwilling to alert Grant to his presence if indeed they were tucked away in there. He edged closer and strained to listen.

His high hopes deflated when he couldn't hear anything but silence.

Just as he was about to give up, he heard a weird scratching noise.

Something was inside the crevasse, but was it animal?

Or human?

JANELLE SILENTLY PRAYED over and over again as she waited from inside Devon's squad car for news. Any news. Being here alone wasn't nearly as frightening as wondering what was going on in the woods.

Sebastian was well overdue for his peritoneal dialysis exchange. Would he be feeling sick as a result? Or just tired? She had been meticulous about doing his exchanges so she had no idea what to expect him to feel like when he missed one.

Deep down, she hoped he was asleep, dreaming of good things rather than being huddled someplace, alone and afraid.

She took a small measure of comfort in knowing that he had his stuffed angel with him. And of course, she firmly believed God was watching over him.

What was taking them so long? She stared blindly through the windshield, the darkness so complete that she couldn't see more than a few feet in any direction.

Headlights shimmered on the horizon and she couldn't deny feeling relieved that more deputies were on their way to help search. She was so afraid they'd decide to hold off and wait until morning.

When the car pulled up and parked alongside the others, she slid out of the car to greet them, a bit surprised when she realized that Sheriff Luke Torretti was walking toward her.

"Hi Sheriff," she greeted him. "Devon asked me to stay here, to show you the map so you'd know where they're searching."

The Sheriff nodded and then reached out to take her chilly hand in his. "I'm sorry that you have to go through this, Janelle," he said in a low voice full of sympathy. "I want you to know we're doing everything in our power to find your son."

Tears threatened and she rapidly blinked them away. "Thank you. Is the K9 unit here? I have Sebastian's jacket."

"Right here, Ma'am," a deep voice said from behind the sheriff. A tall man with jet black hair stepped forward, a large yellow Lab at his side. "I'm Seth Bertram and this is my dog, Buck. Will you hand me the boy's jacket?"

Janelle was impressed at how well behaved Buck was. He sat motionless beside his master. Seth took the jacket and then held it for Buck to sniff.

The dog buried his nose in the fabric for several long moments before Seth straightened. "I'll keep the jacket with me, if you don't mind," he said.

"Of course I don't mind. Thanks for your help."

"It's no problem, Ma'am. This is what we've trained for."

Seth turned toward the Sheriff. "We'll start out by walking back and forth to see if Buck picks up the scent."

"Sounds good." Sheriff Torretti turned to Janelle. "Any news yet?"

"Nothing." She couldn't begin to say how much the lack of information haunted her. She'd assumed there would be regular updates, but at this point, it was clear the deputies didn't have anything to report.

What if they were looking in the wrong place? She reviewed the brief, disjointed conversation she'd had with Grant. Technically, he hadn't said, "Meet us in the woods."

She reminded herself that they'd already searched all the other possible places: the vacant properties, the motel, the campground, and up and down Main Street. They hadn't checked the hiking trail along the lake, since the wildfire last fall had destroyed the area.

Where else could they be?

The woods made the most sense, but suddenly she was overwhelmed with doubt. Since when had Grant ever been logical?

Since never.

"Good boy," Seth's deep voice cut through the night.

Janelle rushed over. "Did you find something?"

Seth nodded. "Buck here picked up the boy's scent. Sheriff, do you want to come along?"

Sheriff Torretti nodded. "Yes. Janelle, stay here and let the others know the K9 dog picked up the boy's scent. We'll be in touch as soon as we have something."

She resisted the urge to beg him to stay. Better that Seth and Buck have all the help and support they need. She returned to the car, watching as the two men bearing flashlights followed the yellow lab's lead through the trees.

She did as she was told, using the radio to let all the

deputies know that the K9 unit was following Sebastian's scent. Both Zack and Ian responded affirmatively.

But she hadn't heard anything from Devon.

The bobbing of the Sheriff's and the K9 cop's flashlights grew dim, until the darkness swallowed them up. She bit her lip to keep from crying out in despair. Tilting her head back so she could gaze up at the stars hovering in the inky sky, she prayed once again.

Please keep Sebastian safe in Your care!

Minutes crawled by slowly, and the night air grew chilly, forcing her once again back inside Devon's squad car. His male, musky scent lingered inside, giving her a small measure of comfort.

When her radio crackled a few minutes later, she nearly jumped out of her skin. It took a minute for her to recognize Devon's voice. "Janelle? Do you copy?"

Eagerly she pressed the button. "Yes, Devon, I'm here. What happened? You didn't respond earlier, did you find something?"

"Yes. I have Sebastian, over."

She clenched her fingers on the radio with excitement. "You found him? Is he okay?"

"He's okay," there was a brief pause before he continued "I'm carrying him out now."

The hesitancy in his tone caused a frisson of worry to snake down her spine. Sebastian was just okay? What did that mean? Was the boy unconscious? Unable to talk?

Had going too long without his exchange caused some sort of harm? And if so, was it temporary?

Or permanent?

She leaped out of the front passenger seat to grab the backpack of supplies she brought from home out of the back. The minute Devon arrived with Sebastian, she intended to be ready.

Once she had everything ready to go, she turned and gazed toward the woods, trying to catch the glimmer of light that would indicate they were close. She desperately needed to see her son for herself, to touch him, to hold him.

But as she stood there, looking at nothing, she realized that Devon hadn't said anything about Grant. Because he was there but unconscious and unable to put up a fight?

Or because he'd disappeared, leaving Sebastian alone to die?

13

Devon carried Sebastian, the stuffed angel firmly wedged between them, his long strides eating up the ground as he made his way back toward the squad car where Janelle was waiting.

"Hang in there, Sebastian," he murmured, wrapping his coat more tightly around the child. The boy's hands had been like ice when he'd arrived, but they were beginning to warm up nicely.

"Okay," the child's voice was faint and he was so sleepy that Devon couldn't be sure that Gardner hadn't drugged him up to keep him quiet.

Not that the guy would be drugging anyone ever again. When Devon arrived, he'd found Grant dead of what Dev could only assume was an accidental drug overdose.

He felt sad that Grant had died so young, like so many others who ended up hooked on drugs. But thankfully, Sebastian hadn't seemed to notice the guy who'd taken him from Janelle was dead.

A light from the west grew brighter and soon Devon

realized that the K9 unit was coming toward him. "Armbruster?" a familiar voice called out. "Is that you?"

"Yes, Sheriff. I have Sebastian, but the guy who kidnapped him is dead."

"Dead, how?" Sheriff Torretti asked, frowning as he approached. "I don't recall hearing a gunshot."

"No sir, I didn't shoot him. He was crumpled up on the ground when I arrived with a syringe hanging out of his arm. I'm pretty sure it was an accidental overdose, but we'll need to notify the ME to verify that."

Sheriff Torretti blew out a heavy breath. "What a waste."

Devon silently agreed. He glanced at the K9 officer. "I'm Deputy Armbruster. I can take you back to where Grant's body is located as soon as I hand Sebastian over to Janelle. He was pretty cold when I found him."

"I'm Deputy Seth Bertram, and this is my partner, Buck. We can probably find the dead guy ourselves, Buck is pretty good at that kind of thing," Seth said. "No need to rush back."

Devon nodded. "Let me know if you can't find it for some reason." He edged past the two men, grateful when Sebastian squirmed a bit against him.

"Dev?" Sebastian asked in a whisper.

"Yeah, buddy, I'm here. You're safe now, nothing to worry about, okay?"

"'Kay," the boy mumbled.

Devon's heart squeezed in his chest as he pressed a kiss to the top of Sebastian's head. In the short time that he'd been around the child, he'd come to care about him, deeply.

He cared to the point where the thought of not seeing him, or Janelle again, was intolerable.

Yet could he really stay here in Crystal Lake for the rest of his life? Janelle made it clear she loved the small town, with its community atmosphere. And up until recently, he'd enjoyed it, too.

But what about his dream of making a difference, like his brother Steven had done? Was that God's plan for him?

Or had God's plan been about staying here to find Sebastian?

Dev knew there was time to think about the future, but right now, he needed to pick up the pace. Janelle would want to get started on Sebastian's dialysis exchange right away.

When he emerged from the woods, Janelle came running toward him, her eyes full of gratitude. "Oh, Devon, thank you for finding him. Thank you so much!"

"Let me carry him to the car," he said, when she reached up to take Sebastian. "He was chilled when I found him, so I've wrapped him up in my coat. We'll need to keep him as warm as possible."

"Okay." She kept her hand on the child's arm, as if she couldn't bear to be separated from him for another second. When they reached his squad car, he waited for her to open the back door before he crouched down and gently set the boy inside.

"Oh, Sebastian," Janelle murmured, kissing his cheek. "I'm so glad you're okay. Let's get this catheter connected to a drainage bag."

Dev stepped back, watching for a moment as Janelle washed her hands with sanitizer before moving Sebastian's clothing just enough to expose his catheter. It didn't take long to begin draining the fluid from his abdomen and she gently pulled the coat back around him for warmth.

"Mommy?" Sebastian asked, reaching his hand toward Janelle.

She leaned in and took his hand, pressing a kiss to his fingers. "Yes, Sebastian, I'm right here."

A faint smile crossed his features. "I wuv you."

"Oh sweetie, I love you, too." Janelle's voice broke and Devon quickly stepped forward to draw her into his embrace.

Janelle turned and wrapped her arms around his waist. "What happened to Grant?" she asked in soft voice, obviously not wanting Sebastian to overhear.

"He's dead, Janelle," Dev informed her. "Looks like he killed himself by overdosing on drugs."

She buried closer, tightening her grip on him. "That's so terrible," she whispered. "But I can't deny being glad he's no longer a threat to us. To Sebastian."

"I know, it's awful to lose someone so young, especially when he might have been able to turn his life around with treatment. But the important thing is, we have Sebastian back, unharmed. And I don't think Sebastian knows Grant's dead, either. He was pretty groggy when I found him."

That news caused her head to come up. "Groggy? Did Grant drug him?"

Dev hesitated and shrugged. "I honestly don't know. Sebastian was chilled when I found him, so it could be that he was a bit hypothermic, or exhausted, or even because he was late in getting his exchange."

She drew a deep breath. "Most likely, a combination of all three," she agreed. She stared up at him for a moment. "How did you find him so fast? The K9 unit had barely gotten started."

He flashed a wry grin. "I got lucky," he admitted. "I remembered how Steven and I played in this area when we were younger. We found this crevasse in the side of a hill, shallow enough to be safe from predators. I was so glad I managed to get there in time to get Sebastian out of the cold."

"Me, too." She levered up on her tiptoes to brush his cheek with her lips. "Words can't express how much I appreciate what you've done for me, Devon."

He longed to kiss her properly, but wasn't sure if she really felt the same way. Right now, she was simply grateful for having her son back, safe and sound.

For all he knew, she still only cared about him as a friend, while his feelings for her had somehow become much more complicated than that.

JANELLE GLANCED at the dashboard clock, wincing when she realized that the hour was approaching midnight. As much as she needed to get a paycheck, she couldn't go into work the next morning.

She was exhausted, as was Sebastian, but that wasn't the real reason. After everything that had transpired in the last few hours, there was no way she could bear to leave Sebastian with Mrs. Alice.

Yet she hated the thought of calling in to work, asking for yet another unpaid personal day. But what choice did she have? It was too late to find someone to switch shifts for her.

Devon pulled into her driveway and then shut off the car. "I'll carry Sebastian in for you," he offered.

Since she needed to haul in all the supplies, she nodded. "Okay, thanks."

They both climbed out of the car and she pulled the backpack up from between her knees and looped it over her shoulder. Sebastian had been so tired he'd barely eaten any of the fish crackers she'd brought along.

He was safe, and that was all that mattered, she reminded herself. No doubt, he'd wake up starving for breakfast.

She used her key to unlock the door and held it for Devon as he carried Sebastian inside. She flipped on the kitchen light, then went down the hall to help tuck Sebastian into bed.

"G'night, Dev. G'night, Mommy," Sebastian murmured before snuggling into the blankets she brought up beneath his chin.

That was the second time he'd called her *Mommy*, and as much as she rejoiced in the endearment, she knew that it was possible Sebastian was confused.

In the morning she'd be Nana again.

She leaned down to press a gentle kiss on his forehead before straightening up to ease out of the room. Devon waited at the doorway, a tender smile on his face.

"I'm glad he's doing all right," Devon whispered as she closed the bedroom door part way, leaving it open an inch in case Sebastian suffered from any nightmares as the night wore on.

"You and me, both," she agreed. As she headed for the kitchen, she pulled out her phone. "I need to call the hospital to let them know I won't be in tomorrow morning."

"I thought you had that woman all lined up to watch Sebastian?" Devon asked with a puzzled frown.

"I just can't do it," she confided. "Sebastian didn't like her and after everything he's been through, I can't just leave him with her in the morning. I'll have to try and find someone else to watch him."

"I'll come and stay until 2:30," Devon offered in a low husky voice.

She appreciated his generosity, but she couldn't just

leave work early, either. "No, that's not necessary. I'm lucky to get home by four in the afternoon, so we'd need someone to watch him for that period of time." It took her a minute to notice she'd used the pronoun *we*, as if they were really in this together.

But they weren't. A fact she needed to remember.

She cleared her throat, hoping Devon hadn't noticed her subconscious slip. "Don't worry, I'm sure I'll find someone to watch Sebastian. I can always offer to pick up some other shift." She frowned, wondering if Tina, the young woman who finished her certified nursing assistant training would get back to her soon enough to possibly pick up a shift over the weekend?

Devon didn't seem inclined to leave, but stood leaning against the kitchen counter while she called into work.

Thankfully, the charge nurse didn't seem too upset by the news. "We're actually staffed okay for the day shift tomorrow, Janelle," Kimberly said. "But we're short staffed this weekend, so let us know if you can help out at all."

She let out her breath in a relieved sigh. "I'm hoping to find someone to watch Sebastian over the weekend, so that is a definite possibility. I'll let you know for sure when I have someone lined up."

"Okay, sounds good," Kimberly said cheerfully.

Janelle disconnected from the call. Then she called Mrs. Alice, wincing at the late hour. Thankfully the woman didn't answer so she left a brief message, cancelling her for the next morning. Then she glanced at Devon who was staring at her intently.

"I'm off this weekend," he said in a casual tone. "I'd be happy to watch Sebastian."

She would have liked nothing better, but she shook her head. "I don't think that's a good idea," she protested.

His gaze darkened. "Why not?"

Her heart literally ached in her chest, but she knew she needed to stand firm "because Sebastian is already getting too attached to you, Devon."

"So? I'm pretty attached to him, too."

Was he being obtuse on purpose? "And what about when you move away for your new job?" she asked in a challenging tone. "I'll tell you what will happen you'll break his tiny heart into a zillion pieces."

He opened his mouth to protest, but then closed it again. He pushed himself upright and then walked past her toward the door.

She wanted to call out to him, to stop him from leaving, but at the same time, she wasn't about to prevent him from pursuing his future.

Too bad Devon didn't care about her in the same way she cared for him.

And when he left the townhouse, shutting the door quietly behind him, she collapsed into a chair and covered her face with her hands.

Sebastian was safe there was no reason to cry.

But she couldn't hold back the tears that trickled down her cheeks, anyway.

DEVON LEFT Janelle's townhouse feeling as if he'd been kicked in the gut.

When his cell phone rang, he answered it with a growl. "Armbruster."

"Hey Dev, I'd like your statement before you head home," Sheriff Torretti said in a tone that didn't leave room for argument. "We found Grant Gardner's body and are sending it to Dr. Hauf, the medical examiner."

Duty calls, he thought with a sigh. "Sure thing. I'll get right on that."

"By the way, Captain Mark Anderson from the Madison PD called asking me to give you a reference," the sheriff continued. "Of course I gave you high marks."

The news should have cheered him up, but it didn't. "Thank you, sir."

There was a brief pause, and Devon stood by his squad car, waiting for the sheriff to finish up the conversation. "I'm sorry to see you go, Armbruster. I'll miss having you on my team, you're a good cop."

Dev rubbed the back of his neck. "Thank you, sir. I want you to know that I've enjoyed working for you."

"Then why are you so anxious to leave?"

He repeated what he'd told Janelle just a few days ago. "I guess I feel like I should be making a bigger difference in people's lives. You're a good sheriff Hope County doesn't have a lot of crime."

"But we have some crime, and you might want to think about the fact that helping people you know on a first name basis can be more rewarding than helping strangers," Sheriff Torretti pointed out. "In fact, I'm not sure what would have happened to Sebastian if you hadn't known where to look for him."

He thought back to how chilled the boy was when he'd arrived. What if he'd been a few hours later? He didn't want to think about the fact that Sebastian may have died.

"Someone else may have thought of that hiding spot, too," he said breaking the silence.

"Not sure I agree with you on that. Zack grew up here, too, but he didn't know anything about that crevasse in the side of the hill. Frankly, I have no idea how Gardner managed to stumble upon it."

Dev was shocked to hear that Zack Crain didn't have any knowledge of that area of the woods. "Pure luck, probably," he said in response to the sheriff's comment about Gardner. "I'm on my way to headquarters now," he said, changing the subject as he slid behind the wheel. "You'll have my report tonight, sir."

Another slight pause, before the sheriff responded. "Thanks, Devon. You did a good job, tonight."

The sheriff disconnected from the call before he could respond, and Devon set his phone aside and turned the key in the ignition.

As he drove, he kept thinking about what Sheriff Torretti had said about helping people you know being more rewarding than helping total strangers.

Was he right about that? Hadn't Janelle mentioned something similar?

The thought nagged at him as he drove into the parking lot and trudged into the building. When he booted up his computer, he was surprised to see that he had a message from the Madison Police Department, asking him to call them as soon as possible if he was still interested in the position.

And he was interested, wasn't he?

He stared at the e-mail, belatedly realizing that he hadn't checked his computer prior to responding to Janelle's panicked phone call. Of course, it was too late to do anything about the message now. He'd have to remember to call first thing in the morning.

And do what? Agree to take the job if they offered it to him?

He couldn't believe he was having second thoughts about moving away from Crystal Lake. He'd sent out his resume months ago. He'd be foolish to turn down the opportunity.

But truthfully, he wasn't nearly as thrilled with the idea of moving any longer not since getting to know Janelle and Sebastian.

His heart clenched in his chest. He hadn't intended to fall in love ever again. So why was he picturing a future with Janelle and Sebastian?

Ignoring the message wasn't easy, but he needed to write up his report for the Sheriff. When something this big happened in their small county, he knew that there would be lots of scrutiny on how they'd handled the case.

Devon couldn't deny there were a few things he could have done differently.

But he didn't have many regrets, since he'd found a way to deliver on his promise to bring Sebastian home to Janelle.

And she'd turned around and refused his offer to watch Sebastian over the weekend while she went to work.

Maybe he was fooling himself, thinking that he had a reason to stay here in Crystal Lake.

He finished his report, printed it out and set a copy on the Sheriff's desk.

And as he drove home to his dark, empty house, he tried not to think about the fact that if he took the job in Madison, he'd just be trading one dark, empty, lonely house for another.

14

Janelle didn't sleep well that night, thanks in part to the way Devon had left so abruptly when she'd declined his offer to babysit over the weekend. In the early morning light, she found herself second-guessing her decision not to have Devon stay with Sebastian while she went to work.

She wanted to do the right thing for Sebastian. He was already emotionally attached to Devon, would one more weekend hurt? Even if Dev did get another job he'd have to give a two week notice to the Sheriff, wouldn't he?

The thought of not seeing Devon again after a few weeks, filled her with sorrow. Not just because she'd miss his friendship and support, which she would.

But she'd miss his hugs, and his kisses, even more.

She gave a little sigh, wishing she'd gotten rid of Lane long before Sebastian came into her life. Maybe she would have noticed Devon earlier, and gotten to know him better, before he'd made the decision to move on to a big city.

Although truthfully, she had no reason to believe Devon

felt remotely the same way about her. She knew from Josie just how much Devon had loved Debra, his fiancée.

"Mommy?" Sebastian's weak voice calling her from his bedroom interrupted her thoughts.

A warm glow settled in the region of her heart at the way he said *Mommy*, and she hoped he'd continue calling her that from now on. She hurried down the hall to his bedroom. "Good morning, sweetie, how are you feeling?"

"Hungry," he said rubbing his eyes with his chubby fists.

She lifted him up and gave him a hug and a kiss, which he returned enthusiastically, before carrying him into the living room. There was no reason he couldn't walk, but she wanted to keep him close after everything that had happened the night before. "What would you like for breakfast?" she asked as she placed him on the sofa.

"French toast, please." He gazed up at her, his wide blue eyes filled with hope. "Is Dev here, too?"

She was caught off guard by the question, why would he think Devon stayed here over night? Maybe Sebastian's memory was a bit fuzzy. "No, he went home last night after he rescued you." She hadn't asked Sebastian about what happened, figuring that he'd tell her when he was ready to talk. The last thing she wanted to do was to bring up bad memories. "Dev has to work again today, so I don't know if he'll have time to stop by."

Sebastian's expression reflected his disappointment. "Couldn't you call him?"

She hesitated, unsure of the right approach. Last night she'd wanted to protect Sebastian from getting even more attached to Devon than he was already. But was it better to wean him slowly over the next few days? Or cut the ties cold turkey?

Janelle knew that if she called Devon, he'd come to see

Sebastian, regardless of how they'd parted last night. He'd never let his anger keep him from seeing Sebastian.

Just one of the many reason's he'd be a great father.

"It's too early to call him now," she said. "But maybe later, okay?"

"Okay," he said in a dejected tone.

Janelle felt bad for him, and toyed with the idea of asking Devon to stop by for a few minutes before work. Not long enough to play a game, but to at least say hi and maybe toss a few baseballs. Maybe he'd even bring his nephew's baseball mitt over.

Warming to the idea, she headed into the kitchen to begin making French toast, deciding to wait until after breakfast to do Sebastian's exchange in order to get him back on a reasonable schedule. From what she could tell, the little boy hadn't suffered any ill effects from the delay in his exchange last night.

Thankfully, no nightmares, either.

Once breakfast was finished and she'd completed Sebastian's exchange, Janelle decided to try calling the teenager, Tina Jamison one more time. The girl hadn't returned her call, which wasn't too encouraging. But it was possible that she'd been busy with homework, or after school activities.

"Oh, yes, I'll get Tina for you," her mother said. "She's off school today and tomorrow."

After a minute a young woman's voice came over the line. "Hello?"

Janelle drew a deep breath and tried to think of the best way to get the girl to agree. "Hi Tina, my name is Janelle Larson and I left your mother a message about possibly doing some babysitting for my son, Sebastian. He has kidney failure and needs peritoneal dialysis exchanges three times a day. Since I knew you recently passed the certified nursing assistant program in Madison, I thought you might be interested in putting some of those patient care skills to good use."

"Oh, yes, my mom just told me you called last night. I would love to help you out, I've recently been accepted into UW Madison starting this fall and I'm hoping to get into the nursing program."

Janelle perked up at this news, even though obviously having Tina babysit was little more than a short term solution. "I love nursing," she confided. "I work in the ER here at Hope County Hospital."

"Really" Tina sounded excited. "I'd love to get a nursing assistant job there for the summer."

"I could give you a reference," Janelle offered, even though she knew that if Tina did get a nursing assistant job she might not have any time to help her out with Sebastian.

"That would be awesome, although I'm sure you'd have to wait and see how well I do with Sebastian first."

Hope bloomed in her chest. "So you'll do it? You'll learn how to do Sebastian's exchanges and maybe watch him on the weekends?"

"Sure, I could even do some evenings if needed," Tina agreed.

Janelle did a quick fist-pump. "Great, thank you so much! I need to work this weekend, is that too soon?"

"Just a minute," Tina said. In the background Janelle heard Tina talking to her mother as they discussed the weekend plans. "I can do Saturday if that helps," Tina said.

"Saturday is perfect. But I'll need you to come over sometime today or tomorrow to learn how to do his exchanges. You're off school, right?"

"Yes, we're off school, but I have plans today. Can I come over tomorrow, instead?"

"Sure." Janelle couldn't believe how things were falling into place at least temporarily. She made plans to meet with Tina tomorrow at one o'clock in the afternoon and then broke the news to Sebastian.

"Tina? Not Mrs. Alice?"

She hesitated, wondering if she should give the retired nurse another chance. "You might need both of them to alternate," she admitted. "I know you don't like Mrs. Alice so I promise I'll keep looking for someone to replace her, okay?"

"Okay," he said, surprising her by his acquiescence. "What happened to my daddy?"

Janelle sucked in a quick breath, unprepared for that question. "I'm not sure," she hedged. "I think he might be sick."

Sebastian's stared at her. "He wasn't very nice to me," he confided. "I was hungry, but he didn't have any food. He kept telling me to shut up and be quiet."

Her heart squeezed in her chest and she quickly crossed over to sit beside him on the sofa. "I'm sorry we argued, Sebastian," she said, hugging him close. "But I want you to know that I love you, very much. I'll never hurt you, but sometimes I will make you do things you don't like to do."

Sebastian burrowed close. "I luv you too, Mommy. And I'm never going to leave you again."

Her eyes went misty with emotion as she pressed a kiss to the top of his head. He'd called her Mommy, again.

She hoped and prayed he'd never stop.

There was a knock at the door, so she regretfully pulled away from Sebastian to answer it. Her pulse jumped when she saw Devon standing on her front porch.

She was a little surprised he wasn't wearing his uniform. He looked so wonderful in a pair of black well-worn jeans and a white button down shirt with the cuffs rolled up, exposing his tanned forearms. It was all she could do not to throw herself into his arms.

"Hi Dev," she greeted him in what she hoped was a casual tone. "Come on, in."

He nodded and stepped over the threshold, glancing over her shoulder at where Sebastian was seated on the sofa. The little boy was playing the racing game, and didn't seem to realize Devon was there. "How is he doing?"

"Pretty well," she informed him. "Do you want to talk to him?"

"If you don't mind."

The hesitancy in his tone made her wince. "Listen, Dev, I'm sorry about last night," she said softly. "It's just that Sebastian idolizes you so much, I'm worried how he's going to handle it when you're gone."

"I know," Devon said, tucking his hands in his back pockets. "Madison offered me a job this morning."

Her stomach sank to the soles of her feet, although she did her best to paste a smile on her face. "That's great news, Devon. I'm so happy for you."

His deep brown gaze searched hers. "I didn't accept the job, yet."

Her mouth dropped open. "You didn't? She echoed in shock. "Why not? I thought that was exactly what you wanted."

He shrugged. "To be honest, another opportunity has come up that I'm considering as well."

Hope deflated quicker than a popped balloon. "Oh, I see. Well, it's good that you're taking your time and considering all your options." She hoped her keen disappointment wasn't too obvious.

"Dev! You came!" Sebastian finally noticed they had

company and slid off the sofa to come running toward Devon. The way Dev picked up her son and held him close made her throat tighten with emotion.

"Did Mommy call you?" Sebastian asked.

Devon glanced at her in surprise. "Uh, no, she didn't. But I do have a couple of questions for you, Sebastian. Do you mind talking to me for a few minutes?"

A tingle of alarm skittered across her nerves. "What do you need to talk to him about?" she asked.

"I'd like to ask him what he remembers from last night," Devon admitted. "It's not my intent to upset him, you can listen in if you like."

Knowing this was a professional visit instead of a personal one stung. But of course she couldn't blame Devon for needing to tie up loose ends from last night, either.

Her problem, if she wanted something more than he was willing to give.

Devon searched Janelle's face, trying to figure out how she felt about his dropping by unexpectedly.

Sheriff Torretti had asked someone else to work his second shift duties, so that he could finish up the investigation against Grant Gardner. In addition, the sheriff had asked him to talk to the Feds about the possibility of collaborating on an anti-drug task force they were creating which was part of the reason he hadn't accepted the job in Madison yet.

The task force sounded intriguing and would span multiple jurisdictions, including their very own Hope County.

But if he were honest with himself, he'd admit that the

real reason he hadn't accepted the Madison job was because of Sebastian and Janelle.

He cared about the boy, but it was Janelle that he couldn't seem to get out of his mind.

Had he imagined the flash of relief in her eyes when he told her he hadn't accepted the Madison job yet?

He forced himself to concentrate on the task at hand, dreading the need to ask Sebastian about what he remembered about last night.

Janelle hovered close, and he didn't blame her. Sebastian admitted that he'd gone along with his daddy when Grant tapped on his window. From there, Sebastian pretty much confirmed their working theory that once Grant had the boy he dragged him out into the woods, claiming they were going camping.

When Sebastian said that his daddy was mean to him, Devon had to work hard not to show his anger. There was nothing he could do about it now, especially considering the fact that Grant would never hurt anyone again.

"Where's my daddy, now?" Sebastian asked. "He's not coming back here, is he?"

"No, your daddy can't come here ever again," Dev assured the boy.

"I don't wanna live wif him," Sebastian persisted, his gaze earnest. "I wanna stay wif my mom."

Dev glanced over at Janelle, who looked as if she might burst into tears any minute. "Sebastian, your daddy is gone forever, so you don't need to worry about him, okay?" He sent a helpless glance at Janelle, unsure of how to tell the boy his father was actually dead.

"He's up in heaven, Sebastian," Janelle spoke up, coming to his rescue.

The boy seemed satisfied with that response. Dev closed his notebook. "That's all I needed, thanks."

"Do you wanna play a game wif me?" Sebastian asked, picking up the controller.

"Dev has to work today, remember?" Janelle said quickly. "Maybe some other time."

"Okay." Sebastian picked up the controller and went back to his racing game.

Devon rose to his feet and headed into the kitchen, hoping to speak to Janelle alone. "Actually, I don't have to report in for my regular shift, Sheriff Torretti gave me some time to finish up the investigation, which included getting Sebastian's statement."

"Oh, I see." She gestured toward the fridge. "Do you want something to drink? I have ice tea or lemonade."

Since she had lemonade on the table, he nodded. "Lemonade would be great, thanks."

When she handed him the glass, he took a sip and then set it down. He felt ridiculously nervous. "Do you have a few minutes to talk?"

She lifted her eyebrow in surprise. "Sure, do you need my statement too?"

"No." He waited until she sat down, then took the seat next to her, so he could take her hand in his. "Janelle, I need to ask you something, and I want you to be completely honest with me, okay?"

She looked a bit apprehensive, but nodded "of course."

He couldn't ever remember feeling this uncertain about a woman. Maybe because he and Debra had known each other for a long time, dated since college. Being with his fiancée had been comfortable, familiar.

Sitting next to Janelle, getting ready to pour his heart and soul out to her, was way outside of his comfort zone. But he wasn't a coward. "Would you consider going out with me?"

She blinked. "You mean, on a date?"

Wasn't it obvious? "Yes, on a date. I don't want to take the job in Madison," he blurted. "I don't want to leave you."

"Me? Or Sebastian?"

"Both of you. I care about Sebastian, but it's you that I keep thinking about." He tightened his grip on her hand. "But if you don't feel the same way, I'll understand."

She looked surprised. "I care about you, too, Devon, but all this time, I thought you were still in love with your fiancée. Wasn't that part of the reason you wanted to move away from here?"

"Not exactly" he knew it was time to tell her the truth. "The Feds want me to help them work on a multi-district task force that would keep me here in Crystal Lake. I wasn't trying to avoid the area, I just wanted to do something important with my life, the way my older brother did."

She didn't look as if she believed him. "I'm sure you have memories of Debra everywhere you look."

He knew it was time to put his past to rest. "I loved Debra, and I was devastated when she was killed. No one knows this, but she was pregnant, just eight weeks along, when she died. And I blamed God for taking her and our child away from me."

"Oh, Dev," she whispered, her eyes full of sympathy. "I'm so sorry for your loss."

"Thank you, but you've shown me the way back to God and my faith. I was wrong to avoid going back to church. But I have to be honest, Janelle. When I realized you had taken custody of Sebastian, I tried to stay away because I couldn't stop thinking about my unborn child a little girl or a boy who would have been close to his age if he or she had lived."

Her gaze was full of compassion. "Those hours that Sebastian was gone were the longest of my entire life. I can't even imagine what you must have gone through."

He was glad she seemed to understand. "Janelle, I didn't intend to open myself up to loving anyone ever again, but somehow, you wiggled your way under my skin and into my heart. I know that it's probably too soon for you to hear this, but I've fallen in love with you. I'm willing to be patient, to give you the time you need to see if you feel the same way."

Janelle's face filled with joy. "Oh, Devon, it's not too soon at all. And I don't need time, I feel the same way. I was so upset about the thought of you moving away from Crystal Lake, I tried to ignore my feelings, but I love you, too. More than I can possibly say."

He surged to his feet, drawing her up and into his arms. "Janelle," he murmured, before leaning down and covering her mouth with his.

She wound her arms around his neck and kissed him back, showing him without words that he wasn't in this alone. Her citrusy scent filled his senses and Devon couldn't believe how blessed he was to have been given a second chance.

A second chance to love and to have a family.

He prolonged the kiss, completely forgetting the fact that they weren't alone until Sebastian interrupted them.

"Why are you kissing Mommy?"

Devon lifted his head, struggling to catch his breath. Janelle hid her face in his shoulder, shaking with repressed laughter.

What kind of question was that? He tried to pull his scrambled brain cells together. "Because I love her," Devon finally responded.

"Me, too," Sebastian agreed.

Dev held his hand out to Sebastian, encouraging him to come over to join them. Using one arm, he lifted the boy up and held him close, keeping his other arm firmly around Janelle.

"Sebastian, I love your mommy very much. How do you feel about us being a family?"

Janelle's face broke into a wide smile, and she put her arm around Sebastian, including him in the three-way hug.

"Would we live together like a real family?" Sebastian asked.

Devon nodded. "I'd be your new daddy," he added "if that's okay with you."

"Yay!" Sebastian cried out. "God answered my prayers!"

Devon tightened his grip on Janelle and Sebastian, knowing that God had answered his prayers, too.

EPILOGUE

Janelle stood in the back of the church, smoothing a hand over her white gown as she waited for Lexi Ryerson, Julie and Derek's daughter, and Sebastian to walk down the aisle. They looked so cute, even though Lexi hadn't wanted anything to do with holding Sebastian's hand.

When Sebastian reached the front of the church, Devon stepped forward to take the wedding rings from the little boy, then he drew Sebastian to his side, where he would participate in their wedding ceremony.

The music swelled, and Janelle stepped forward to make her way down the aisle. Devon's dark gaze captured hers, admiration and happiness shining from his eyes.

She smiled, anxious to begin a new life with Devon. The past few months had passed in a whirlwind of wedding plans, since neither one of them had wanted a long engagement.

Janelle was so thankful the Lord had brought them together, and with their friends and the Crystal Lake townsfolk watching, they'd vow to love and honor each other for the rest of their lives.

Devon couldn't wait, but stepped forward to take her hand in his. She let him draw her up to the front of the church where Pastor John waited for them.

The ceremony was sweetly poignant. "This ring is a sign of my love and fidelity, for as long as we both shall live," Devon murmured, slipping her wedding band on the third finger of her left hand.

She took his ring, and repeated the vow to him. "This ring is a sign of my love and fidelity, for as long as we both shall live."

Pastor John's grin was broad as he lifted his hands to encompass the crowd packed into the church. "I know pronounce you husband and wife. Please welcome Devon and Janelle Armbruster."

The crowd broke into wild applause, and Devon bent his head to give her a firm kiss. "I love you, Mrs. Armbruster," he whispered.

"I love you, too, Deputy Armbruster," she replied. She placed her hand in the crook of Devon's arm, then she grasped Sebastian's hand so the three of them could walk down the aisle, together. They made their way to the back of the church, where everyone would gather for their reception.

"Are you ready for your wedding present?" Devon asked in a low tone as they took their place in the receiving line.

She glanced at him in surprise. "A present? But I didn't get you anything," she protested.

Devon grinned. "This present is for our family. I didn't want to say anything until I knew for sure, but I had my blood and tissue testing done to see if I'm a potential match for Sebastian. Turns out, my blood type is O negative. I've been approved to donate a kidney for our son."

"What?" Janelle could hardly believe what he was saying. "Are you sure?"

"Yes, the doctors assured me that my kidney would absolutely work for Sebastian. We can schedule the surgery any time."

"Oh, Devon, that's amazing news, but are you absolutely sure you want to do this?" Janelle was surprised and humbled by his willingness to donate a kidney for Sebastian. "This isn't something to take lightly, there are risks. Not just surgical risks, but the risk of you suffering kidney failure later in life."

"I know, the transplant surgeon explained everything to me, and I know there's a possibility I'll have more complications as I get older, but Janelle, it's worth the risk to provide Sebastian a healthy life." He stared down at her intently. "You would do this for our son if you were a match, so why shouldn't I?"

She didn't have an argument for that one, so she simply threw her arms around his neck and kissed him again. "I love you so much," she whispered.

"I love you, too," he whispered back.

Janelle was forced to release him when the wedding guests filed out of the church and lined up to wish them well.

As she thanked everyone for coming, she knew deep in her heart that everything would work out fine, because she and Devon loved each other.

There was no doubt God was watching over them.

Dear Reader,

I hope you enjoyed all the books in my Crystal Lake Series. Many readers have been asking for Deputy Devon Armbruster's story, so I decided to give him a second chance at love and faith. As a critical care nurse, I also worked with transplant recipients so I decided to give the story a bit of a twist with ER nurse Janelle's nephew, Sebastian, requiring peritoneal dialysis and hopefully one day being given the gift of life with a kidney transplant. And of course, there is nothing better than falling in love and becoming a family.

If you would be so kind as to leave a review from the site where you purchased this book, I'd greatly appreciate it. Reviews are very important for sales although trust me, I understand customers are being reviewed to death.

I love hearing from my readers. You can write to me and sign up for my newsletter through my website at www.laurascottbooks.com. Or find me on Facebook at Laura Scott Books Author, and on Twitter @laurascottbooks. Lastly, I offer a free exclusive Crystal Lake Novella for all subscribers.

Yours in faith,
Laura Scott